*Lieutenant John Grimes of the Federation
Survey Service: fresh out of the Academy —
and as green as they come!*

"What do you think you're playing at?"

"Captain," said Wolverton, "I can no more
than guess at what you intend to do—but I have
decided not to help you do it."

"Give me the initiator, Wolverton. That's an
order!

"A *law*ful command, Captain? As lawful as
those that armed this ship?"

"Hold him, Grimes!"

. . . . They hung there, clinging to each other, but
more in hate than in love. Wolverton's back was to
the machine; he could not see, as could Grimes,
that there was an indraught of air into the shimmering, spinning complexity. Grimes felt the beginnings of panic . . . all that mattered was that there
was nothing to prevent him and Wolverton from
being drawn into the machine. . . .Violently Grimes
shoved away. To the action, there was a reaction. . .

When he had finished retching, Grimes forced
himself to look again at the slimy, bloody obscenity that was a man turned inside out—heart still
beating, intestines still writhing . . .

THE ROAD TO THE RIM

by

A. Bertram Chandler

SF
ace books
A Division of Charter Communications Inc.
A GROSSET & DUNLAP COMPANY
360 Park Avenue South
New York, New York 10010

DEDICATION:

For ADMIRAL LORD HORNBLOWER, R.N.

I

HIS UNIFORM was new, too new, all knife-edged creases, and the braid and buttons as yet undimmed by time. It sat awkwardly upon his chunky body—and even more awkwardly his big ears protruded from under the cap that was set too squarely upon his head. Beneath the shiny visor his eyes were gray (but not yet hard), and his face, for all its promise of strength, was as yet unlined, had yet to lose its immature softness. He stood at the foot of the ramp by which he had disembarked from the transport that had carried him from the Antarctic Base to Port Woomera, looking across the silver towers that were the ships, interplanetary and interstellar, gleaming in the desert. The westering sun was hot on his back, but he did not notice the discomfort. There were the ships, the *real* ships—not obsolescent puddle-jumpers like the decrepit cruiser in which he, with the other midshipmen of his class, had made the training cruise to the moons of Saturn. There were the ships, the star ships, that span their web of commerce from Earth to the Centaurian planets, to the Cluster Worlds, to the Empire of Waverley, to the Shakespearian Sector and beyond.

(*But they're only merchantmen*, he thought, with a young man's snobbery.)

He wondered in which one of the vessels he would be taking passage. Merchantman or not, that big ship, the one that stood out from her neighbors like a city skyscraper among village church steeples, looked a likely enough craft. He pulled the folder containing his orders from his inside breast pocket, opened it, read (not for the second time, even), the relevant page.

. . . *you are to report on board the Interstellar Transport Commission's* Delta Orionis . . .

He was not a spaceman yet, in spite of his uniform, but he knew the Commission's system of nomenclature. There was the *Alpha* class, and the *Beta* class, and there were the *Gamma* and *Delta* classes. He grinned wryly. His ship was one of the smaller ones. Well, at least he would not be traveling to Lindisfarne Base in an *Epsilon* class tramp.

Ensign John Grimes, Federation Survey Service, shrugged his broad shoulders and stepped into the ground car waiting to carry him and his baggage from the airport to the spaceport.

II

GRIMES LOOKED at the officer standing just inside *Delta Orionis'* airlock, and she looked at him. He felt the beginnings of a flush spreading over his face, a prickling of the roots of his close-cropped hair, and felt all the more embarrassed by this public display of his embarrassment. But spaceborn female officers, at this time, were almost as scarce as hens' teeth in the Survey Service—and such few as he had met all looked as though they shared a common equine ancestry. It was all wrong, thought Grimes. It was unfair that this girl (this attractive girl) should already be a veteran of interstellar voyages while he, for all his uniform and commission, should be embarking upon his first, his very first trip outside the bounds of the Solar System. He let his glance fall from her face (but not without reluctance), to the braid on her shoulderboards. Gold on a white facing. So it wasn't too bad. She was only some sort of paymaster—or, to use Merchant Service terminology, only some sort of purser.

She said, her clear, high voice almost serious, "Welcome aboard the *Delia O'Ryan*, Admiral."

"Ensign," corrected Grimes stiffly. "Ensign Grimes . . ."

". . . of the Federation Survey Service," she finished for him. "But you are all potential admirals." There was the faintest of smiles flickering

upon her full lips, a barely discernible crinkling at
the corners of her eyes. *Her brown eyes,* thought
Grimes. *Brown eyes, and what I can see of her hair
under that cap seems to be auburn . . .*

She glanced at her wristwatch. She told him, her
voice now crisp and businesslike, "We lift ship in
precisely ten minutes' time, Ensign."

"Then I'd better get my gear along to my cabin,
Miss . . . ?"

"I'll look after that, Mr. Grimes. Meanwhile,
Captain Craven sends his compliments and invites
you to the Control Room."

"Thank you." Grimes looked past and around
the girl, trying to discover for himself the door that
gave access to the ship's axial shaft. He was determined not to ask.

"It's labeled," she told him with a faint smile.
"And the cage is waiting at this level. Just take it
up as far as it goes, then walk the rest. Or do you
want a pilot?"

"I can manage," he replied more coldly than he
had intended, adding, "thank you." He could see
the sign over the door now. It was plain enough.
AXIAL SHAFT. So was the button that he had to
press to open the door—but the girl pressed it for
him. He thanked her again—and this time his coldness was fully intentional—and stepped into the
cage. The door slid shut behind him. The upper-
most of the studs on the elevator's control panel
was marked CAPTAIN'S DECK. He pushed it, then
stood there and watched the lights flashing on the
panel as he was swiftly lifted to the nose of the
ship.

When he was carried no further he got out,
found himself on a circular walk surrounding the

upper extremity of the axial shaft. On the outside of the shaft itself there was a ladder. After a second's hesitation he climbed it, emerged through a hatch into the control room.

It was like the control room of the cruiser in which he had made his training cruise—and yet subtly (or not so subtly), unlike it. Everything—but so had it been aboard the Survey Service vessel—was functional, but there was an absence of high polish, of polishing for polishing's sake. Instruments gleamed—but it was the dull gleam that comes from long and continual use, and matched the dull gleam of the buttons and rank marks on the uniforms of the officers already seated at their stations, the spacemen to whom, after all, a uniform was no more (and no less), than an obligatory working rig.

The big man with the four gold bars on each shoulder half turned his head as Grimes came up through the hatch. "Glad to have you aboard, Ensign," he said perfunctorily. "Grab yourself a seat—there's a spare one alongside the Mate's. Sorry there's no time for introductions right now. We're due to get upstairs."

"Here!" grunted one of the officers.

Grimes made his way to the vacant acceleration chair, dropped into it, strapped himself in. While he was so doing he heard the Captain ask, "All secure, Mr. Kennedy?"

"No, sir."

"Then why the hell not?"

"I'm still waiting for the purser's report, sir."

"Are you?" Then, with a long-suffering sigh, "I suppose she's still tucking some passenger into her—or *his*—bunk. . . . "

"She could still be stowing some passenger's gear, sir," contributed Grimes. "Mine," he added.

"Indeed?" The Captain's voice was cold and elaborately uninterested.

Over the intercom came a female voice. "Purser to Control. All secure below."

"And bloody well time," grumbled the shipmaster. Then, to the officer at the transceiver, Mr. Digby, kindly obtain clearance."

"Obtain clearance, sir," acknowledged that young man brightly. Then, into his microphone, "*Delta Orionis* to Port Control. Request clearance to lift ship. Over."

"Port Control to *Delta Orionis*. You may lift. Bon voyage. Over."

"Thank you, Port Control. Over and out."

Then the ship was throbbing to the rhythmic beat of her Inertial Drive, and Grimes felt that odd sense of buoyancy, of near weightlessness, that persisted until the vessel broke contact with the ground—and then the still gentle acceleration induced the reverse effect. He looked out through the nearest viewport. Already the ocher surface of the desert, streaked by the long, black shadows of ships and spaceport buildings, was far below them, with the vessels and the immobile constructions looking like toys, and one or two surface vehicles like scurrying insects. Far to the north, dull-ruddy against the blue of the sky, there was a sandstorm. *If that sky were darker*, thought Grimes, *this would look like Mars*, and the mental comparison reminded him that he, too, was a spaceman, that he, too, had been around (although only within the bounds of Sol's planetary system). Even x, he was Survey Service, and these others with him in Control were only merchant officers, fetchers and carriers, interstellar coach and truck drivers. (But he envied them their quiet competency.)

Still the ship lifted, and the spaceport below her dwindled, and the land horizon to the north and the now visible sea horizon to the south began to display the beginnings of curvature. Still she lifted, and overhead the sky was dark, and the first bright stars, Sirius and Canopus, Alpha and Beta Centauri, were sparkling there, beckoning, as they had beckoned for ages immemorial before the first clumsy rocket clambered heavenward up the ladder of its own fiery exhaust, before the first airplane spread its flimsy wings, before the first balloon was lifted by the hot, expanding gases from its airborne furnace. . . .

"Mr. Grimes," said the Captain suddenly, his voice neither friendly nor unfriendly.

"Sir?"

"We lift on I.D. until we're clear of the Van Allens."

"I know, sir," said Grimes—then wished that he could unsay the words. But it was too late. He was conscious of the shipmaster's hostile silence, of the amused contempt of the merchant officers. He shrank into his chair, tried to make himself as inconspicuous as possible. The ship's people talked among themselves in low voices, ignoring him. They allowed themselves a period of relaxation, producing and lighting cigarettes. Nobody offered the Ensign one.

Sulkily he fumbled for his pipe, filled it, lighted it. The Chief Officer coughed with quite unnecessary vigor. The Captain growled, "Put that out, please," and muttered something about stinking out the control room. He, himself, was puffing at a villainous black cigar.

The ship lifted, and below her the Earth was now a great sphere, three-quarters in darkness, the line of the terminator drawn across land masses, cloud formations and oceans. City lights twinkled in the gloom like star clusters, like nebulae. In a quiet voice an officer was calling readings from the radar altimeter.

To the throbbing of the Inertial Drive was added the humming, shrilling to a whine, of the directional gyroscopes as the ship turned about her short axis hunting the target star. The pseudo-gravity of centrifugal force was at an odd angle to that of acceleration—and the resultant was at an odder angle still. Grimes began to feel sick—and was actually thankful that the Captain had made him put his pipe out. Alarm bells sounded, and then somebody was saying over the intercom. "Prepare for acceleration. Prepare for acceleration. Listen for the countdown."

The countdown. Part of the long tradition of space travel, a hangover from the days of the first, unreliable rockets. Spaceships still used rockets—but only as auxiliaries, as a means of delivering thrust in a hurry, of building up acceleration in a short time.

At the word *Zero!* the Inertial Drive was cut and, simultaneously, the Reaction Drive flared into violent life. The giant hand of acceleration bore down heavily upon all in the ship—then, suddenly, at a curt order from the Captain, lifted.

Grimes became aware of a thin, high keening, the song of the ever-precessing gyroscopes of the Mannschenn Drive. He knew the theory of it—as what spaceman did not?—although the mathematics of it were beyond the comprehension of all but a handful of men and women. He knew what was happening, knew that the ship, now that speed had been built up, was, as one of his instructors had put it, going ahead in space and astern in time. He felt, as he had been told that he would feel, the uncanny sensation of *déja vu,* and watched the outlines of the control room and of every person and instrument in the compartment shift and shimmer, the colors sagging down the spectrum.

Ahead, the stars were pulsating spirals of opalescence, astern, Earth and Moon were frighteningly distorted, uncanny compromises between the sphere and the tesseract. But this was no more than the merest subliminal glimpse; in the twinkling of an eye the Home Planet and her daughter were no more than dust motes whirling down the dark dimensions.

The Captain lit a fresh cigar. "Mr. Kennedy," he said, "you may set normal Deep Space watches." He turned to Grimes. His full beard almost hid his expression, that of one performing a social duty with no enthusiasm. "Will you join me in my day cabin, Ensign?"

"It will be my pleasure, sir," lied Grimes.

III

HANDLING HIS BIG BODY with easy grace in the Free Fall conditions, the Captain led the way from the control room. Grimes followed slowly and clumsily, but with a feeling of great thankfulness that after his training cruise he was no longer subject to spacesickness. There were drugs, of course, and passengers used them, but a spaceman was expected to be independent of pharmaceutical aids. Even so, the absence of any proper "up" or "down" bothered him more than he cared to admit.

The shipmaster slid open the door to his accommodation, motioned to Grimes to enter, murmuring sardonically, "Now you see how the poor live." The so-called poor, thought Grimes, didn't do at all badly. This Deep Space sitting room was considerably larger than the day cabin of the Survey Service cruiser's Captain had been. True, it was also shabbier—but it was far more comfortable. Its decorations would never have been approved aboard a warship, were obviously the private property of the Master. There were a full dozen holograms on the bulkhead, all of them widely differing but all of them covering the same subject matter. Not that the subject matter was covered.

"My harem," grunted the Captain. "That one there, the redhead, I met on Caribbea. Quite a stopover that was. The green-haired wench—and you can see that it's not a dye job, although I've often wondered why women can't be *thorough*—isn't human, of course. But indubitably humanoid, and indubitably mammalian. Belongs to Brrrooonooorrrooo—one of the worlds of the Shaara Empire. The local Queen Mother offered to sell Lalia—that's her name—to me for a case of Scotch. And I was tempted . . ." He sighed. "But you Service Survey types aren't the only ones who have to live by Regulations."

Grimes said nothing, tried to hide his interest in the art gallery.

"But take a pew, Ensign. Spit on the mat and call the cat a bastard—this is Liberty Hall."

Grimes pulled himself to one of the comfortable chairs, strapped himself in. He said lamely, "I don't see any cat, sir."

"A figure of speech," growled the Captain, seating himself next to what looked like a drink cabinet. "Well, Mr. Grimes, your Commandant at the Academy, Commodore Bradshaw, is an old friend and shipmate of mine. He said that you were a very promising young officer"—like a balloon in a comic strip the unspoken words, "God knows why," hung between them—"and asked me to keep an eye on you. But I have already gained the impression that there is very little that a mere merchant skipper such as myself will be able to teach you."

Grimes looked at the bulky figure seated opposite him, at the radiation-darkened skin of the face above the black, silver-streaked beard, at the fiercely jutting nose, at the faded but bright and intelligent blue eyes, the eyes that were regarding him with more than a hint of amused contempt. He blushed miserably as he recalled his brash, "I know, sir," in this man's own control room. He said, with an effort, "This is my first Deep Space voyage, sir."

"I know." Surprisingly the Captain chuckled—and as though to celebrate this minor scoring over his guest opened the liquor cabinet. "Pity to have to suck this excellent Manzanila out of a bulb—but that's one of the hardships of Free Fall. Here!" He tossed a little pear-shaped container to Grimes, kept one for himself. "Your health, Ensign!"

"And yours, sir."

The wine was too dry for Grimes' taste, but he made a pretense of enjoying it. He was thankful that he was not asked to have a second drink. Meanwhile, his host had pulled a typewritten sheet from a drawer of his desk and was looking at it. "Let me see, now . . . You're in cabin 15, on D Deck. You'll be able to find your own way down, won't you?"

Grimes said that he would and unbuckled his lapstrap. It was obvious that the party was over.

"Good. Now, as an officer of the Survey Service you have the freedom of the control room and the engine rooms . . . . "

"Thank you, sir."

"Just don't abuse the privilege, that's all."

After that, thought Grimes, *I'm not likely to take advantage of it, let alone abuse it*. He let himself float up from his chair, said, "Thank you, sir." (For the drink, or for the admonition? What did it matter?) "I'll be getting down to my cabin, sir.

I've some unpacking to do."

"As you please, Mr. Grimes."

The Captain, his social duty discharged, had obviously lost interest in his guest. Grimes let himself out of the cabin and made his way, not without difficulty, to the door in the axial shaft. He was surprised at the extent to which one not very large drink had interfered with the control of his body in Free Fall. Emerging from the elevator cage on D Deck he stumbled, literally, into the purser. "Let go of me," she ordered, "or I shall holler rape!"

That, he thought, *is all I need to make this trip a really happy one.*

She disengaged herself, moved back from him, her slim, sandaled feet, magnetically shod, maintaining contact with the steel decking, but gracefully, with a dancing motion. She laughed. "I take it that you've just come from a home truth session with B.B."

"B.B.?"

"The Bearded Bastard. But don't take it too much to heart. He's that way with *all* junior officers. The fact that you're Survey Service is only incidental."

"Thank you for telling me."

"His trouble," she went on. "His *real* trouble is that he's painfully shy."

He's not the only one, thought Grimes, looking at the girl. She seemed even more attractive than on the occasion of their first meeting. She had changed into shorts-and-shirt shipboard uniform—and she was one of the rare women who could wear such a rig without looking lumpy and clumpy. There was no cap now to hide her hair—

smooth, lustrous, with coppery glints, with a straight white part bisecting the crown of her finely shaped head.

She was well aware of his scrutiny. She said, "You must excuse me, Ensign. I have to look after the other customers. They aren't seasoned spacemen like you."

Suddenly bold, he said, "But before you go, what is your name?"

She smiled dazzlingly. "You'll find a list of all ship's personnel posted in your cabin. I'm included." Then she was gone, gliding rapidly around the curve of the alleyway.

He looked at the numbers over the cabin doors, outboard from the axial shaft, making a full circuit of that hollow pillar before he realized that this was only the inner ring, that he would have to follow one of the radial alleyways to reach his own accommodation. He finally found No. 15 and let himself in.

His first action was to inspect the framed notices on the bulkhead.

I.S.S. Delta Orionis, he read.

Captain J. Craven, O.G.S., S.S.R.

So the Old Man held a Reserve commission. And the Order of the Golden Star was awarded for something more than good attendance.

Mr. P. Kennedy, Chief Officer.

He ignored the other names on the list while he searched for one he wanted. Ah, here it was.

Miss Jane Pentecost, Purser.

He repeated the name to himself, thinking that, despite the old play on words, this Jane was not plain. (But Janes rarely are.) *Jane Pentecost . . .* Then, feeling that he should be showing some professional interest, he acquainted himself with the names of the other members of the ship's crew. He was intrigued by the manning scale, amazed that such a large vessel, relatively speaking, could be run by such a small number of people. But this was not a warship; there were no weapons to be manned, there would never be the need to put a landing party ashore on the surface of a hostile planet. The Merchant Service could afford to automate, to employ machinery in lieu of ratings. The Survey Service could not.

Virtuously he studied the notices dealing with emergency procedures, ship's routine, recreational facilities and all the rest of it, examined with care the detailed plan of the ship. Attached to this was a card, signed by the Master, requesting passengers to refrain, as much as possible, from using the elevator in the axial shaft, going on to say that it was essential, for the good of their physical health, that they miss no opportunity for taking exercise. (In a naval vessel, thought Grimes, with a slight sneer, that would not be a request—it would be an order. And, in any case, there would be compulsory calisthenics for all hands.)

He studied the plan again and toyed with the idea of visiting the bar before dinner. He decided against it; he was still feeling the effects of the drink that the Captain had given him. So, to pass the time, he unpacked slowly and carefully, methodically stowing his effects in the drawers under the bunk. Then, but not without reluctance, he changed from his uniform into his one formal civilian suit. One of the officer-instructors at the Academy had advised this. "Always wear civvies when you're traveling as passenger. If you're in uniform, some old duck's sure to take you for one of the ship's officers and ask you all sorts of technical questions to which you don't know the answers."

While he was adjusting his frilled cravat in front of the mirror the sonorous notes of a gong boomed from the intercom.

IV

THE DINING SALOON was much more ornate than the gunroom of that training cruiser had been, and more ornate than her wardroom. The essentials were the same, of course, as they are in any ship—tables and chairs secured to the deck, each seat fitted with its strap so that the comforting pressure of buttocks on padding could give an illusion of gravity. Each table was covered with a gaily colored cloth—but beneath the fabric there was the inevitable stainless steel to which the stainless steel service would be held by its own magnetic fields. But what impressed Grimes was the care that had been taken, the ingenuity that had been exercised to make this compartment look like anything but part of a ship.

The great circular pillar of the axial shaft was camouflaged by trelliswork, and the trelliswork itself almost hidden by the luxuriance of some broad-level climbing plant that he could not identify. Smaller pillars were similarly covered, and there was a further efflorescence of living decoration all around the circular outer wall—the wall that must be the inner skin of the ship. And there were windows in this wall. No, Grimes decided, not windows, but holograms. The glowing, three dimensional pictures presented and maintained the illusion that this was a hall set in the middle of some great park. But on what world? Grimes could not say. Trees, bushes and flowers were unfamiliar, and the color of the sky subtly strange.

He looked around him at his fellow diners, at the dozen passengers and the ship's officers, most of whom were already seated. The officers were in neat undress uniform. About half the male passengers were, like himself, formally attired; the others were sloppy in shorts and shirts. But this was the first night out and some laxity was allowable. The women, however, all seemed to have decided to outshine the glowing flowers that flamed outside the windows that were not windows.

There was the Captain, unmistakable with his beard and the shimmering rainbow of ribbons on the left breast of his blouse. There were the passengers at his table—the men inclined to portliness and pomposity, their women sleek and slim and expensive looking. Grimes was relieved to see that there was no vacant place—and yet, at the same time, rather hurt. He knew that he was only an Ensign, a one-ringer, and a very new Ensign at that—but, after all, the Survey Service was the Survey Service.

He realized that somebody was addressing him. It was a girl, a small, rather chubby blonde. She was in uniform—a white shirt with black shoulder-boards, each bearing a narrow white stripe, sharply creased slacks, and black, highly polished shoes. Grimes assumed, correctly, that she was a junior member of the purser's staff. "Mr. Grimes," she said, "will you follow me, please? You're at Miss Pentecost's table."

Willingly he followed the girl. She led him around the axial shaft to a table for four at which the purser with two passengers, a man and a woman, was already seated. Jane Pentecost was attired as was his guide, the severity of her gold-trimmed black and white in pleasing contrast to the pink and blue frills and flounces that clad the other woman, her slenderness in still more pleasing contrast to the other's untidy plumpness.

She smiled and said pleasantly, "Be seated, Admiral."

"Admiral?" asked the man at her left, unpleasantly incredulous. He had, obviously, been drinking. He was a rough looking customer, in spite of the attempt that he had made to dress for dinner. He was twice the Ensign's age, perhaps, although the heavily lined face under the scanty sandy hair made him look older. "Admiral?" He laughed, revealing irregular yellow teeth. "In what? The Space Scouts?"

Jane Pentecost firmly took control. She said, "Allow me to introduce Ensign Grimes, of the Survey Service . . . "

"Survey Service . . . Space Scouts . . . S.S. . . . . What's the difference?"

"Plenty!" answered Grimes hotly.

The purser ignored the exchange. "Ensign, this is Mrs. Baxter . . . ."

"Pleased to meet you, I'm sure," simpered the woman.

"And Mr. Baxter."

Baxter extended his hand reluctantly and Grimes took it reluctantly. The amenities observed, he pulled himself into his seat and adjusted his lapstrap. He was facing Jane Pentecost. The man was on his right, the woman on his left. He glanced first at her, then at her husband, wondering how to start and to maintain a conversation. But this was the purser's table, and this was her responsibility.

She accepted it. "Now you're seeing how the poor live, Admiral," she remarked lightly.

Grimes, taking a tentative sip from his bulb of consomme, did not think that the self-styled poor did at all badly, and said as much. The girl grinned and told him that the first night out was too early to draw conclusions. "We're still on shoreside meat and vegetables," she told him, "and you'll not be getting your first taste of our instant table wine until tomorrow. Tonight we wallow in the unwonted luxury of a quite presentable Montrachet. When we start living on the produce of our own so-called farm, washing it down with our own reconstituted plonk, you'll see the difference."

The Ensign replied that, in his experience, it didn't matter if food came from tissue-culture vats or the green fields of Earth—what *was* important was the cook.

"Wide experience, Admiral?" she asked sweetly.

"Not very," he admitted. "But the gunroom cook in my last ship couldn't boil water without burning it."

Baxter, noisily enjoying his dinner, said that this preoccupation with food and drink was symptomatic of the decadence of Earth. As he spoke his knife grated unpleasantly on the steel spines that secured his charcoal broiled steak to the surface of his plate.

Grimes considered inquiring if the man thought that good table manners were also a symptom of decadence, then thought better of it. After all, this was not *his* table. Instead, he asked, "And where are you from, Mr. Baxter?"

"The Rim Worlds, Mr. Grimes. Where we're left to sink or swim—so we've no time for much else than keeping ourselves afloat." He sucked noisily from his bulb of wine. "Things might be a little easier for us if your precious Survey Service did something about keeping the trade routes open."

"That is our job," said Grimes stiffly. "And we do it."

"Like hell! There's not a pirate in the Galaxy but can run rings around you!"

"Practically every pirate has been hunted down and destroyed," Grimes told him coldly.

"Practically every pirate, the man says! A few small-time bunglers, he means!"

"Even the notorious Black Bart," persisted Grimes.

"Black Bart!" Baxter, spluttering through his full mouth, gestured with his laden fork at Grimes. "Black Bart! He wasn't much. Once he and that popsy of his split brass rags he was all washed up. I'm talkin' about the *real* pirates, the ones whose ships wear national colors instead o' the Jolly Roger, the ones that your precious Survey Service daren't say boo to. The ones who do the dirty work for the Federation."

"Such as?" asked Grimes frigidly.

"So now you're playin' the bleedin' innocent. Never heard o' the Duchy o' Waldegren, Mr. Ensign Grimes?"

"Of course. Autonomous, but they and the Federation have signed what's called a Pact of Perpetual Amity."

"Pretty words, ain't they? Suppose we analyze them. Suppose we analyze by analogy. D'yer know much about animals, Mr. Ensign Grimes?"

"Animals?" Grimes was puzzled. "Well, I suppose I do know something. I've taken the usual courses in xenobiology . . . ."

"Never mind that. You're a Terry. Let's confine

ourselves to a selection of yer own Terran four-footed friends.''

"What the hell are you driving at?" flared Grimes, losing his temper. He threw an apologetic glance in Jane Pentecost's direction, saw that she was more amused than shocked.

"Just think about a Pact of Perpetual Amity between an elephant and a tom cat," said Baxter. "A fat an' lazy elephant. A lean, scrawny, vicious tom cat. If the elephant wanted to he could convert that cat into a fur bedside rug just by steppin' on him. But he doesn't want to. He leaves the cat alone, just because the cat is useful to him. He does more than just leave him alone. He an' this feline pull out their pens from wherever they keep 'em an' sign their famous Pact.

"In case you haven't worked it out for yourself, the elephant's the Federation, and the tom cat's the Duchy of Waldegren."

"But why?" asked Grimes. *"Why?"*

"Don't they teach you puppies any interstellar politics? Or are those courses reserved for the top brass? Well, Mr. Grimes, I'll tell you. There's one animal that has the elephant *really* worried. Believe it or not, he's scared o' mice. An' there're quite a few mice inside the Federation, mice that make the elephant nervous by their rustlings an' scurryings an' their squeaky demands for full autonomy. That's where the cat comes in. By his free use of his teeth an' claws, by his very presence, he keeps the mice quiet."

"And just who are these famous mice, Mr. Baxter?" asked Grimes.

"Don't they teach you nothin' in your bleedin' Academy? Well, I'll tell you. In *our* neck o' the woods, the mice are the Rim Worlds, an' the tom cat, as I've already made clear, is the Duchy o' Waldegren. The Duchy gets away with murder—murder an' piracy. But accordin' to the Duchy, an accordin' to your big, stupid elephant of a Federation, it's not piracy. It's—now, lemme see, what fancy words have been used o' late? Contraband Control. Suppression of Espionage. Violation of the Three Million Mile Limit. Every time that there's an act of piracy there's some quote legal unquote excuse for it, an' it's upheld by the Federation's tame legal eagles, an' you Survey Service sissies just sit there on your big, fat backsides an' don't lift a pinkie against your dear, murderous pals, the Waldegrenese. If you did, they send you screaming back to Base, where some dear old daddy of an Admiral'd spank your little plump bottoms for you."

"Please, Mr. Baxter!" admonished Jane Pentecost.

"Sorry, Miss. I got sort of carried away. But my young brother was Third Reaction Drive Engineer of the old *Bunyip* when she went missing. Nothin' was ever proved—but the Waldegrenese Navy was holdin' fleet maneuvers in the sector she was passin' through when last heard from. Oh, they're cunnin' bastards. They'll never go for one o' these ships, or one of the Trans-Galactic Clippers; it'll always be some poor little tramp that nobody'll ever miss but the friends an' relatives o' the crew. And, I suppose, the underwriters—but Lloyds makes such a packet out o' the ships that don't get lost that they can well afford to shell out now an' again. Come to that, it must suit 'em. As long as there're a few 'overdues' an' 'missings' they can keep the premiums up."

"But I still can't see how piracy can possibly

pay," protested Grimes.

"O' course it pays. Your friend Black Bart made it pay. An' if you're goin' to all the expense of building and maintaining a war fleet, it might just as well earn its keep. Even your famous Survey Service might show a profit if you were allowed to pounce on every fat merchantman who came within range o' your guns."

"But for the Federation to condone piracy, as you're trying to make out . . . That's utterly fantastic."

"If you lived on the Rim, you might think different," snarled Baxter.

And Jane Pentecost contributed, "Not piracy. Confrontation."

V

AS SOON AS the meal was finished the Baxters left rather hastily to make their way to the bar, leaving Grimes and Jane Pentecost to the leisurely enjoyment of their coffee. When the couple was out of earshot Grimes remarked, "So those are Rim Worlders. They're the first I've met."

"They're not, you know," the girl told him.

"But they are. Oh, there are one or two in the Survey Service, but I've never run across them. Now I don't particularly want to."

"But you did meet one Rim Worlder before you met the Baxters."

"The Captain?"

She laughed. "Don't let him hear you say that—not unless you want to take a space walk without a suit!"

"Then who?"

"Who could it be, Admiral? Whom have you actually met, to talk to, so far in this ship? Use your crust."

He stared at her incredulously. "Not you?"

"Who else?" She laughed again, but with a touch of bitterness. "We aren't all like our late manger companions, you know. Or should know. Even so, you'd count yourself lucky to have Jim Baxter by your side in any real jam. It boils down to this. Some of us have acquired veneer. Some of us haven't. Period."

"But how did you . . . ?" He groped for words that would not be offensive to conclude the sentence.

"How did I get into this galley? Easily enough. I started my spacefaring career as a not very competent Catering Officer in *Jumbuk*, one of the Sundowner Line's more ancient and decrepit tramps. I got sick in Elsinore. Could have been my own cooking that put me in the hospital. Anyhow, I was just about recovered when the Commission's *Epsilon Serpentis* blew in—and she landed *her* purser with a slightly broken leg. She'd learned the hard way that the Golden Rule—*stop whatever you're doing and secure everything when the acceleration warning sounds*—is meant to be observed. The Doctor was luckier. She broke his fall. . . . "

Grimes was about to ask what the Doctor and the purser had been doing, then was thankful that he had not done so. He was acutely conscious of the crimson blush that burned the skin of his face.

"You must realize," said the girl dryly, "that merchant vessels with mixed crews are not monastic institutions. But where was I? Oh, yes. On Elsinore. Persuading the Master of the *Snaky Eppy* that I was a fit and proper person to take over his pursering. I managed to convince him that I was at least proper—I still can't see what my predecessor saw in that lecherous old goat of a quack, although the Second Mate had something. . . ." Grimes felt a sudden twinge of jealousy. Anyhow, he signed me on, as soon as I agreed to waive repatriation.

"It was a long voyage; as you know, the *Epsilon* class ships are little better than tramps themselves. It was a long voyage, but I enjoyed it—seeing all the worlds that I'd read about and heard about and always wanted to visit. The Sundowner Line doesn't venture far afield—just the four Rim Worlds, and now and again the Shakespearian Sector, and once in a blue moon one of the drearier planets of the Empire of Waverley. The Commission's tramps, of course, run *everywhere*.

"Anyhow, we finally berthed at Woomera. The Old Man must have put in a good report about me, because I was called before the Local Superintending Purser and offered a berth, as a junior, in one of the *Alpha* class liners. *Alpha Centauri*, if you must know. She was on the Sol-Sirius service. Nothing very glamorous in the way of ports of call, but she was a fine ship, beautifully kept, efficiently run. A couple of years there knocked most of the sharp corners off me. After that—a spell as Assistant Purser of *Beta Geminorum*. Atlanta, Caribbea Carinthia and the Cluster Worlds. And then my first ship as Chief Purser. This one."

One of Jane's girls brought them fresh bulbs of coffee and ampuls of a sweet, potent liqueur. When she was gone Grimes asked, "Tell me, what are the Rim Worlds like?"

She waited until he had applied the flame of his lighter to the tip of her long, thin cigar, then answered, "Cold. Dark. Lonely. But . . . they have something. The feeling of being on a frontier. *The* frontier. The last frontier."

"The frontier of the dark . . . " murmured Grimes.

"Yes. The frontier of the dark. And the names of our planets. They have something too. A . . . poetry? Yes, that's the word. Lorn, Ultimo, Faraway and Thule . . . And there's that night sky of ours, especially at some times of the year. There's the Galaxy—a great, dim-glowing lenticulate nebula, and the rest is darkness. At other times of the year there's only the darkness, the blackness that's made even more intense by the sparse, faint stars that are the other Rim Suns, by the few, faint luminosities that are the distant island universes that we shall never reach. . . . ''

She shivered almost imperceptibly. ''And always there's that sense of being on the very edge of things, of hanging on by our fingernails with the abyss of the eternal night gaping beneath us. The Rim Worlders aren't a spacefaring people; only a very few of us ever get the urge. It's analogous, perhaps, to your Maoris—I spent a leave once in New Zealand and got interested in the history of the country. The Maoris come of seafaring stock. Their ancestors made an epic voyage from their homeland paradise to those rather grim and dreary little islands hanging there, all by themselves, in the cold and stormy Southern Ocean, lashed by frigid gales sweeping up from the Antarctic. And something—the isolation? the climate?—killed the wanderlust that was an essential part of the makeup of their race. You'll find very few Maoris at sea—or in space—although there's no dearth of Polynesians from the home archipelagoes aboard the surface ships serving the ports of the Pacific. And there are quite a few, too, in the Commission's ships. . . . ''

''We have our share in Survey Service,'' said Grimes. ''But tell me, how do you man your vessels? This Sundowner Line of yours . . . ''

''There are always the drifters, the no-hopers, the castoffs from the Interstellar Transport Commission, and Trans-Galactic Clippers, and Waverley Royal Mail and all the rest of them.''

''And from the Survey Service?''

The question lifted her out of her sombre mood. ''No,'' she replied with a smile. ''Not yet.''

''Not ever,'' said Grimes.

VI

ONCE HIS INITIAL shyness had worn off—and with it much of his Academy-induced snobbery—Grimes began to enjoy the voyage. After all, Survey Service or no Survey Service, this was a ship and he was a spaceman. He managed to accept the fact that most of the ship's officers, even the most junior of them, were far more experienced spacemen than he was. Than he was *now,* he often reminded himself. At the back of his mind lurked the smug knowledge that, for all of them, a captaincy was the very limit of promotion, whereas he, one day, would be addressed in all seriousness as Jane Pentecost now addressed him in jest.

He was a frequent visitor to the control room but, remembering the Master's admonition, was careful not to get in the way. The watch officers accepted him almost as one of themselves and were willing to initiate him into the tricky procedure of obtaining a fix with the interstellar drive in operation—an art, he was told, rather than a science.

Having obtained the permission of the Chief Engineers he prowled through the vessel's machinery spaces, trying to supplement his theoretical knowledge of reaction, inertial and interstellar drives with something more practical. The first two, of course, were idle, and would be until the ship emerged from her warped Space-Time back into the normal continuum—but there was the

Pile, the radio-active heart of the ship, and there was the auxiliary machinery that, in this tiny, man-made planet, did the work that on a natural world is performed by winds, rivers, sunlight and gravity.

There was the Mannschenn Drive Room—and, inside this holy of holies, no man need fear to admit that he was scared by the uncanny complexity of ever-precessing gyroscopes. He stared at the tumbling rotors, the gleaming wheels that seemed always on the verge of vanishing into nothingness, that rolled down the dark dimensions, dragging the ship and all aboard her with them. He stared, hypnotized, lost in a vague, disturbing dream in which Past and Present and Future were inextricably mingled—and the Chief Interstellar Drive Engineer took him firmly by the arm and led him from the compartment. "Look at the time-twister too long," he growled, "and you'll be meeting yourself coming back!"

There was the "farm"—the deck of yeast—and tissue-culture vats which was no more (and no less), than a highly efficient protein factory, and the deck where stood the great, transparent globes in which algae converted the ship's organic waste and sewage back into usable form (processed as nutriment for the yeasts and the tissue-cultures and as fertilizer for the hydroponic tanks, the biochemist was careful to explain), and the deck where luxuriant vegetation spilled over from the trays and almost barricaded the inspection walks, the source of vitamins and of flowers for the saloon tables and, at the same time, the ship's main air-conditioning unit.

Grimes said to Jane Pentecost, who had accompanied him on this tour of inspection, "You know, I envy your Captain."

"From you, Admiral," she scoffed, "that *is* something. But why?"

"How can I put it? You people do the natural way what we do with chemicals and machinery. The Captain of a warship is Captain of a warship. Period. But your Captain Craven is absolute monarch of a little world."

"A warship," she told him, "is supposed to be able to go on functioning as such even with every compartment holed. A warship cannot afford to depend for the survival of her crew upon the survival of hosts of other air-breathing organisms."

"Straight from the book," he said. Then, puzzled, "But for a . . . " He hesitated.

"But for a woman, or for a purser, or for a mere merchant officer I know too much," she finished for him. "But I can read, you know. And when I was in the Sundowner Line, I, as well as all the other officers, was supposed to keep up with all the latest Survey Service publications."

"But why?" he asked.

"But why not? We'll have a Navy of our own, one day. Just stick around, Admiral."

"Secession?" he inquired, making it sound like a dirty word.

"Once again—why not?"

"It'd never work," he told her.

"The history of Earth is full of secessions that did work. So is the history of Interstellar Man. The Empire of Waverley, for example. The Duchy of Waldegren, for another—although that's one that should have come to grief. We should all of us be a great deal happier if it had."

"Federation policy . . . " he began.

"Policy, shmolicy! Don't let's be unkind to the Waldegrenese, because as long as they're in being they exercise a restraining influence upon the Empire of Waverley and the Rim Worlds . . . " Her pace slackened. Grimes noticed that they were passing through the alleyway in which she and her staff were accommodated. She went on, "But all this talking politics is thirsty work. Come in for a couple of drinks before lunch."

"Thank you. But, Jane"—she didn't seem to have noticed the use of her given name—"I don't think that either of us is qualified to criticize the handling of foreign and colonial affairs."

"Spoken like a nice, young, well-drug-up future admiral. Oh, I know, I know. You people are trained to be the musclemen of the Federation. Yours not to reason why, yours but to do and die, and all the rest of it. But I'm a Rim Worlder—and out on the Rim you learn to think for yourself." She slid her door open. "Come on in. This is Liberty Hall—you can spit on the mat and call the cat a bastard."

Her accommodation was a suite rather than a mere cabin. It was neither as large nor as well fitted as the Captain's, but it was better than the Chief Officer's quarters, in which Grimes had already been a guest. He looked with interest at the holograms on the bulkhead of the sitting room. They were—but in an altogether different way—as eye-catching as Captain Craven's had been. There was one that was almost physically chilling, that induced the feeling of utter cold and darkness and loneliness. It was the night sky of some planet—a range of dimly seen yet sharply serrated peaks bisecting a great, pallidly glowing, lenticulate nebula. "Home, sweet home," murmured the girl, seeing what he was looking at. "The Desolation Mountains on Faraway, with the Galactic Lens in the background."

"And you feel homesick for *that?*"

"Darn right I do. Oh, not all the time. I like warmth and comfort as well as the next woman. But . . . " She laughed. "Don't stand around gawking—you make the place look untidy. Pull yourself into a chair and belay the buttocks."

He did so, watching her as she busied herself at the liquor cabinet. Suddenly, in these conditions of privacy, he was acutely conscious of the womanliness of her. The rather right and rather short shorts, as she bent away from him, left very little to the imagination. And her legs, although slender, were full where they should be full, with the muscles working smoothly under the golden skin. He felt the urge, which he sternly suppressed, to plant a kiss in the delectable hollow behind each knee. She turned suddenly. "Here! Catch!" He managed to grab the bulb that was hurtling toward his face, but a little of the wine spurted from the nipple and struck him in the right eye. When his vision cleared he saw that she was seated opposite him, was laughing (at or with him?). At, he suspected. A real demonstration of sympathy would have consisted of tears, not laughter. Her face grew momentarily severe. "Not the mess," she said reprovingly. "But the waste."

Grimes examined the bulb. "I didn't waste much. Only an eyeful."

She raised her drink in ritual greeting. "Here's mud in your eye," adding, "for a change."

"And in yours."

In the sudden silence that followed they sat looking at each other. There was a tension, some odd resultant of centrifugal and centripitel forces. They were on the brink of something, and both of them knew it, and there was the compulsion to go forward countered by the urge to go back.

She asked tartly, "Haven't you ever seen a woman's legs before?"

He shifted his regard to her face, to the eyes that, somehow, were brown no longer but held the depth and the darkness of the night through which the ship was plunging.

She said, "I think you'd better finish your drink and go."

He said, "Perhaps you're right."

"You better believe I'm right." She managed a smile. "I'm not an idler, like some people. I've work to do."

"See you at lunch, then. And thank you."

"Don't thank me. It was on the house, as the little dog said. Off with you, Admiral."

He unbuckled his lapstrap, got out of the chair and made his way to the door. When he was out of her room he did not go to his own cabin but to the bar, where he joined the Baxters. They, rather to his surprise, greeted him in a friendly manner. Rim Worlders, Grimes decided, had their good points.

It was after lunch when one of the purserettes told him that the Captain wished to see him. *What have I done now?* wondered Grimes—and answered his own question with the words, *Nothing. Unfortunately.*

Craven's manner, when he admitted Grimes into his dayroom, was severe. "Come in, Ensign. Be seated."

"Thank you, sir."

"You may smoke if you wish."

"Thank you, sir."

Grimes filled and lighted his pipe; the Captain ignited one of his pungent cigars, studied the eddying coils of smoke as though they were writing a vitally important message in some strange language.

"Er, Mr. Grimes, I believe that you have been seeing a great deal of my purser, Miss Pentecost."

"Not a great deal, sir. I'm at her table, of course."

"I am told that she has entertained you in her quarters."

"Just one bulb of sherry, sir. I had no idea that we were breaking ship's regulations."

"You were not. All the same, Mr. Grimes, I have to warn you."

"I assure you, sir, that nothing occurred between us."

Craven permitted himself a brief, cold smile. "A ship is not a Sunday school outing—especially a ship under my command. Some Masters, I know, do expect their officers to comport themselves like Sunday school pupils, with the Captain as the principal—but *I* expect *my* senior officers to behave like intelligent and responsible adults. Miss Pentecost is quite capable of looking after herself. It is you that I'm worried about."

"There's no need to be worried, sir."

The Captain laughed. "I'm not worried about your morals, Mr. Grimes. In fact, I have formed the opinion that a roll in the hay would do you far more good than harm. But Miss Pentecost is a dangerous woman. Before lifting ship, very shortly before lifting ship, I received a confidential report concerning her activities. She's an efficient purser, a highly efficient purser, in fact, but she's even more than that. Much more." Again he studied the smoke from his cigar. "Unfortunately there's no *real* proof, otherwise she'd not be sailing with us. Had I insisted upon her discharge I'd have been up against the Interstellar Clerical and Supply Officers' Guild."

"Surely not," murmured Grimes.

Craven snorted. "You people are lucky. You haven't a mess of Guilds to deal with, each and every one of which is all too ready to rush to the defense of a Guild member, no matter what he or she is supposed to have done. As a Survey Service Captain you'll never have to face a suit for wrongful dismissal. You'll never be accused of victimization."

"But what has Miss Pentecost done, sir?" asked Grimes.

"Nothing—or too damn much. You know where she comes from, don't you? The Rim Worlds. The planets of the misfits, the rebels, the nonconformists. There's been talk of secession of late—but even those irresponsible anarchists know full well that secession will never succeed unless they build up their own space power. There's the Duchy of Waldegren, which would pounce as soon as the Federation withdrew its protection. And even the Empire of Waverley might be tempted to extend its boundaries. So . . .

"They have a merchant fleet of sorts, these Rim Worlders. The Sundowner Line. I've heard rumors that it's about to be nationalized. But they have no fighting navy."

"But what's all this to do with Miss Pentecost, sir?"

"If what's more than just hinted at in that confidential report is true—plenty. She's a recruiting sergeant, no less. Any officer with whom she's shipmates who's disgruntled, on the verge of throwing his hand in—or on the verge of being emptied out—she'll turn on the womanly sympathy for, and tell him that there'll always be a job waiting out on the Rim, that the Sundowner Line is shortly going to expand, so there'll be quick promotion and all the rest of it."

"And what's that to do with *me,* Captain?

"Are all Survey Service ensigns as innocent as you, Mr. Grimes? Merchant officers the Rim Worlds want, and badly. Naval officers they'll want more badly still once the balloon goes up."

Grimes permitted himself a superior smile. "It's extremely unlikely, sir, that I shall ever want to leave the Survey Service."

"Unlikely perhaps—but not impossible. So bear in mind what I've told you. I think that you'll be able to look after yourself now that you know the score."

"I think so too," Grimes told him firmly. He thought, *The old bastard's been reading too many spy stories.*

VII

THEY WERE DANCING.

Tables and chairs had been cleared from the ship's saloon, and from the big, ornate playmaster throbbed the music of an orchestra so famous that even Grimes had heard of it—The Singing Drums.

They were dancing.

Some couples shuffled a sedate measure, never losing the contact between their magnetically shod feet and the polished deck. Others—daring or foolhardy—cavorted in Nul-G, gamboled fantastically but rarely gracefully in Free Fall.

They were dancing.

Ensign Grimes was trying to dance.

It was not the fault of his partner that he was making such a sorry mess of it. She, Jane Pentecost, proved the truth of the oft-made statement that spacemen and spacewomen are expert at this form of exercise. He, John Grimes, was the exception that proves the rule. He was sweating, and his feet felt at least six times their normal size. Only the fact that he was holding Jane, and closely, saved him from absolute misery.

There was a pause in the music. As it resumed Jane said, "Let's sit this one out, Admiral."

"If you wish to," he replied, trying not to sound too grateful.

"That's right I wish to. I don't mind losing a little toenail varnish, but I think we'll call it a day while I still have a full set of toenails."

"I'm sorry," he said.

"So am I." But the flicker of a smile robbed the words of their sting.

She led the way to the bar. It was deserted save for the bored and sulky girl behind the gleaming counter. "All right, Sue," Jane told her. "You can join the revels. The Admiral and I will mind the shop."

"*Thank* you, Miss Pentecost." Sue let herself out from her little cage, vanished gracefully and rapidly in the direction of the saloon. Jane took her place.

"I *like* being a barmaid," she told the ensign, taking two frosted bulbs out of the cooler.

"I'll sign for these," offered Grimes.

"You will not. This comes under the heading of entertaining influential customers."

"But I'm not. Influential, I mean."

"But you will be." She went on dreamily. "I can see it. I can just see it. The poor old *Delia O'Ryan*, even more decrepit that she is now, and her poor old purser, about to undergo a fate worse than death at the hands of bloody pirates from the next Galaxy but three. . . . But all is not lost. There, light years distant, is big, fat, Grand Admiral Grimes aboard his flagship, busting a gut, to say nothing of his Mannschenn Drive unit, to rush to the rescue of his erstwhile girlfield. 'Dammitall,' I can hear him muttering into his beard. 'Dammitall. That girl used to give me free drinks when I was a snotty nosed ensign. I will repay. Full speed ahead, Gridley, and damn the torpedoes!' "

Grimes laughed—then asked sharply, "Admiral in which service?"

"What do you mean, John?" She eyed him warily.

"*You* know what I mean."

"So . . . " she murmured. "So . . . I know that you had another home truth session with the Bearded Bastard. I can guess what it was about."

"And is it true?" demanded Grimes.

"Am I Olga Popovsky, the Beautiful Spy? Is that what you mean?"

"More or less."

"Come off it, John. How the hell can I be a secret agent for a non-existent government?"

"You can be a secret agent for a subversive organization."

"What *is* this? Is it a hangover from some half-baked and half-understood course in counter-espionage?"

"There was a course of sorts," he admitted. "I didn't take much interest in it. At the time."

"And now you wish that you had. Poor John."

"But it wasn't espionage that the Old Man had against you. He had some sort of story about your acting as a sort of recruiting sergeant, luring officers away from the Commission's ships to that crumby little rabble of star tramps calling itself the Sundowner Line. . . . "

She didn't seem to be listening to him, but was giving her attention instead to the music that drifted from the saloon. It was one of the old, Twentieth Century melodies that were enjoying a revival. She began to sing in time to it.

> *"Goodbye, I'll run*
> *To seek another sun*
> *Where I*
> *May find*
> *There are hearts more kind*
> *Than the ones left behind . . . "*

She smiled somberly and asked, "Does that answer your question?"

"Don't talk in riddles," he said roughly.

"Riddles? Perhaps—but not very hard ones. That, John, is a sort of song of farewell from a very old comic opera. As I recall it, the guy singing it was going to shoot through and join the French Foreign Legion. (But there's no French Foreign Legion anymore. . . .) We, out on the Rim, have tacked our own words on to it. It's become almost a national anthem to the Rim Runners, as the people who man our ships—such as they are—are already calling themselves.

"There's no French Foreign Legion anymore—but the misfits and the failures have to have somewhere to go. I haven't *lured* anybody away from this service—but now and again I've shipped with officers who've been on the point of getting out, or being emptied out, and when they've cried into my beer I've given them advice. Of course, I've a certain natural bias in favor of my own home world. If I were Sirian born I'd be singing the praises of the Dog Star Line."

"Even so," he persisted, "your conduct seems to have been somewhat suspect."

"Has it? And how? To begin with, *you* are not an officer in this employ. And if you were, I should challenge you to find anything in the Commission's regulations forbidding me to act as I have been doing."

"Captain Craven warned me," said Grimes.

"Did he, now? That's his privilege. I suppose that he thinks that it's also his duty. I suppose he has the idea that I offered you admiral's rank in the Rim Worlds Navy as soon as we secede. *If* we had our own Navy—which we don't—we might just take you in an Ensign, Acting, Probationary."

"Thank you."

She put her elbows on the bar counter, propping her face between her hands, somehow conveying the illusion of gravitational pull, looking up at him. "I'll be frank with you, John. I admit that we do take the no-hopers, the drunks and the drifters into our merchant fleet. I know far better than you what a helluva difference there is between those rustbuckets and the well-found, well-run ships of the Commission and, come to that, Trans-Galactic Clippers and Waverley Royal Mail. But when we do start some kind of a Navy we shall want better material. Much better. We shall want highly competent officers who yet, somehow, will have the Rim World outlook. The first batch, of course, will have to be outsiders, to tide us over until our own training program is well under way."

"And I don't qualify?" he asked stiffly.

"Frankly, no. I've been watching you. You're too much of a stickler for rules and regulations, especially the more stupid ones. Look at the way you're dressed now, for example. Evening wear, civilian, junior officers, for the use of. No individuality. You might as well be in uniform. Better, in fact. There'd be some touch of brightness."

"Go on."

"And the way you comport yourself with women. Stiff. Starchy. Correct. And you're all too conscious of the fact that I, even though I'm a mere merchant officer, and a clerical branch at that, put up more gold braid than you do. I noticed that especially when we were dancing. I was having to lead all the time."

He said defensively, "I'm not a very good dancer."

"You can say that again." She smiled briefly. "So there you have it, John. You can tell the Bearded Bastard, when you see him again, that you're quite safe from my wiles. I've no doubt that you'll go far in your own Service—but you just aren't Rim Worlds material."

"I shouldn't have felt all that flattered if you'd said that I was," he told her bluntly—but he knew that he was lying.

VIII

"YES?" JANE WAS SAYING. "Yes, Mr. Letourneau?"

Grimes realized that she was not looking at him, that she was looking past him and addressing a newcomer. He turned around to see who it was. He found—somehow the name hadn't registered—that it was the Psionic Radio Officer, a tall, pale, untidily put together young man in a slovenly uniform. He looked scared—but that was his habitual expression, Grimes remembered. They were an odd breed, these trained telepaths with their Rhine Institute diplomas, and they were not popular, but they were the only means whereby ships and shore stations could communicate instantaneously over the long light years. In the Survey Service they were referred to, slightingly, as Commissioned Teacup Readers. In the Survey Service and in the Merchant Service they were referred to as Snoopers. But they were a very necessary evil.

"Yes, Mr. Letourneau?"

"Where's the Old Man? He's not in his quarters."

"The Master"—Jane emphasized the title—"is in the saloon." Then, a little maliciously, "Couldn't you have used your crystal ball?"

Letourneau flushed. "You know very well, Miss Pentecost, that we have to take an oath that we will always respect the mental privacy of our shipmates. . . . But I must find him. Quickly."

"Help yourself. He's treading the light fantastic in there." When he was gone she said, "Typical. Just typical. If it were a real emergency he could get B.B. on the intercom. But no. Not him. He has to parade his distrust of anything electronic and, at the same time, make it quite clear that he's not breaking his precious oath. . . . Tell me, how do you people handle your spaceborne espers?"

He grinned. "We've still one big stick that you people haven't. A court martial followed by a firing party. Not that I've ever seen it used."

"Hardly, considering that you've only been in Space a dog watch." Her face froze suddenly. "Yes, Sue?"

It was the girl whom Jane had relieved in the bar. "Miss Pentecost, will you report to the Captain in Control, please. At once."

"What have I done now?"

"It's some sort of emergency, Miss Pentecost. The Chief Officer's up there with him, and he's sent for the Doctor and the two Chief Engineers."

"Then I must away, John. Look after the bar again, Sue. Don't let the Admiral have too many free drinks."

She moved fast and gracefully, was gone before Grimes could think of any suitable repartee. He said to the girl, "What *is* happening, Sue?"

"I don't know, Ad—" She flushed. "Sorry, Ensign. And, in any case, I'm not supposed to talk to the passengers about it."

"But I'm not a real passenger," he said—and asked himself, *Am I a* real *anything?*

"No, I suppose you're not, Mr. Grimes. But you're not on duty."

"An officer of the Survey Service is *always* on duty," he told her, with some degree of truth.

"Whatever happens on the spacelanes is our concern." It sounded good.

"Yes," she agreed hesitantly. "That's what my fiancé—he's a Lieutenant J.G.—is always telling me."

"So what's all the flap about?"

"Promise not to tell anybody?"

"Of course."

"Mr. Letourneau came wandering into the Saloon. He just stood there staring about, the way he does, then he spotted the Captain. He was actually dancing with me at the time. . . ." She smiled reminiscently, and added, "He's a very good dancer."

"He would be. But go on."

"He came charging across the dance floor—Mr. Letourneau, I mean. He didn't care whose toes he trod on or who he tripped over. I couldn't help overhearing when he started babbling away to Captain Craven. It's a distress call. From one of our ships—*Epsilon Sextans*." Her voice dropped to a whisper. "And it's piracy."

"Piracy? Impossible."

"But, Mr. Grimes, it's what he said."

"Psionic Radio Officers have been known to go around the bend before now," Grimes told her, "and to send false alarm calls. And to receive non-existent ones."

"But the *Sexy Eppy*—sorry, *Epsilon Sextans*—has a cargo that'd be worth pirating. Or so I heard. The first big shipment of Antigeriatridine to Waverly. . . ."

Antigeriatridine, the so-called Immortality Serum. Manufactured in limited, but increasing quantities only on Marina (often called by its colonists Submarina), a cold, unpleasantly watery world in orbit about Alpha Crucis. The fishlike creatures from which the drug was obtained bred and flourished only in the seas of their own world.

But piracy. . . .

But the old legends were full of stories of men who had sold their souls for eternal youth.

The telephone behind the bar buzzed sharply. Sue answered it. She said, "It's for you, Mr. Grimes."

Grimes took the instrument. "That you, Ensign?" It was Captain Craven's voice. "Thought I'd find you there. Come up to Control, will you?" It was an order rather than a request.

All the ship's executive officers were in the Control Room, and the Doctor, the purser and the two Chief Engineers. As Grimes emerged from the hatch he heard Kennedy, the Mate, say, "Here's the Ensign now."

"Good. Then dog down, Mr. Kennedy, so we get some privacy." Craven turned to Grimes. "You're on the Active List of the Survey Service, Mister, so I suppose you're entitled to know what's going on. The situation is this. *Epsilon Sextans,* Marina to Waverley with a shipment of Antigeriatridine, has been pirated." Grimes managed, with an effort, to refrain from saying "I know." Craven went on. "Her esper is among the survivors. He says that the pirates were two frigates of the Waldegren Navy. Anyhow, the Interstellar Drive Engineers aboard *Epsilon Sextans* managed to put their box of tricks on random precession, and they got away. But not in one piece. . . ."

"Not in one piece?" echoed Grimes stupidly.

"What the hell do you expect when an unarmed

merchantman is fired upon, without warning, by
two warships? The esper says that their Control
has had it, and all the accommodation spaces. By
some miracle the Psionic Radio Officer's shack
wasn't holed, and neither was the Mannschenn
Drive Room."

"But even one missile . . ." muttered Grimes.

"If you want to capture a ship and her cargo
more or less intact," snapped Craven, "you don't
use missiles. You use laser. It's an ideal weapon if
you aren't fussy about how many people you kill."

"Knowing the Waldegrenese as *we* do," said
Jane Pentecost bitterly, "there wouldn't have
been any survivors anyhow."

"Be quiet!" roared Craven. Grimes was puzzled by his outburst. It was out of character. True,
he could hardly expect a shipmaster to react to the
news of a vicious piracy with equanimity—but this
shipmaster was an officer of the Reserve, had seen
service in warships and had been highly decorated
for outstanding bravery in battle.

Craven had control of himself again. "The situation is this. There are people still living aboard
Epsilon Sextans. Even though all her navigators
have been killed I think that I shall be able to find
her in time. Furthermore, she has a very valuable
cargo and, in any case, cannot be written off as a
total loss. There is little damage that cannot be
repaired by welded patches. I have already sent a
message to Head Office requesting a free hand. I
have salvage in mind. I see no reason why the ship
and her cargo should not be taken on to Waverley."

"A prize crew, sir?"

"If you care to put it that way. This will mean
cutting down the number of officers aboard my

own vessel—but I am sure, Mr. Grimes, that you will be willing to gain some practical watch-keeping experience. All that's required is your autograph on the ship's Articles of Agreement."

"Thank you, sir."

"Don't thank me. I may be thanking you before the job's over and done." He turned to his Chief Officer. "Mr. Kennedy, keep in touch with Mr. Letourneau and let me know if anything further comes through either from *Epsilon Sextans* or from Head Office. The rest of you—keep this to yourselves. No sense in alarming the passengers. I'm sure that the Doctor and Miss Pentecost between them can concoct some soothing story to account for this officers' conference."

"Captain Craven," said Jane Pentecost.

"Well?"

"The other man at my table, Mr. Baxter. I knew him out on the Rim. He holds Chief Reaction Drive Engineer's papers."

"Don't tell him anything yet. But I'll keep him in mind. Now, Mr. Grimes, will you join me in my day cabin?"

IX

THE HOLOGRAMS were all gone from the bulkheads of Captain Craven's cabin. To replace them there was just one picture—of a woman, not young, but with the facial bone structure that defies age and time. She was in uniform, and on her shoulderboards were the two and a half stripes of a Senior Purser. The shipmaster noticed Grimes' interest and said briefly and bitterly. "She was too senior for an *Epsilon* class ship—but she cut her leave short, just to oblige, when the regular purser went sick. She should have been back on Earth at the same time as me, though. Then we were going to get married. . . ."

Grimes said nothing. He thought, *Too senior for an* Epsilon *class ship?* Epsilon Sextans, *for example?* What could he say?

"And that," said Craven savagely, "*was* that."

"I'm sorry, sir," blurted Grimes, conscious of the inadequacy of his words. Then, foolishly, "But there are survivors, sir."

"Don't you think that I haven't got Letourneau and his opposite number checking? And have *you* ever seen the aftermath of a Deep Space battle, Mister? Have you ever boarded a ship that's been slashed and stabbed to death with laser beams?" He seemed to require no answer; he pulled himself into the chair by his desk, strapped himself in and motioned to Grimes to be seated. Then he pulled out from a drawer a large sheet of paper, which he unfolded. It was a cargo plan. "Current voyage," he grunted. "And we're carrying more to Lindisfarne than one brand-new ensign."

"Such as, sir?" ventured Grimes.

"Naval stores. I don't mind admitting that I'm more than a little rusty insofar as Survey Service procedure is concerned, even though I still hold my Reserve Commission. You're more familiar with fancy abbreviations than I am. Twenty cases RERAT, for example. . . . "

"Reserve rations, sir. Canned and dehydrated."

"Good. And ATREG?"

"Atmospheric regeneration units, complete."

"So if *Epsilon Sextans'* 'farm' has been killed we shall be able to manage?"

"Yes, sir."

"Do you think you'd be able to install an ATREG unit?"

"Of course, sir. They're very simple, as you know. Just synthetic chlorophyl and a UV source. . . . In any case, there are full instructions inside every container."

"And this? A double M, Mark XV?"

"Anti-Missile Missile."

"And ALGE?"

"Anti-Laser Gas Emitter."

"The things they do think of. I feel more at home with these AVMs—although I see that they've got as far as Mark XVII now."

"Anti-Vessel Missiles," said Grimes. A slight enthusiasm crept into his voice. "The XVII's a real honey."

"What does it do?"

"I'm sorry, sir. Even though you are a Reserve Officer, I can't tell you."

"But they're effective?"

"Yes. Very."

"And I think you're Gunnery Branch, Mr. Grimes, aren't you?"

"I am sir." He added hastily, "But I'm still quite capable of carrying out a watch officer's duties aboard this vessel should the need arise."

"The main thing is, you're familiar with naval stores and equipment. When we find and board *Epsilon Sextans* I shall be transshipping certain items of cargo . . . "

"RERAT and ATREG, sir?"

"Yes. And the others."

"But, sir, I can't allow it. Not unless I have authority from the Flag Officer commanding Lindisfarne Base. As soon as your Mr. Letourneau can be spared I'll get him to try and raise the station there."

"I'm afraid that's out of the question, Mr. Grimes. In view of the rather peculiar political situation, I think that the answer would be No. Even it it were Yes, you know as well as I how sluggishly the tide flows through official channels. Furthermore, just in case it has escaped your notice, *I* am the Master."

"And I, sir, represent the Survey Service. As the only commissioned officer aboard this vessel *I* am responsible for Survey Service cargo."

"As a Reserve Officer, Mr. Grimes, I rank you."

"Only when you have been recalled to Active Service. Sir."

Craven said, "I was rather afraid that you'd take this attitude. That's why I decided to get this interview over and done with, just so we all know where we stand." He put away the cargo plan, swiveled his chair so that he could reach out to his liquor cabinet. He pulled out two bulbs, tossed one to Grimes. "No toasts. If we drank to Law and Order we should mean different things. So just drink. And listen.

"To begin with, *Epsilon Sextans* doesn't know where she is. But Letourneau is one of the rare telepaths with the direction finding talent, and as soon as he's able to get lined up we shall alter course to home on the wreck. That's what he's trying to do now.

"When we find her, we shall synchronize and board, of course. The first thing will be medical aid to the survivors. Then we patch the ship up. And then we arm her. And then, with a prize crew under myself, we put ourselves on the trajectory for Waverley—hoping that those Waldegrenese frigates come back for another nibble."

"They'd never dare, sir."

"Wouldn't they? The original piracy they'll try to laugh off by saying that it was by *real* pirates— no, that's not quite right, but you know what I mean—wearing Waldegren colors. The second piracy—they'll make sure that there are no survivors."

"But I still can't see how they can hope to get away with it. It's always been an accepted fact that the main weapon against piracy has been psionic radio."

"And so it was—until some genius developed a jamming technique. *Epsilon Sextans* wasn't able to get any messages out until her crazy random precession pulled her well clear."

"And you hope, sir, that they *do* attack you?"

"I do, Mr. Grimes. I had hoped that I should have a good gunnery officer under me, but"—he shrugged his massive shoulders—"I think that I shall be able to manage."

"And you hope that you'll have your weapons," persisted Grimes.

"I see no reason why I should not, Ensign."

"There is one very good reason, sir. That is that I, a commissioned officer of the Survey Service, am aboard your vessel. I insist that you leave the tracking down and destruction of the pirates to the proper authorities. I insist, too, that no Survey Service stores be discharged from this ship without my written authority."

For the first time the hint of a smile relieved the somberness of Craven's face. "And to think that I believed that Jane Pentecost could recruit *you*," he murmured. Then, in a louder voice, "And what if I just go ahead without your written authority, Ensign?"

Grimes had the answer ready. "Then, sir, I shall be obliged to order your officers not to obey your unlawful commands. If necessary, I shall call upon the male passengers to assist me in any action that is necessary."

Craven's bushy eyebrows went up and stayed up. "Mr. Grimes," he said in a gritty voice, "it is indeed lucky for you that I have firsthand experience of the typical Survey Service mentality. Some Masters I know would, in these circumstances, send you out on a spacewalk without a suit. But, before I take drastic action, I'll give you one more chance to cooperate." His tone softened. "You noticed the portrait I've put up instead of all the temporary popsies. Every man, no matter how much he plays around, has one woman who is *the* woman. Gillian was *the* woman as far as I was concerned—as far as I *am* concerned. I've a chance to bring her murderers under my guns—

and, by God, I'm taking that chance, no matter what it means either to my career or to the somewhat odd foreign policy of the Federation. I used to be annoyed by Jane Pentecost's outbursts on that subject—but now I see that she's right. And she's right, too, when it comes to the Survey Service's reluctance to take action against Waldegren.

"So I, Mr. Grimes, am taking action."

"Sir, I forbid you . . . "

"*You* forbid *me*? Ensign, you forget yourself. Perhaps this will help you remember."

This was a Minetti automatic that had appeared suddenly in the Captain's hand. In his hairy fist the little, glittering weapon looked no more than a toy—but Grimes knew his firearms, knew that at the slightest pressure of Craven's finger the needle-like projectiles would stitch him from crown to crotch.

"I'm sorry about this, Mr. Grimes." As he spoke, Craven pressed a button set in his desk with his free hand. "I'm sorry about this. But I realize that I was expecting rather too much of you. After all, you have your career to consider. . . . Time was," he went on, "when a naval officer could put his telescope to his blind eye as an excuse for ignoring orders—and get away with it. But the politicians had less power in those days. We've come a long way—and a wrong way—since Nelson."

Grimes heard the door behind him slide open. He didn't bother to look around, not even when hard hands were laid on his shoulders.

"Mr. Kennedy," said Craven, "things turned out as I feared that they would. Will you and Mr. Ludovic take the Ensign along to the Detention Cell?"

"I'll see you on trial for piracy, Captain!" flared Grimes.

"An interesting legal point, Ensign—especially since you are being entered in my Official Log as a mutineer."

X

THE DETENTION CELL was not uncomfortable, but it was depressing. It was a padded cell—passengers in spacecraft have been known to exhibit the more violent symptoms of mania—which detracted from its already inconsiderable cheerfulness if not from its comfort. However, Grimes was not mad—not in the medical sense, that is—and so was considered able to attend to his own bodily needs. The little toilet was open to him, and at regular intervals a bell would sound and a container of food would appear in a hatch recessed into the bulkhead of the living cabin. There was reading matter too—such as it was. The Ensign suspected that Jane Pentecost was the donor. It consisted of pamphlets published by some organization calling itself The Rim Worlds Secessionist Party. The almost hysterical calls to arms were bad enough—but the ones consisting mainly of columns of statistics were worse. Economics had never been Grimes' strong point.

He slept, he fed at the appointed times, he made a lengthy ritual of keeping himself clean, he tried to read—and, all the time, with only sounds and sensations as clues, he endeavored to maintain a running plot of the ship's maneuvers.

Quite early there had been the shutting down of the Mannschenn Drive, and the consequent fleeting sensation of temporal disorientation. This had been followed by the acceleration warning—the cell had an intercom speaker recessed in the padding—and Grimes, although it seemed rather pointless in his sponge rubber environment, had strapped himself into his couch. He heard the directional gyroscopes start up, felt the effects of centrifugal force as the ship came around to her new heading. Then there was the pseudo-gravity of acceleration, accompanied by the muffled thunder of the reaction drive. It was obvious, thought the Ensign, that Captain Craven was expending his reaction mass in a manner that, in other circumstances, would have been considered reckless.

Suddenly—silence and Free Fall, and almost immediately the off-key keening of the Mannschenn Drive. Its note was higher, much higher, than Grimes remembered it, and the queasy feeling of temporal disorientation lasted much longer than it had on previous occasions.

And that, for a long time, was all.

Meals came, and were eaten. Every morning—according to his watch—the prisoner showered and applied depilatory cream to his face. He tried to exercise—but to exercise in a padded cell, with no apparatus, in Free Fall, is hard. He tried to read—but the literature available was hardly more interesting to him than a telephone directory would have been. And, even though he never had been gregarious, the lack of anybody to talk to was wearing him down.

It was a welcome break from the monotony when he realized that, once again, the ship was maneuvering. This time there was no use of the directional gyroscopes; there were no rocket blasts, but there was a variation of the whine of the Drive as it hunted, hunted, as the temporal precession rate was adjusted by tens of seconds, by seconds, by microseconds.

And then it locked.

The ship shuddered slightly—once, twice.

Grimes envisaged the firing of the two mooring rockets, one from the bow and one from the stern, each with the powerful electromagnet in its nose, each trailing its fathoms of fine but enormously strong cable. Merchant vessels, he knew, carried this equipment, but unlike naval ships rarely used it. But Craven, as a Reservist, would have seen and taken part in enough drills.

The ship shuddered again—heavily.

So the rendezvous had been made. So *Delta Orionis* and *Epsilon Sextans*, their Drives synchronized, bound together by the rescue ship's cables, were now falling as one unit through the dark immensities.

So the rendezvous had been made—and already the survivors of the wreck were being brought aboard the *Delia O'Ryan*, were being helped out of their stinking spacesuits, were blurting out their story to Craven and his officers. Grimes could visualize it all, almost as clearly as though he were actually watching it. He could visualize, too, the engineers swarming over the wreck, the flare of their burning and welding torches, the cannibalizing of nonessential plating from the ship's structure for hull patches. It was all laid down in the Survey Service's Damage Control Manual—and Captain Craven, at least, would know that book as thoroughly as did Grimes.

And what of the cargo, the Survey Service stores, *Grimes'* stores? A trembling in the ship's structure, a barely felt vibration, told him that

gantries and conveyor belts were being brought
into operation. There would be no great handling
problems. Lindisfarne was *Delta Orionis'* first
port of call, and the Survey Service consignment
would be top stowage. But there was nothing that
Grimes could do about it—not a thing. In fact, he
was beginning to doubt the legality of the stand he
had made against the Master. And he was the small
frog in this small puddle, while Captain Craven
had made it quite clear that he was the big frog.
Grimes wished that he was better versed in as-
tronautical law—although a professional lawyer's
knowledge would be of no use to him in his present
situation.

So, with some hazy idea that he might need all
his strength, both mental and physical, for what
was to befall him (but *what?*), in the near future, he
strapped himself into his bunk and did his best to
forget his worries in sleep. He was well enough
acquainted with the psychiatrists' jargon to know
that this was no more than a return to the womb
but, before dropping off into a shallow slumber,
shrugged, *So what?*

He jerked into sudden wakefulness.

Jane Pentecost was there by his bunk, looking
down at him.

"Come in," he said. "Don't bother to knock.
Now you see how the poor live. This is Liberty
Hall; you can spit on the mat and call the cat a
bastard."

She said, "That's not very funny."

"I know it's not. Even the first time that I heard
it aboard this blasted ship I was able to refrain from
rolling in the aisles."

She said, "There's no need to be so bitchy, John."

"Isn't there? Wouldn't you be bitchy if you'd been thrown into this padded cell?"

"I suppose I would be. But you asked for it, didn't you?"

"If doing my duty—or trying to do my duty—is asking for it, I suppose that I did. Well—and has our pirate Captain cast off yet, armed to the teeth with the weapons he's stolen?"

"No. The weapons are still being mounted. But let's not argue legalities, John. There's not enough time. I . . . I just wanted to say goodbye."

"Goodbye?" he echoed.

"Yes. Somebody has to do the cooking aboard *Epsilon Sextans*—and I volunteered."

"You?"

"And why the hell not?" she flared. "Captain Craven has been pushed over to *our* side of the fence, and it'd be a pretty poor show if we Rim Worlders weren't prepared to stand by him. Baxter's gone across to take over as Reaction Drive Engineer; the only survivor in that department was the Fourth, and he's only a dog watch in Space."

"And who else?"

"Nobody. The *Sexy Eppy's* Chief, Second and Third Interstellar Drive Engineers survived, and they're willing—anxious, in fact, now that their ship's being armed—to stay on. And the Psionic Radio Officer came through, and is staying on. All of our executive officers volunteered, of course, but the Old Man turned them down. He said that, after all, he could not hazard the safety of this ship by stripping her of her trained personnel. Especially since we carry passengers.''

''That's his worry,'' said Grimes without much sympathy. ''But how does he hope to fight his ship if those frigates pounce again?''

''He thinks he'll be able to manage—with remote controls for every weapon brought to his main control panel.''

''Possible,'' admitted Grimes, his professional interest stirred. ''But not very efficient. In a naval action the Captain has his hands full just handling the ship alone, without trying to control her weaponry.''

''And you'd know, of course.''

''Yes.''

''Yes, you've read the books. And Captain Craven commanded a light cruiser during that trouble with the Dring, so he knows nothing.''

''He still hasn't got four hands and two heads.''

''Oh, let's stop talking rubbish,'' she cried. ''I probably shan't see you again, John and . . . and . . . oh, hell, I want to say goodbye properly, and I don't want you to think too badly about either the Old Man or . . . or myself.''

''So what are we supposed to do about it?''

''Damn you, Grimes, you snotty-nosed, stuck-up spacepuppy! Look after yourself!''

Suddenly she bent down to kiss him. It was intended to be no more than a light brushing of lips, but Grimes was suddenly aware, with his entire body, of the closeness of her, of the warmth and the scent of her, and almost without volition his arms went about her, drawing her closer still to him. She tried to break away, but it was only a halfhearted effort. He heard her murmur, in an odd, sardonic whisper, ''wotthehell, wotthehell.'' and then, ''toujours gai.'' It made no sense at the

time but, years later, when he made the acquaint-
ance of the Twentieth Century poets, he was to
remember and to understand. What was important
now was that her own arms were about him.

Somehow the buttons of her uniform shirt had
come undone, and her nipples were taut against
Grimes' bare chest. Somehow her shorts had been
peeled away from her hips—unzippered by
whom? and how?—and somehow Grimes' own
garments were no longer the last barrier between
them.

He was familiar enough with female nudity; he
was one of the great majority who frequented the
naked beaches in preference to those upon which
bathing costumes were compulsory. He knew
what a naked woman looked like—but this was
different. It was not the first time that he had
kissed a woman—but it was the first time that he
had kissed, and been kissed by, an unclothed one.
It was the first time that he had been alone with
one.

What was happening he had read about often
enough—and, like most young men, he had seen
his share of pornographic films. But this was different. This was happening to *him*.

And for the first time.

When it was over, when, still clasped in each
others' arms they drifted in the center of the little
cabin, impelled there by some odd resultant of
forces, their discarded clothing drifting with
them, veiling their perspiration-moist bodies,
Grimes was reluctant to let her go.

Gently, Jane tried to disengage herself.

She whispered, "That was a warmer goodbye
that I intended. But I'm not sorry. No. I'm not
sorry. . . ."

Then, barely audibly, "It was the first time for you, wasn't it?"

"Yes."

"Then I'm all the more glad it happened. But this *is* goodbye."

"*No.*"

"Don't be a fool, John. You can't keep me here."

"But I can come with you."

She pushed him from her. Somehow he landed back on the bed. Before he could bounce he automatically snapped one of the confining straps about his middle. Somehow—she was still wearing her sandals but nothing else—she finished up standing on the deck, held there by the contact between the magnetic soles and the ferrous fibers in the padding. She put out a long, graceful arm and caught her shirt. She said harshly, "*I'm* getting dressed and out of here. *You* stay put. Damn you, Grimes, for thinking that I was trying to lure you aboard the *Sexy Eppy* with the body beautiful. I told you before that I am not, repeat now, Olga Popovsky, the Beautiful Spy. And I'm not a prostitute. There's one thing I wouldn't *sell* if I were offered the services of the finest Gunnery Officer (which you aren't), in the whole bloody Galaxy in payment!"

"You're beautiful when you flare up like that," said Grimes sincerely. "But you're *always* beautiful." Then, in a louder voice, "Jane, I love you."

"Puppy love," she sneered. "And I'm old enough to be your . . . " A faint smile softened her mouth. "Your maiden aunt."

"Let me finish. All right, it's only puppy love—*you* say. But it's still love. But"—he was extemporizing—convincingly, he hoped—"but my real reason for wanting to come with you is this. I can appreciate now what Captain Craven lost when *Epsilon Sextans* was pirated. I can see—I can *feel*—why he's willing to risk his life and his career to get his revenge. And I think that it's worth it. And I want to help him."

She stood there, her shirt half on, eying him suspiciously. "You mean that? You really mean that?"

"Yes."

"Then you're a liar, Grimes."

"No," he said slowly. "No. Not altogether. I want to help the Old Man—and I want to help *you*. This piracy has convinced me that you Rim Worlders *are* getting the dirty end of the stick. I may not be the finest Gunnery Officer in the whole Galaxy—but I'm better acquainted with the new stuff than Captain Craven is."

Her grin was openly derisive. "First it's fellow-feeling for another spaceman, then it's international politics. What next?"

"Where we started. I *do* love you, Jane. And if there's going to be any shooting, I want to be on hand to do the shooting back on your behalf. I'll admit that . . . that what's happened has influenced my decision. But you didn't buy me, or bribe me. Don't think that. Don't ever think that." There was a note of pleading in his voice. "Be realistic, Jane. With another officer along, especially an officer with recent gunnery training, you stand a damn sight better chance than you would otherwise."

"I . . . I suppose so. But I still don't like it."

"You don't have to. But why look a gift horse in the mouth?"

"All right. You win. Get your clothes on and come and see the Old Man."

XI

JANE PENTECOST led Grimes to the airlock. The ship seemed oddly deserted, and he remarked on this. The girl explained that the passengers had been requested to remain in their accommodations, and that most of *Delta Orionis'* personnel were employed in work aboard *Epsilon Sextans*.

"So I haven't been the only one to be kept under lock and key," commented Grimes sardonically.

"You're the only one," retorted the girl, "who's been compensated for his imprisonment."

There was no answer to that, so the Ensign remained silent. Saying nothing, he inspected with interest the temporary tunnel that had been rigged between the airlocks of the two ships. So *Epsilon Sextans'* pressure hull had been made good, her atmosphere restored. That meant that the work of installing the armament had been completed. He hoped that he would not have to insist upon modifications.

The wreck—although she was a wreck no longer—bore her scars. The worst damage had been repaired, but holes and slashes that did not impair her structural strength were untouched, and spatters of once molten metal still made crazy patterns on beams and frames, stanchions and bulkheads. And there were the scars made by Craven's engineers—the raw, bright cicatrices of new welding.

Forward they made their way, deck after deck. The elevator in the axial shaft was not yet working, so Grimes had time and opportunity to appreciate the extent of the damage. They passed through the wreckage of the "farm"—the burst algae tanks, the ruptured vats in which yeast and tissue cultures were black and dead, frostbitten and dehydrated. They brushed through alleyways choked with the brittle fronds of creeping plants killed by the ultimate winter.

And then they were passing through the accommodation levels. Bulkheads had been slashed through, destroying the privacy of the cabins that they had once enclosed. Destroying the privacy—and the occupants. There were no longer any bodies; for this Grimes was deeply thankful. (He learned later that Craven's first action had been to order and conduct a funeral service.) There were no bodies—but there were still stains. Men and women die quickly in hard vacuum—quickly and messily.

Captain Craven was alone in the Control Room. He was working, rather slowly and clumsily, wiring up an obviously makeshift panel that was additional to the original one installed before the Master's acceleration chair. It was obvious what it was—the remote controls for the newly fitted weaponry. Grimes said quickly, "There's no need for that, sir."

Craven started, let go of his screwdriver, made a fumbling grab for it as it drifted away from him. He stared at Grimes, then growled, "So it's *you*, is it?" Then, to Jane, "What the hell do you mean by letting this puppy out of his kennel?"

"Captain Craven," she told him quietly, "Mr. Grimes wants to come with us."

"*What*? I warn you, Miss Pentecost, I'm in no mood for silly jokes."

"This is not a silly joke, Captain," said Grimes.

"I've had time to think things over. I feel, I really feel that you have a far better chance if there's a qualified officer along to handle the gunnery."

Craven looked at them, from the girl to Grimes, then back again. He said, "Ensign, didn't I warn you?"

"It's not that way at all, sir," Grimes told him, flushing. "In fact, Miss Pentecost has been trying hard to dissuade me."

"*Oh?*"

"It's true," said Jane. "But he told me that we couldn't afford to look a gift horse in the mouth."

"I don't know what's been happening," rasped Craven. "I don't want to know what's been happening between the pair of you. This change of mind, this change of heart is rather . . . sudden. No matter. One volunteer, they say, is worth ten pressed men." He glared coldly at the Ensign. "And you volunteer?"

"Yes, Captain."

"I believe you. I have no choice in the matter. But you realize the consequences?"

"I do."

"Well, I *may* be able to do something to clear your yardarm. I've still to make my last entries in the Official Log of *Delta Orionis*, before I hand over to Captain Kennedy. And when it comes to such documentation, nobody cares to accuse a shipmaster of being a liar. Not out loud." He paused, thinking. "How does this sound, Miss Pentecost? Date, Time, Position, etc., etc. Mr. John Grimes, passenger, holding the rank of Ensign in the Federation Survey Service, removed by force from this vessel to *Epsilon Sextans*, there to supervise the installation and mounting of the armament, Survey Service property, discharged on my orders from No. 1 hold, also to advise upon the use of same in the subsequent event of an action's being fought. Signed, etc., etc. And witnessed."

"Rather long-winded, sir. But it seems to cover the ground."

"I intend to do more than advise!" flared Grimes.

"Pipe down. Or, if you must say it, make sure that there aren't any witnesses around when you say it. Now, when it comes to the original supervision, you see what I'm trying to do. Will it work?"

"After a fashion, sir. But it will work much better if the fire control panel is entirely separate from maneuvering control."

"You don't think that I could handle both at once?"

"You *could*. But not with optimum efficiency. No humanoid could. This setup of yours might just work if we were Shaara, or any of the other multi-limbed arthropods. But even the Shaara, in their warships, don't expect the Queen-Captain to handle her ship *and* her guns simultaneously."

"You're the expert. I just want to be sure that you're prepared to, quote, advise, unquote, with your little pink paws on the actual keyboard of your battle organ."

"That's just the way that I propose to advise."

"Good. Fix it up to suit yourself, then. I should be able to let you have a mechanic shortly to give you a hand."

"Before we go any further, sir, I'd like to make an inspection of the weapons themselves. Just in case . . . "

"Just in case I've made some fantastic bollix,

eh?'' Craven was almost cheerful. ''Very good. But try to make it snappy. It's time we were on our way.''

"Yes," said Jane, and it seemed that the Captain's discarded somberness was hanging about her like a cloud. "It's time."

XII

AT ONE TIME, before differentiation between the mercantile and the fighting vessel became pronounced, merchant vessels were built to carry a quite considerable armament. Today, the mounting of weapons on a merchantman presents its problems. After his tour of inspection Grimes was obliged to admit that Captain Craven had made cunning use of whatever spaces were available— but Craven, of course, was a very experienced officer, with long years of service in all classes of spacecraft. Too—and, perhaps, luckily—there had been no cannon among the Survey Service ordnance that had been requisitioned, so recoil had not been among the problems.

When he was finished, Grimes returned to the Control Room. Craven was still there, and with him was Jane Pentecost. They had, obviously, been discussing something. They could, perhaps, have been quarreling; the girl's face was flushed and her expression sullen.

"Yes?" snapped the Captain.

"You've done a good job, sir. She's no cruiser, but she should be able to defend herself."

"Thank you. Then we'll be on our way."

"Not so fast, sir. I'd like to wire up my control panel properly before we shove off."

Craven laughed. "You'll have time, Mr. Grimes. I still have a few last duties to discharge aboard *Delta Orionis*. But be as quick as you can."

He left the compartment, followed by Jane

Pentecost. She said, over her shoulder, "I'll send Mr. Baxter to help you, John."

The Rim Worlder must have been somewhere handy; in a matter of seconds he was by Grimes' side, an already open tool satchel at his belt. As he worked, assisting deftly and then taking over as soon as he was sure of what was required, he talked. He said, "Mum wanted to come along, but I soon put the damper on that. But I was bloody amazed to find *you* here."

"Were you?" asked Grimes coldly.

"You bet I was. Never thought you were cut out to be a bloody pirate." He cursed briefly as a spatter of hot metal from his sizzling soldering iron stung his hand. "A cold weld'd be better, but it'd take too much time. But where was I? Oh, yes. The shock to me system when I saw you comin' aboard this wagon."

"I have my quite valid reasons," Grimes told him stiffly.

"You're tellin' me. Just as my missus had quite valid reasons for wantin' to come with me. But she ain't a gunnery expert." He added piously, "Thank Gawd."

"And I am one," said the Ensign, trying to change the drift of the conversation before he lost his temper. "Yes. that's right. Just stick to the color code. The blue wiring's the ALGE . . . "

"I know," Baxter told him. "Tell me, is it any good?"

"Yes. Of course, if an enemy held us in her beams for any prolonged period we should all be cooked, but as far as it goes it's effective enough."

"Hope you're right." He made the last connections, then replaced the panel on the open shallow box. "Here's yer magic cabinet, Professor. All we have ter see now is what rabbits yer can pull outer the hat.''

''Plenty, I hope,'' said Captain Craven, who had returned to Control. ''And are you ready now, Mr. Grimes?''

''Yes, sir.''

''Good. Then we'll make it stations. If you will take the copilot's chair, while Mr. Baxter goes along to look after his rockets.''

''Will do, Skipper,'' said the engineer, packing away his tools as he pulled himself toward the exit hatch.

The ship's intercom came to life, in Jane Pentecost's voice. ''Connection between vessels severed. Airlock door closed.''

''We're still connected,'' grumbled Craven. ''*Delia 'O'Ryan* still has her magnetic grapnels out.'' He spoke into the transceiver microphone: ''*Epsilon Sextans* to *Delta Orionis*. Cast off, please. Over.''

''*Delta Orionis* to *Epsilon Sextans*. Casting off.'' Through a viewport Grimes could see one of the bright mooring wires snaking back into its recess. ''All clear, Captain.''

''Thank you, *Captain* Kennedy.'' And in a softer voice, ''And I hope you keep that handle to your name, Bill.''

''Thank you, sir. And all the best, Captain, from all of us, to all of you. And good hunting.''

''Thanks. And look after the old *Delia*, Captain. And yourself. Over—and out.''

''*Delia Orionis* to *Epsilon Sextans*. Over and out.''

(There was something very final, thought Grimes, about those outs.)

He was aware that the ships were drifting slowly

apart. Now he could see all of *Delta Orionis* from his viewport. He could not help recalling the day on which he had first seen her, at the Woomera spaceport. So much had happened since that day. (And so much was still to happen—he hoped.) He heard Craven say into the intercom, "Stand by for temporal precession. We're desynchronizing." Then, there was the giddiness, and the off-beat whine of the Mannschenn Drive that pierced his eardrums painfully, and beyond the viewports the great, shining shape of the other ship shimmered eerily and was suddenly warped into the likeness of a monstrous Klein flash—then vanished. Where she had been (where she still was, in space but not in time) shone the distant stars, the stars that in this distorted continuum were pulsing spirals of iridescence.

"Mannschenn Drive. *Cut!*"

The thin, high keening died abruptly. Outside, the stars were glittering points of light, piercingly bright against the blackness.

"Mr. Grimes!" Craven's voice was sharp. "I hope that you take more interest in gunnery than you do in ship handling. In case it has escaped your notice, I would remind you that you are second in command of this vessel, and in full charge in the event of my demise."

"Sorry, sir," stammered Grimes. Then, suddenly bold, "But I'm not your second in command, sir. I've signed no Articles."

Surprisingly, Craven laughed. "A spacelawyer, yet! Well, Mr. Grimes, as soon as we get this vessel on course we'll attend to the legal formalities. Meanwhile, may I request your close attention to what I am doing?"

"You may, sir."

Thereafter he watched and listened carefully. He admired the skill with which Craven turned the ship on her directional gyroscopes until the red-glowing target star was centered exactly in the cartwheel sight. He noted that the Captain used his reaction drive at a longer period and at a higher rate of acceleration than usual, and said as much. He was told, the words falling slowly and heavily in the pseudo-gravity, "They . . . will . . . expect . . . us . . . to . . . be . . . in . . . a . . . hurry We must . . . not . . . disappoint . . . them."

Speed built up, fast—but it was a velocity that, in the context of the interstellar distances to be traversed, was no more than a snail's crawl. Then—and the sudden silence was like a physical blow—the thunder of the rockets ceased. The screaming roar had died, but the ship was not quiet. The whine of the Mannschenn Drive pervaded her every compartment, vibrated through every member of her structure. She was falling, falling through space and time, plunging through the warped continuum to her rendezvous with Death. . . .

And whose death? wondered Grimes.

He said, "I should have asked before, sir. But how are . . . how are *they* going to find us?"

"I don't know," said Craven. "I don't know. But they've found other ships when they've wanted to. They've never used the old pirate's technique of lying in wait at breaking-out points. A Mass Proximity Indicator? Could be. It's theoretically possible. It could be for a ship under Mannschenn Drive what radar is for a ship in normal space-time. Or some means of homing on a temporal precession field? That's more like it, I think, as this vessel was able to escape when she went random.

"But if they want us—and they will—they'll find us. And then"—he looked at Grimes, his blue gaze intense—"and then it's up to you, Ensign."

"To all of us," said Grimes.

XIII

SHE WAS UNDERMANNED, this *Epsilon Sextans*, but she functioned quite efficiently. Craven kept a Control Room watch himself, and the other two watchkeepers were Grimes and Jane Pentecost. Four on and eight off were their hours of duty—but there was plenty of work to be done in the off duty periods. The Captain, of course, was in over-all charge, and was trying to bring his command to the pitch of efficiency necessary for a fighting ship. Jane Pentecost was responsible for meals—although these, involving little more than the opening of cans, did not take up too much of her time. She had also taken over biochemist's duties, but called now and again upon Grimes to help her with the ATREG unit. Its operation was simple enough, but it was inclined to be tempermental and, now and again, allowed the carbon dioxide concentration to reach a dangerous level. Grimes' main concern was his armament. He could not indulge in a practice shot—the expulsion of mass by a ship running under interstellar drive is suicidal; even the employment of laser weapons is dangerous. But there were tests that he could make; there was, in the ship's stores, a spare chart tank that he was able to convert to a battle simulator.

Craven helped him, and set up targets in the tank, glowing points of light that were destroyed by the other sparks that represented Grimes' missiles. After one such drill he said, "You seem to know your stuff, Ensign. Now, what's your grasp of the tactical side of it?''

Grimes considered his words before speaking. ''Well, sir, we *could* use laser with the Drive in operation—but we haven't got laser. The pirates have. They can synchronize and just carve us up at leisure. This time, I think they'll go for the interstellar drive engine room first, so that we can't get away by the use of random precession.''

''Yes. That's what they'll do. That's why I have that compartment literally sealed in a cocoon of insulation. Oh, I know it's not effective, but it will give us a second or so of grace. No more.''

''We can't use our reflective vapor,'' went on Grimes. ''That'd be almost as bad, from our viewpoint, as loosing off a salvo of missiles. But, sir, when this ship was first attacked there must have been a considerable loss of mass when the atmosphere was expelled through the rents in the shell plating . . . the Drive was running. How was it that the ship wasn't flung into some other space-time?''

''Come, come, Mr. Grimes. You should know the answer to that one. She was held by the powerful temporal precession fields of the drive units of the two pirates. And then, of course, when the engineers managed to set up their random precession there was no mass left to be expelled.''

''H'm. I see. Or I think I see. Then, in that case, why shouldn't I use my ALGE as soon as we're attacked?''

''No. Better not. Something might just go wrong—and I don't want to become one of my own ancestors.''

''Then . . . ?''

''You tell me, Mr. Grimes.''

''Cut our Drive . . . ? Break out into the normal

continuum? Yes . . . it could work." He was becoming enthusiastic. "And then we shall be waiting for them, with our missile batteries, when *they* break out."

"We'll make an admiral of you yet, young Grimes."

With watchkeeping and with off-watch duties time was fully occupied. And yet there was something missing. There was, Grimes said to himself, one hell of a lot missing. Jane Pentecost had her own watch to keep, and her own jobs to do when she was not in the control room—but she and Grimes had some free time to share. But they did not share it.

He broached the subject when he was running a test on the artificial chlorophyl in the ATREG. "Jane, I was hoping I'd see more of you."

"You're seeing plenty of me."

"But not enough."

"Don't be tiresome," she snapped. Then, in a slightly softer voice, "Don't . . . "

" . . . spoil everything?" he finished for her sardonically.

"You know what I mean," she told him coldly.

"Do I?" He groped for words. "Jane . . . Damn it all, I hoped . . . After what happened aboard the *Delia O'Ryan* . . . "

"That," she said, "was different." Her face flushed. "I tell you this, Grimes, if I'd known that you were coming along with us it never would have happened."

"No?"

"*NO!*"

"Even so . . . I don't see any reason why we shouldn't . . . "

"Why we shouldn't what? Oh, all right, all right. I know what you mean. But it's out of the question. I'll tell you why, in words of one syllable. In a ship such as *Delta Orionis* discreet fun and games were permissible, even desirable. No shortage of women—both crew and passengers. Here, I'm the only female. Your friend Mr. Baxter has been sniffing after me. And Mr. Wolverton, the Interstellar Chief. *And* his Second. And even, bereaved though he is, the Bearded Bastard. *He* might get away with it—the privileges of rank and all that. But nobody else would—most certainly not yourself. How long would it remain a secret if we went to bed together?"

"I suppose you're right, but . . ."

"But what? Oh John, John, you *are* a stubborn cow."

"*Cow?*"

"Sorry. Just Rimworldsese. Applicable to both sexes."

"Talking of sex . . ."

"Oh, shut *up!*"

"I'll not." She looked desirable standing there. A small smudge of grease on her flushed cheek was like a beauty spot. "I'll not," he said again. She was close to him, and he was acutely conscious that beneath the thin uniform shirt and the short shorts there was only Jane. He had only to reach out. He did so. At first she did not resist—and then exploded into a frenzy of activity. Before he could let go of her a hard, rough hand closed on his shirt collar and yanked him backwards.

"Keep yer dirty paws off her!" snarled a voice. It was Baxter's. "Keep yer dirty paws off her! If we didn't want yer ter let off the fireworks I'd do yer, here an' now."

"And keep *your* dirty paws off me!" yelped Grimes. It was meant to be an authentic quarter-deck bark, but it didn't come out that way.

"Let him go, Mr. Baxter," said Jane, adding, "please."

"Oh, orl right. If yer says so. But I still think we should run him up ter the Old Man."

"No. Better not." She addressed Grimes, "Thank you for your help on the ATREG, Mr. Grimes. And thank *you*, Mr. Baxter, for your help. It's time that I started looking after the next meal."

She left, not hastily, but not taking her time about it either. When she was gone Baxter released Grimes. Clumsily the Ensign turned himself around, with a wild flailing motion. Unarmed combat had never been his specialty, especially unarmed combat in Free Fall conditions. But he knew that he had to fight, and the rage and the humiliation boiling up in him made it certain that he would do some damage.

But Baxter was laughing, showing all his ugly, yellow teeth. "Come orf it, Admiral! An' if we must have a set-to—not in here. Just smash the UV projector—an' bang goes our air conditioning! Simmer down, mate. Simmer down!"

Grimes simmered down, slowly. "But I thought you were out for my blood, Mr. Baxter."

"Have ter put on a show for the Sheilas now an' again. Shouldn't mind puttin' on another kind o' show *with* her. But not in public—like you was goin' to. It just won't do—not until the shootin' is over, anyhow. An' even then.... So, Admiral, it's paws off as far as you're concerned. An' as far as I'm concerned—*an'* the Chief Time Twister an' his sidekick. But, if yer can spare the time, I propose we continue the conversation in my palatial dogbox."

Grimes should have felt uneasy as he followed the engineer to his accommodation but, oddly enough, he did not. The rough friendliness just could not be the prelude to a beating up. And it wasn't.

"Come in," said Baxter, pulling his sliding door to one side. "Now yer see how the poor live. This is . . . "

"No," protested Grimes. "No."

"Why? I was only goin' to say that this is me 'umble 'umpy. An' I'd like yer to meet a coupla friends o' mine—and there's more where they came from."

The "friends" were two drinking bulbs. Each bore proudly no less than four stars on its label. The brandy was smooth, smooth and potent. Grimes sipped appreciatively. "I didn't know that we had any of *this* aboard *Delia O'Ryan*."

"An' nor did we. You'll not find this tipple in the bar stores of any merchantman, nor aboard any of yer precious Survey Service wagons. Space stock for the Emperor's yacht, this is. So here's ter the Waverley taxpayers!"

"But where did you get this from, Mr. Baxter?"

"Where d'yer think? I've had a good fossick around the holds o' this old bitch, an' there's quite a few things too good to let fall inter the hands o' those bloody Waldegrenese."

"But that's pillage."

"It's common sense. Mind yer, I doubt if Captain Craven would approve, so yer'd better chew some dry tea—that's in the cargo too—before yer see the Old Man again. All the bleedin' same—it's no worse than him borrowing your Survey Service stores an' weapons from *his* cargo."

"I suppose it's not," admitted Grimes. All the same, he still felt guilty when he was offered a second bulb of the luxurious spirit. But he did not refuse it.

XIV

HE WAS A GOOD FOSSICKER, was Baxter.

Two days later, as measured by the ship's chronometer, he was waiting for Grimes as he came off watch. "Ensign," he announced without preamble, "I've found somethin' in the cargo."

"Something new, you mean?" asked Grimes coldly. He still did not approve of pillage, although he had shared the spoils.

"Somethin' that shouldn't be there. Somethin' that's up *your* alley, I think."

"There's no reason why equipment for the Waverley Navy shouldn't be among the cargo."

"True enough. But it wouldn't be in a case with *Beluga Caviar* stenciled all over it. I thought I'd found somethin' to go with the vodka I half inched, but it won't."

"Then what is it?"

"Come and see."

"All right." Briefly Grimes wondered if he should tell Craven, who had relieved the watch, then decided against it. The Old Man would probably insist on making an investigation in person, in which case Grimes would have to pass another boring hour or so in the Control Room.

The two men made their way aft until they came to the forward bulkhead of the cargo spaces. Normally these would have been pressurized, but, when *Epsilon Sextans'* atmosphere had been replenished from *Delta Orionis'* emergency cylinders, it had seemed pointless to waste precious oxygen. So access was through an airlock that had a locker outside, in which suits, ready for immediate use, were stowed.

Grimes and Baxter suited up, helping each other as required. Then the engineer put out his gloved hand to the airlock controls. Grimes stopped him, bent forward to touch helmets. He said, "Hang on. If we open the door it'll register on the panel in Control."

"Like hell it will!" came the reply. "Most of the wiring was slashed through during the piracy. I fixed the hold lights—but damn all else." Grimes, through the transparency of the visors, saw the other's grin. "For obvious reasons."

Grimes shrugged, released Baxter. Everything was so irregular that one more, relatively minor irregularity hardly mattered. He squeezed with the engineer into the small airlock, waited until the atmosphere it held had been pumped back into the body of the ship, then himself pushed the button that actuated the mechanism of the inner valve.

This was not the first time that he had been in the cargo spaces. Some of the weapons "borrowed" from *Delta Orionis*' cargo had been mounted in the holds. When he had made his inspections it had never occurred to him that the opening and closing of the airlock door had not registered in Control.

He stood back and let Baxter lead the way. The engineer pulled himself to one of the bins in which he had been foraging. The door to it was still open, and crates and cartons disturbed by the pillager floated untidily around the opening.

"You'll have to get all this restowed," said Grimes sharply. "If we have to accelerate there'll be damage." But he might as well have been speaking to himself. The suit radios had not been switched on and, in any case, there was no air to carry sound waves, however faintly.

Baxter had scrambled into the open bin. Grimes followed him, saw him standing by the case, its top prized open, that carried the lettering, BELUGA CAVIAR. PRODUCE OF THE RUSSIAN SOCIAL DEMOCRATIC REPUBLIC. Baxter beckoned. Grimes edged his way past the drifting packages to join him.

There was something in the case—but it was not jars or cans of salted sturgeon's eggs. It looked at first like a glittering, complex piece of mobile statuary, although it was motionless. It was a metal mismating of gyroscope and Moëbius Strip. It did not look wrong—nothing functional ever does—but it did look *odd*.

Grimes was standing hard against Baxter now. Their helmets were touching. He asked, "What . . . what is it?"

"I was hopin' you'd be able ter tell me, Admiral." Then, as Grimes extended a cautious hand into the case, "Careful! Don't touch nothin'!"

"Why not?"

" 'Cause this bloody lot was booby-trapped, that's why. See that busted spring? An' see that cylinder in the corner? That's a thermite bomb, or somethin' worse. Shoulda gone orf when I pried the lid up—but luckily I buggered the firin' mechanism with me bar when I stuck it inter just the right crack. But I think the bastard's deloused now."

"It looks as though it—whatever it is—is hooked up to one of the electrical circuits."

"Yair. An' it's not the lightin' circuit. Must be the airlock indicators."

"Must be." As a weapons expert, Grimes could see the thermite bomb—if that was what it was—had been rendered ineffective. It hadn't been an elaborate trap, merely a device that would destroy the—the *thing* if the case housing it were tampered with. Baxter had been lucky—and, presumably, those who had planted the—what the hell was it?—unlucky.

With a cautious finger he nudged the rotor.

It turned—and he was reminded of those other rotors, the ever-precessing gyroscopes of the Mannschenn Drive.

He remembered, then. He remembered a series of lectures at the Academy on future weapons and navigational devices. Having decided upon his specialty he had been really interested only in the weapons. But there had been talk of a man called Carlotti, who was trying to develop a device that would induce temporal precession in radio signals, so that instantaneous communications would be possible throughout the Galaxy without ships and shore stations having to rely upon the temperamental and unreliable telepaths. And beacons, employing the same principle, could be used for navigation by ships under interstellar drive. . . .

So this could be one of Signor Carlotti's gadgets. Perhaps the Empire of Waverley had offered him a higher price than had the Federation. But why the BELUGA CAVIAR? To deter and confuse industrial spies? But *Epsilon Sextans* possessed excellent strong rooms for the carriage of special cargo.

And why was the thing wired up?

Suddenly it was obvious. Somehow, the Duchy of Waldegren possessed Carlotti equipment. This . . . this beacon had been transmitting, unknown to anybody aboard the ship, during the voyage.

The frigates had homed upon her. When, inadvertently, its power supply had been shut off the victim, using random precession, had been able to make her escape.

So, if the pirates were to make a second attack it would have to be reactivated.

"We'd better throw this lot on to the Old Man's plate," said Grimes.

Captain Craven listened intently as Grimes and Baxter told their story. They feared that he was going to lose his temper when told of the engineer's cargo pillaging, but he only remarked, in a dry voice, "I guess that the consignees can afford to compensate us for our time and trouble. Even so, Mr. Baxter, I insist that this practice must cease forthwith." And then, when Grimes described the device, he said, "Yes, I have heard of Carlotti's work. But I didn't think that he'd got as far as a working model. But the thing could have been developed by Waldegrenese scientists from the data in his published papers."

"So you agree, sir, that it is some kind of beacon upon which the pirates can home?"

"What else can it be? Now, gentlemen, we find ourselves upon the horns of a dilemma. If we don't reactivate the bloody thing, the chances are that we shall deliver the ship and cargo intact, at no great risk to ourselves, and to the joy of the underwriters. If we *do* reactivate it—then the chances are that we shall have to fight our way through. And there's no guarantee that we shall be on the winning side."

"I was shanghaied away here as a gunnery officer," said Grimes.

"Shanghaied—or press-ganged?" queried Craven.

"The technique was more that of the shanghai," Grimes told him.

"Indeed?" Craven's voice was cold. "But no matter. You're here, and you're one of my senior officers. What course of action do *you* recommend?"

Grimes replied slowly and carefully. "Legally speaking, what we're involved in isn't a war. But it *is* a war, of sorts. And a just war. And, in any case, the Master of a merchant vessel has the legal right to resist illegal seizure or destruction by force of arms. Of course, we have to consider the illegal circumstances attending the arming of this ship. . . ."

"Let's not get bogged down in legalities and illegalities," said Craven, with a touch of impatience. "The lawyers can sort it all out eventually. Do we reactivate?"

"Yes," said Grimes.

"And you, Mr. Baxter. What do you say?"

"We Rim Worlders just don't like Waldegren. I'll not pass up a chance ter kick the bastards in the teeth. Reactivate, Skipper."

"Good. And how long will it take you to make good the circuit the beacon's spliced in to?"

"Twenty minutes. No more. But d'yer think we oughter put the whole thing to the vote first?"

"No. Everybody here was under the impression that we should be fighting. With one possible exception, they're all volunteers."

"But I did volunteer, sir," objected Grimes.

"Make your mind up, Ensign. You were telling me just now that you'd been shanghaied. All right.

Everybody is a volunteer. So we just rebait the trap without any more yapping about it. Let me know as soon as you're ready, Mr. Baxter. Will you require assistance?"

"I'll manage, Skipper."

When he was gone Craven turned to Grimes. "You realize, Ensign, that this puts me in rather a jam. Let me put it this way. Am I justified in risking the lives of all my officers to carry out a private act of vengeance?"

"I think that you can take Mr. Baxter and myself as being representative, sir. As for the others—Miss Pentecost's a Rim Worlder, and her views will coincide with Baxter's. And the original crew members—they're just as entitled to vengeance as you are. I know that if I'd been an officer of this ship at the time of the original piracy I'd welcome the chance of hitting back."

"*You* would. Yes. Even if, as now, an alternative suddenly presented itself. But . . . "

"I honestly don't see what you're worrying about, sir."

"You wouldn't. It's a matter of training. But, for all my Reserve commission, I'm a merchant officer. Oh, I know that any military commander is as responsible for the lives of his men as I am—but he also knows that those lives, like his own, are expendable."

"It's a pity that Baxter found the beacon," said Grimes.

"It is—and it isn't. If he hadn't found it, I shouldn't be soliloquizing like a spacefaring Hamlet. And we should have brought the ship in intact and, like as not, all been awarded Lloyd's Medals. On the other hand—if he hadn't found it we—or

I?—should have lost our chance of getting back at the pirates."

"You aren't Hamlet, sir." Grimes spoke with the assurance of the very young, but in later years he was to remember his words, and to feel neither shame nor embarrassment, but only a twinge of envy and regret. "You aren't Hamlet. You're Captain Craven, Master under God. Please, sir, for once in your life do something you want to do, and argue it out later with the Almightly if you must."

"And with my owners?" Grimes couldn't be sure, but he thought he saw something like a smile beneath Craven's full beard. "And with my owners?"

"Master Astronauts' certificates aren't all that common, sir. If worst comes to worst, there's always the Rim Worlds. The Sundowner Line, isn't it?"

"I'd already thought of that." There was no doubt about it. Craven was smiling. "After all that you've been saying to me, I'm surprised that *you* don't join forces with our Miss Pentecost."

"Go out to the Rim, sir? Hardly."

"Don't be so sure, young Grimes. Anyhow, you'd better get Miss Pentecost up here now so that we can see how friend Baxter is getting on. There's always the risk that he'll find a few more things among the cargo that aren't nailed down."

XV

GRIMES CALLED Jane Pentecost on the intercom;
after a minute or so she made her appearance in
Control. Craven told her what Baxter had discovered and what he, Craven, intended doing about it.
She nodded in emphatic agreement. "Yes," she
said. "The thing's here to be used—and to be used
the way that *we* want to use it. But I don't think
that we should make it public."

"Why not, Miss Pentecost?"

"I could be wrong, Captain, but in my opinion
there are quite a few people in this ship who'd
welcome the chance of wriggling out of being the
cheese in the mousetrap. When there's no alternative they're brave enough. When there's a face-
saving alternative . . ."

Baxter's voice came from the intercom speaker.
"Chief Reaction Drive Engineer to Control. Repairs completed. Please check your panel."

Yes, the circuit had been restored. The buzzer
sounded, and on the board a glowing red light
showed that the outer door to the cargo hold airlock was open. How much of the failure of the
indicators was due to battle damage and how much
to Baxter's sabotage would never be known.
Craven's heavy eyebrows lifted ironically as he
looked at Grimes, and Grimes shrugged in reply.

Then, the watch handed over to the girl, the two
men made their way aft from the Control Room.
Outside the airlock they found Baxter, already
suited up save for his helmet. There had been only
two suits in the locker, and the engineer had

brought another one along for the Captain from somewhere.

The little compartment would take only two men at a time. Craven and Grimes went through first, then were joined by Baxter. There was no longer any need for secrecy, so the suit radios were switched on. The only person likely to be listening in was Jane Pentecost in Control.

Grimes heard Craven muttering angrily as they passed packages that obviously had been opened and pillaged, but the Captain did no more than mutter. He possessed the sense of proportion so essential to his rank—and a few bulbs of looted liquor were, after all, relatively unimportant.

They came to the bin in which the case allegedly containing caviar had been stowed, in which some secret agent of Waldegren had tapped the circuit supplying power to the beacon. Inside the box the gleaming machine was still motionless. Craven said, "I thought you told me the current was on."

"It is, Skipper." Baxter's voice was pained. "But I switched it off before I fixed the wiring." He extended a gloved finger, pressed a little toggle switch.

And nothing happened.

"Just a nudge." whispered the engineer.

The oddly convoluted rotor turned easily enough, and as it rotated it seemed almost to vanish in a mist of its own generating—a mist that was no more than an optical illusion.

It rotated, slowed—and stopped.

Baxter cast aspersions upon the legitimacy of its parenthood. Then, still grumbling, he produced a volt-meter. Any doubt that power was being delivered to the machine was soon dispelled. Power was being delivered—but it was not being used.

"Well, Mr. Baxter?" demanded Craven.

"I'm a fair mechanic, Skipper—but I'm no physicist."

"Mr. Grimes?"

"I specialized in gunnery, sir."

Craven snorted, the sound unpleasantly loud in the helmet phones. He said sarcastically, "I'm only the Captain, but I have some smatterings of Mannschenn Drive maintenance and operation. This thing isn't a Mannschenn Drive unit—but it's first cousin to one. As I recall it, some of the earlier models couldn't be started without the employment of a small, temporal precession field initiator. Furthermore, these initiators, although there is no longer any need for them, are still carried as engine room spares in the Commission's ships."

"And that gadget'll start *this* little time-twister, Skipper?" asked the engineer.

"It might, Mr. Baxter. It might. So, Mr. Grimes, will you go along to the Mannschenn Drive room and ask Mr. Wolverton for his initiator? No need to tell him what it's for."

Wolverton was in the Mannschenn Drive room, staring moodily at the gleaming complexity of precessing rotors. Grimes hastily averted his eyes from the machine. It frightened him, and he didn't mind admitting it. And there was something about the engineer that frightened him, too. The tall, cadaverous man, with the thin strands of black hair drawn over his gleaming skull, looked more like a seer than a ship's officer, looked like a fortune-teller peering into the depths of an uncannily mobile crystal ball. He was mumbling, his voice a low, guttural muttering against the thin, high keening of his tumbling gyroscopes. The Ensign at last was able to make out the words.

"Divergent tracks. . . . To be, or not to be, that is the question—"

Grimes thought, *This ship should be renamed the* State of Denmark. *There's something rotten here.* . . . He said sharply, "Mr. Wolverton!"

Slowly the Chief Interstellar Drive Engineer turned his head, stared at Grimes unseeingly at first. His eyes came into focus. He whispered, "It's you."

"Who else, Chief? Captain's compliments, and he'd like to borrow your temporal precession field initiator."

"He would, would he? And why?"

"An—an experiment." said Grimes, with partial truth. The fewer people who knew the whole truth the better.

"An experiment?"

"Yes. If you wouldn't mind letting me have it now, Chief. . . . "

"But it's engine room stores. It's the Commission's stores. It's a *very* delicate instrument. It is against the Commission's regulations to issue it to unqualified personnel."

"But Mr. Baxter is helping with the . . . experiment."

"Mr. Baxter! That letter-off of cheap fireworks. That . . . *Rim Runner*! No. No. Mr. Baxter is not qualified personnel."

"Then perhaps you could lend us one of your juniors."

"No. No, I would not trust them. Why do you think that I am here, Mr. Grimes? Why do you think that I have been tied to my gyroscopes? Literally tied, almost. If I had not been here, keeping my own watch, when the pirates struck, this ship would have been utterly destroyed. I *know* the Drive, Mr. Grimes." He seized the Ensign's arm, turned him so that he was facing the gleaming, spinning rotors, endlessly precessing, endlessly tumbling down the dark dimensions, shimmering on the very verge of invisibility. Grimes wanted to close his eyes, but could not. "I *know* the Drive, Mr. Grimes. It talks to me. It shows me things. It warned me, that time, that Death was waiting for this ship and all in her. And now it warns me again. But there is a . . . a divergence. . . ."

"Mr. Wolverton, please! There is not much time."

"But what is Time, Mr. Grimes? What *is* Time? What do you know of the forking World Lines, the Worlds of If? I've lived with this machine, Mr. Grimes. It's part of me—or am I part of *it?* Let me show you. . . ." His grip on the Ensign's arm was painful. "Let me show you. Look. Look into the machine. What do you see?"

Grimes saw only shadowy, shimmering wheels and a formless darkness.

"I see you, Mr. Grimes," almost sang the engineer. "I see you—but not as you *will* be. But as you might be. I see you on the bridge of your flagship, your uniform gold-encrusted and medal-bedecked, with commodores and captains saluting you and calling you 'sir' . . . but I see you, too, in the control room of a shabby little ship, a single ship, in shabby clothes, and the badge on your cap is one that I have never seen, is one that does not yet exist. . . ."

"Mr. Wolverton! That initiator. *Please!*"

"But there is no hurry, Mr. Grimes. There is no

hurry. There is time enough for everything—for everything that is, that has been, that will be and that might be. There is time to decide, Mr. Grimes. There is time to decide whether or not we make our second rendezvous with Death. The initiator is part of it all, Mr. Grimes, is it not? The initiator is the signpost that stands at the forking of the track. You weren't here, Mr. Grimes, when the pirates struck. You did not hear the screams, you did not smell the stench of burning flesh. You're young and foolhardy; all that you want is the chance to play with your toys. And all that I want, now that I know that alternatives exist, is the chance to bring this ship to her destination with no further loss of life.''

''Mr. Wolverton . . . ''

''Mr. Grimes!'' It was Captain Craven's voice, and he was in a vile temper. ''What the hell do you think you're playing at?''

''Captain,'' said Wolverton. ''I can no more than guess at what you intend to do—but I have decided not to help you to do it.''

''Then give us the initiator. We'll work it ourselves.''

''No, Captain.''

''Give me the initiator, Mr. Wolverton. That's an order.''

''A *lawful* command, Captain? As lawful as those commands of yours that armed this ship?''

''Hold him, Grimes!'' (*And who's supposed to be holding whom?* wondered the Ensign. Wolverton's grip was still tight and painful on his arm.) ''Hold him, while I look in the storeroom!''

''Captain! Get away from the door! You've no right . . . ''

Wolverton relinquished his hold on Grimes who, twisting with an agility that surprised himself, contrived to get both arms about the engineer's waist. In the scuffle the contact between their magnetic shoe soles and the deck was broken. They hung there, helpless, with no solidity within reach of their flailing limbs to give them purchase. They hung there, clinging to each other, but more in hate than in love. Wolverton's back was to the machine; he could not see, as could Grimes, that there was an indraught of air into the spinning, shimmering complexity. Grimes felt the beginnings of panic, more than the mere beginnings. There were no guardrails; he had read somewhere why this was so, but the abstruse physics involved did not matter—all that mattered was that there was nothing to prevent him and Wolverton from being drawn into the dimension-twisting field of the thing.

He freed, somehow, his right hand, and with an effort that sprained his shoulder brought it around in a sweeping, clumsy and brutal blow to the engineer's face. Wolverton screamed and his grip relaxed. Violently, Grimes shoved away. To the action there was reaction.

Craven emerged from the storeroom, carrying something that looked like a child's toy gyroscope in a transparent box. He looked around for Grimes and Wolverton at deck level and then, his face puzzled, looked up. He did not, as Grimes had been doing for some seconds, vomit—but his face, behind the beard went chalk-white. He put out his free hand and, not ungently, pulled Grimes to the deck.

He said, his voice little more than a whisper,

"There's nothing we can do. Nothing—except to get a pistol and finish him off. . . ."

Grimes forced himself to look again at the slimy, bloody obscenity that was a man turned, literally, inside-out—heart (if it was the heart) still beating, intestines still writhing.

XVI

IT WAS GRIMES who went for a pistol, fetching a Minetti from the weapons rack that he, himself, had fitted up in the Control Room. He told Jane Pentecost what he wanted it for. He made no secret of either his horror or his self blame.

She said, "But this is a war, even if it's an undeclared one. And in a war you must expect casualties."

"Yes, yes. I know. But *I* pushed him into the field."

"It was an accident. It could easily have been you instead of him. And I'm glad that it wasn't."

"But you haven't seen . . ."

"And I don't want to." Her voice hardened. "Meanwhile, get the hell out of here and back to the Mannschenn Drive room. If you're so sorry for the poor bastard, do something about putting him out of his misery."

"But . . ."

"Don't be such a bloody coward, Grimes."

The words hurt—mainly because there was so much truth in them. Grimes was dreading having to see again the twisted obscenity that had once been a man, was dreading having to breathe again the atmosphere of that compartment, heavy with the reek of hot oil, blood and fecal matter. But, with the exception of Craven, he was the only person in the ship trained in the arts of war. He recalled the words of a surgeon-commander who had lectured the midshipmen of his course on the handling of battle casualties—and recalled, too, how afterward the young gentlemen had sneered at the bloodthirstiness of one who was supposed to be a professional healer. "*When one of your ship-mates has really had it, even if he's your best friend, don't hesitate a moment about finishing him off. You'll be doing him a kindness. Finish him off—and get him out of sight. Shockingly wounded men are bad for morale.*"

"What are you waiting for?" demanded Jane Pentecost. "Do you want *me* to do it?"

Grimes said nothing, just hurried out of the Control Room.

Craven was still in the Mannschenn Drive room when Grimes got back there. With him were two of the interstellar drive engineers—the Second and the Third. Their faces were deathly white, and the Second's prominent Adam's apple was working spasmodically, but about them there was an air of grim resolution. The Third—how could he bear to touch that slimy, reeking mess?—had hold of its shoulders (white, fantastically contorted bone gleaming pallidly among red convolutions of flesh), while the Second, a heavy spanner in his hand, was trying to decide where to strike.

The Captain saw Grimes. "Give me that!" he snapped, and snatched the pistol from the Ensign's hand. Then, to the engineers, "Stand back!"

The little weapon rattled sharply and viciously. To the other smells was added the acridity of burned propellant. What had been Wolverton was driven to the deck by the impact of the tiny projectiles, and adhered there. There was surprisingly little blood, but the body had stopped twitching.

Craven handed the empty pistol back to the Ensign. He ordered, "You stay here, Mr. Grimes, and organize the disposal of the body." He went to the locker where he had put the initiator, took out the little instrument and, carrying it carefully, left the Mannschenn Drive room. Neither of the engineers, still staring with horrified fascinators at their dead Chief, noticed.

"How . . . how did it happen?" asked the Second, after a long silence.

"He fell into the field," said Grimes.

"But how? How? He was always getting on us about being careless, and telling us what was liable to happen to us, and now it's happened to him—"

"That's the way of it," contributed the Third, with a certain glum satisfaction. "Don't do as I do, do as I say."

"Have you a box?" asked Grimes.

"A box?" echoed the Second.

"Yes. A box." Now that he was doing something, doing something useful, Grimes was beginning to feel a little better. "We can't have a funeral while we're running under interstellar drive. We have to . . . to put him somewhere." *Out of sight,* he mentally added.

"That chest of spares?" muttered the Second

"Just the right size," agreed the Third.

"Then get it," ordered Grimes.

The chest, once the spares and their packing had been removed and stowed elsewhere, was just the right size. Its dimensions were almost those of a coffin. It was made of steel, its bottom magnetized, and remained where placed on the deck while the three men, fighting down their recurring nausea, handled the body into it. All of them sighed audibly in relief when, at last, the close-fitting lid covered the remains. Finally, the Third ran a welding torch around the joint. As he was doing so the lights flickered.

Was it because of the torch? wondered Grimes. Or was it because the beacon in the hold had been reactivated?

Somehow he could not feel any real interest.

Cleaned up after a fashion, but still feeling physically ill, he was back in the Control Room. Craven was there, and Baxter was with him. Jane Pentecost had been relieved so that she could attend to her duties in the galley. "Not that *I* feel like a meal," the Captain had said. "And I doubt very much that Mr. Grimes does either."

"Takes a lot ter put *me* off me tucker," the engineer declared cheerfully as he worked on the airlock door telltale panel.

"You didn't see Mr. Wolverton, Mr. Baxter," said Craven grimly.

"No, Skipper. An' I'm not sorry I didn't." He paused in his work to rummage in his tool bag. He produced bulbs of brandy. "But I thought you an' the Ensign might need some o' this."

Craven started to say something about cargo pillage, then changed his mind. He accepted the liquor without further quibbling. The three men sipped in silence.

Baxter carelessly tossed his squeezed empty bulb aside, continued with what he had been doing. The Captain said to Grimes, "Yes. We got the thing started again. And we've improved upon it."

"Improved upon it, sir? How?"

"It's no longer only a beacon. It's also an alarm. As soon as it picks up the radiation from the similar pieces of apparatus aboard the enemy frigates, the buzzer that Mr. Baxter is fitting up will sound, the red light will flash. We shall have ample warning. . . ."

"She'll be right, Skipper," said the engineer.

"Thank you, Mr. Baxter. And now; if you don't mind, I'd like a few words in private with Mr. Grimes."

"Don't be too hard on him, Skipper."

Baxter winked cheerfully at Grimes and left the control room.

"Mr. Grimes," Craven's voice was grave. "Mr. Grimes, today, early in your career, you have learned a lesson that some of us never have to learn. You have killed a man—yes, yes, I know that it was not intentional—and you have been privileged to see the end result of your actions.

"There are many of us who are, who have been, killers. There are many of us who have pushed buttons but who have never seen what happens at the other end of the trajectory. Perhaps people slaughtered by explosion or laser beam do not look quite so horrible as Wolverton—but, I assure you, they often look horrible enough, and often die as slowly and as agonizingly. You know, now, what violent death looks like, Mr. Grimes. So tell me, are you still willing to push your buttons, to play pretty tunes on your battle organ?"

"And what did the bodies in this ship look like, Captain?" asked Grimes. Then, remembering that one of the bodies had belonged to the woman whom Craven had loved, he bitterly regretted having asked the question.

"Not pretty," whispered Captain Craven. "Not at all pretty."

"I'll push your buttons for you," Grimes told him.

And for Jane Pentecost, he thought. *And for the others. And for myself? The worst of it all is that I haven't got the excuse of saying that it's what I'm paid for . . . .*

XVII

DOWN THE DARK dimensions fell *Epsilon Sextans,* falling free through the warped continuum. But aboard the ship time still possessed meaning, the master chronometer still ticked away the seconds, minutes and hours; the little man-made world was still faithful to that puissant god of scientific intelligences everywhere in the universe—the Clock. Watch succeeded watch in Control Room and engine room. Meals were prepared and served on time. There was even, toward the end, a revival of off-duty social activities: a chess set was discovered and brought into use, playing cards were produced and a bridge school formed.

But there was one social activity that, to Grimes' disappointment was not resumed—the oldest social activity of them all. More than once he pleaded with Jane—and every time she laughed away his pleas. He insisted—and that made matters worse. He was (as he said), the donkey who had been allowed one nibble of the carrot and who could not understand why the carrot had been snatched away. He was (she said), a donkey. Period.

He should have guessed what was happening, but he did not. He was young, and inexperienced in the ways of women—of men *and* women. He just could not imagine that Jane would spare more than a casual glance for any of the engineers or for the flabby, pasty youth who was the psionic radio officer—and in this he was right.

Epsilon Sextans was, for a ship of her class, very well equipped. In addition to the usual intercom system she was fitted with closed circuit television. In the event of emergency the Captain or watch officer, by the flip of a switch, could see what was happening in any compartment of the vessel. Over the control panel, in big, red letters, were the words: EMERGENCY USE ONLY. Grimes did not know what was the penalty for improper use of the apparatus in the Merchant Navy—but he did know that in the Survey Service officers had been cashiered and given an ignominious discharge for this offense. The more cramped and crowded the conditions in which men—and women—work and live, the more precious is privacy.

It was Grimes' watch.

When he had taken over, all the indications were that it would be as boring as all the previous watches. All that was required of the watchkeeper was that he stay awake. Grimes stayed awake. He had brought a book with him into Control, hiding it inside his uniform shirt, and it held his attention for a while. Then, following the example of generations of watch officers, he set up a game of three dimensional tic-tac-toe in the chart tank and played, right hand against left. The left hand was doing remarkably well when a buzzer sounded. The Ensign immediately cleared the tank and looked at the airlock indicator panel. But there were no lights on the board, and he realized that it was the intercom telephone.

"Control," he said into his microphone.

"P.R.O. here. I . . . I'm not happy, Mr. Grimes. . . ."

"Who is?" quipped Grimes.

"I . . . I feel . . . smothered."

"Something wrong with the ventilation in your shack?"

"No. NO. It's like . . . it's like a heavy blanket soaked in ice-cold water. . . . You can't move . . . you can't shout . . . you can't *hear*. . . . *It's like it was before*. . . ."

"*Before what*?" snapped Grimes—and then as the other buzzer sounded, as the additional red light flashed on the telltale panel, he realized the stupidity of his question.

At once he pressed the alarm button. This was it, at last. Action Stations! Throughout the ship the bells were shrilling, the klaxons squawking. Hastily Grimes vacated the pilot's chair, slipped into the one from which he could control his weapons—and from which he could reach out to other controls. But where was the Old Man? Where was Captain Craven? This was the moment that he had longed for, this was the consummation toward which all his illegalities had been directed. Damn it all, *where was he*?

Perhaps he was floating stunned in his quarters—starting up hurriedly from sleep he could have struck his head upon some projection, knocked himself out. If this were the case he, Grimes, would have to call Jane from her own battle station in Sick Bay to render first aid. But there was no time to lose.

The Ensign reached out, flipped the switches that would give him the picture of the interior of the Captain's accommodation. The screen brightened, came alive. Grimes stared at the luminous presentation in sick horror. Luminous it was—with that peculiar luminosity of naked female flesh. Jane was dressing herself with almost ludicrous haste. Of the Captain there was no sign—*on the screen.*

Craven snarled, with cold ferocity, "You damned, sneaking, prurient puppy!" Then, in a louder voice, "Switch that damn thing off! I'll deal with you when this is over."

"But, sir . . ."

"Switch it off, I say!"

Cheeks burning, Grimes obeyed. Then he sat staring at his armament controls, fighting down his nausea, his physical sickness. Somehow, he found time to think bitterly, *So I was the knight, all set and ready to slay dragons for his lady. And all the time, she* . . . He did not finish the thought.

He heard a voice calling over the intercom, one of the engineers. "Captain, they're trying to lock on! Same as last time. Random precession, sir?"

"No. Cut the Drive!"

"Cut the Drive?" Incredulously.

"You heard me. *Cut!*" Then, to Grimes, "And what the hell are *you* waiting for?"

The Ensign knew what he had to do; he had rehearsed it often enough. He did it. From the nozzles that pierced the outer shell spouted the cloud of reflective vapor, just in time, just as the enemy's lasers lashed out at their target. It seemed that the ship's internal temperature rose suddenly and sharply—although that could have been illusion, fostered by the sight of the fiery fog glimpsed through the viewports before the armored shutters slammed home.

There were targets now on Grimes' fire control screen, two of them, but he could not loose a missile until the tumbling rotors of the Drive had ceased to spin, to precess. The use of the anti-laser vapor screen had been risky enough. Abruptly the screens went blank—which signified that the temporal precession rates of hunted and hunters were no longer in synchronization, that the fields of the pirates had failed to lock on. In normal spacetime there would be no need to synchronize—and then the hunters would discover that their quarry had claws and teeth.

Aboard *Epsilon Sextans* the keening note of the Drive died to a whisper, a barely audible murmur, fading to silence. There was the inevitable second or so of utter disorientation when, as soon as it was safe, the engineers braked the gyroscopes.

Craven acted without hesitation, giving his ship headway and acceleration with Inertial Drive. He was not running—although this was the impression that he wished to convey. He was inviting rather than evading combat—but if the Waldegren captains chose to assume that *Epsilon Sextans* was, as she had been, an unarmed merchantman (after all, the anti-laser screen could have been jury rigged from normal ship's stores and equipment), taking evasive action, that was *their* error of judgment.

Grimes watched his screens intently. Suddenly the two blips reappeared, astern, all of a hundred kilos distant, but closing. This he reported.

"Stand by for acceleration!" ordered Craven. "Reaction Drive—stand by!"

It was all part of the pattern—a last, frantic squandering of reaction mass that could do no more than delay the inevitable. It would look good from the enemy control rooms.

"Reaction Drive ready!" reported Baxter over the intercom.

"Thank you. Captain to all hands, there will be no countdown. *Fire!*"

From the corner of his eye Grimes saw Craven's hand slam down on the key. Acceleration slammed him brutally back into his chair. There was a roar that was more like an explosion than a normal rocket firing, a shock that jarred and rattled every fitting in the Control Room.

Craven remarked quietly. "That must have looked convincing enough—but I hope that Baxter didn't really blow a chamber."

There was only the Inertial Drive now, and the two blips that, very briefly, had fallen astern, were now creeping up again, closing the range.

"Anti-laser," ordered Craven briefly.

"But, sir, it'll just be wasting it. They'll not be using laser outside twenty kilometers."

"They'll not be expecting a gunnery specialist aboard this wagon, either."

Once again the nozzles spouted, pouring out a cloud that fell rapidly astern of the running ship, dissipating uselessly.

Craven looked at his own reens, frowned, muttered, "They're taking their sweet time about it . . . probably low on reaction mass themselves." He turned to Grimes. "I think a slight breakdown of the I.D.'s in order."

"As you say, sir." The Ensign could not forget having been called a damned, sneaking, prurient puppy. Let Craven make his own decisions.

"Stand by for Free Fall," ordered the Captain quietly. The steady throbbing of the Inertial Drive faltered, faltered and ceased. There were two long minutes of weightlessness, and then, for five minutes, the Drive came back into operation. *A breakdown*, the enemy must be thinking. *A breakdown, and the engineers sweating and striving to get the ship under way again.* A breakdown—it

would not be surprising after the mauling she had
endured at the first encounter.

She hung there, and although her actual speed
could be measured in kilometers a second she was,
insofar as her accelerating pursuers were concerned, relatively motionless. Grimes wondered
why the warships did not use their radio, did not
demand surrender—*Epsilon Sextans'* transceiver
was switched on, but no sound issued from the
speaker but the hiss and crackle of interstellar
static. He voiced his puzzlement to Craven.

Craven laughed grimly. "They know who *we*
are—or they think that they know. And they know
that we know who *they* are. After what happened
before, why should we expect mercy? All that we
can do now—they think—is to get the Mannschenn Drive going again. But with that comic
beacon of theirs working away merrily they'll be
able to home on us, no matter how random our
precession." He laughed again. "They haven't a
care in the world, bless their little black hearts."

Grimes watched his screens. Forty
kilometers—thirty—"Sir, the ALGE?" he asked.

"Yes. It's your party now."

For the third time reflective vapor gushed from
the nozzles, surrounding the ship with a dense
cloud. Craven, who had been watching the dials of
the external temperature thermometers, remarked
quietly, "They've opened fire. The shell plating's
heating up. Fast."

And in the Control Room it felt hot—and hotter,
Grimes pressed the button that unmasked his batteries. The gas screen, as well as affording protection from laser, hid the ship from visual observation. The enemy would not be expecting defense
by force of arms.

He loosed his first salvo, felt the ship tremble as the missiles ejected themselves from their launching racks. There they were on the screens—six tiny sparks, six moronic mechanical intelligences programmed to home upon and destroy, capable of countering evasive action so long as their propellant held out. There they were on the screens—six of them, then four, then one. This last missile almost reached its target—then it, too, blinked out. The Waldegren frigates were now using their laser for defense, not attack.

"I don't think," remarked Craven quietly, "that they'll use missiles. Not yet, anyhow. They want our cargo intact." He chuckled softly. "But we've got them worried."

Grimes didn't bother to reply. The telltale lights on his panel told him that the six AVM launchers were reloaded. The AMMs—the anti-missile missiles—had not yet been fired. Dare he risk their use against big targets? He carried in his magazines stock sufficient for three full salvos only— and with no laser for anti-missile work dare he deplete his supply of this ammunition?

He had heard the AMMs described as "vicious little brutes." They were to the Anti-Vessel Missiles as terriers are to mastiffs. Their warheads were small, but this was compensated for by their greater endurance. They were, perhaps, a little more "intelligent" than the larger rockets—and Grimes, vaguely foreseeing this present contingency, had made certain modifications to their "brains."

He pushed the button that actuated his modifications, that overrode the original programming. He depressed the firing stud. He felt the vibration as the war-rockets streaked away from the ship, and on his screens watched the tiny points of light closing the range between themselves and the two big blips that were the targets. They were fast, and they were erratic. One was picked off by laser within the first ten seconds, but the others carried on, spurting and swerving, but always boring toward their objectives. Grimes could imagine the enemy gunnery officers flailing their lasers like men, armed only with sticks, defending themselves against a horde of small, savage animals. There was, of course, one sure defense—to start up the Mannschenn Drive and to slip back into the warped continuum where the missiles could not follow. But, in all probability, the Waldegren captains had yet to accept the fact, emotionally, that this helpless merchantman had somehow acquired the wherewithal to strike back.

Two of the AMMs were gone now, picked off by the enemy laser. Three were still closing on the target on *Epsilon Sextans'* port quarter, and only one of the target abaft the starboard beam. Grimes loosed his second flight of AMMs, followed it with a full salvo of AVMs. Then, knowing that the protective vapor screen must have been thinned and shredded by his rocketry, he sent out a replenishing gush of reflective gas.

He heard Craven cry out in exultation. The three AMMs of the first flight had hit their target, the three sparks had fused with the blip that represented the raider to port. The three sparks that were the second flight were almost there, and overtaking them were the larger and brighter sparks of the second AVM salvo. The Anti-Missile Missiles would cause only minor damage to a ship—but, in all probability, they would throw fire control out of kilter, might even destroy laser projectors. In theory, one AVM would suffice to destroy a frigate; a hit by three at once would make destruction a certainty.

And so it was.

Seen only on the radar screen, as a picture lacking in detail painted on a fluorescent surface by an electron brush, it was anticlimactic. The blips, the large one, the three small ones and the three not so small, merged. And then there was an oddly shaped blob of luminescence that slowly broke up into a cluster of glowing fragments, a gradually expanding cluster, a leisurely burgeoning flower of pale fire.

Said Craven viciously, "The other bastard's got cold feet. . . ."

And so it was. Where she had been on the screen was only darkness, a darkness in which the sparks that were missiles and anti-missiles milled about aimlessly. They would not turn upon each other—that would have been contrary to their programming. They would not, in theory, use their remaining fuel to home upon the only worthwhile target remaining—*Epsilon Sextans* herself. But, as Craven knew and as Grimes knew, theory and practice do not always coincide. Ships have been destroyed by their own missiles.

With reluctance Grimes pushed the DESTRUCT button. He said to the Captain, gesturing toward the wreckage depicted on the screen, "Pick up survivors, sir? If there are any."

"If there are any," snarled Craven, "that's their bad luck. No—we give chase to the other swine!"

XVIII

GIVE CHASE . . .

It was easier said than done. The surviving frigate had restarted her Mannschenn Drive, had slipped back into the warped continuum where, unless synchronization of precession rates was achieved and held, contact between vessels would be impossible. The Carlotti Beacon in *Epsilon Sextans'* hold was worse than useless; it had been designed to be homed upon, not to be a direction-finding instrument. (In any case, it could function as such only if the beacon aboard the Waldegren ship were working.) Neither Craven nor Grimes knew enough about the device to effect the necessary modifications. The interstellar drive engineers thought that they could do it, but their estimates as to the time required ranged from days to weeks. Obviously, as long as it was operating it would be of value to the enemy only.

So it was switched off.

There was only one method available to Craven to carry out the pursuit—psionic tracking. He sent for his Psionic Radio Officer, explained the situation. The telepath was a young man, pasty faced, unhealthy looking, but not unintelligent. He said at once, "Do you think, Captain, that the other officers and myself are willing to carry on the fight? After all, we've made our point. Wouldn't it be wisest to carry on, now, for Waverley?"

"Speaking for meself," put in Baxter, who had accompanied Jane Pentecost to Control, "an' fer any other Rim Worlders present, I say that now the bastards are on the run it's the best time ter smack 'em again. An' hard. An' the tame time-twisters think the same as we do. I've already had words with 'em.'' He glared at the telepath. ''Our snoopin' little friend here should know very well what the general consensus of opinion is.''

''We do not pry,'' said the communications officer stiffly. ''But I am willing to abide by the will of the majority.''

''And don't the orders of the Master come into it?'' asked Craven, more in amusement than anger.

''Lawful commands, sir?'' asked Grimes who, until now, had been silent.

''Shut up!'' snapped Jane Pentecost.

''Unluckily, sir,'' the young man went on, ''I do not possess the direction-finding talent. It is, as you know, quite rare.''

''Then what *can* you do?'' demanded Craven.

''Sir, let me finish, please. The psionic damping device—I don't know what it was, but I suspect that it was the brain of some animal with which I am unfamiliar—was in the ship that was destroyed. The other vessel carries only a normal operator, with normal equipment—himself and some sort of organic amplifier. He is still within range, and I can maintain a listening watch—''

''And suppose *he* listens to you?'' asked the Captain. ''Even if you transmit nothing—as you will not do, unless ordered by myself—there could be stray thoughts. And that, I suppose, applies to all of us.''

The telepath smiled smugly. ''Direction-finding is not the only talent. I'm something of a damper myself—although not in the same class as the one that was blown up. I give you my word, sir, that this vessel is psionically silent." He raised his hand as Craven was about to say something. "Now, sir, I shall be able to find out where the other ship is heading. I know already that her Mannschenn Drive unit is not working at full capacity; it sustained damage of some kind during the action. I'm not a navigator, sir, but it seems to me that we could be waiting for her when she reemerges into the normal continuum."

"You're not a navigator," agreed Craven, "and you're neither a tactician nor a strategist. We should look rather silly, shouldn't we, hanging in full view over a heavily fortified naval base, a sitting duck. Even so . . . " His big right hand stroked his beard. "Meanwhile, I'll assume that our little friends are headed in the general direction of Waldegren, and set course accordingly. If Mr. Grimes will be so good as to hunt up the target star in the Directory . . . "

Grimes did as he was told. He had made his protest, such as it was, and, he had to admit, he was in favor of continuing the battle. It was a matter of simple justice. Why should one shipload of murderers be destroyed, and the other shipload escape unscathed? He was still more than a little dubious of the legality of it all, but he did not let it worry him.

He helped Craven to line the ship up on the target star, a yellow, fifth magnitude spark. He manned the intercom while the Captain poured on the acceleration and then, with the ship again falling free, cut in the Mannschenn Drive. When the vessel was on course he expected that the Old Man would give the usual order—"Normal Deep Space routine, Mr. Grimes,"—but this was not forth-coming.

"Now," said Craven ominously.

"Now *what*, sir?"

"You have a short memory, Ensign. A conveniently short memory, if I may say so. Mind you, I was favorably impressed by the way you handled your armament, but that has no bearing upon what happened before."

Grimes blushed miserably. He knew what the Captain was driving at. But, playing for time, he asked, "What do you mean, sir?"

Craven exploded. "What do I mean? You have the crust to sit there and ask me that! Your snooping, sir. Your violation of privacy. Even worse, your violation of the Master's privacy! I shall not tell Miss Pentecost; it would be unkind to embarrass her. But . . ."

Grimes refrained from saying that he had seen Miss Pentecost wearing even less than when, inadvertently, he had spied upon her. He muttered, "I can explain, sir."

"You'd better. Out with it."

"Well, sir, it was like this. I knew that we'd stumbled on the enemy—or that the enemy had stumbled upon us. I'd sounded Action Stations. And when you were a long time coming up to Control I thought that you must have hurt yourself, somehow . . . there have been such cases, as you know. So I thought I'd better check—"

"You thought . . . *you* thought. I'll not say that you aren't paid to think—because that's just what an officer *is* paid for. But you didn't think hard enough, or along the right lines." Grimes could see that Craven had accepted his explanation and that all would be well. The Captain's full beard could not hide the beginnings of a smile. "Did you ever hear of Sir Francis Drake, Ensign?"

"No, sir."

"He was an admiral—one of Queen Elizabeth's admirals. The first Elizabeth, of course. When the Spanish Armada was sighted he did not rush down to his flagship yelling 'Action Stations!' He knew that there was time to spare, and so he quietly finished what he was doing before setting sail."

"And what was he doing, sir?" asked Grimes innocently.

Craven glared at him, then snapped, "Playing bowls."

Then, suddenly, the tension was broken and both men collapsed in helpless laughter. In part it was reaction to the strain of battle—but in greater part it was that freemasonry that exists only between members of the same sex, the acknowledgment of shared secrets and shared experiences.

Grimes knew that Jane Pentecost was not for him—and wished Craven joy of her and she of the Captain. Perhaps they had achieved a permanent relationship, perhaps not—but, either way, his best wishes were with them.

Craven unbuckled his seat strap.

"Deep Space routine, Mr. Grimes. It is your watch, I believe."

"Deep Space routine it is, sir."

Yes, it was still his watch (although so much had happened). It was still his watch, although there were barely fifteen minutes to go before relief. He was tired, more tired than he had ever been in his life before. He was tired, but not unhappy. He knew that the fact that he had killed men should be weighing heavily upon his conscience—but it did not. They, themselves, had been killers—and they had had a far better chance then any of their own victims had enjoyed.

He would shed no tears for them.

XIX

CRAVEN CAME BACK to the Control Room at the change of watch, when Grimes was handing over to Jane Pentecost. He waited until the routine had been completed, then said, "We know where our friends are headed. They were, like us, running for Waldegren—but they're having to change course." He laughed harshly. "There must be all hell let loose on their home planet."

"Why? What's happened?" asked Grimes.

"I'll tell you later. But, first of all, we have an alteration of course ourselves. Look up Dartura in the Directory, will you, while I get the Drive shut down."

Epsilon Sextans was falling free through normal spacetime before Grimes had found the necessary information. And then there was the hunt for and the final identification of the target star, followed by the lining up by the use of the directional gyroscopes. There was the brief burst of acceleration and then, finally, the interstellar drive was cut in once more.

The Captain made a business of selecting and lighting a cigar. When the pungent combustion was well under way he said, "Our young Mr. Summers is a good snooper. Not as good as some people I know, perhaps." Grimes flushed and Jane Pentecost looked puzzled. "He's a supersensitive. He let me have a full transcript of all the signals, out and in. It took us a little time to get them sorted out—but not too long, considering.

Adler—that's the name of the surviving frigate—
was running for home. Her Captain sent a rather
heavily edited report of the action to his Admiral.
It seems that *Adler* and the unfortunate *Albatross*
were set upon and beaten up by a heavily armed
Survey Service cruiser masquerading as an innocent merchantman. The Admiral, oddly enough,
doesn't want a squadron of Survey Service
battlewagons laying nuclear eggs on his base. So
Adler has been told to run away and lose herself
until the flap's over. . . . ''

"And did they send all that *en clair?*" demanded
Grimes. "They must be mad!"

"No, they aren't mad. The signal's weren't *en
clair.*"

"But . . . "

"Reliable merchant captains," said Craven,
"are often entrusted with highly confidential naval
documents. There were some such in my safe
aboard *Delta Orionis*, consigned to the Commanding Officer of Lindisfarne Base. The officer who
delivered them to me is an old friend and shipmate
of mine, and he told me that among them was the
complete psionic code used by the Waldegren
Navy. Well, when I had decided to take over this
ship, I'd have been a bloody fool not to have
photostated the whole damned issue.

"So that's the way of it. Herr Kapitan von Leid-
nitz thinks he can say what he likes to his superiors
without anybody else knowing what he's saying.
And all the while . . . " Craven grinned wolfishly.
"It seems that there's a minor base, of sorts, on
Dartura. Little more than repair yards, although I
suppose that there'll be a few batteries for their
protection. I can imagine the sort of personnel
they have running the show—passed-over com-

manders and the like, not overly bright. By the time that we get there we shall have concocted a convincing story—convincing enough to let us hang off in orbit until *Adler* appears on the scene. After all, we have their precious code. Why should they suspect us?''

''Why shouldn't *we* be *Adler*?'' asked Grimes.

''What do you mean, Ensign?''

''The Waldegren Navy's frigates are almost identical, in silhouette, with the Commission's *Epsilon* class freighters. We could disguise this ship a little by masking the dissimilarities by a rough patching of plating. After all, *Adler* was in action and sustained some damage—''

''Complicated,'' mused the Captain. ''Too complicated. And two *Adlers*—each, presumably, in encoded psionic communication with both Waldegren and Dartura. . . . You've a fine, devious mind, young Grimes—but I'm afraid you've out-fixed yourself on that one.''

''Let me talk, sir. Let me think out loud. To begin with—a ship running on Mannschenn Drive *can* put herself into orbit about a planet, but it's not, repeat not, recommended.''

''Damn right it's not.''

''But we have the heels of *Adler*? Yes? Then we could afford a slight delay to carry out the modifications—the disguise—that I've suggested. After all, forty odd light years is quite a long way.''

''But what do we gain, Mr. Grimes?''

''The element of confusion, sir. Let me work it out. We disguise ourselves as well as we can. We find out, from intercepted and decoded signals, *Adler's* ETA—*and* the coordinates of her break-through into the normal continuum. We contrive matters to be more or less in the same place at exactly the same time. And when the shore batteries and the guardships see no less than two *Adlers* slugging it out, each of them yelling for help in the secret code, they won't know which of us to open fire on."

"Grimes," said Craven slowly, "I didn't know you had it in you. All I can say is that I'm glad that you're on *our* side."

"Am I?" asked Grimes wonderingly, suddenly deflated. He looked at the Captain who, after all, was little better than a pirate, whose accomplice he had become. He looked at the girl, but for whom he would not be here. "Am I? Damn it all, whose side *am* I on?"

"You'd better go below," Craven told him gently. "Go below and get some sleep. You need it. You've earned it."

"Jeremy," said Jane Pentecost to Craven, "would you mind looking after the shop for half an hour or so? I'll go with John."

"As you please, my dear. As you please."

It was the assurance in the Captain's voice that hurt. *It won't make any difference to us,* it implied. *It can't make any difference. Sure, Jane, go ahead. Throw the nice little doggie a bone . . . we can spare it.*

"No thank you," said Grimes coldly, and left the Control Room.

But he couldn't hate these people.

XX

AFTER A LONG SLEEP Grimes felt better. After a
meal he felt better still. It was a good meal, even
though the solid portion of it came from tins. Craven's standards were slipping, thought the Ensign.
He was reasonably sure that such items as caviar,
escargots, paté de foie gras, Virginia ham, Brie,
and remarkably alcoholic cherries were not included in the Commission's inventory of
emergency stores. And neither would be the quite
reasonable Montrachet, although it had lost a little
by being decanted from its original bottles into
standard squeeze bulbs. But if the Captain had
decided that the laborer was worthy of his hire,
with the consignees of the cargo making their
contribution toward that hire, that was his privilege . . .? Responsibility?—call it what you will.

Jane Pentecost watched him eat. As he was
finishing his coffee she said, "Now that our young
lion has fed, he is required in the Control Room."

He looked at her both gratefully and warily.
"What have I done now?"

"Nothing, my dear. It is to discuss what
you—we—will do. Next."

He followed her to Control. Craven was there,
of course, and so were Baxter and Summers. The
Captain was enjoying one of his rank cigars, and a
limp, roll-your-own cigarette dangled from the engineer's lower lip. The telepath coughed pointedly
every time that acrid smoke expelled by either
man drifted his way. Neither paid any attention to

him, and neither did Grimes when he filled and lighted his own pipe.

Craven said, "I've been giving that scheme of yours some thought. It's a good one."

"Thank you, sir."

"Don't thank me. I should thank you. Mr. Summers, here, has been maintaining a careful listening watch. *Adler's* ETA is such that we can afford to shut down the Drive to make the modifications that you suggest. To begin with, we'll fake patching plates with plastic sheets—we can't afford to cannibalize any more of the ship's structure—so as to obscure our name and identification letters. We'll use more plastic to simulate missile launchers and laser projectors—luckily there's plenty of it in the cargo."

"We found more than plastic while we were lookin' for it," said the engineer, licking his lips.

"That will do, Mr. Baxter. Never, in normal circumstances, should I have condoned . . ."

"These circumstances ain't normal, Skipper, an' we all bloody well know it."

"That will do, I say." Craven inhaled deeply, then filled the air of the Control Room with a cloud of smoke that, thought Grimes, would have reflected laser even at close range. Summers almost choked, and Jane snapped, "Jeremy!"

"This, my dear, happens to be *my* Control Room." He turned again to the Ensign. "It will not be necessary, Mr. Grimes, to relocate the real weapons. They functioned quite efficiently where they are and, no doubt, will do so again. And now, as soon as I have shut down the Drive, I shall hand the watch over to you. You are well rested and refreshed."

"Come on," said Jane to Baxter. "Let's get

suited up and get that sheeting out of the airlock."

"Couldn't Miss Pentecost hold the fort, sir?" asked Grimes. He added, "I've been through the camouflage course at the Academy."

"And so have I, Mr. Grimes. Furthermore, Miss Pentecost has had experience in working outside, but I don't think that you have."

"No, sir. But . . ."

"That will be all, Mr. Grimes."

At Craven's orders the Drive was shut down, and outside the viewports the sparse stars became stars again, were no longer pulsing spirals of multi-colored light. Then, alone in Control, Grimes actuated his scanners so that he could watch the progress of the work outside the hull, and switched on the transceiver that worked on the spacesuit frequency.

This time he ran no risk of being accused of being a Peeping Tom.

He had to admire the competence with which his shipmates worked. The plastic sheeting had no mass to speak of, but it was awkward stuff to handle. Torches glowed redly as it was cut, and radiated invisibly in the infrared as it was shaped and welded. The workers, in their bulky, clumsy suits, moved with a grace that was in startling contrast to their attire—a Deep Space ballet, thought Grimes, pleasurably surprised at his own way with words. From the speaker of the transceiver came Craven's curt orders, the brief replies of the others. "*This way a little . . . that's it.*" "*She'll do, Skipper.*" "*No she won't. Look at the bend on it!*" Then Jane's laughing voice. "*Our secret weapon, Jeremy. A laser that fires around corners!*" "*That will do, Miss Pentecost. Straighten it, will you?*" "*Ay, ay, sir. Captain, sir.''* The two interstellar drive engineers were working in silence, but with efficiency. Aboard the ship were only Grimes and Summers, the telepath.

Grimes felt out of it, but somebody had to mind the shop, he supposed. But the likelihood of any customers was remote.

Then he stiffened in his chair. One of the spacesuited figures was falling away from the vessel, drifting out and away, a tiny, glittering satellite reflecting the harsh glare of the working floods, a little, luminous butterfly pinned to the black velvet of the Ultimate Night. Who was it? He didn't know for certain, but thought that it was Jane. The ship's interplanetary drives—reaction and inertial—were on remote control, but reaction drive was out; before employing it he would have to swing to the desired heading by use of the directional gyroscopes. But the inertial drive was versatile.

He spoke into the microphone of the transceiver. ''Secure yourselves. I am proceeding to rescue.''

At once Craven's voice snapped back, ''Hold it, Grimes. Hold it! There's no danger.''

''But, sir . . . ''

''Hold it!''

Grimes could see the distant figure now from a viewport, but it did not seem to be receding any longer. Hastily he checked with the radar. Range and bearing were not changing. Then, with relative bearing unaltered, the range was closing. He heard Jane call out, ''Got it! I'm on the way back!''

Craven replied, ''Make it snappy—otherwise young Grimes'll be chasing you all over the Universe!''

Grimes could see, now, the luminous flicker of a suit reaction unit from the lonely figure.

Later, he and the others examined the photographs that Jane had taken.

Epsilon Sextans looked as she was supposed to look—like a badly battle-scarred frigate of the Waldegren Navy.

XXI

IN TERMS OF SPACE and of time there was not much longer to go.

The two ships—one knowing and one unknowing—raced toward their rendezvous. Had they been plunging through the normal continuum there would have been, toward the finish, hardly the thickness of a coat of paint between them, the adjustment of a microsecond in temporal precession rates would have brought inevitable collision. Craven knew this from the results of his own observations and from the encoded position reports, sent at six hourly intervals, by *Adler*. Worried, he allowed himself to fall astern, a mere half kilometer. It would be enough—and, too, it would mean that the frigate would mask him from the fire of planet-based batteries.

Summers maintained his listening watch. Apart from the position reports he had little of interest to tell the Captain. *Adler*, once or twice, had tried to get in contact with the Main Base on Waldegren—but, other than from a curt directive to proceed as ordered there were no signals from the planet to the ship. Dartura Base was more talkative. That was understandable. There was no colony on the planet and the Base personnel must be bored, must be pining for the sight of fresh faces, the sound of fresh voices. They would have their excitement soon enough, promised Craven grimly.

Through the warped continuum fell the two

ships, and ahead the pulsating spiral that was the Dartura sun loomed ever brighter, ever larger. There were light years yet to go, but the Drive-induced distortions made it seem that tentacles of incandescent gas were already reaching out to clutch them, to drag them into the atomic furnace at the heart of the star.

In both Control Rooms watch succeeded watch—but the thoughts and the anticipations of the watchkeepers were not the same. Aboard *Adler* there was the longing for rest, for relaxation—although *Adler's* Captain must have been busy with the composition of a report that would clear him (if possible) of blame for his defeat. Aboard *Epsilon Sextans* there was the anticipation of revenge—insofar as Craven, Baxter, Jane Pentecost and the survivors of the ship's original personnel were concerned. Grimes? As the hour of reckoning approached he was more and more dubious. He did not know what to think, what to feel. There was the strong personal loyalty to Craven—and, even now, to Jane Pentecost. There was the friendship and mutual respect that had come into being between himself and Baxter. There was the knowledge that *Adler's* crew were no better than pirates, were murderers beyond rehabilitation. There was the pride he felt in his own skill as a gunnery officer. (But, as such, was he, himself, any better than a pirate, a murderer? The exercise of his craft aboard a warship would be legal—but here, aboard a merchantman, and a disguised merchantman at that, the legality was doubtful. What had his motives been when he volunteered—and as a commissioned officer of the Survey Service he had had no right to do so—and what were his motives now?)

He, Grimes, was not happy. He had far too much time to ponder the implications. He was an accessory before, during and after the fact. He had started off correctly enough, when he had tried to prevent Craven from requisitioning the Survey Service cargo aboard *Delta Orionis*, but after that . . . after he and Jane . . . (that, he admitted, was a memory that he wanted to keep, always, just as that other memory, of the bright picture of naked female flesh on the screen, he wished he could lose forever.)

He had started off correctly enough—and then, not only had he helped install the purloined armament but had used it. (*And used it well*, he told himself with a brief resurgence of pride.) Furthermore, the disguise of *Epsilon Sextans* had been his idea.

Oh, he was in it, all right. He was in up to his neck. What the final outcome of it all would be he did not care to contemplate.

But it would soon be over. He had no fears as to the outcome of the battle. The element of surprise would be worth at least a dozen missile launchers. *Adler* would never have the chance to use her laser.

Adler, reported Summers, had shut down her Mannschenn Drive and emerged briefly into normal spacetime to make her final course adjustment. She was now headed not for the Dartura Sun but for the planet itself—or where the planet would be at the time of her final—and fatal—reemergence into the continuum. The last ETA was sent, together with the coordinates of her planetfall. *Epsilon Sextans* made her own course adjustment—simultaneity in time and a half kilometer's divergence in space being Craven's objective. It was finicky work, even with the use of the ship's computer, but the Captain seemed satisfied.

The race—the race that would culminate in a dead heat—continued. Aboard the frigate there was, reported Summers, a lessening of tension, the loosening up that comes when a voyage is almost over. Aboard the merchantman the tension increased. The interstellar drive engineers, Grimes knew, were no happier about it all than he was—but they could no more back out than he could. Craven was calm and confident, and Baxter was beginning to gloat. Jane Pentecost assumed the air of dedication that in women can be so infuriating. Grimes glumly checked and rechecked his weaponry. It passed the time.

Dartura itself was visible now—not as tiny disk of light but as a glowing annulus about its distorted primary. The thin ring of luminescence broadened, broadened. The time to go dwindled to a week, to days, to a day, and then to hours . . .

To minutes . . .

To seconds. . . .

Craven and Grimes were in the Control Room; the others were at their various stations. From the intercom came the telepath's voice, "He's cutting the Drive—"

"Cut the Drive!" ordered the Captain.

In the Mannschenn Drive room the spinning, precessing gyroscopes slowed, slowed, ceased their endless tumbling, assumed the solidity that they exhibited only when at rest. For perhaps two seconds there was temporal confusion in the minds of all on board as the precession field died, and past, present and future inextricably mingled.

Then there was a sun glaring through the view-ports, bright in spite of the polarization—a sun, and, directly ahead, a great, green-orange planet. There was a ship. . . .

There were ships—ahead of them, astern, on all sides.

There were ships—and, booming from the intership transceiver, the transceiver that was neither tuned nor switched on (but navies could afford induction transmitters with their fantastic power consumption), came the authorative voice: "*Inflexible* to *Adler*! Heave to for search and seizure! Do not attempt to escape—our massed fields will hold you!"

The effect was rather spoiled when the same voice added, in bewilderment, "Must be seeing double . . . there's two of the bastards." The bewilderment did not last long. "*Inflexible* to *Adler* and to unidentified vessel. Heave to for search and seizure!"

"Hold your fire, Mr. Grimes," ordered Craven, quietly and bitterly. "It's the Survey Service."

"I know," replied Grimes—and pressed the button.

XXII

HE NEVER KNEW just why he had done so.

Talking it over afterward, thinking about it, he was able to evolve a theory that fitted the facts. During the brief period immediately after the shutting down of the Drive, during the short session of temporal disorientation, there had been prescience, of a sort. He had known that *Adler*, come what may, would attempt one last act of defiance and revenge, just as *Adler's* Captain or Gunnery Officer must have known, in that last split second, that Nemesis was treading close upon his heels.

He pushed the button—and from the nozzles in the shell plating poured the reflective vapor, the protective screen that glowed ruddily as *Adler's* lasers slashed out at it.

From the speaker of the dead transceiver, the transceiver that should have been dead, roared the voice of the Survey Service Admiral. "*Adler!* Cease fire! Cease fire, damn you!" There was a pause, then: "You've asked for it!"

She had asked for it—and now she got it. Suddenly the blip on Grimes' screen that represented the Waldegren frigate became two smaller blips, and then four. The rolling fog outside *Epsilon Sextans'* viewports lost its luminosity, faded suddenly to drab grayness. The voice from the transceiver said coldly, "And now *you*, whoever you are, had better identify yourself. And fast."

Craven switched on the communications equipment. He spoke quietly into the microphone.

"Interstellar Transport Commission's *Epsilon Sextans*. Bound Waverly, with general cargo . . ."

"Bound Waverley? Then what the hell are you doing here? And what's that armament you're mounting?"

"Plastic," replied the Captain. "Plastic dummies."

"And I suppose your ALGE is plastic, too. Come off it, Jerry. We've already boarded your old ship, and although your ex-Mate was most reluctant to talk we got a story of sorts from him."

"I thought I recognized your voice, Bill. May I congratulate you upon your belated efforts to stamp out piracy?"

"And may I deplore your determination to take the law into your own hands? Stand by for the boarding party."

Grimes looked at Craven, who was slumped in his seat. The Master's full beard effectively masked his expression. "Sir," asked the Ensign. "What can they do? What will they do?"

"You're the space lawyer, Grimes. You're the expert on Survey Service rules and regulations. What will it be, do you think? A medal—or a firing squad? Praise or blame?"

"You know the Admiral, sir?"

"Yes. I know the Admiral. We're old shipmates."

"Then you should be safe."

"Safe? I suppose so. Safe from the firing squad—but not safe from my employers. I'm a merchant captain, Grimes, and merchant captains aren't supposed to range the spacelanes looking for trouble. I don't think they'll dare fire me—but I know that I can never expect command of anything better than *Delta* class ships, on the drearier runs.'' Grimes saw that Craven was smiling. "But there're still the Rim Worlds. There's still the Sundowner Line, and the chance of high rank in the Rim Worlds Navy when and if there is such a service.''

"You have . . . inducements, sir?''

"Yes. There are . . . inducements. Now.''

"I thought, once,'' said Grimes, "that I could say the same. But not now. Not any longer. Even so . . . I'm Survey Service, sir, and I should be proud of my service. But in this ship, this merchant vessel, with her makeshift armament, we fought against heavy odds, and won. And, just now, we saved ourselves. It wasn't the Survey Service that saved us.''

"Don't be disloyal,'' admonished Craven.

"I'm not being disloyal, sir. But . . . or, shall we say, I'm being loyal. You're the first captain under whom I served under fire. If you're going out to the Rim Worlds I'd like to come with you.''

"Your commission, Grimes. You know that you must put in ten years' service before resignation is possible.''

"But I'm dead.''

"*Dead*?''

"Yes. Don't you remember? I was snooping around in the Mannschenn Drive room and I got caught in the temporal precession field. My body still awaits burial; it's in a sealed metal box in the deep freeze. It can never be identified.''

Craven laughed. "I'll say this for you. You're ingenious. But how do we account for the absence of the late Mr. Wolverton? And your presence aboard this ship?''

"I can hide, sir, and . . . ''

"And while you're hiding you'll concoct some story that will explain everything. Oh Grimes, Grimes—you're an officer I wish I could always have with me. But I'll not stand in the way of your career. All I can do, all I will do, is smooth things over on your behalf with the Admiral. I should be able to manage that."

Jane Pentecost emerged from the hatch in the Control Room deck. Addressing Craven she said formally, "Admiral Williams, sir." She moved to one side to make way for the flag officer.

"Jerry, you bloody pirate!" boomed Williams, a squat, rugged man the left breast of whose shirt was ablaze with ribbons. He advanced with outstretched hand.

"Glad to have you aboard, Bill. This is Liberty Hall—you can spit on the mat and call the cat a bastard!"

"Not again!" groaned Grimes.

"And who is this young man?" asked the Admiral.

"I owe you—or your Service—an apology, Bill. This is Ensign Grimes, who was a passenger aboard *Delta Orionis*. I'm afraid that I . . . er . . . press-ganged him into my service. But he has been most . . . cooperative? Uncooperative? Which way do you want it?

"As we are at war with Waldegren—I'd say cooperative with reservations. Was it he, by the way, who used the ALGE? Just as well for you all that he did."

"At war with Waldegren?" demanded Jane Pentecost. "So you people have pulled your fingers out at last."

The Admiral raised his eyebrows.

"One of my Rim Worlders," explained Craven.

"But I shall be a Rim Worlder myself shortly."

"You're wise, Jerry. I've got the buzz that the Commission is taking a very dim view of your piracy or privateering or whatever it was, and my own lords and masters are far from pleased with you. You'd better get the hell out before the lawyers have decided just what crimes you are guilty of."

"As bad as that?"

"As bad as that."

"And young Grimes, here?"

"We'll take him back. Six months' strick discipline aboard my flagship will undo all the damage that you and your ideas have done to him. And now, Jerry, I'd like your full report."

"In my cabin, Bill. Talking is thirsty work."

"Then lead on. It's your ship."

"And it's your watch, Mr. Grimes. She'll come to no harm on this trajectory while we get things sorted out."

Grimes sat with Jane Pentecost in the Control Room. Through the ports, had he so desired, he could have watched the rescue teams extricating the survivors from the wreckage of *Adler*; he could have stared out at the looming bulk of Dartura on the beam. But he did not do so, and neither did he look at his instruments.

He looked at Jane. There was so much about her that he wanted to remember—and, after all, so very little that he was determined to forget.

The intercom buzzed. "Mr. Grimes, will you pack whatever gear you have and prepare to transfer with Admiral Williams to the flagship? Hand the watch over to Miss Pentecost."

"But you'll be shorthanded, sir."

"The Admiral is lending me a couple of officers for the rest of the voyage."

"Very good, sir."

Grimes made no move. He looked at Jane—a somehow older, a tireder, a more human Jane than the girl he had first met. He said, "I'd have liked to have come out to the Rim with you. . . ."

She said, "It's impossible, John."

"I know. But . . ."

"You'd better get packed."

He unbuckled his seat belt, went to where she was sitting. He kissed her. She responded, but it was only the merest flicker of a response.

He said, "Goodbye."

She said, "Not goodbye. We'll see you out on the Rim, sometime."

With a bitterness that he was always to regret he replied, "Not very likely."

THE HARD
WAY UP

by

A. Bertram Chandler

WITH GOOD INTENTIONS

Pathfinder was not a happy ship.

Pathfinder's Captain was not a happy man, and made this glaringly obvious.

Young Lieutenant Grimes, newly appointed to the Survey Service cruiser, was also far from happy. During his few years in Space he had served under strict commanding officers as well as easy going ones, but never under one like Captain Tolliver.

"You must make allowances, John," Paymaster Lieutenant Beagle told him as the two young men were discussing matters over a couple or three drinks in Grimes's cabin.

"Make allowances?" echoed Grimes. "I don't know what's biting him—but I know what's biting me. Him, that's what."

"All the same, you should make allowances."

"It's all very well for you to talk, Peter—but you idlers can keep out of his way. We watchkeepers can't."

"But he's a Worrallian," said Beagle. "Didn't you know?"

"No," admitted Grimes. "I didn't."

He knew now. He knew, too, that there were only a hundred or so Worrallians throughout the entire Galaxy. Not so long ago the population of Worrall had been nudging the thirty million mark. Worrall had been a prosperous planet—also it had been among the few Man-colonised worlds of the Interstellar Federation upon which the concepts of race and nationality had been allowed to take hold and develop. "It makes for healthy competition," had been the claim of the Worrallian delegations—three of them—whenever the subject came up at the meetings of the Federation Grand Council. And so they had competed happily among themselves on their little ball of mud and rock and water—North Worrall, and South Worrall, and Equatorial Worrall—until all three nations laid simultaneous claim to a chain of hitherto worthless islands upon which flourished the stinkbird colonies. The stinkbird—it was more of a flying reptile really, although with certain mammalian characteristics—had always been regarded as more unpleasant than useful, and if anybody had wanted those barren, precipitous rocks lashed by the perpetually stormy seas the stinkbird would soon have gone the way of many another species unlucky enough to get in Man's way. The stinkbird—along with everything and everybody else on Worrall—finally was unlucky, this being when a bright young chemist discovered that a remarkably effective rejuvenating compound was secreted by certain glands in its body. Worrall, although a prosperous enough closed economy, had always been lacking, until this time, in exports that would fetch high prices on the interstellar market.

So there was a squabble—with words at first, and then with weapons. In its ultimate stage somebody pushed some sort of button—or, quite possibly, three buttons were pushed. The only Worrallians to survive were those who were elsewhere at the time of the button-pushing.

And Captain Tolliver was a Worrallian.

Grimes sighed. He felt sorry for the man. He

could visualise, but dimly, what it must be like to have no place in the entire Galaxy to call home, to know that everything, but everything had been vaporised in one hellish blast of fusion flame—parents, friends, lovers, the house in which one was brought up, the school in which one was educated, the bars in which one used to drink. Grimes shuddered.

But he still felt sorry for himself.

Grimes realised that Captain Tolliver had come into the control room. But, as the commanding officer had not announced his presence, the young man went on with what he was doing—the midwatch check of the ship's position. Carefully, trying hard not to fumble, Grimes manipulated the Carlotti Direction Finder—an instrument with which he was not yet familiar—lining up the antenna, an elliptical Mobius Strip rotating about its long axis, with the Willishaven beacon, finally jotting down the angle relative to the fore-and-aft line of the ship. Then, still working slowly and carefully, he took a reading on Brownsworld and, finally, on Carlyon. By this time he was perspiring heavily and his shirt was sticking to his body, and his prominent ears were flushed and burning painfully. He swivelled his chair so that he could reach the chart tank, laid off the bearings. The three filaments of luminescence intersected nicely, exactly on the brighter filament that marked *Pathfinder's* trajectory. Decisively Grimes punched the keys that caused the time of the observation, in tiny, glowing figures, to appear alongside the position.

"Hrrmph."

Grimes simulated a start of surprise, swung

round in his chair to face the Captain. "Sir?"

Tolliver was a tall, gangling scarecrow of a man, and even though his uniform was clean and correct in every detail it hung on him like a penitent's sackcloth and ashes. He stared down at his officer from bleak grey eyes. He said coldly, "Mr. Grimes, I checked the time it took you to put a position in the tank. It was no less than eleven minutes, forty-three point five seconds. Objective speed is thirty-five point seven six lumes. Over what distance did this ship travel from start to finish of your painfully slow operations?"

"I can work it out, sir . . . " Grimes half got up from his chair to go to the control room computer.

"Don't bother, Mr. Grimes. Don't bother. I realise that watchkeepers have more important things with which to exercise their tiny minds than the boresome details of navigation—the girl in the last port, perhaps, or the girl you hope to meet in the next one . . . "

More than Grimes's ears was flushed now. A great proportion of his watch had been spend reminiscing over the details of his shore leave on New Capri.

"This cross of yours looks suspiciously good. I would have expected an inexpert navigator such as yourself to produce more of a cocked hat. I suppose you did allow for distance run between bearings?"

"Of course, sir."

"Hrrmph. Well, Mr. Grimes, we will assume that this fix of yours is reasonably accurate. Put down a D.R. from it for 1200 hours, then lay off a trajectory from there to Delta Sextans."

"Delta Sextans, sir?"

"You heard me."

"But aren't we bound for Carlyon?"

"We were bound for Carlyon, Mr. Grimes. But—although it may well have escaped your notice—the arm of our lords and masters in Admiralty House is a long one, extending over many multiples of light years. For your information, we have been ordered to conduct a survey of the planetary system of Delta Sextans."

"Will there be landings, sir?" asked Grimes hopefully.

"Should it concern you, Mr. Grimes, you will be informed when the time comes. Please lay off the trajectory."

Lieutenant Commander Wanger, the ship's Executive Officer, was more informative than the Captain had been. Convening off-duty officers in the wardroom he gave them a run-down on the situation. He said, "No matter what the biologists, sociologists and all the rest of 'em come up with, population keeps on exploding. And so we, as well as most of the other survey cruisers presently in commission, have been ordered to make more thorough inspections of habitable planets which, in the past, were filed away, as it were, for future reference.

"Delta Sextans has a planetary family of 10 worlds. Of these, only two—Delta Sextans IV and Delta Sextans V—could possibly meet our requirements. According to Captain Lovell's initial survey IV could be rather too hot, and V more than a little too cold. Both support oxygen-breathing life forms, although V, with its mineral wealth, has greater industrial potential than IV. In any case it is doubtful if IV will be selected as the site for the Delta Sextans colony; Captain Lovell said that in his opinion, and in that of his biologists, at least one of the indigenous species comes into the third category."

"And what is that?" asked a junior engineer.

"Any being in the third category," explained the Executive Officer, "is considered capable of evolving into the second category."

"And what is the second category?" peristed the engineer.

"The likes of us. And the first category is what we might become—or, if we're very unlucky, run into. Anyhow, the ruling is that third category beings may be observed, but not interfered with. And taking somebody else's world is classed as interference. Will somebody pour me some more coffee?"

Somebody did, and after lubricating his throat Wanger went on. "The drill will be this. We establish a camp of observers on IV—according to the initial surveys there's nothing there that could be at all dangerous to well-equipped humans—and then the ship shoves off for V to get on with the real work. There's no doubt that V will be selected for the new colony—but it will be as well if the colonists know something about their next-door neighbours."

"Any idea who'll be landed on IV?" asked Grimes.

"Haven't a clue, John. There'll be a team of biologists, ethologists, cartographers, geologists, and whatever. If the Old Man abides by Regulations—and he will—there'll be an officer of the military branch officially in charge of the camp. Frankly, it's not a job that I'd care for—I've had experience of it. Whoever goes with the boggins will soon find that he's no more than chief cook and bottle washer—quite literally.''

Nonetheless, Grimes was pleased when he was told, some days later, that he was to be in charge of the landing party.

Pathfinder hung in orbit about Delta Sextans IV until the boat was safely down, until Grimes reported that the camp was established. To start with, Grimes enjoyed his authority and responsibility—then found that once the turbulent atmospheric approach had been negotiated and the landing craft was sitting solidly and safely on the bank of a river it was responsibility only. The scientists—not at all offensively—soon made it clear that once they were away from the ship gold braid and brass buttons meant less than nothing. When the stores and equipment were unloaded each of them was concerned only with his own treasures. They cooperated, after a fashion, in setting up the inflatable tents that were living quarters and laboratory. Reluctantly they agreed to defer their initial explorations until the following morning. (The boat, following the Survey Service's standard practice, had landed at local dawn, but by the time that Grimes had things organised to his liking the sun, a blur of light and heat heavily veiled by the overcast, was almost set.)

It was Grimes who cooked the evening meal—and even though the most important tool employed in its preparation was a can opener he rather resented it. Three of the six scientists were women, and if anybody had ever told them that a woman's place is in the kitchen they had promptly forgotten it. He resented it, too, when nobody showed any appreciation of his efforts. His charges gobbled their food without noticing what it was, intent upon their shop talk. The only remark addressed to Grimes was a casual suggestion that he have the flitters ready for use at first light.

The Lieutenant left the surveying party, still talking nineteen to the dozen, in the mess tent, hoping that they would eventually get around to stacking the dishes and washing up. (They didn't.) Outside it was almost dark and, in spite of the heat of the past day, there was a damp chill in the air. Something was howling in the forest of cabbage-like trees back from the river bank, and something else flapped overhead on wide, clattering wings. There were insects, too—or things analogous to insects. They did not bite, but they were a nuisance. They were attracted, Grimes decided, by his body heat. He muttered to himself, "If the bastards like warmth so much, why the hell can't they come out in the daytime?"

He decided to switch on the floods. With this perpetual overcast he might have trouble recharging the batteries during the hours of daylight, but they should hold out until *Pathfinder's* return. He was able to work easily in the harsh glare and made a thorough check of the alarm system. Anything trying to get into the camp would either be electrocuted or get a nasty shock, according to size. (The same applied, of course, to anything or anybody trying to get out—but he had warned the scientists.) Finally he opened the boxes in which the flitters were stowed, started to assemble the first of the machines. He did not like them much himself—they were flimsy, one-person helicopters, with a gas bag for greater lift—but he doubted that he would get the chance to use one. Already he could see that he would be confined to camp for the duration of the party's stay on IV.

With the camp secure for the night and the flitters assembled he returned to the mess tent—to find that the scientists had retired to their sleeping tents and left him with all the washing up.

Came the dawn, such as it was, and Grimes was rudely awakened by Dr. Kortsoff, one of the biologists. "Hey, young Grimes," shouted the bearded, burly scientist. "Rise and shine! What about some breakfast? Some of us have to work for our livings, you know!"

"I know," grumbled Grimes. "That's what I was doing most of last night."

He extricated himself from his sleeping bag, pulled on yesterday's shirt and shorts (still stiff with dried sweat, but they would have to do until he got *himself* organised) and thrust his feet into sandals, stumbled out of his tent—and was surrounded by a mob of naked women. There were only three of them, as a matter of fact, but they were making enough noise for a mob. One of them, at least—the red-haired Dr. Margaret Lazenby—possessed the sort of good looks enhanced by anger, but Grimes was not in an appreciative mood.

"Mr. Grimes!" she snapped. "Do you want to *kill* us?"

"What do you mean, Dr. Lazenby?" he asked meekly.

"That bloody force field of yours, or whatever it is. When we were trying to go down to the river for our morning swim Jenny and I were nearly electrocuted. Turn the bloody thing off, will you?"

"I warned you last night that I'd set it up . . ."

"We never heard you. In any case, there aren't any dangerous animals here . . ."

"Never take anything for granted . . . " Grimes began.

"You can say that again, Grimes. Never take it for granted, for example, that everybody knows all about the odd things you do during the night when sensible people are sleeping. Setting up force fields on a world where there's nothing more dangerous than a domestic cat!"

"What about some *coffee*, Mr. Grimes?" somebody else was yelling.

"I've only one pair of hands," muttered Grimes as he went to switch off the force field.

And so it went on throughout the day—fetch this, fix that, do this, don't do that, lend a hand here, there's a good fellow . . . Grimes remembered, during a very brief smoke, what Maggie Lazenby had told him once about the pecking order, claiming that what was true for barnyard fowls was also true for human beings. "There's the boss bird," she had said, "and she's entitled to peck everybody. There's the number two bird— and she's pecked by the boss, and pecks everybody else. And so on, down the line, until we come to the poor little bitch who's pecked by *everybody*." "But that doesn't apply to humans," Grimes had demurred. "Doesn't it just, duckie! In schools, aboard ships . . . I've nothing to do with the administration of this wagon—thank all the Odd Gods of the Galaxy!—but even I can see now that poor Ordinary Spaceman Wilkes is bullied by everybody . . . "

Grimes had never, so far as he knew, bullied that hapless rating—but he found himself wishing that the man were here. As he was not, Grimes was bottom bird in the pecking order. There was no malice about it—or no conscious malice. It was just that Grimes was, by the standards of the scientific party, only semi-literate, his status that of a hewer of wood, a drawer of water. He was in an environment where his qualifications counted for little or nothing, where the specialists held sway. And these same specialists, Grimes realised, must have resented the very necessary discipline aboard the ship. Although they would never have admitted it to themselves they were dogs having their day.

The next day wasn't so bad. Six of the flitters were out—which meant that Grimes had the camp to himself. Two by two the scientists had lifted from the camp site, ascending into the murk like glittering, mechanical angels. Carrying a portable transceiver—and a projectile pistol, just in case—Grimes went for a stroll along the river bank. He felt a little guilty about deserting his post, but should any of his charges get into trouble and yell for help he would know at once. He decided that he would walk to the first bend in the wide stream, and then back.

Delta Sextans IV was not a pretty world. The sky was grey, with a paler blur that marked the passage of the hot sun across it. The river was grey. The fleshy-leaved vegetation was grey, with the merest hint of dull green. There was little distinction between blossom and foliage as far as a non-botanist like Grimes was concerned.

But it was good to get away from the camp, from that huddle of plastic igloos, and from the multitudinous chores. It was good to walk on the surface of a world unspoiled by Man, the first time that Grimes had done so. Captain Lovell's survey had been, after all, a very superficial effort and so, thought Grimes, there was a chance that he, even he, would find something, some plant or animal, that would be named after him. He grinned wryly. If any Latin tags were to be affixed to local fauna and flora his own name would be the last to be considered.

He came to the bend in the river, decided to carry on for just a few yards past it. *Well, he thought with a glow of pleasure, I have found something—something which the others, flapping around on their tin wings, have missed* . . . The something was an obvious game trail leading through the jungle to the water's edge. But why in this particular spot? Grimes investigated. Elsewhere the bank was steep—here there was a little bay, with a gently shelving beach. Here, too, growing in the shallow water, was a clump of odd-looking plants—straight, thick stems, each a few feet high, each topped by a cluster of globules varying in size from grape to orange. And here, too, something had died or been killed. Only the bones were left—yellowish, pallidly gleaming. There was a rib cage, which must have run the entire length of a cylindrical body. There was a skull, almost spherical. There were jaws, with teeth—the teeth of a herbivore, thought Grimes. The beast, obviously, had been a quadruped, and about the size of a Terran Shetland pony.

Suddenly Grimes stiffened. Something was coming along that trail through the jungle— something that rustled and chattered. As he backed away from the skeleton he pulled out his pistol, thumbed back the safety catch. He re-treated to the bend of the river and waited there, ready to fight or run—but curious as to what sort of animal would appear.

There were more than one of them. They spilled out on to the river bank—about a dozen grey, shaggy brutes, almost humanoid. Mostly they walked upright, but now and again dropped to all fours. They chattered and gesticulated. They varied in size from that of a small man to that of a young child—but somehow Grimes got the idea that there were no children among them.

They had not come to drink. They went straight to the plants, started tearing the largest—the ripest?—fruit from the stems, stuffing them into their wide mouths, gobbling them greedily. There was plenty for all—but, inevitably, there was one who wasn't getting any. It was not that he was the smallest of the tribe—but neither was he the largest. Even so, his trouble seemed to be psychological rather than physical; he seemed to be hampered by a certain diffidence, a reluctance to join in the rough and tumble scramble.

At last, when all his mates were busy gorging themselves, he shambled slowly through the shallows to the fruit plants. Glancing timorously around to see that nobody was watching he put out a hand, wrenched one of the spheroids from its stem. He was not allowed to even taste it. A hairy paw landed on the side of his head with a loud *hunk*, knocking him sprawling into the muddy water. The brute who had attacked him snatched the fruit from his hand, bit into it, spat and grimaced and threw it out into the river. No less than three times there was a roughly similar sequence of events—and then, as though in response to some inaudible signal, the troop scampered back into the jungle, the victim of the bullies looking back wistfully to the fruit that he had not so much as tasted.

That evening Grimes told the scientists about his own minor exploration, but none of them was interested. Each was too engrossed in his own project—the deposit of rich, radioactive ores, the herds of food animals, the villages of the simian-like creatures. Maggie Lazenby did say that she would accompany Grimes as soon as she had a spare five minutes—but that would not be until her real work had been tidied up. And then, after dinner, Grimes was left with the washing up as usual.

That night he set an alarm to wake him just before sunrise, so that he was able to switch off the force fields to allow the women to leave the camp for their morning swim, to make coffee and get breakfast preparations under way. After the meals he was left to himself again.

He was feeling a certain kinship with the native who was bottom bird in the pecking order. He thought smugly: "If Maggie were right, I'd kick him around myself. But I'm civilised." This time he took with him a stun-gun instead of a projectile pistol, setting the control for mini minimum effect.

The natives had not yet arrived at the little bay when he got there. He pulled off his shoes and stockings, waded out through the shallow water to where the fruit-bearing plants were growing. He plucked two of the largest, ripest-seeming globes. He didn't know whether or not they would be dangerous to the human metabolism, and was not tempted to find out. Even with their tough skins intact they stank. Then he retired a few yards from the end of the trail, sat down to wait.

At almost exactly the same time the gibbering, gesticulating troop debouched from the jungle. As before, the timid member hung back, hovering on the outskirts of the scrum, awaiting his chance—

his slim chance—to get some fruit for himself.
Grimes got slowly to his feet. The primitive
humanoids ignored him, save for the timorous
one—but even he stood his ground. Grimes
walked carefully forward, the two ripe fruit extended in his left hand. He saw a flicker of interest,
of greed, in the creature's yellow eyes, the glisten
of saliva at the corners of the wide, thin-lipped
mouth. And then, warily, the thing was shambling
towards him. "Come and get it," whispered
Grimes. "Come and get it."

Was the native telepathic? As soon as he was
within snatching distance of the spaceman he
snatched, his long nails tearing the skin of Grimes's
left hand. Were his fellows telepathic? Growling,
the leader of the troop dropped the fruit that he had
been guzzling, scampered through the shallows
and up the bank towards the recipient of Grimes's
gift. That miserable being whined and cringed,
extended the fruit towards the bully in a placatory
gesture.

Grimes growled too. His stun-gun was ready,
and aiming it was a matter of microseconds. He
pressed the stud. The bully gasped, dropped to the
ground, twitching. "Eat your bloody fruit, damn
you!" snarled Grimes. This time the timorous one
managed a couple of bites before another bully—
number two in the pecking order?—tried to steal
his meal. By the time the fruit were finished no less
than half a dozen bodies were strewn on the moss-
like ground-covering growth. They were not dead,
Grimes noted with some relief. As he watched the
first two scrambled unsteadily to their feet, stared
at him reproachfully and then shambled away to
feed on what few ripe fruit were left. Characteris-
tically they did not pluck these for themselves but

snatched them from the weaker members of the troop. Oddly enough they made no attempt to revenge themselves on Grimes's protégé.

The next day Grimes continued his experiment. As before, he plucked two tempting—but not to him—fruit. As before, he presented them to Snuffy. (It was as good a name as any.) This time, however, he was obliged to use his stun-gun only once. Grimes thought that it was the troop leader—again—who was least capable of learning by experience. The third day he did not have to use the weapon at all, and Snuffy allowed him to pat him, and patted him back. The fourth day he did not think that he would be using the gun—and then one of the smaller humanoids, one who had taken Snuffy's place as tribal butt, screamed angrily and flew at Snuffy, all claws and teeth. Snuffy dropped his fruit and tried to run—and then the whole troop was on him, gibbering and hitting and kicking. Grimes—the gun set on wide beam, shocked them all into unconsciousness. When they recovered all of them scampered back into the jungle.

On the fifth day Grimes was all ready for the next stage of his experiment. He was glad that the scientists were still fully occupied with their own games; he suspected that they—especially Maggie Lazenby—would want to interfere, would want things done their way, would complicate an essentially simple situation. It was all so glaringly obvious to the young Lieutenant. Snuffy would have to be taught to defend himself, to protect his own rights.

He picked the two fruits as usual. He used the stun-gun to deter the bullies—and then he used the weapon on Snuffy, giving him another shock every time that he showed signs of regaining consciousness. He realised that the creature—as he had hoped would be the case—was not popular with his troop fellows; when the time came for them to return to their village or whatever it was they vanished into the jungle without a backward glance. Grimes lifted Snuffy—he wasn't very heavy—and carried him to where the skeleton of the horse-like animal lay on the bank like the bones of a wrecked and stranded ship. He felt a tickling on his skin under his shirt, was thankful that he had thought to make a liberal application of insect-repellent before leaving the camp. He deposited the hairy body on the thick moss, then went to work on the skeleton. Using his knife to sever the dry, tough ligaments he was able to detach the two thigh bones. They made good clubs—a little too short and too light for a man's use, but just right for a being of Snuffy's size. Finally he picked some more fruit—there were a few ripe ones that had been missed by the troop.

At last Snuffy came round, making his characteristic snuffling sound. He stared at Grimes. Grimes looked calmly back, offered him what he had come to think of as a stink-apple. Snuffy accepted it, bit into it. He belched. Grimes regretted that he was not wearing a respirator. While the humanoid was happily munching, Grimes juggled with one of the thigh bones. Snuffy finally condescended to notice what he was doing, to evince some interest. With a sharp *crack* Grimes brought his club down on the skeleton's rib cage. Two of the ribs were broken cleanly in two.

Snuffy extended his hands toward the club. Grimes gave it to him, picking up the other one.

The native was a good pupil. Finally, without any prompting from the spaceman, he was flailing

away at the skull of the dead animal, at last cracking it. Grimes looked guiltily at his watch. It was
time that he was getting back to the camp to get the
preparations for the evening meal under way. Still
feeling guilty, he wondered how Snuffy would
make it back to his own living place, what his
reception would be. But he was armed now, would
be able to look after himself—Grimes hoped.

And then it became obvious that the native had
no intention of going home by himself. Still carrying his bone club he shambled along at Grimes's
side, uttering an occasional plaintive *eek*. He
would not be chased off, and Grimes was reluctant
to use the stun-gun on him. But there was a spare
tent that would be used eventually for the storage
of specimens. Snuffy would have to sleep there.

To Grimes's surprise and relief the native did not
seem to mind when he was taken into the plastic
igloo. He accepted a bowl of water, burying his
wrinkled face in it and slurping loudly. Rather
dubiously he took a stick of candy, but once he had
sampled it it soon disappeared. (Grimes had
learned from the scientists that anything eaten by
the life form of Delta Sextans IV could be handled
by the human metabolism; it was logical to suppose that a native of IV could eat human food with
safety.) More water, and more candy—and Snuffy
looked ready to retire for the night, curling up on
the floor of the tent in a foetal posture. Grimes left
him to it.

He did not sleep at all well himself. He was
afraid that his . . . guest? prisoner? would awake
during the hours of darkness, would awaken the
whole camp by howling or other anti-social conduct. Grimes was beginning to have an uneasy
suspicion that the scientists would not approve of

his experiments. But the night was as silent as night on Delta Sextans IV ever was, and after their usual early breakfast the scientific party flapped off on its various occasions.

Grimes went to the spare tent, opened the flap. The stench that gusted out made him retch, although Snuffy did not seem to be worried by it. The native shambled into the open on all fours, and then, rising to an approximately erect posture, went back inside for his previous club. With his free hand he patted Grimes on the arm, grimacing up at him and whining. Grimes led him to where a bucket of water was standing ready, and beside it two candy bars.

The spaceman, fighting down his nausea, cleaned up the interior of the tent. It had been bad enough washing up after the scientists—but this was too much. From now on Snuffy would have to look after himself. He had no occasion to change his mind as the aborigine followed him around while he coped with the camp chores. The humanoid displayed an uncanny genius for getting in the way.

At last, at long last, it was time to get down to the river. Grimes strode along smartly, Snuffy shuffling along beside him, winging his club. Their arrival at the little bay coincided with that of the troop of humanoids. Snuffy did not hang back. He got to the fruit before the others did. The troop leader advanced on him menacingly. For a moment it looked as though Snuffy were going to turn and run—then he stood his ground, seeming suddenly to gain inches in stature as he did so. Clumsily he raised his club, and even more clumsily brought it crashing down. More by luck than otherwise the blow fell on the bully's shoulder. The second blow caught him squarely on the side of the head, felling him. Grimes saw the glisten of yellow blood in the grey, matted fur.

Snuffy screamed—but it was not a scream of fear. Brandishing the club he advanced on those who had been his tormentors. They broke and ran, most of them. The two who did not hastily retreated after each had felt the weight of the primitive weapon.

Grimes laughed shakily. "That's my boy," he murmured. "That's my boy . . ."

Snuffy ignored him. He was too busy stuffing himself with the pick of the ripe fruit.

When you have six people utterly engrossed in their own pursuits and a seventh person left to his own devices, it is easy for that seventh person to keep a secret. Not that Grimes even tried to do so. More than once he tried to tell the scientists about his own experiment in practical ethology, and each time he was brushed aside. Once Maggie Lazenby told him rather tartly, "You're only our bus driver, John. Keep to your astronautics and leave real science to us."

Then—the time of *Pathfinder's* return from Delta Sextans V was fast approaching—Grimes was unable to spend much, if any, time on the river bank. The preliminaries to shutting up shop were well under way with specimens and records and unused stores to be packed, with the propulsion unit of the landing craft to be checked. Nonetheless, Grimes was able to check up now and again on Snuffy's progress, noted with satisfaction that the native was making out quite well.

In all too short a time the cruiser signalled that she was establishing herself in orbit about IV, also that the Captain himself would be coming down in the pinnace to inspect the camp. Grimes worked as he had never worked before. He received little help from the others—and the scientists were such untidy people. There should have been at least six general purpose robots to cope with the mess, but there was only one. Grimes. But he coped.

When the pinnace dropped down through the grey overcast the encampment was as near to being shipshape and Bristol fashion as it ever could be. Grimes barely had time to change into a clean uniform before the boat landed. He was standing to attention and saluting smartly when Captain Tolliver strode down the ramp.

Tolliver, after acknowledging the salute, actually smiled. He said, "You run a taut shore base, Mr. Grimes. I hope that when the time comes you will run a taut ship."

"Thank you, sir."

Grimes accompanied the Captain on his rounds of the encampment, the senior officer grunting his approval of the tidiness, the neatly stacked items all ready to be loaded into the landing craft and the pinnace in the correct order. And the scientists— thank the Odd Gods of the Galaxy!—were no longer their usual slovenly selves. Just as the camp was a credit to Grimes, so were they. Maggie Lazenby winked at him when Captain Tolliver was looking the other way. Grimes smiled back gratefully.

Said Tolliver, "I don't suppose that you've had time for any projects of your own, Mr. Grimes. Rather a pity . . ."

"But he has found time, sir," said the Ethologist.

"Indeed, Dr. Lazenby. What was it?"

"Er . . . We were busy ourselves, sir. But we gained the impression that Mr. Grimes was engaged upon research of some kind."

"Indeed? And what was it, Mr. Grimes?"

Grimes looked at his watch. It was almost time. He said, "I'll show you, sir. If you will come this way. Along the river . . . "

"Lead the way, Mr. Grimes," ordered Tolliver jovially. In his mind's eye Grimes saw the glimmer of that half ring of gold braid that would make him a Lieutenant Commander. Promotions in the Survey Service were the result of Captain's Reports rather than seniority.

Grimes guided Tolliver along the river bank to where the trail opened from the jungle to the little bay. "We wait here, sir," he said. He looked at his watch again. It shouldn't be long. And then, quite suddenly, Snuffy led the way out of the jungle. He was proudly carrying his bone club, holding it like a sceptre. He was flanked by two smaller humanoids, each carrying a crude bone weapon, followed by two more, also armed. He went to the fruit plants, tore at them greedily, wasted more than he ate. The others looked on hungrily. One tried to get past the guards, was clubbed down viciously. Grimes gulped. In a matter of only three days his experiment was getting out of hand.

"I have studied Captain Lovell's films of these beings," said Tolliver in a cold voice. "Are *you* responsible for this?"

"Yes, sir. But . . ."

"You will be wise to apply for a transfer, Mr. Grimes. Should you continue in the Service, which is doubtful, I sincerely hope that you discover the legendary fountain of youth."

"Why, sir?"

"Because it's a bloody pity that otherwise you won't be around to see the end results of what you started," said Tolliver bitterly.

THE SUBTRACTER

The Federation's Survey Service Cruiser *Pathfinder* returned to Lindisfarne Base, and Lieutenant Grimes was one of the officers who was paid off there. He was glad to leave the ship; he had not gotten on at all well with Captain Tolliver. Yet he was far from happy. What was going to happen to him? Tolliver—who, for all his faults, was a just man—had shown Grimes part of the report that he had made on *Pathfinder's* officers, and this part of the report was that referring to Grimes.

"Lieutenant Grimes shows initiative," Tolliver had written, "and has been known to be zealous. Unfortunately his initiative and zeal are invariably misdirected."

Grimes had decided not to make any protest. There had been occasions, he knew very well, when his initiative and zeal had not been misdirected—but never under Tolliver's command. But the Captain, as was his right—his duty—was reporting on Grimes as *he* had found him. His report was only one of many. Nonetheless Grimes was not a little worried, was wondering what his next appointment would be, what his future career in the Survey Service (if any) would be like.

Dr. Margaret Lazenby had also paid off *Pathfinder*, at the same time as Grimes. (Her Service rank was Lieutenant Commander, but she preferred the civilian title.) As old shipmates, with shared experiences, she and Grimes tended to knock about in each other's company whilst they were on Lindisfarne. In any case, the Lieutenant liked the handsome, red-haired ethologist, and was pleased that she liked him. With a little bit of luck the situation would develop favorably, he thought. Meanwhile, she was very good company, even though she would permit nothing more than the briefest goodnight kiss.

One night, after a drink too many in the almost deserted B.O.Q. wardroom, he confided his troubles to her. He said, "I don't like it, Maggie . . . "

"What don't you like, John?"

"All this time here, and no word of an appointment. I told you that I'd seen Tolliver's report on me . . . "

"At least six times. But what of it?"

"It's all right for you, Maggie. For all your two and a half rings you're not a spacewoman. *You* don't have to worry about such sordid details as promotion. I do. I'm just a common working stiff of a spaceman, a trade school boy. Space is all I know."

"And I'm sure you know it well, duckie." She laughed. "But not to worry. Everything will come right in the end. Just take Auntie Maggie's word for it."

"Thank you for trying to cheer me up," he said. "But I can't help worrying. After all, it's *my* career."

She grinned at him, looking very attractive as she did so. "All right. I'll tell you. Your precious Captain Tolliver wasn't the only one to put in a report on your capabilities. Don't forget that the Delta Sextans IV survey was carried out by the Scientific Branch. You, as the spaceman, were officially in command, but actually it was *our* show. Dr. Kortsoff—or Commander Kortsoff if you'd rather call him that—was the real head of our little expedition. *He* reported on you too."

"I can imagine it," said Grimes. "I can just imagine it. This officer, with no scientific training whatsoever, took it upon himself to initiate a private experiment which, inevitably, will disastrously affect the ecology, ethology, zoology and biology of the planet.' Have I missed any 'ologies' out?"

"We all liked you," said the girl. "I still like you, come to that. Just between ourselves, we all had a good laugh over your 'private experiment.' You might have given your friend Snuffy and his people a slight nudge on to the upward path—but no more than a slight nudge. Sooner or later—sooner rather than later, I think—they'd have discovered weapons by themselves. It was bound to happen.

"Do you want to know what Dr. Kortsoff said about you?"

"It can't be worse than what Captain Tolliver said."

" 'This officer,' " quoted Maggie Lazenby, " 'is very definitely command material.' "

"You're not kidding?" demanded Grimes.

"Most certainly not, John."

"Mphm. You've made me feel a little happier."

"I'm glad," she said.

And so Grimes, although he did not get promotion, got command. The Survey Service's Couriers, with their small crews, were invariably captained by two ringers, mere lieutenants. However, as the twentieth century poet Gertrude Stein might have said, "a captain is a captain is a captain . . ." The command course which Grimes went through prior to his appointment made this quiet clear.

There was one fly in the ointment, a big one. His name was Damien, his rank was Commodore, his function was Officer Commanding Couriers. He knew all about Grimes; he made this quite clear at the first interview. Grimes suspected that he knew more about Grimes than he, Grimes, did himself.

He had said, toying with the bulky folder on the desk before him, "There are so many conflicting reports about you, Lieutenant. Some of your commanding officers are of the opinion that you'll finish up as the youngest Admiral ever in the Service, others have said that you aren't fit to be Third Mate in Rim Runners. And then we have the reports from high-ranking specialist officers, most of whom speak well of you. But these gentlemen are not spacemen.

"There's only one thing to do with people like you, Lieutenant. We give you a chance. We give you the command of something small and relatively unimportant—and see what sort of a mess you make of it. I'm letting you have *Adder*. To begin with you'll be just a galactic errand boy, but if you shape well, *if* you shape well, you will be entrusted with more important missions.

"Have I made myself clear?"

"Yes, sir."

"Then try to remember all that we've tried to teach you, and try to keep your nose clean. That's all."

Grimes stiffened to attention, saluted, and left Damien's office.

Grimes had come to love his first command, and

was proud of her, even though she was only a little ship, a Serpent Class Courier, lightly armed and manned by a minimal crew. In addition to Grimes there were two watch-keeping officers, both Ensigns, an engineering officer, another one ringer, and two communications officers, Lieutenants both. One was in charge of the vessel's electronic equipment, but could be be called upon to stand a control room watch if required. The other was the psionic radio officer, a very important crew member, as *Adder* had yet to be fitted with the Carlotti Deep Space Communications and Direction Finding System. In addition to crew accommodation there was more than merely adequate passenger accommodation; one function of the Couriers is to get V.I.P.s from Point A to Point B in a hurry, as and when required.

"You will proceed," said Commodore Damien to Grimes, "from Lindisfarne Base to Doncaster at maximum speed, but considering at all times the safety of your vessel."

"And the comfort of my passenger, sir?" asked Grimes.

"That need not concern you, Lieutenant." Damien grinned, his big teeth yellow in his skull-like face. "Mr. Alberto is . . . tough. Tougher, I would say, than the average spaceman."

Grimes's prominent ears flushed. The Commodore had managed to imply that he, Grimes, was below average. "Very well, sir," he said. "I'll pile on the Gees and the Lumes."

"Just so as you arrive in one piece," growled Damien. "That's all that our masters ask of you. Or, to more exact, just so as Mr. Alberto arrives in one piece, and functioning." He lifted a heavily sealed envelope off his desk, handed it to Grimes.

"Your Orders, to be opened after you're on trajectory. But I've already told you most of it." He grinned again. "On your bicycle, spaceman!"

Grimes got to his feet, put on his cap, came stiffly to attention. He saluted with his free right hand, turned about smartly and marched out of the Commodore's office.

This was his first Sealed Orders assignment.

Clear of the office, Grimes continued his march, striding in time to martial music audible only to himself. Then he paused, looking towards the docking area of the spaceport. There was his ship, already positioned on the pad, dwarfed by a huge *Constellation* Class cruiser to one side of her, a *Planet* Class transport to the other. But she stood there bravely enough on the apron, a metal spire so slender as to appear taller than she actually was, gleaming brightly in the almost level rays of the westering sun. And she was *his*. It did not matter that officers serving in larger vessels referred to the couriers as flying darning needles.

So he strode briskly to the ramp extruded from the after airlock of his flying darning needle, his stocky body erect in his smart—but not too smart—uniform. Ensign Beadle, his First Lieutenant, was there to greet him. The young man threw him a smart salute. Grimes returned it with just the right degree of sloppiness.

"All secure for lift off—Captain!"

"Thank you, Number One. Is the passenger aboard?"

"Yes, sir. And his baggage."

Grimes fought down the temptation to ask what he was like. Only when one is really senior can one unbend with one's juniors. "Very well, Number One." He looked at his watch. "My lift off is scheduled for 1930 hours. It is now 1917. I shall go straight to Control, Mr. Beadle . . . ''

"Mr. von Tannenbaum and Mr. Slovotny are waiting for you there, sir, and Mr. McCloud is standing by in the engine room."

"Good. And Mr. Deane is tucked safely away with his poodle's brain in aspic?"

"He is, sir."

"Good. Then give Mr. Alberto my compliments, and ask him if he would like to join us in Control during lift off."

Grimes negotiated the ladder in the axial shaft rapidly, without losing breath. (The *Serpent* Class couriers were too small to run to an elevator.) He did not make a stop at his own quarters. (A courier captain was supposed to be able to proceed anywhere in the Galaxy, known or unknown, at a second's notice.) In the control room he found Ensign von Tannenbaum ("The blond beast") and Lieutenant Slovotny (just "Sparks") at their stations. He buckled himself into his own chair. He had just finished doing so when the plump, lugubrious Beadle pulled himself up through the hatch. He addressed Grimes. "I asked Mr. Alberto if he'd like to come up to the office, Captain . . . "

"And is he coming up, Number One?" Grimes looked pointedly at the clock on the bulkhead.

"No, Captain. He said . . . "

"Out with it man. It's time we were getting up them stairs."

"He said, 'You people look after your job, and I'll look after mine.' "

Grimes shrugged. As a courier captain he had learned to take V.I.P.s as they came. Some—a very few of them—he would have preferred to have left. He asked, "Are Mr. Alberto and Mr. Deane secured for lift off?"

"Yes, Captain, although Spooky's not happy about the shockproof mount for his amplifier . . ."

"He never is. Clearance, Sparks . . ."

"Clearance, Captain." The wiry little radio officer spoke quietly into his microphone. "Mission 7DKY to Tower. Request clearance."

"Tower to Mission 7DKY. You have clearance. Bon voyage."

"Thank him," said Grimes. He glanced rapidly around the little control room. All officers were strapped in their acceleration chairs. All tell-tale lights were green. "All systems *Go* . . ." he muttered, relishing the archaic expression.

He pushed the right buttons, and *went*.

It was a normal enough courier lift off. The inertial drive developed maximum thrust within microseconds of its being started. Once his radar told him that the ship was the minimum safe altitude above the port, Grimes cut in his auxiliary rockets. The craft was built to take stresses that, in larger vessels, would have been dangerous. Her personnel prided themselves on their toughness. And the one outsider, the passenger. Grimes would have grinned had it not been for the acceleration flattening his features. Commodore Damien had said that Mr. Alberto was tough—so Mr. Alberto would just have to take the Gs and like it.

The ship drove up through the last, high wisps of cirrus, into the darkling, purple sky, towards the sharply bright, unwinking stars. She plunged outward through the last, tenuous shreds of atmosphere, and the needles of instruments flickered briefly as she passed through the van Allens. She was out and clear now, out and clear, and Grimes cut both inertial and reaction drives, used his gyroscopes to swing the sharp prow of the ship on to the target star, the Doncaster sun, brought that far distant speck of luminosity into the exact center of his spiderweb sights. Von Tannenbaum, who was Navigator, gave him the corrections necessitated by Galactia Drift; it was essential to aim the vessel at where the star was *now*, not where it was some seventy-three years ago.

The Inertial Drive was restarted, and the ever-precessing rotors of the Mannschenn Drive were set in motion. There was the usual brief queasiness induced by the temporal precession field, the usual visual shock as colors sagged down the spectrum, as the hard, bright stars outside the viewports became iridescent nebulosities. Grimes remained in his chair a few minutes, satisfying himself that all was as it should be. Slowly and carefully he filled and lit his foul pipe, ignoring a dirty look from Beadle who, in the absence of a Bio-Chemist, was responsible for the ship's air-regeneration system.

Then, speaking through a swirl of acrid smoke, he ordered. ''Set Deep Space watches, Number One. And tell Mr. Deane to report to Lindisfarne Base that we are on trajectory for Doncaster.''

''E.T.A. Doncaster, Captain?'' asked Beadle.

Grimes pulled the sealed envelope from the pouch at the side of his chair, looked at it. He thought, *For Your Eyes Only. Destroy By Fire Before Reading.* He said, ''I'll let you know after I've skimmed through this bumf.'' After all, even in a small ship informality can be allowed to go only so far. He unbuckled himself, got up from his seat, then went down to his quarters to read the Orders.

There was little in them that he had not already been told by Commodore Damien. Insofar as the E.T.A. was concerned, this was left largely to his own discretion, although it was stressed that the courier was to arrive at Doncaster not later than April 23, Local Date. And how did the Doncastrian calendar tally with that used on Lindisfarne? Grimes, knowing that the Blond Beast was now on watch, called Control and threw the question on to von Tannenbaum's plate, knowing that within a very short time he would have an answer accurate to fourteen places of decimals, and that as soon as he, Grimes, made a decision regarding the time of arrival the necessary adjustment of velocity would be put in hand without delay. Von Tannenbaum called back. "April 23 on Doncaster coincides with November 8 on Lindisfarne. I can give you the exact correlation, Captain . . . "

"Don't bother, Pilot. My Orders allow me quite a bit of leeway. Now, suppose we get Mr. Alberto to his destination just three days before the deadline . . . It will give him time to settle in before he commences his duties, whatever they are, in the High Commissioner's office. As far as I can gather, we're supposed to stay on Doncaster until directed elsewhere—so an extra three days in port will do us no harm."

"It's a pleasant planet, I've heard, Captain." There was a pause, and Grimes could imagine the burly, flaxen-headed young man running problems through the control room computer, checking the results with his own slipstick. "This calls for a reduction of speed. Shall I do it by cutting down the temporal precession rate, or by reducing actual acceleration?"

"Two G *is* a little heavy," admitted Grimes.

"Very well, Captain. Reduce to 1.27?"

"That will balance?"

"It will balance."

"Then make it so."

Almost immediately the irregular throbbing of the Inertial Drive slowed. Grimes felt his weight pressing less heavily into the padding of his chair. He did not need to glance at the accelerometer mounted among the other tell-tale instruments on the bulkhead of his cabin. Von Tannenbaum was a good man, a good officer, a good navigator.

There was a sharp rap on his door.

"Come in," called Grimes, swivelling his seat so that he faced the caller. This, he realised, would be his passenger, anticipating the captain's invitation to an introductory drink and talk.

He was not a big man, this Mr. Alberto, and at first he gave an impression of plumpness, of softness. But it was obvious from the way that he moved that his bulk was solid muscle, not fat. He was clad in the dark grey that was almost a Civil Service uniform—and even Grimes, who knew little of the niceties of civilian tailoring, could see that both the material and the cut of Alberto's suit were superb. He had a broad yet very ordinary looking face; his hair was black and glossy, his eyes black and rather dull. His expression was petulant. He demanded rather then asked, "Why have we slowed down?"

Grimes bit back a sharp retort. After all, he was only a junior officer, in spite of his command, and his passenger probably piled on far more Gs than a mere lieutenant. He replied, "I have adjusted to a comfortable actual velocity, Mr. Alberto, so as to arrive three days, local, before the deadline. I trust that this suits your plans."

"Three days . . ." Alberto smiled—and his face was transformed abruptly from that of a sulky baby to that of a contented child. It was, Grimes realised, no more than a deliberate turning of charm—but, he admitted to himself, it was effective. "Three days . . . That will give me ample time to settle down, Captain, before I start work. And I know, as well as you do, that overly heavy acceleration can be tiring."

"Won't you sit down, Mr. Alberto? A drink, perhaps?"

"Thank you, Captain. A dry sherry, if I may . . ."

Grimes grinned apologetically. "I'm afraid that these Couriers haven't much of a cellar. I can offer you gin, scotch, brandy . . ."

"A gin and lime, then."

The Lieutenant busied himself at his little bar, mixed the drinks, gave Alberto his glass, raised his own in salute. "Here's to crime!"

Alberto smiled again. "Why do you say that, Captain?"

"It's just one of those toasts that's going the rounds in the Service. Not so long ago it was, "Down the hatch!' Before that it was, 'Here's mud in yer eye . . ."

"I see." Alberto sipped appreciatively. "Good gin, this."

"Not bad. We get it from Van Diemen's Planet." There was a brief silence. Then, "Will you be long on Doncaster, Mr. Alberto? I rather gained the impression that we're supposed to wait there until you've finished your . . . business."

"It shouldn't take long."

"Diplomatic?"

"You could call it that." Again the smile—but

why should those white teeth look so carnivorous?
Imagination, thought Grimes.

"Another drink?"

"Why, yes. I like to relax when I can."

"Yours is demanding work?"

"And so is yours, Captain."

The brassy music of a bugle drifted into the
cabin through the intercom.

"Mess call," said Grimes.

"You do things in style, Captain."

Grimes shrugged. "We have a tape for all the
calls in general use. As for the tucker . . . " He
shrugged again. "We don't run to a cook in a ship
of this class. Sparks—Mr. Slovotny—prepares
the meals in space. As a chef he's a good radio
officer . . . "

"Do you think he'd mind if I took over?" asked
Alberto. "After all, I'm the only idler aboard this
vessel."

"We'll think about it," said Grimes.

"You know what I think, Captain . . . " said
Beadle.

"I'm not a telepath, Number One," said
Grimes. "Tell me."

The two men were sitting at ease in the Courier's
control room. Each of them was conscious of a
certain tightness in the waistband of his uniform
shorts. Grimes was suppressing a tendency to
burp gently. Alberto, once he had been given a free
hand in the galley, had speedily changed shipboard
eating from a a necessity to a pleasure. (He insisted that somebody else always do the washing
up, but this was a small price to pay.) This evening,
for example, the officers had dined on *saltim-
bocca*, accompanied by a rehydrated rough red

that the amateur chef had contrived, somehow, to make taste like real wine. Nonetheless he had apologised—actually apologised!—for the meal. "I should have used *prosciutto*, not any old ham. And *fresh* sage leaves, not dried sage . . ."

"I think" said Beadle, "that the standard of the High Commissioner's entertaining has been lousy. Alberto must be a *cordon bleu* chef, sent out to Doncaster to play merry hell in the High Commissioner's kitchen."

"Could be," said Grimes. He belched gently. "Could be. But I can't see our lords and masters laying on a ship, even a lowly *Serpent* Class Courier, for a cook, no matter how talented. There must be cooks on Doncaster just as good."

"There's one helluva difference between a chef and a cook."

"All right. There must be chefs on Doncaster."

"But Alberto is *good*. You admit that."

"Of course I admit it. But one can be good in quite a few fields and still retain one's amateur status. As a matter of fact, Alberto told me that he was a mathematician . . ."

"A mathematician?" Beadle was scornfully incredulous. "You know how the Blond Beast loves to show off his toys to anybody who'll evince the slightest interest. Well, Alberto was up in the control room during his watch; you'll recall that he said he'd fix the coffee maker. Our Mr. von Tannenbaum paraded his pets and made them do their tricks. He was in a very disgruntled mood when he handed over to me when I came on. How did he put it? 'I don't expect a very high level of intelligence in planetlubbers, but that Alberto is in a class by himself. I doubt if he could add two and two and get four twice running. . . .'"

"Did he fix the machinetta?"

"As a matter of fact, yes. It makes beautiful coffee now."

"Then what are you complaining about, Number One?"

"I'm not complaining, Captain. I'm just curious."

And so am I, thought Grimes, *so am I*. And as the commanding officer of the ship he was in a position to be able to satisfy his curiosity. After Mr. Beadle had gone about his multifarious duties Grimes called Mr. Deane on the telephone. "Are you busy, Spooky?" he asked.

"I'm always busy, Captain," came the reply. This was true enough. Whether he wanted it or not, a psionic radio officer was on duty all the time, sleeping and waking, his mind open to the transmitted thoughts of other telepaths throughout the Galaxy. Some were powerful transmitters, others were not, some made use, as Deane did, of organic amplifiers, others made do with the un-aided power of their own minds. And there was selection, of course. Just as a wireless operator in the early days of radio on Earth's seas could pick out his own ship's call sign from the babble and Babel of Morse, could focus all his attention on an S.O.S. or T.T.T., so the trained telepath could "listen" selectively. At short ranges he could, too, receive the thoughts of the non-telepaths about him—but, unless the circumstances were exceptional, he was supposed to maintain the utmost secrecy regarding them.

"Can you spare me a few minutes, Spooky? After all, you can maintain your listening watch anywhere in the ship, in my own quarters as well as in yours."

"Oh, all right, Captain. I'll be up. I already know what you're going to ask me."

You would, thought Grimes.

A minute or so later, Mr. Deane drifted into his day cabin. His nickname was an apt one. He was tall, fragile, so albinoid as to appear almost translucent. His white face was a featureless blob.

"Take a pew, Spooky," ordered Grimes. "A drink?"

"Mother's ruin, Captain."

Grimes poured gin for both of them. In his glass there was ice and a generous sprinkling of bitters. Mr. Deane preferred his gin straight, as colorless as he was himself.

The psionic radio officer sipped genteelly. Then: "I'm afraid that I can't oblige you, Captain."

"Why not, Spooky?"

"You know very well that we graduates of the Rhine Institute have to swear to respect privacy."

"There's no privacy aboard a ship, Spooky. There cannot be."

"There can be, Captain. There must be."

"Not when the safety of the ship is involved."

It was a familiar argument—and Grimes knew that after the third gin the telepath would weaken. He always did.

"We got odd passengers aboard this ship, Spooky. Surely you remember that Waldegren diplomat who had the crazy scheme of seizing her and turning her over to his Navy . . ."

"I remember, Captain." Deane extended his glass which, surprisingly, was empty. Grimes wondered, as he always did, if its contents had been teleported directly into the officer's stomach, but he refilled it.

"Mr. Alberto's another odd passenger," he went on.

"But a Federation citizen," Deane told him.

"How do we know? He could be a double agent. Do *you* know?"

"I don't." After only two gins Spooky was ready to spill the beans. This was unusual. "I don't know *anything*."

"What do you mean?"

"Usually, Captain, we have to shut our minds to the trivial, boring thoughts of you psionic morons. No offense intended, but that's the way we think of you. We get sick of visualisations of the girls you met in the last port and the girls you hope to meet in the next port." He screwed his face up in disgust, made it evident that he did, after all, possess features. "Bums, bellies and breasts! The Blond Beast's a tit man, and *you* have a thing about *legs* . . ."

Grimes's prominent ears reddened, but he said nothing.

"And the professional wishful thinking is even more nauseating. *When do I get my half ring? When do I get my brass hat? When shall I make Admiral?*"

"Ambition . . ." said Grimes.

"Ambition, shambition! And of late, of course, *I wonder what Alberto's putting on for breakfast? For lunch? For dinner?*"

"What *is* he putting on for dinner?" asked Grimes. "I've been rather wondering if our tissue culture chook could be used for *Chicken Cacciatore* . . ."

"I don't know."

"No, you're not a chef. As well we know, after

the last time that you volunteered for galley
duties.''

"I mean, I don't know what the menus will be."
It was Deane's turn to blush. "As a matter of fact,
Captain, I *have* been trying to get previews. I have
to watch my diet . . . ''

Grimes tried not to think uncharitable thoughts.
Like many painfully thin people, Deane enjoyed a
voracious appetite.

He said, "You've been *trying* to eavesdrop?"

"Yes. But there are non-telepaths, you know,
and Alberto's one of them. *True* non-telepaths, I
mean. Most people transmit, although they can't
receive. Alberto doesn't transmit.''

"A useful qualification for a diplomat," said
Grimes. "If he is a diplomat. But could he be using
some sort of psionic jammer?"

"No. I'd know if he were."

Grimes couldn't ignore that suggestively held
empty glass any longer. He supposed that Deane
had earned his third gin.

The Courier broke through into normal space/
time north of the plane of Doncaster's ecliptic. In
those days, before the Carlotti Beacons made FTL
position fixing simple, navigation was an art rather
than a science—and von Tannenbaum was an art-
ist. The little ship dropped into a trans-polar orbit
about the planet and then, as soon as permission to
land had been granted by Aerospace Control, descended to Port Duncannon. It was, Grimes told
himself smugly, one of his better landings. And so
it should have been; conditions were little short of
ideal. There was no cloud, no wind, not even any
clear air turbulence at any level. The ship's instru-

ments were working perfectly, and the Inertial Drive was responding to the controls with no time lag whatsoever. It was one of those occasions on which the Captain feels that his ship is no more— and no less—than a beautifully functioning extension of his own body. Finally, it was morning Local Time, with the sun just lifting over the verdant, rolling hills to the eastward, bringing out all the color of the sprawling city a few miles from the spaceport, making it look, from the air, like a huge handful of gems spilled carelessly on a green carpet.

Grimes set the vessel down in the exact center of the triangle marked by the blinkers, so gently that, until he cut the drive, a walnut under the vaned landing gear would not have been crushed. He said quietly, "Finished with engines."

"Receive boarders, Captain?" asked Beadle.

"Yes, Number One." Grimes looked out through the viewport to the ground cars that were making their way from the Administration Block. Port Health, Immigration, Customs . . . The Harbourmaster paying his respects to the Captain of a visiting Federation warship . . . And the third vehicle? He took a pair of binoculars from the rack, focused them on the flag fluttering from the bonnet of the car in the rear. It was dark blue, with a pattern of silver stars, the Federation's colours. So the High Commissioner himself had come out to see the ship berth. He wished that he and his officers had dressed more formally, but it was too late to do anything about it now. He went down to his quarters, was barely able to change the epaulettes of his shirt, with their deliberately tarnished braid, for a pair of shining new ones before the High Commissioner was at his door.

Mr. Beadle ushered in the important official with all the ceremony that he could muster at short notice. "Sir, this is the Captain, Lieutenant Grimes. Captain, may I introduce Sir William Willoughby, Federation High Commissioner on Doncaster?"

Willoughby extended a hand that, like the rest of him was plump. "Welcome aboard, Captain. Ha, ha. I hope you don't mind my borrowing one of the favorite expressions of you spacefaring types!"

"We don't own the copyright, sir."

"Ha, ha. Very good."

"Will you sit down, Sir William?"

"Thank you, Captain, thank you. But only for a couple of minutes. I shall be out of your hair as soon as Mr. Alberto has been cleared by Port Health, Immigration and all the rest of 'em. Then I'll whisk him off to the Residence." He paused, regarding Grimes with eyes that, in the surrounding fat, were sharp and bright. "How did you find him, Captain?"

"Mr. Alberto, sir?" What was the man getting at? "Er . . . He's a very good cook . . ."

"Glad to hear you say it, Captain. That's why I sent for him. I have to do a lot of entertaining, as you realise, and the incompetents I have in my kitchens couldn't boil water without burning it. It just won't do, Captain, it just won't do, not for a man in my position."

"So he *is* a chef, sir."

Again those sharp little eyes bored into Grimes's skull. "Of course. What else? What did you think he was?"

"Well, as a matter of fact we were having a yarn the other night, and he sort of hinted that he was some sort of a mathematician . . ."

"Did he?" Then Willoughby chuckled. "He was having you on. But, of course, a real chef *is* a mathematician. He has to get his equations just right—this quantity, that quantity, this factor, that factor . . ."

"That's one way of looking at it, Sir William."

Beadle was back then, followed by Alberto. "I must be off, now, Captain," said the passenger, shaking hands. "Thank you for a very pleasant voyage."

"Thank *you*," Grimes told him, adding, "We shall miss you."

"But you'll enjoy some more of his cooking," said the High Commissioner genially. "As officers of the only Federation warship on this world you'll have plenty of invitations—to the Residence as well as elsewhere. Too, if Mr. Alberto manages to train my permanent staff in not too long a time you may be taking him back with you."

"We hope so," said Grimes and Beadle simultaneously.

"Good day to you, then. Come on, Mr. Alberto—it's time you started to show my glorified scullions how to boil an egg!"

He was gone, and then the Harbourmaster was at the door. He was invited in, took a seat, accepted coffee. "Your first visit to Doncaster," he announced rather than asked.

"Yes, Captain Tarran. It looks a very pleasant planet."

"Hphm." That could have meant either "yes" or "no."

"Tell me, sir, *is* the cooking in the High Commissioner's Residence as bad as he makes out?"

"I wouldn't know, Captain. I'm just a merchant skipper in a shore job, I don't get asked to all the posh parties, like you people." The sudden white grin in the dark, lean face took the rancor out of the words. "And I thank all the Odd Gods of the Galaxy for that!"

"I concur with your sentiments, Captain Tarran. One never seems to meet any *real* people at the official bunstruggle . . . it's all stiff collars and best behavior and being nice to nongs and drongoes whom normally you'd run a mile to avoid . . ."

"Still," said Mr. Beadle, "the High Commissioner seems to have the common touch . . ."

"How so?" asked Grimes.

"Well, coming out to the spaceport in person to pick up his chef . . ."

"Cupboard love," Grimes told him. "Cupboard love."

There were official parties, and there were unofficial ones. Tarran may not have been a member of the planet's snobocracy, but he knew people in all walks of life, in all trades and professions, and the gatherings to which, through him, Grimes was invited were far more entertaining affairs than the official functions which, now and again, Grimes was obliged to attend. It was at an informal supper given by Professor Tolliver, who held the Chair of Political Science at Duncannon University, that he met Selma Madigan.

With the exception of Tarran and Grimes and his officers all the guests were university people, students as well as instructors. Some were human and some were not. Much to his surprise Grimes found that he was getting along famously with a Shaara Princess, especially since he had cordially detested a Shaara Queen to whom he had been introduced at a reception in the Mayor's Palace. ("And there I was," he had complained afterwards to Beadle, "having to say nice things to a bedraggled old oversized bumblebee loaded down with more precious stones than this ship could lift . . . and with all that tonnage of diamonds and the like she couldn't afford a decent voice box; it sounded like a scratched platter and a worn-out needle on one of those antique record players . . .") This Shreen was—beautiful. It was an inhuman beauty (of course), that of a glittering, intricate mobile. By chance or design—design thought Grimes—her voice box produced a pleasant, almost seductive contralto, with faintly buzzing undertones. She was an arthroped, but there could be no doubt about the fact that she was an attractively female member of her race.

She was saying, "I find you humans so fascinating, Captain. There is so much similarity between yourselves and ourselves, and such great differences. But I have enjoyed my stay on this planet . . ."

"And will you be here much longer, Your Highness?"

"Call me Shreen, Captain," she told him.

"Thank you, Shreen. My name is John. I shall feel honored if you call me that." He laughed. "In any case, my real rank is only Lieutenant."

"Very well, Lieutenant John. But to answer your question. I fear that I shall return to my own world as soon as I have gained my degree in Socio-Economics. Our Queen Mother decided that this will be a useful qualification for a future ruler. The winds of change blow through our hives, and we must trim our wings to them."

And very pretty wings, too, thought Grimes.

But Shreen was impossibly alien, and the girl who approached gracefully over the polished floor was indubtitably human. She was slender, and tall for a woman, and her gleaming auburn hair was piled high in an intricate coronal. Her mouth was too wide for conventional prettiness, the planes of her thin face too well defined. Her eyes were definitely green. Her smile, as she spoke, made her beautiful.

"Another conquest, Shreen?" she asked.

"I wish it were, Selma," replied the Princess. "I wish that Lieutenant John were an arthroped like myself."

"In that case," grinned Grimes, "I'd be a drone."

"From what I can gather," retorted the human girl, "that's all that spaceship captains are anyhow."

"Have you met Selma?" asked Shreen. Then she performed the introductions.

"And are you enjoying the party, Mr. Grimes?" inquired Selma Madigan.

"Yes, Miss Madigan. It's a very pleasant change from the usual official function—but don't tell anybody that I said so."

"I'm glad you like us. We try to get away from that ghastly Outposts of Empire atmosphere. Quite a number of our students are like Shreen here, quote aliens unquote . . ."

"On *my* world *you* would be the aliens."

"I know, my dear, and I'm sure that Mr. Grimes does too. But all intelligent beings can make valuable contributions to each other's cultures. No one race has a sacred mission to civilise the Galaxy . . ."

"I wish you wouldn't *preach*, Selma." It was

amazing how much expression the Princess could get out of her mechanical voice box. "But if you must, perhaps you can make a convert out of Lieutenant John." She waved a thin, gracefully articulated fore limb and was away, gliding off to join a group composed of two human men, a young Hallichek and a gaudy pseudo-saurian from Dekkovar.

Selma Madigan looked directly at Grimes. "And what do you think of our policy of integration?" she asked.

"It has to come, I suppose."

"It has to come," she mimicked. "You brassbound types are all the same. You get along famously with somebody like Shreen, because she's a real, live Princess. But the Shaara royalty isn't royalty as we understand it. The Queens are females who've reached the egg-laying stage, the Princesses are females who are not yet sexually developed. Still—Shreen's a Princess. You have far less in common with her, biologically speaking, than you have with Oona—but you gave Oona the brush-off and fawned all over Shreen."

Grimes flushed. "Oona's a rather smelly and scruffy little thing like a Terran chimpanzee. Shreen's—beautiful."

"Oona has a brilliant mind. Her one weakness is that she thinks that Terrans in pretty, gold-braided uniforms are wonderful. You snubbed her. Shreen noticed. I noticed."

"As far as I'm concerned," said Grimes, "Oona can be Her Imperial Highness on whatever world she comes from, but I don't *have* to like her."

Professor Tolliver, casually clad in a rather grubby toga, smoking a pipe even fouler than

Grimes's, joined the discussion. He remarked, "Young Grimes has a point . . ."

"Too right I have," agreed Grimes. "As far as I'm concerned, people are people—it doesn't matter a damn if they're humanoid, arachnoid, saurian or purple octopi from the next galaxy but three. If they're our sort of people, I like 'em. If they ain't—I don't."

"Oona's our sort of people," insisted Selma.

"She doesn't smell like it."

The girl laughed. "And how do you think *she* enjoys the stink of your pipe—and, come to that, Peter's pipe?"

"Perhaps she does enjoy it," suggested Grimes.

"As a matter of fact she does," said Professor Tolliver.

"*Men* . . ." muttered Selma Madigan disgustedly.

Tolliver drifted off then, and Grimes walked with the girl to the table on which stood a huge punchbowl. He ladled out drinks for each of them. He raised his own glass in a toast. "Here's to integration!"

"I wish that you really meant that."

"Perhaps I do . . ." murmured Grimes, a little doubtfully. "Perhaps I do. After all, we've only one Universe, and we all have to live in it. It's not so long that blacks and whites and yellows were at each other's throats on the Home Planet—to say nothing of the various subdivisions within each color groups. Von Tannenbaum—that's him over there, the Blond Beast we call him. He's an excellent officer, a first class shipmate, and a very good friend. But *his* ancestors were very unkind to mine, on my mother's side. And mine had quite a long record of being unkind to other people. I could be wrong—but I think that much of Earth's bloody history was no more—and no less—than xenophobia carried to extremes . . . ''

"Quite a speech, John." She sipped at her drink. "It's a pity that the regulations of your Service forbid you to play any active part in politics."

"Why?"

"You'd make a very good recruit for the new Party we're starting. LL . . . ''

"LL . . . ?"

"The obvious abbreviation. The League of Life. You were talking just now of Terran history. Even when Earth's nations were at war there were organisations—religions, political parties, even fraternal orders—with pan-national and pan-racial memberships. The aim of the League of Life is to build up a membership of all intelligent species."

"Quite an undertaking."

"But a necessary one. Doncaster could be said to be either unfortunately situated, or otherwise, according to the viewpoint. Here we are, one Man-colonised planet on the borders of no less than two . . . yes, I'll use that word, much as I dislike it . . . no less than two alien empires. The Hallichek Hegemony, the Shaara Super-Hive. We know that Imperial Earth is already thinking of establishing Fortress Doncaster, converting this world into the equivalent of a colossal, impregnably armored and fantastically armed dreadnought with its guns trained upon both avian and arthroped, holding the balance of power, playing one side off against the other and all the rest of it. But there are those of us who would sooner live in peace and friendship with our neighbours. That's why Duncannon University has always tried to attract non-Terran students—and that's why the League of Life was brought into being." She smiled. "You could, I suppose call it enlightened self-interest."

"Enlightened," agreed Grimes.

He liked this girl. She was one of those women whose physical charm is vastly enhanced by enthusiasm. She did far more to him, for him, than the sort of female equally pretty or prettier, whom he usually met.

She said, "I've some literature at home, if you'd like to read it."

"I should—Selma."

She took the use of her given name for granted. Was that a good sign, or not?

"That's splendid—John. We could pick it up now. The party can get along without us."

"Don't you . . . er . . . live on the premises?"

"No. But it's only a short walk from here. I have an apartment in Heathcliff Street."

When Grimes had collected his boat cloak and cap from the cloakroom she was waiting for him. She had wrapped herself in a green academic gown that went well with her hair, matched her eyes. Together they walked out into the misty night. There was just enough chill in the air to make them glad of their outer garments, to make them walk closer together than they would, otherwise— perhaps—have done. As they strode over the damp-gleaming cobblestones Grimes was conscious of the movements of her body against his. *Political literature*, he thought with an attempt at cynicism. *It makes a change from etchings*. But he could not remain cynical for long. He had already recognised in her qualities of leadership, had no doubt in his mind that she would achieve high political rank on the world of her birth. Nonetheless, this night things could happen between them, probably would happen between them, and he, most certainly, would not attempt to stem the course of Nature. Neither of them would be the poorer; both of them, in fact, would be the richer. Meanwhile, it was good to walk with her through the soft darkness, to let one's mind dwell pleasurably on what lay ahead at the end of the walk.

"Here we are John," she said suddenly.

The door of the apartment house was a hazy, golden-glowing rectangle in the dimness. There was nobody in the hallway—not that it mattered. There was an elevator that bore them swiftly upwards, its door finally opening on a richly carpeted corridor. There was another door—one that, Grimes noted, was opened with an old-fashioned metal key. He remembered, then, that voice-actuated locks were not very common on Doncaster.

The furnishing of her living room was austere but comfortable. Grimes, at her invitation, removed his cloak and cap, gave them to her to hang up somewhere with her own gown, sat down on a well-sprung divan. He watched her walk to the window that ran all along one wall, press the switch that drew the heavy drapes aside, press another switch that caused the wide panes to sink into their housing.

She said, "The view of the city is good from here—especially on a misty night. And I like it when you can smell the clean tang of fog in the air . . ."

"You're lucky to get a clean fog," said Grimes, Earth-born and Earth-raised.

He got up and went to stand with her. His arm

went about her waist. She made no attempt to disengage it. Nonetheless, he could still appreciate the view. It was superb; it was like looking down at a star cluster enmeshed in a gaseous nebula . . .

"Smell the mist . . . " whispered Selma.

Dutifully, Grimes inhaled. *Where did that taint of garlic come from?* It was the first time that he had smelled it since Alberto ceased to officiate in the ship's galley. *It must come from a source in the room with them . . .*

Grimes could act fast when he had to. He sensed rather than saw that somebody was rushing at him and the girl from behind. He let go of her, pushed her violently to one side. Instinctively he fell into a crouch, felt a heavy body thud painfully into his back. He dropped still lower, his arms and the upper part of his torso hanging down over the windowsill. What followed was the result of luck rather than of any skill on the spaceman's part— good luck for Grimes, the worst of bad luck for his assailant. The assassin slithered over Grimes's back, head down, in an ungraceful dive. The heel of a shoe almost took one of the Lieutenant's prominent ears with it. And then he was staring down, watching the dark figure that fell into the luminous mist with agonising slowness, twisting and turning as it plunged, screaming. The scream was cut short by a horridly fluid *thud*.

Frantically, Selma pulled Grimes back to safety.

He stood there, trembling uncontrollably. The reek of garlic was still strong in the air. He broke away from her, went back to the window and was violently sick.

"There are lessons," said Commodore Damien drily, "that a junior officer must learn if he wishes to rise in the Service. One of them is that it is unwise to throw a monkey wrench into the machinations of our masters."

"How was I to know, sir?" complained Grimes. He flushed. "In any case, I'd do it again!"

"I'm sure that you would, Mr. Grimes. No man in his right senses submits willingly to defenstration—and no gentleman stands by and does nothing while his companion of the evening is subjected to the same fate. Even so . . . " He drummed on his desk top with his skeletal fingers. "Even so, I propose to put you in the picture, albeit somewhat belatedly.

"To begin with, the late Mr. Alberto was criminally careless. Rather a neat play on words, don't you think? Apparently he officiated as usual in the High Commissioner's kitchen on the night in question, and Sir William had, earlier in the day, expressed a wish for *pasta* with one of the more redolent sauces. As a good chef should, Alberto tasted, and tasted, and tasted. As a member of his *real* profession he should have deodorised his breath before proceeding to Miss Madigan's apartment—where, I understand, he concealed himself in the bathroom, waiting until she returned to go through her evening ritual of opening the window of her living room. He was not, I think, expecting her to have company—not that it would have worried him if he had . . . "

"What happened served the bastard right," muttered Grimes.

"I'm inclined to agree with you, Lieutenant. But we are all of us no more than pawns insofar as Federation policy is concerned. Or, perhaps, Alberto was a knight—in the chess sense of the word, although the German name for that piece, *springer,* would suit him better.

"Alberto was employed by the Department of Socio-Economic Science, and directly responsible only to its head, Dr. Barratin. Dr. Barratin is something of a mathematical genius, and uses a building full of computers to extrapolate from the current trends on all the worlds in which the Federation is interested. Doncaster, I need hardly tell you, is such a world, and the League of Life is a current trend. According to the learned Doctor's calculations, this same League of Life will almost certainly gain considerable influence, even power, in that sector of the Galaxy, under the leadership of your Miss Madigan . . . "

"She's not *my* Miss Madigan, sir. Unfortunately."

"My heart fair bleeds for you. But, to continue. To Dr. Barratin the foreign and colonial policies of the Federation can all be worked out in advance like a series of equations. As you will know, however, equations are apt, at times, to hold undesirable factors. Alberto was employed to remove such factors, ensuring thereby that the good Doctor's sums came out. He was known to his employers as the Subtracter . . . "

"Very funny," said Grimes. "Very funny. Sir."

"Isn't it?" Damien was laughing unashamedly. "But when things went so very badly wrong on Doncaster, Barratin couldn't see the joke, even after I explained it to him. You see, Grimes, that *you* were a factor that wasn't allowed for in the equation. Alberto travelled to Doncaster in *your* ship, a Serpent Class Courier. *You* were with Miss Madigan when Alberto tried to . . . subtract her.

"And you were captain of the *Adder!*"

"I'm afraid, Lieutenant," said Commodore Damien, "that your passenger, this trip, won't be able to help out in the galley."

"As long as he's not another assassin, he'll do me," said Grimes. "But I've found, sir, that anybody who likes to eat also likes now, and again, to prepare his own favorite dishes . . ."

"This one does. All the time."

Grimes looked at his superior dubiously. He suspected the Commodore's sense of humor. The older man's skull-like face was stiffly immobile, but there was a sardonic glint in the pale grey eyes.

"If he wants galley privileges, sir, it's only fair that he shares, now and again, what he hashes up for himself."

Damien sighed. "I've never known officers so concerned about their bellies as you people in the *Adder*. All you think about is adding to your weight . . ." Grimes winced—as much because of the unfairness of the imputation as in reaction to the pun. The Couriers—little, very fast ships—did not carry cooks, so their officers, obliged to cook for themselves, were more than usually food-conscious. *Adder's* crew was no exception to this rule. Damien went on, "I've no doubt that Mr. Adam would be willing to share his . . . er . . . nutriment with you, but I don't think that any of you, catholic as your tastes may be, would find it palatable. Or, come to that, nourishing. But who started this particularly futile discussion?"

"You did, sir," said Grimes.

"You'll never make a diplomat, Lieutenant. It is doubtful that you'll ever reach flag rank in this Service, rough and tough spacemen though we be, blunt and outspoken to a fault, the glint of honest iron showing through the work-worn fabric of our velvet gloves . . . H'm. Yes. Where was I?"

"Talking about iron fists in velvet gloves, sir."

"Before you side-tracked me, I mean. Yes, your passenger. He is to be transported from Lindisfarne Base to Delacron. You just dump him there, then return to Base forthwith." The Commodore's bony hand picked up the heavily sealed envelope from his desk, extended it. "Your Orders."

"Thank you, sir. Will that be all, sir?"

"Yes. Scramble!"

Grimes didn't exactly scramble; nonetheless he walked briskly enough to where his ship, the Serpent Class Courier *Adder*, was berthed. Dwarfed as she was by the bigger vessels about her she still stood there, tall, proud and gleaming. Grimes knew that she and her kind were referred to, disparagingly, as "flying darning needles," but he loved the slenderness of her lines, would not have swapped her for a hulking dreadnought. (In a dreadnought, of course, he would have been no more than one of many junior officers.) She was *his*.

Ensign Beadle, his First Lieutenant, met him at the airlock ramp, saluted. He reported mournfully (nobody had ever heard Beadle laugh, and he smiled but rarely), "All secure for lift off, Captain."

"Thank you, Number One."

"The . . . The passenger's aboard . . . "

"Good. I suppose we'd better extend the usual courtesy. Ask him if he'd like the spare seat in Control when we shake the dust of Base off our tail vanes."

"I've already done so, Captain. It says that it'll be pleased to accept the invitation."

"*It*, Number One. *It*? Adam is a good Terran name."

Beadle actually smiled. "Technically speaking, Captain, one could not say that Mr. Adam is of Terran birth. But he is of Terran manufacture."

"And what does he eat?" asked Grimes, remembering the Commodore's veiled references to the passenger's diet. "A.C. or D.C.? Washed down with a noggin of light lubricating oil?"

"How did you guess, Captain?"

"The Old Man told me, in a roundabout sort of way. But . . . A passenger, not cargo . . . There must be some mistake."

"There's not, Captain. It's intelligent, all right, and it has a personality. I've checked its papers, and officially it's a citizen of the Interstellar Federation, with all rights, privileges and obligations."

"I suppose that our masters know best," said Grimes resignedly.

It was intelligent, and it had a personality, and Grimes found it quite impossible to think of Mr. Adam as "it." This robot was representative of a type of which Grimes had heard rumors, but it was the first one that he had ever seen. There were only a very few of them in all the worlds of the Federation—and most of that few were of Earth itself. To begin with, they were fantastically expensive. Secondly, their creators were scared of them, were plagued by nightmares in which they saw themselves as latter day Frankensteins. Intelligent robots were not a rarity—but intelligent robots with imagination, intuition, and initiative were. They had been developed mainly for research and exploration, and could survive in environments that would be almost immediately lethal to even the most heavily and elaborately armored man.

Mr. Adam sat in the spare chair in the control room. There was no need for him to sit, but he did so, in an astonishingly human posture. Perhaps, thought Grimes, he could sense that his hosts would feel more comfortable if something that looked like an attenuated knight in armor were not looming tall behind them, peering over their shoulders. His face was expressionless—it was a dull-gleaming ovid with no features to be expressive with—but it seemed to Grimes that there was the faintest flicker of luminosity behind the eye lenses that could betoken interest. His voice, when he spoke, came from a diaphragm set in his throat.

He was speaking now. "This has been very interesting, Captain. And now, I take it, we are on trajectory for Delacron." His voice was a pleasant enough baritone, not quite mechanical.

"Yes, Mr. Adam. That is the Delacron sun there, at three o'clock from the center of the cartwheel sight."

"And that odd distortion, of course, is the resultant of the temporal precession field of your Drive . . . " He hummed quietly to himself for a few seconds. "Interesting."

"You must have seen the same sort of thing on your way out to Lindisfarne from Earth."

"No, Captain. I was not a guest, ever, in the

control room of the cruiser in which I was transported." The shrug of his gleaming, metal shoulders was almost human. "I . . . I don't think that Captain Grisby trusted me."

That, thought Grimes, was rather an odd way of putting it. But he knew Grisby, had served under him. Grisby, as a naval officer of an earlier age, on Earth's seas, would have pined for the good old days of sail, of wooden ships and iron men—and by "iron men" he would not have meant anything like this Mr. Adam . . .

"Yes," the robot went on musingly, "I find this not only interesting, but amazing . . . "

"How so?" asked Grimes.

"It could all be done—the lift off, the setting of trajectory, the delicate balance between acceleration and temporal precession—so much . . . faster by one like myself . . . "

You mean "better" rather than faster, thought Grimes, *but you're too courteous to say it.*

"And yet . . . and yet . . . You're flesh and blood creatures, Captain, evolved to suit the conditions of just one world out of all the billions of planets. Space is not your natural environment."

"We carry our environment around with us, Mr. Adam." Grimes noticed that the other officers in Control—Ensign von Tannenbaum, the Navigator, Ensign Beadle, the First Lieutenant, and Lieutenant Slovotny, the radio officer—were following the conversation closely and expectantly. He would have to be careful. Nonetheless, he had to keep his end up. He grinned. "And don't forget," he said, "that Man, himself, is a quite rugged, self-maintaining, self-reproducing, all-purpose robot."

"There are more ways than one of reproducing," said Mr. Adam quietly.

"I'll settle for the old-fashioned way!" broke in von Tannenbaum.

Grimes glared at the burly, flaxen-headed young man—but too late to stop Slovotny's laughter. Even Beadle smiled.

John Grimes allowed himself a severely rationed chuckle. Then: "The show's on the road, gentlemen. I'll leave her in your capable hands. Number One. Set Deep Space watches. Mr. Adam, it is usual at this juncture for me to invite any guests to my quarters for a drink and a yarn . . ."

Mr. Adam laughed. "Like yourself, Captain, I feel the occasional need for a lubricant. But I do not make a ritual of its application. I shall, however, be very pleased to talk with you while you drink."

"I'll lead the way," said Grimes resignedly.

In a small ship passengers can make their contribution to the quiet pleasures of the voyage, or they can be a pain in the neck. Mr. Adam, at first, seemed pathetically eager to prove that he could be a good shipmate. He could talk—and he did talk, on anything and everything. Mr. Beadle remarked about him that he must have swallowed an encyclopedia. Mr. McCloud, the Engineering Officer, corrected this statement, saying that he must have been built around one. And Mr. Adam could listen. That was worse than his talking—one always had the impression of invisible wheels whirring inside that featureless head, of information either being discarded as valueless or added to the robot's data bank. He could play chess (of course)—and on the rare occasions that he lost a game it was strongly suspected that he had done so out of politeness. It was the same with any card game.

Grimes sent for Spooky Deane, the psionic communications officer. He had the bottle and the glasses ready when the tall, fragile young man seeped in through the doorway of his day cabin, looking like a wisp of ectoplasm decked out in Survey Service uniform. He sat down when invited, accepted the tumbler of neat gin that his captain poured for him.

"Here's looking up your kilt," toasted Grimes coarsely.

"A *physical* violation of privacy, Captain," murmured Deane. "I see nothing objectionable in that."

"And just what are you hinting at, Mr. Deane?"

"I know, Captain, that you are about to ask me to break the Rhine Institute's Privacy Oath. And this knowledge has nothing to do with my being a telepath. Every time that we carry passengers it's the same. You always want me to pry into their minds to see what makes them tick."

"Only when I feel that the safety of the ship might be at stake." Grimes refilled Deane's glass, the contents of which had somehow vanished.

"You are . . . frightened of our passenger?"

Grimes frowned. "Frightened" was a strong word. And yet mankind has always feared the robot, the automaton, the artificial man. A premonitory dread? Or was the robot only a symbol of the machines—the *mindless* machines—that with every passing year were becoming more and more dominant in human affairs?

Deane said quietly, "Mr. Adam is not a mind-less machine."

Grimes glared at him. He almost snarled, "How the hell do you know what I'm thinking?"—then thought better of it. Not that it made any difference.

The telepath went on, "Mr. Adam has a mind, as well as a brain."

"That's what I was wondering."

"Yes. He broadcasts, Captain, as all of you do. The trouble is that I haven't quite got his . . . frequency."

"Any . . . hostility towards us? Towards humans?"

Deane extended his empty glass. Grimes refilled it. The telepath sipped daintily, then said, "I . . . I don't think so, but, as I've already told you, his mind is not human. Is it contempt he feels? No . . . Not quite. Pity? Yes, it could be. A sort of amused affection? Yes . . . "

"The sort of feelings that we'd have towards— say—a dog capable of coherent speech?"

"Yes."

"Anything else?"

"I could be wrong, Captain. I most probably am. This is the first time that I've eavesdropped on a non-organic mind. There seems to be a strong sense of . . . mission . . . "

"*Mission?*"

"Yes. It reminds me of that priest we carried a few trips back—the one who was going out to convert the heathen Tarvarkens . . . "

"A dirty business," commented Grimes. "Wean the natives away from their own, quite satisfactory local gods so that they stop lobbing missiles at the trading post, which was established without their consent anyhow . . . ''

''Father Cleary didn't look at it that way.''

''Good for him. I wonder what happened to the poor bastard?''

''Should you be talking like this, Captain?''

''I shouldn't. But with you it doesn't matter. You know what I'm thinking, anyhow. But this Mr. Adam, Spooky. A missionary? It doesn't make sense.''

''That's just the *feeling* I get.''

Grimes ignored this. ''Or, perhaps, it does make sense. The robots of Mr. Adam's class are designed to be able to go where Man himself cannot go. In our own planetary system, for example, they've carried out explorations on Mercury, Jupiter, and Saturn. A robot missionary on Tarvark would have made sense, being impervious to poisoned arrows, spears, and the like. But on Delacron, an Earth colony? No.''

''But I still get that *feeling*,'' insisted Deane.

''There are feelings *and* feelings,'' Grimes told him. ''Don't forget that this is non-organic mind that you're prying into. Perhaps you don't know the code, the language . . . ''

''Codes and languages don't matter to a telepath.'' Deane contrived to make his empty glass obvious. Grimes refilled it. ''Don't forget, Captain, that there are machines on Delacron, *intelligent* machines. Not a very high order of intelligence, I admit, but . . . And you must have heard of the squabble between Delacron and its nearest neighbour, Muldoon . . . ''

Grimes had heard of it. Roughly midway between the two planetary systems was a sun with only one world in close orbit about it—and that solitary planet was a fantastic treasure house of radio-active ores. Both Delacron and Muldoon had laid claim to it. Delacron wanted the rare metals for its own industries, the less highly industrialized Muldoon wanted them for export to other worlds of the Federation.

And Mr. Adam? Where did he come into it? Officially, according to his papers, he was a programmer, on loan from the Federation's Grand Council to the Government of Delacron. A programmer . . . A teacher of machines . . . An intelligent machine to teach other intelligent machines . . . To teach other intelligent machines *what*?

And who had programmed *him*—or had he just, as it were, happened?

A familiar pattern—vague, indistinct, but nonetheless there—was beginning to emerge. It had all been done before, this shipping of revolutionaries into the places in which they could do the most harm by governments absolutely unsympathetic towards their aspirations. . . .

"Even if Mr. Adam had a beard," said Deane, "he wouldn't *look* much like Lenin . . . "

And Grimes wondered if the driver who brought that train into the Finland Station knew what he was doing.

Grimes was just the engine driver, and Mr. Adams was the passenger, and Grimes was tied down as much by the Regulations of his Service as was that long ago railwayman by the tracks upon which his locomotive ran. Grimes was blessed—or cursed—with both imagination and a conscience, and a conscience is too expensive a luxury for a junior officer. Those who can afford such a luxury all too often decide that they can do quite nicely without it.

Grimes actually wished that in some way Mr. Adam was endangering the ship. Then he, Grimes, could take action, drastic action if necessary. But the robot was less trouble than the average human passenger. There were no complaints about monotonous food, stale air and all the rest of it. About the only thing that could be said against him was that he was far too good a chess player, but just about the time that Grimes was trying to find excuses for not playing with him he made what appeared to be a genuine friendship, and preferred the company of Mr. McCloud to that of any the other officers.

"Of course, Captain," said Beadle, "they belong to the same clan."

"What the hell do you mean, Number One?"

Deadpan, Beadle replied, "The Clan MacHinery."

Grimes groaned, then, with reluctance, laughed. He said, "It makes sense. A machine will have more in common with our Engineering Officer than the rest of us. Their shop talk must be fascinating." He tried to initiate McCloud's accent. "An' tell me, Mr. Adam, whit sorrt o' lubricant d'ye use on yon ankle joint?"

Beadle, having made his own joke, was not visibly amused. "Something suitable for heavy duty I should imagine, Captain."

"Mphm. Well, if Mac keeps him happy, he's out of our hair for the rest of the trip."

"He'll keep Mac happy, too, Captain. He's always moaning that he should have an assistant."

"Set a thief to catch a thief," cracked Grimes. "Set a machine to . . . to . . . "

"Work a machine?" suggested Beadle.

Those words would do, thought Grimes, but after the First Lieutenant had left him he began to consider the implications of what had been discussed. McCloud was a good engineer—but the better the engineer, the worse the psychological shortcomings. The Machine had been developed to be Man's slave—but ever since the twentieth century a peculiar breed of Man had proliferated that was all too ready and willing to become the Machine's servants, far too prone to sacrifice human values on the altar of Efficiency. Instead of machines being modified to suit their operators, men were being modified to suit the machines. And McCloud? He would have been happier in industry than in the Survey Service, with its emphasis on officer-like qualities and all the rest of it. As it was, he was far too prone to regard the ship merely as the platform that carried his precious engines.

Grimes sighed. He didn't like what he was going to do. It was all very well to snoop on passengers, on outsiders—but to pry into the minds of his own people was not gentlemanly.

He got out the gin bottle and called for Mr. Deane.

"Yes, Captain?" asked the telepath.

"You know what I want you for, Spooky."

"Of course. But I don't like it."

"Neither do I." Grimes poured the drinks, handed the larger one to Deane. The psionic communications officer sipped in an absurdly genteel manner, the little finger of his right hand extended. The level of the transparent fluid in his glass sank rapidly.

Deane said, his speech ever so slightly slurred,

"And you think that the safety of the ship is jeopardised?"

"I do." Grimes poured more gin—but not for himself.

"If I have your assurance, Captain, that such is the case . . ."

"You have."

Deanne was silent for a few seconds, looking through rather than at Grimes, staring at something . . . elsewhere. Then: "They're in the computer room. Mr. Adam and the Chief. I can't pick up Adam's thoughts—but I feel a sense of . . . rightness? But I can get into Mac's mind . . ." On his almost featureless visage the grimace of extreme distaste was startling. "I . . . I don't understand . . ."

"You don't understand what, Spooky?"

"How a man, a human being, can regard a hunk of animated ironmongery with such reverence . . ."

"You're not a very good psychologist, Spooky, but go on."

"I . . . I'm looking at Adam through Mac's eyes. He's bigger, somehow, and he seems to be self-luminous, and there's a sort of circle of golden light around his head . . ."

"That's the way that Mac sees him?"

"Yes. And his voice. Adam's voice. It's not the way that *we* hear it. It's more like the beat of some great engine . . . And he's saying, 'You believe, and you will serve.' And Mac has just answered, 'Yes, Master. I believe, and I will serve.' "

"What are they *doing*?" demanded Grimes urgently.

"Mac's opening up the computer. The memory bank, I think it is. He's turned to look at Adam again, and a panel over Adam's chest is sliding away and down, and there's some sort of storage bin in there, with rows and rows of pigeonholes. Adam has taken something out of one of them . . . A ball of greyish metal or plastic, with connections all over its surface. He's telling Mac where to put it in the memory bank, and how to hook it up . . . ''

Grimes, his glass clattering unheeded to the deck, was out of his chair, pausing briefly at his desk to fling open a drawer and to take from it his .50 automatic. He snapped at Deane, ''Get on the intercom. Tell every officer off duty to come to the computer room, armed if possible.'' He ran through the door out into the alleyway, then fell rather than clambered down the ladder to the next deck, and to the next one, and the next. At some stage of his descent he twisted his ankle, painfully, but kept on going.

The door to the computer room was locked, from the inside—but Grimes, as Captain, carried always on his person the ship's master key. With his left hand—the pistol was in his right—he inserted the convoluted sliver of metal into the slot, twisted it. The panel slid open.

McCloud and Adam stared at him, at the weapon in his hand. He stared back. He allowed his gaze to wander, but briefly. The cover plate had been replaced over the memory bank—but surely that heavily insulted cable leading to and through it was something that had been added, was an additional supply of power, too much power, to the ship's electronic bookkeeper.

McCloud smiled—a vague sort of smile, yet somehow exalted, that looked odd on his rough-hewn features. He said, ''You and your kind are finished, Captain. You'd better tell the dinosaurs, Neanderthal Man, the dodo, the great auk, and all the others to move over to make room for you.''

"Mr. McCloud," ordered Grimes, his voice (not without effort on his part) steady, "switch off the computer, then undo whatever it is that you have done."

It was Adam who replied. "I am sorry, genuinely sorry, Mr. Grimes, but it is too late. As Mr. McCloud implied, you are on the point of becoming extinct."

Grimes was conscious of the others behind him in the alleyway. "Mr. Beadle?"

"Yes, Captain?"

"Take Mr. Slovetny with you down to the engine room. Cut off all power to this section of the ship."

"You can try," said Mr. Adam. "But you will not be allowed. I give notice now; I am the Master."

"You are the Master," echoed McCloud.

"Mutiny," stated Grimes.

"Mutiny?" repeated Adam, iron and irony in his voice. He stepped towards the Captain, one long, metallic arm upraised.

Grimes fired. He might as well have been using a pea-shooter. He fired again, and again. The bullets splashed like pellets of wet clay on the robot's armor. He realised that it was too late for him to turn and run; he awaited the crushing impact of the steel fist that would end everything.

There was a voice saying, "No . . . *No* . . ."

Was it his own? Dimly, he realised that it was not.

There was the voice saying, "*No!*"

Surprisingly Adam hesitated—but only for a second. Again he advanced—and then, seemingly from the computer itself, arced a crackling discharge, a dreadful, blinding lightning. Grimes, in the fleeting instant before his eyelids snapped shut, saw the automaton standing there, arms outstretched rigidly from his sides, black amid the electric fire that played about his body. Then, as he toppled to the deck, there was a metallic crash.

When, at long last, Grimes regained his eyesight he looked around the computer room. McCloud was unharmed—physically. The engineer was huddled in a corner, his arms over his head, in a foetal position. The computer, to judge from the wisps of smoke still trickling from cracks in its panels, was a total write-off. And Adam, literally welded to the deck, still in that attitude of crucifixion, was dead.

Dead . . . thought Grimes numbly. *Dead* . . . Had he ever been alive, in the real sense of the word?

But the ship, he knew, had been briefly alive, had been aware, conscious, after that machine which would be God had kindled the spark of life in her electronic brain. And a ship, unlike other machines, always has personality, a pseudo-life derived from her crew, from the men who live and work, hope and dream within her metal body.

This vessel had known her brief minutes of full awareness, but her old virtues had persisted, among them loyalty to her rightful captain.

Grimes wondered if he would dare to put all this in the report that he would have to make. It would be a pity not to give credit where credit was due.

THE SLEEPING BEAUTY

Commodore Damien, Officer Commanding Couriers, was not in a very good mood. This was not unusual—especially on the occasions when Lieutenant Grimes, captain of the Serpent Class Courier *Adder*, happened to be on the carpet.

"Mr. Grimes . . . " said the Commodore in a tired voice.

"Sir!" responded Grimes smartly.

"Mr. Grimes, you've been and gone and done it *again*."

The Lieutenant's prominent ears reddened. "I did what I could to save my ship and my people, sir."

"You destroyed a *very* expensive piece of equipment, as well as playing merry hell with the Federation's colonial policy. My masters—who, incidentally, are also *your* masters—are not, repeat not, amused."

"I saved my ship," repeated Grimes stubbornly.

The Commodore looked down at the report on his desk. A grim smile did little, if anything, to soften the harsh planes of his bony face. "It says here that your ship saved you."

"She did," admitted Grimes. "It was sort of mutual . . . "

"And it was your ship that killed—I suppose that 'kill' is the right word to use regarding a highly intelligent robot—Mr. Adam . . . H'm. A *slightly* extenuating circumstance. Nonetheless, Grimes,

were it not for the fact that you're a better than
average spaceman you'd be O-U-bloody-T, trying
to get a job as Third Mate in Rim Runners or some
such outfit." He made a steeple of his skeletal
fingers, glared at the Lieutenant coldly over the
bony erection. "So, in the interests of all concerned, I've decided that your *Adder* will not be
carrying any more passengers for a while—at
least, not with you in command of her. Even so,
I'm afraid that you'll not have much time to enjoy
the social life—such as it is—of Base . . . "

Grimes sighed audibly. Although a certain Dr.
Margaret Lazenby was his senior in rank he was
beginning to get on well with her.

"As soon as repairs and routine maintenance
are completed, Mr. Grimes, you will get the hell
off this planet."

"What about my officers, sir? Mr. Beadle is
overdue for Leave . . . "

"My heart fair bleeds for him."

"And Mr. McCloud is in hospital . . . "

"Ensign Vitelli, your new Engineering Officer,
was ordered to report to your vessel as soon as
possible, if not before. The work of fitting a re-
placement computer to *Adder* is already well in
hand." The Commodore looked at his watch. "It
is now 1435. At 1800 hours you will lift ship."

"My Orders, sir . . . "

"Oh, yes, Grimes. Your Orders. A matter of
minor importance, actually. As long as you get out
of *my* hair that's all that matters to me. But I
suppose I have to put you in the picture. The
Shaara are passing through a phase of being nice to
humans, and we, of the Federation, are reciprocat-
ing. There's a small parcel of *very* important cargo
to be lifted from Droomoor to Brooum, and for

some reason or other our arthropedal allies haven't a fast ship of their own handy. Lindisfarne Base is only a week from Droomoor by Serpent Class Courier. So . . . ''

So Viper, Asp *and* Cobra *have all been in port for weeks*, thought Grimes bitterly, *but I get the job.*

The Commodore had his telepathic moments. He smiled again, and this time there was a hint of sympathy. He said, "I want you off Lindisfarne, young Grimes, before there's too much of a stink raised over this Mr. Adam affair. You're too honest. I can bend the truth better than you can."

"Thank you, sir," said Grimes, meaning it.

"Off you go, now. Don't forget these." Grimes took the heavily sealed envelope. "And try not to make too much of a balls of this assignment."

"I'll try, sir."

Grimes saluted, marched smartly out of the Commodore's office, strode across the apron to where his "flying darning needle," not yet shifted to a lay-up berth (not that she would be now), was awaiting him.

Mr. Beadle met him at the airlock. He rarely smiled—but he did so, rather smugly, when he saw the Orders in Grimes's hand. He asked casually, "Any word of my relief, Captain?"

"Yes. You're not getting it, Number One," Grimes told him, rather hating himself for the pleasure he derived from being the bearer of bad tidings. "And we're to lift off at 1800 hours. Is the new engineer aboard yet?"

Beadle's face had resumed its normal lugubrious case. "Yes," he said. "But stores, Captain . . . Repairs . . . Maintenance . . ."

"Are they in hand?"

"Yes, but . . ."

"Then if we aren't ready for space, it won't be our fault." But Grimes knew—and it made him feel as unhappy as his first lieutenant looked—that the ship would be ready.

Adder lifted at precisely 1800 hours. Grimes, sulking hard—he had not been able to see Maggie Lazenby—did not employ his customary, spectacular getting-upstairs-in-a-hurry technique, kept his fingers off the auxiliary reaction drive controls. The ship drifted up and out under inertial drive only, seemingly sharing the reluctance to part of her officer. Beadle was slumped gloomily in his chair, von Tannenbaum, the navigator, stared at his instruments with an elaborate lack of interest, Slovotny, the electronic communications officer, snarled every time that he had occasion to hold converse with Aerospace Control.

And yet, once the vessel was clear of the atmosphere, Grimes began to feel almost happy. *Growl you may*, he thought, *but go you must*. He had gone. He was on his way. He was back in what he regarded as his natural element. Quite cheerfully he went through the motions of lining *Adder* up on the target star, was pleased to note that von Tannenbaum was cooperating in his usual highly efficient manner. And then, once trajectory had been set, the Mannschenn Drive was put into operation and the little ship was falling at a fantastic speed through the warped Continuum, with yet another mission to be accomplished.

The captain made the usual minor ritual of lighting his pipe. He said, "Normal Deep Space routine, Number One."

"Normal Deep Space routine, sir."

"Who has the watch?"

"Mr. von Tannenbaum, Captain."

"Good. Then come to see me as soon as you're free."

When Beadle knocked at his door Grimes had the envelope of instructions open. He motioned the first lieutenant to a chair, said, "Fix us drinks, Number One, while I see what's in this bumf . . ." He extended a hand for the glass that the officer put into it, sipped the pink gin, continued reading. "Mphm. Well, we're bound for Droomoor, as you know . . ."

"As well I know." Beadle then muttered something about communistic bumblebees.

"Come, come, Mr. Beadle. The Shaara are our brave allies. And they aren't at all bad when you get to know them."

"I don't want to get to know them. If I couldn't have my leave I could have been sent on a mission to a world with real human girls and a few bright lights . . ."

"Mr. Beadle, you shock me. By your xenophobia as well as by your low tastes. However, as I was saying, we are to proceed to Droomoor at maximum velocity consistent with safety. There we are to pick up a small parcel of very important cargo, the loading of which is to be strictly supervised by the local authorities. As soon as possible thereafter we are to proceed to Brooum at maximum velocity &c &c."

"Just delivery boys," grumbled Beadle. "That's us."

"Oh, well," Grimes told him philosophically, "it's a change from being coach drivers. And after the trouble we've had with passengers of late it should be a welcome one.''

Droomoor is an Earth-type planet, with the usual seas, continents, polar icecaps and all the rest of it. Evolution did not produce any life-forms deviating to any marked degree from the standard pattern; neither did it come up with any fire-making, tool-using animals. If human beings had been the first to discover it, it would have become a Terran colony. But it was a Shaara ship that made the first landing, so it was colonised by the Shaara, as was Brooum, a very similar world.

Grimes brought *Adder* in to Port Sherr with his usual competence, receiving the usual co-operation from the Shaara version of Aerospace Control. Apart from that, things were not so usual. He and his officers were interested to note that the aerial traffic which they sighted during their passage through the atmosphere consisted of semi-rigid airships rather than heavier-than-air machines. And the buildings surrounding the landing apron at the spaceport were featureless, mud-coloured domes rather than angular constructions of glass and metal. Beadle mumbled something about a huddle of bloody beehives, but Grimes paid no attention. As a reasonably efficient captain he was interested in the lay-out of the port, was trying to form some idea of what facilities were available. A ship is a ship is a ship, no matter by whom built or by whom manned—but a mammal is a mammal and an arthroped is an arthroped, and each has its own separate requirements.

''Looks like the Port Officials on their way out to us,'' remarked von Tannenbaum.

A party of Shaara had emerged from a circular opening near the top of the nearer dome. They flew slowly towards the ship, their gauzy wings almost invisible in the sunlight. Grimes focused his binoculars on them. In the lead was a Princess, larger than the others, her body more slender, glittering with the jeweled insignia of her rank. She was followed by two drones, so hung about with precious stones and metal that it was a wonder that they were able to stay airborne. Four upper caste workers, less gaudily caparisoned than the drones, but with sufficient ornamentation to differentiate them from the common herd, completed the party.

"Number One," said Grimes, "attend the air-lock, please. I shall receive the boarding party in my day cabin."

He went down from the control room to his quarters, got out the whisky—three bottles, he decided, should be sufficient, although the Shaara drones were notorious for their capacity.

The Princess was hard, businesslike. She refused to take a drink herself, and under her glittering, many-faceted eyes the workers dare not accept Grimes's hospitality, and even the drones limited themselves to a single small glass apiece. She stood there like a gleaming, metallic piece of abstract statuary, motionless, and the voice that issued from the box strapped to her thorax was that of a machine rather than of a living being.

She said, "This is an important mission, Captain. You will come with me, at once, to the Queen Mother, for instructions."

Grimes didn't like being ordered around, especially aboard his own ship, but was well aware that it is foolish to antagonise planetary rulers. He said:

"Certainly, Your Highness. But first I must give instructions to my officers. And before I can do so I must have some information. To begin with, how long a stay do we have on your world?"

"You will lift ship as soon as the consignment has been loaded." She consulted the jewelled watch that she wore strapped to a forelimb. "The underworkers will be on their way out to your vessel now." She pointed towards the four upper caste working Shaara. "These will supervise stowage. Please inform your officers of the arrangements."

Grimes called Beadle on the intercom, asked him to come up to his cabin. Then, as soon as the First Lieutenant put in an appearance, he told him that he was to place himself at the disposal of the supervisors and to ensure that *Adder* was in readiness for instant departure. He then went through into his bedroom to change into a dress uniform, was pulling off his shirt when he realised that the Princess had followed him.

"What are you doing?" she asked coldly.

"Putting on something more suitable, Your Highness," he told her.

"That will not be necessary, Captain. You will be the only human in the presence of Her Majesty, and everybody will know who and what you are."

Resignedly Grimes shrugged himself back into his uniform shirt, unadorned save for shoulder boards. He felt that he should be allowed to make more of a showing, especially among beings all dressed up like Christmas trees themselves, but his orders had been to cooperate fully with the Shaara authorities. And, in any case, shorts and shirt were far more comfortable than long trousers, frock coat, collar and tie, fore-and-aft hat and that ridiculous ceremonial sword. He hung his personal communicator over his shoulder, put on his cap and said, "I'm ready, Your Highness."

"What is that?" she asked suspiciously. "A weapon?"

"No, Your Highness! A radio transceiver. I must remain in touch with my ship at all times."

"I suppose it's all right," she said grudgingly.

When Grimes walked down the ramp, following the princess and her escorting drones, he saw that a wheeled truck had drawn up alongside *Adder* and that a winch mounted on the vehicle was reeling in a small airship, a bloated gasbag from which was slung a flimsy car, at the after end of which a huge, two-bladed propeller was still lazily turning. Workers were scurrying about on the ground and buzzing between the blimp and the truck.

"Your cargo," said the Princess. "And your transport from the spaceport to the palace."

The car of the airship was now only a foot above the winch. From it the workers lifted carefully a white cylinder, apparently made from some plastic, about four feet long and one foot in diameter. Set into its smooth surface were dials, and an indicator light that glowed vividly green even in the bright sunlight. An insulated lead ran from it to the airship's engine compartment where, thought Grimes, there must be either a battery or a generator. Yes, a battery it was. Two workers, their wings a shimmering transparency, brought it out and set it down on the concrete beside the cylinder.

"You will embark," the princess stated.

Grimes stood back and assessed the situation. It would be easy enough to get on to the truck, to clamber on top of the winch and from there into the car—but it would be impossible to do so without getting his white shorts, shirt and stockings filthy. Insofar as machinery was concerned the Shaara believed in lubrication, and plenty of it.

"I am waiting," said the Princess.

"Yes, Your Highness, but . . ."

Grimes did not hear the order given—the Shaara communicated among themselves telepathically—so was somewhat taken aback when two of the workers approached him, buzzing loudly. He flinched when their claws penetrated the thin fabric of his clothing and scratched his skin. He managed to refrain from crying out when he was lifted from the ground, carried the short distance to the airship and dumped, sprawling, on to the deck of the open car. The main hurt was to his dignity. Looking up at his own vessel he could see the grinning faces of von Tannenbaum and Slovotny at the control room viewports.

He scrambled somehow to his feet, wondering if the fragile decking would stand his weight. And then the Princess was with him, and the escorting drones, and the upper caste worker in command of the blimp had taken her place at the simple controls and the frail contraption was ballooning swiftly upwards as the winch brake was released. Grimes, looking down, saw the end of the cable whip off the barrel. He wondered what would happen if the dangling wire fouled something on the ground below, then decided that it was none of his business. These people had been playing around with airships for quite some years and must know what they were about.

The Princess was not in a communicative mood, and obviously the drones and the workers talked only when talked to—by her—although all of them wore voice boxes. Grimes was quite content with the way that things were. He had decided that the Shaaran was a bossy female, and he did not like bossy females, mammalian, arthropedal or whatever. He settled down to enjoy the trip, appreciating the leisurely—by his standards—flight over the lush countryside. There were the green, rolling hills, the great banks of flowering shrubs, huge splashes of colour that were vivid without being gaudy. Thousands of workers were busily employed about the enormous blossoms. There was almost no machinery in evidence—but in a culture such as this there would be little need for the machine, workers of the lower grades being no more than flesh-and-blood robots.

Ahead of them loomed the city.

Just a huddle of domes it was, some large, some small, with the greatest of all of them roughly in the center. This one, Grimes saw as they approached it, had a flattened top, and there was machinery there—a winch, he decided.

The airship came in high, but losing altitude slowly, finally hovering over the palace, its propeller just turning over to keep it stemming the light breeze. Two workers flew up from the platform, caught the end of the dangling cable, snapped it on to the end of another cable brought up from the winch drum. The winch was started and, creaking in protest, the blimp was drawn rapidly down. A set of wheeled steps was pushed into position, its upper part hooked on to the gunwale of the swaying car. The princess and her escort ignored this facility, fluttering out and down in a flurry of gauzy wings. Grimes used the ladder, of course, feeling grateful that somebody had bothered to remember that he was a wingless biped.

"Follow me," snapped the Princess.

The spaceman followed her, through a circular hatch in the platform. The ramp down which she led him was steep and he had difficulty in maintaining his balance, was unable to gain more than a confused impression of the interior of the huge building. There was plenty of light, luckily, a green-blue radiance emanating from clusters of luminescent insects hanging at intervals from the roof of the corridor. The air was warm, and bore an acrid but not unpleasant tang. It carried very few sounds, however, only a continuous, faintly sinister rustling noise. Grimes missed the murmur of machinery. Surely—apart from anything else—a vast structure such as this would need mechanical ventilation. In any case, there was an appreciable air flow. And then, at a junction of four corridors, he saw a group of workers, their feet hooked into rings set in the smooth floor, their wings beating slowly, maintaining the circulation of the atmosphere.

Down they went, and down, through corridors that were deserted save for themselves, through other corridors that were busy streets, with hordes of workers scurrying on mysterious errands. But they were never jostled; the lower caste Shaara always gave the Princess and her party a respectfully wide berth. Even so, there seemed to be little, if any curiosity; only the occasional drone would stop to stare at the Earthman with interest.

Down they went, and down . . .

They came, at last, to the end of a long passageway, closed off by a grilled door, the first that Grimes had seen in the hive. On the farther side of it were six workers, hung about with metal ac-

coutrements. Workers? No, Grimes decided, soldiers, Amazons. Did they, he wondered, have
stings, like their Terran counterparts? Perhaps
they did—but the laser pistols that they held
would be far more effective.

"Who comes?" asked one of them in the sort of
voice that Grimes associated with sergeant-
majors.

"The Princess Shrla, with Drones Brrynn and
Drryhr, and Earth-Drone-Captain Grrimes."

"Enter, Princess Shrla, Enter, Earth-Drone-
Captain Grrimes."

The grille slid silently aside, admitting Grimes
and the Princess, shutting again, leaving the two
drones on its further side. Two soldiers led the way
along a tunnel that, by the Earthman's standards,
was very poorly illuminated, two more brought up
the rear. Grimes was pleased to note that the Princess seemed to have lost most of her arrogance.

They came, then, into a vast chamber, a blue-lit
dimness about which the shapes of the Queen-
Mother's attendants rustled, scurried and crept.
Slowly they walked over the smooth, soft floor—
under Grimes's shoes it felt unpleasantly
organic—to the raised platform on which lay a
huge, pale shape. Ranged around the platform
were screens upon which moved pictures of
scenes all over the planet—one of them showed
the spaceport, with *Adder* standing tall slim and
gleaming on the apron—and banks of dials and
meters. Throne-room this enormous vault was,
and nursery, and the control room of a world.

Grimes's eyes were becoming accustomed to the
near-darkness. He looked with pity at the flabby,
grossly distended body with its ineffectual limbs,
its useless stubs of wings. He did not, oddly

enough, consider obscene the slowly moving belt that ran under the platform, upon which, at regular intervals, a glistening, pearly egg was deposited, neither was he repelled by the spectacle of the worker whose swollen body visibly shrank as she regurgitated nutriment into the mouth of the Shaara Queen—but he was taken aback when that being spoke to him while feeding was still in progress. He should not have been, knowing as he did that the artificial voice boxes worn by the Shaara have no connection with their organs of ingestion.

"Welcome, Captain Grimes," she said in deep, almost masculine tones.

"I am honored, Your Majesty," he stammered.

"You do us a great service, Captain Grimes."

"That is a pleasure as well as an honor, Your Majesty."

"So . . . But, Captain Grimes, I must, as you Earthmen say, put you in the picture." There was a short silence. "On Brooum there is crisis. Disease has taken its toll among the hives, a virus, a mutated virus. A cure was found—but too late. The Brooum Queen-Mother is dead. All Princesses not beyond fertilisation age are dead. Even the royal eggs, larvae and pupae were destroyed by the disease.

"We, of course, are best able to afford help to our daughters and sisters on Brooum. We offered to send a fertilisable Princess to become Queen-Mother, but the Council of Princesses which now rules the colony insists that their new monarch be born, as it were, on the planet. So, then, we are dispatching, by your vessel, a royal pupa. She will tear the silken sheath and emerge, as an imago, into the world over which she will reign."

"Mphm . . ." grunted Grimes absentmindedly.

"Your Majesty," he added hastily.

The Queen-Mother turned her attention to the television screens. "If we are not mistaken," she said, "the loading of the refrigerated cannister containing the pupa has been completed. Princess Shrla will take you back to your ship. You will lift and proceed as soon as is practicable." Again she paused, then went on. "We need not tell you, Captain Grimes, that we Shaara have great respect for Terran spacemen. We are confident that you will carry out your mission successfully. We shall be pleased, on your return to our planet, to confer upon you the Order of the Golden Honeyflower.

"On your bicycle, spaceman!"

Grimes looked at the recumbent Queen dubiously. Where had she picked up *that* expression? But he had heard it said—and was inclined to agree—that the Shaara were more human than many of the humanoids throughout the Galaxy.

He bowed low—then, following the Princess, escorted by the soldiers, made his way out of the throne-room.

It is just three weeks, Terran Standard, from Droomoor to Brooum as the Serpent Class Courier flies. That, of course, is assuming that all systems are Go aboard the said Courier. All systems were not Go insofar as *Adder* was concerned. This was the result of an unfortunate combination of circumstances. The ship had been fitted with a new computer at Lindisfarne Base, a new Engineering Officer—all of whose previous experience had been as a junior in a Constellation Class cruiser—had been appointed to her, and she had not been allowed to stay in port long enough for any real maintenance to be carried out.

The trouble started one evening, ship's time, when Grimes was discussing matters with Spooky Deane, the psionic communications officer. The telepath was, as usual, getting outside a large, undiluted gin. His captain was sipping a glass of the same fluid, but with ice cubes and bitters as additives.

"Well, Spooky," said Grimes, "I don't think that we shall have any trouble with *this* passenger. She stays in her cocoons—the home-grown one and the plastic outer casing—safe and snug and hard-frozen, and thawing her out will be up to her loyal subjects. By that time we shall be well on our way . . . "

"She's alive, you know," said Deane.

"Of course she's alive."

"She's conscious, I mean. I'm getting more and more attuned to her thoughts, her feelings. It's always been said that it's practically impossible for there to be any real contact of minds between human and Shaara telepaths, but when you're cooped up in the same ship as a Shaara, a little ship at that . . . "

"Tell me more," ordered Grimes.

"It's . . . fascinating. You know, of course, that race memory plays a big part in the Shaara culture. The princess, when she emerges as an imago, will *know* just what her duties are, and what the duties of those about her are. She *knows* that her two main functions will be to rule and to breed. Workers exist only to serve her, and every drone is a potential father to her people . . . "

"Mphm. And is she aware of *us*?"

"Dimly, Captain. She doesn't know, of course,

who or what we are. As far as she's concerned
we're just some of her subjects, in close attendance upon her . . . "

"Drones or workers?"

Spooky Deane laughed. "If she were more fully
conscious, she'd be rather confused on that point.
Males are drones, and drones don't work . . . "

Grimes was about to make some unkind re-
marks about his officers when the lights flickered.
When they flickered a second time he was already
on his feet. When they went out he was halfway
through the door of his day cabin, hurrying towards the control room. The police lights came on,
fed from the emergency batteries—but the sudden
cessation of the noise of pumps and fans, the cutting off in mid-beat of the irregular throbbing of the
inertial drive, was frightening. The thin, high
whine of the Mannschenn Drive Unit deepened as
the spinning, precessing gyroscopes slowed to a
halt, and as they did so there came the nauseating
dizziness of temporal disorientation.

Grimes kept going, although—as he put it,
later—he didn't know if it was Christmas Day or
last Thursday. The ship was in Free Fall now, and
he pulled himself rapidly along the guide rail, was
practically swimming in air as he dived through the
hatch into Control.

Von Tannenbaum had the watch. He was busy at
the auxiliary machinery control panel. A fan restarted somewhere, but a warning buzzer began to
sound. The navigator cursed. The fan motor
slowed down and the buzzer ceased.

"What's happened, Pilot?" demanded Grimes.

"The Phoenix jennie I *think*, Captain. Vitelli
hasn't reported yet . . . "

Then the engineer's shrill, excited voice

sounded from the intercom speaker. "Auxiliary engine room to Control! I have to report a leakage of deuterium!"

"What pressure is there in the tank?" Grimes asked.

"The gauges still show 20,000 units. But . . ."

"But what?" Grimes snapped.

"Captain, the tank is empty."

Grimes pulled himself to his chair, strapped himself in. He looked out through the viewports at the star-begemmed blackness, each point of light hard and sharp, no longer distorted by the temporal precession fields of the Drive, each distant sun lifetimes away with the ship in her present conditon. Then he turned to face his officers—Beadle, looking no more (but no less) glum than usual, von Tannenbaum, whose normally ruddy face was now as pale as his hair, Slovotny, whose dark complexion now had a greenish cast, and Deane, ectoplasmic as always. They were joined by Vitelli, a very ordinary looking young man who was, at the moment, more than ordinarily frightened.

"Mr. Vitelli," Grimes asked him. "This leakage—is it into our atmosphere or outside the hull?"

"Outside, sir."

"Good. In that case . . ." Grimes made a major production of filling and lighting his battered pipe. "Now I can think. Mphm. Luckily I've not used any reaction mass this trip, so we have ample fuel for the emergency generator. Got your slipstick ready, Pilot? Assuming that the tanks are full, do we have enough to run the inertial and interstellar drives from here to Brooum?"

"I'll have to use the computer, Captain."

"Then use it. Meanwhile, Sparks and Spooky, can either of you gentlemen tell me what ships are in the vicinity?"

"The Dog Star Line's *Basset*," Slovotny told him. "The cruiser *Draconis*," added Deane.

"Mphm." It would be humiliating for a Courier Service Captain to have to call for help, but *Draconis* would be the lesser of two evils. "Mphm. Get in touch with both vessels, Mr. Deane. I'm not sure that we can spare power for the Carlotti, Mr. Slovotny. Get in touch with both vessels, ask their positions and tell them ours. But don't tell them anything else."

"*Our* position, sir, is . . . ?"

Grimes swivelled his chair so that he could see the chart tank, rattled off the coordinates, adding, "Near enough, until we get an accurate fix . . ."

"I can take one now, Captain," von Tannenbaum told him.

"Thank you, Pilot. Finished your sums?"

"Yes." The navigator's beefy face was expressionless. "To begin with, we have enough chemical fuel to maintain all essential services for a period of seventy-three Standard days. *But* we do not have enough fuel to carry us to Brooum, even using Mannschenn Drive only. We could, however, make for ZX1797—sol-type, with one Earth-type planet, habitable but currently uninhabited by intelligent life forms . . ."

Grimes considered the situation. If he were going to call for help he would be better off staying where he was, in reasonable comfort.

"Mr. Vitelli," he said, "you can start up the emergency generator. Mr. Deane, as soon as Mr. von Tannenbaum has a fix you can get a message out to *Basset* and *Draconis*. . . ."

"But she's properly awake," Deane muttered. "She's torn upon the silk cocoon, and the outer cannister is opening . . ."

"What the hell are you talking about?" barked Grimes.

"The Princess. When the power went off the refrigeration unit stopped. She . . ." The telepath's face assumed an expression of rapt devotion. "We must go to her . . ."

"We must go to her . . ." echoed Vitelli.

"The emergency generator!" almost yelled Grimes. But he, too, could feel that command *inside* his brain, the imperious demand for attention, for . . . love. Here, at last, was something, somebody whom he could serve with all the devotion of which he was, of which he ever would be capable. And yet a last, tattered shred of sanity persisted.

He said gently, "We must start the emergency generator. *She* must not be cold or hungry."

Beadle agreed. "We must start the emergency generator. For *her*."

They started the emergency generator and the ship came back to life—of a sort. She was a small bubble of light and warmth and life drifting down and through the black immensities.

The worst part of it all, Grimes said afterwards, was *knowing* what was happening but not having the willpower to do anything about it. And then he would add, "But it was educational. You can't deny that. I always used to wonder how the Establishment gets away with so much. Now I know. If you're a member of the Establishment you have that inborn . . . arrogance? No, not arrogance. That's not the right word. You have the calm certainty that everybody will do just what you want. With *our* Establishment it could be largely the result of training, of education. With the Shaara Establishment no education or training is necessary.

"Too, the Princess had it easy—almost as easy as she would have done had she broken out of her cocoon in the proper place at the proper time. Here she was in a little ship, manned by junior officers, people used to saluting and obeying officers with more gold braid on their sleeves. For her to impose her will was child's play. Literally child's play in this case. There was a communication problem, of course, but it wasn't a serious one. Even if she couldn't actually speak, telepathically, to the rest of us, there was Spooky Deane. With him she could dot the i's and cross the t's.

"And she did."

And she did.

Adder's officers gathered in the cargo compartment that was now the throne-room. A table had been set up, covered with a cloth that was, in actuality, a new Federation ensign from the ship's flag locker. To it the Princess—the Queen, rather—clung with her four posterior legs. She was a beautiful creature, slim, all the colors of her body undimmed by age. She was a glittering, bejeweled piece of abstract statuary, but she was alive, very much alive. With her great, faceted eyes she regarded the men who hovered about her. She was demanding something. Grimes knew that, as all of them did. She was demanding something—quietly at first, then more and more insistently.

But what?

Veneration? Worship?

"She hungers," stated Deane.

She hungers . . . thought Grimes. His memory was still functioning, and he tried to recall what he knew of the Shaara.

He said, "Tell her that her needs will be satisfied."

Reluctantly yet willingly he left the cargo compartment, making his way to the galley. It did not take him long to find what he wanted, a squeeze bottle of syrup. He hurried back with it.

It did not occur to him to hand the container to the Queen. With his feet in contact with the deck he was able to stand before her, holding the bottle in his two hands, squeezing out the viscous fluid, drop by drop, into the waiting mouth. Normally he would have found that complexity of moving parts rather frightening, repulsive even—but now they seemed to possess an essential rightness that was altogether lacking from the clumsy masticatory apparatus of a human being. Slowly, carefully he squeezed, until a voice said in his mind, *Enough. Enough.*

"She would rest now," said Deane.

"She shall rest," stated Grimes.

He led the way from the cargo compartment to the little wardroom.

In a bigger ship, with a larger crew, with a senior officer in command who, by virtue of his rank, was a member of the Establishment himself, the spell might soon have been broken. But this was only a little vessel, and of her personnel only Grimes was potentially a rebel. The time would come when this potentiality would be realised—just as, later, the time of compromise would come—but it was not yet. He had been trained to obedience—and now there was aboard *Adder* somebody whom he obeyed without question, just as he would have obeyed an Admiral.

In the wardroom the officers disposed of a meal of sorts, and when it was over Grimes, from force of habit, pulled his pipe from his pocket, began to fill it.

Deane admonished him, saying, "*She* wouldn't like it. It taints the air."

"Of course," agreed Grimes, putting his pipe away.

Then they sat there, in silence, but uneasily, guiltily. They should have been working. There was so much to be done about the Hive. Von Tannenbaum at last unbuckled himself from his chair and, finding a soft rag, began, unnecessarily, to polish a bulkhead. Vitelli muttered something about cleaning up the engineroom and drifted away, and Slovotny, saying that he would need help, followed him. Beadle took the dirty plates into the pantry—normally he was one of those who washes the dishes *before* a meal.

"She is hungry," announced Deane.

Grimes went to the galley for another bottle of syrup.

So it went on, for day after day, with the Queen gaining strength and, if it were possible, even greater authority over her subjects. And she was learning. Deane's mind was open to her, as were the minds of the others, but to a lesser degree. But it was only through Deane that she could speak.

"She knows," said the telepath, "that supplies in the Hive are limited, that sooner or later, sooner rather than later, we shall be without heat, without air or food. She knows that there is a planet within reach. She orders us to proceed there, so that a greater Hive may be established on its surface.''

''Then let us proceed,'' agreed Grimes.

He knew, as they all knew, that a general distress call would bring help—but somehow was incapable of ordering it made. He knew that the establishment of a Hive, a colony on a planet of ZX1797 would be utterly impossible—but that was what *she* wanted.

So *Adder* awoke from her sleeping state, vibrating to the irregular rhythm of the inertial drive and, had there been an outside observer, flickered into invisibility as the gyroscopes of the Mannschenn Drive unit precessed and tumbled, falling down and through the warped continuum, pulling the structure of the ship with them.

Ahead was ZX1797, a writhing, multi-hued spiral, expanding with every passing hour.

It was von Tannenbaum who now held effective command of the ship—Grimes had become the Queen's personal attendant, although it was still Deane who made her detailed wishes known. It was Grimes who fed her, who cleansed her, who sat with her hour after hour in wordless communion. A part of him rebelled, a part of him screamed soundlessly and envisaged hard fists smashing those great, faceted eyes, heavy boots crashing through fragile chitin. A part of him rebelled—but was powerless—and *she* knew it. She was female and he was male and the tensions were inevitable, and enjoyable to one if not to the other.

And then Deane said to him, ''She is tiring of her tasteless food.''

She would be, thought Grimes dully. And then there was the urge to placate, to please. Although he had never made a deep study of the arthropedal race he knew, as did all spacemen, which Terran luxuries were appreciated by the Shaara. He went up to his quarters, found what he was looking for. He decanted the fluid from its own glass container into a squeeze bottle. Had it been intended for human consumption this would not have been necessary, now that the ship was accelerating, but Shaara queens do not, ever, feed themselves.

He went back to the throne-room. Deane and the huge arthroped watched him. The Queen's eyes were even brighter than usual. She lifted her forelimbs as though to take the bottle from Grimes, then let them fall to her side. Her gauzy wings were quivering in anticipation.

Grimes approached her slowly. He knelt before her, holding the bottle before him. He raised it carefully, the nippled end towards the working mandibles. He squeezed, and a thin, amber stream shot out. Its odor was rich and heavy in the almost still air of the compartment.

More! the word formed itself in his mind. *More!*

He went on squeezing.

But . . . You are not a worker . . . You are a drone . . .

And that word "drone" denoted masculinity, not idleness.

You are a drone . . . You shall be the first father of the new Hive . . .

"Candy is dandy, but liquor is quicker . . ." muttered Deane, struggling to maintain a straight face.

Grimes glared at the telepath. What was so funny about this? He was feeling, strongly, the stirrings of desire. *She* was female, wasn't she? She was female, and she was beautiful, and he was male. She was female—and in his mind's eye those flimsy wings were transparent draperies enhancing, not concealing, the symmetry of the form of a lovely woman—slim, with high, firm breasts, with long, slender legs. She wanted him to be her mate, her consort.

She wanted him.

She . . .

Suddenly the vision flickered out.

This was no woman spread in alluring, naked abandon.

This was no more than a repulsive insect sprawled in drunken untidiness, desecrating the flag that had been spread over the table that served it for a bed. The wings were crumpled, a dull film was over the faceted eyes. A yellowish ichor oozed from among the still-working mandibles.

Grimes retched violently. To think that he had almost . . .

"Captain!" Deane's voice was urgent. "She's out like a light! She's drunk as a fiddler's bitch!"

"And we must keep her that way!" snapped Grimes. He was himself again. He strode to the nearest bulkhead pick-up. "Attention, all hands! This is the Captain speaking. Shut down inertial and interstellar drive units. Energise Carlotti transceiver. Contact any and all shipping in the vicinity, and request aid as soon as possible. Say that we are drifting, with main engines inoperable due to fuel shortage." He turned to Deane. "I'm leaving you in charge, Spooky. If she shows signs of breaking surface, you know what to do." He looked sternly at the telepath. "I suppose I can trust you . . . "

"You can," the psionic communications officer assured him. "You can. Indeed you can, captain. I wasn't looking forward at all, at all, to ending my days as a worker in some *peculiar*

Terran-Shaara Hive!'' He stared at Grimes
thoughtfully. ''I wonder if the union *would* have
been fertile?''

''That will do, Mr. Deane,'' growled Grimes.

''Fantastic,'' breathed Commodore Damien.
''Fantastic. Almost, Mr. Grimes, I feel a certain
envy. The things you get up to . . . ''

The aroma of good Scotch whisky hung heavily
in the air of the Commodore's office. Damien, although not an abstainer, never touched the stuff.
Grimes's tastes were catholic—but on an occasion
such as this he preferred to be stone cold sober.

''It is more than fantastic,'' snarled the Shaara
Queen-Emissary, the special envoy of the Em-
press herself. Had she not been using a voice-box
her words would have been slurred. ''It is . . .
disgusting. Reprehensible. This officer *forced* liquor down the throat of a member of *our* Royal
family. He . . . ''

''He twisted her arm?'' suggested the Commodore.

. ''I do not understand. But she is now Queen-
Mother of Brooum. A drunken, even alcoholic
Queen-Mother.''

''I saved my ship and my people,'' stated
Grimes woodenly.

Damien grinned unpleasantly. ''Isn't this where
we came in, Lieutenant? But no matter. There are
affairs of far more pressing urgency. Not only do
I have to cope with a direct complaint from
the personal representative of Her Imperial Majesty . . . ''

Even though she was wearing a voice-box, the
Queen-Emissary contrived to hiccough. And all
this, Grimes knew, was going down on tape. It was

unlikely that he would ever wear the ribbon of the Order of the Golden Honeyflower, but it was equally unlikely that he would be butchered to make a Shaara holiday.

"He *weaned* her on Scotch . . . " persisted the Queen-Emissary.

"Aren't you, perhaps, a little jealous?" suggested Damien. He switched his attention back to Grimes. "Meanwhile, Lieutenant, I am being literally bombarded with Carlottigrams from Her not-so-Imperial Majesty on Brooum demanding that I despatch to her, as soon as possible if not before, the only drone in the Galaxy with whom she would dream of mating . . . "

"No!" protested Grimes. "*NO!*"

"Yes, mister. Yes. For two pins I'd accede to her demands." He sighed regretfully. "But I suppose that one must draw some sort of a line somewhere. . . " He sighed again—then, "Get out, you *drone!*" he almost shouted. It was a pity that he had to spoil the effect by laughing.

"We are not amused," said the Shaara Queen.

THE WANDERING BUOY

It shouldn't have been there.

Nothing at all should have been there, save for the sparse drift of hydrogen atoms that did nothing at all to mitigate the hard vacuum of interstellar space, and save for the Courier *Adder*, proceeding on her lawful occasions.

It shouldn't have been there, but it was, and Grimes and his officers were pleased rather than otherwise that something had happened to break the monotony of the long voyage.

"A definite contact, Captain," said von Tannenbaum, peering into the monotony of the long voyage.

"A definite contact, Captain," said von Tannenbaum, peering into the spherical screen of the mass proximity indicator.

"Mphm . . ." grunted Grimes. Then, to the Electronic Communications Officer. "You're quite sure that there's no traffic around, Sparks?"

"Quite sure, Captain," replied Slovotny. "Nothing within a thousand light years."

"Then get Spooky on the intercom, and ask him if *he's* been in touch with anybody—or anything."

"Very good, Captain," said Slovotny rather sulkily. There was always rivalry, sometimes far from friendly, between electronic and psionic communications officers.

Grimes looked over the Navigator's shoulder into the velvety blackness of the screen, at the tiny, blue-green spark that lay a little to one side of

the glowing filament that was the ship's extrapo-
lated trajectory. Von Tannenbaum had set up the
range and bearing markers, was quietly reading
aloud the figures. He said, "At our present velocity we shall be up to it in just over three hours."

"Spooky says that there's no psionic transmission at all from it, whatever it is," reported
Slovotny.

"So if it's a ship, it's probably a derelict," murmured Grimes.

"Salvage . . . " muttered Beadle, looking almost
happy.

"You've a low, commercial mind, Number
One," Grimes told him. *As I have myself*, he
thought. The captain's share of a fat salvage award
would make a very nice addition to his far from
generous pay. "Oh, well, since you've raised the
point you can check towing gear, spacesuits and
all the rest of it. And you, Sparks, can raise Lindisfarne Base on the Carlotti. I'll have the pre-
liminary report ready in a couple of seconds . . . "
He added, speaking as much to himself as to the
others, "I suppose I'd better ask permission to
deviate, although the Galaxy won't grind to a halt
if a dozen bags of mail are delayed in transit . . . "
He took the message pad that Slovotny handed
him and wrote swiftly, *To Officer Commanding
Couriers. Sighted unidentified object coordinates
A1763.5 x ZU97.75 x J222.0 approx. Request authority investigate. Grimes.*

By the time that the reply came Grimes was on
the point of shutting down his Mannschenn Drive
and initiating the maneuvers that would match
trajectory and speed with the drifting object.

It read, *authority granted, but please try to keep
your nose clean for a change. Damien.*

"Well, Captain, we can *try*," said Beadle, not too hopefully.

With the Mannschenn Drive shut down radar, which gave far more accurate readings than the mass proximity indicator, was operable. Von Tannenbaum was able to determine the elements of the object's trajectory relative to that of the ship, and after this had been done the task of closing it was easy.

At first it was no more than a brightening blip in the screen and then, at last, it could be seen visually as *Adder's* probing searchlight caught it and held it. To begin with it was no more than just another star among the stars, but as the ship gained on it an appreciable disc was visible through the binoculars, and then with the naked eye.

Grimes studied it carefully through his powerful glasses. It was spherical, and appeared to be metallic. There were no projections on it anywhere, although there were markings that looked like painted letters or numerals. It was rotating slowly.

"It could be a mine . . . " said Beadle, who was standing with Grimes at the viewport.

"It could be . . . " agreed Grimes. "And it could be fitted with some sort of proximity fuse . . . " He turned to address von Tannenbaum. "You'd better maintain our present distance off, Pilot, until we know better what it is." He stared out through the port again. Space mines are a defensive rather than offensive weapon, and *Adder* carried six of the things in her own magazine. They are a dreadfully effective weapon when the conditions for their use are ideal—which they rarely are. Dropped from a vessel being pursued by an enemy they are an excellent deterrent—provided that the pursuer is not proceeding under interstellar drive. Unless there is temporal synchronisation there can be no physical contact.

Out here, thought Grimes, in a region of space where some sort of interstellar drive *must* be used, a mine just didn't make sense. On the other hand, it never hurt to be careful. He recalled the words of one of the Instructors at the Academy. "There are old spacemen, and there are bold spacemen, but there aren't any old, bold spacemen."

"A sounding rocket . . . " he said.

"All ready, Captain," replied Beadle.

"Thank you, Number One. After you launch it, maintain full control throughout its flight. Bring it to the buoy or the mine or whatever it is *very* gently—I don't want you punching holes in it. Circle the target a few times, if you can manage it, and then make careful contact." He paused. "Meanwhile, restart the Mannschenn Drive, but run it in neutral gear. If there is a big bang we might be able to start precessing before the shrapnel hits us." He paused again, then, "Have any of you gentlemen any bright ideas?"

"It might be an idea," contributed Slovotny, "to clear away the laser cannon. Just in case."

"Do so, Sparks. And you, Number One, don't launch your rocket until I give the word."

"Cannon trained on the target," announced Slovotny after only a few seconds.

"Good. All right, Number One. Now you can practise rocketship handling."

"Beadle returned to the viewport, with binoculars strapped to his eyes and a portable control box in his hands. He pressed a button, and almost at once the sounding rocket swam into the field of view, a sleek, fishlike shape with a pale glimmer of fire at its tail, a ring of bright red lights mounted around its midsection to keep it visible at all times to the aimer. Slowly it drew away from the ship, heading towards the enigmatic ball that hung in the blaze of the searchlight. It veered to one side to pass the target at a respectable distance, circled it, went into orbit about it, a miniscule satellite about a tiny primary.

Grimes started to get impatient. He had learned that one of the hardest parts of a captain's job is to refrain from interfering—even so . . . "Number One," he said at last, "don't you think you could edge the rocket in a little closer?"

"I'm trying, sir," replied Beadle. "But the bloody thing won't answer the controls."

"Do you mind if I have a go?" asked Grimes.

"Of course not, Captain." Implied but not spoken was, "And you're bloody welcome!"

Grimes strapped a set of binoculars to his head, then took the control box. First of all he brought the sounding rocket back towards the ship, then put it in a tight turn to get the feel of it. Before long he was satisfied that he had it; it was as though a tiny extension of himself was sitting in a control room in the miniature spaceship. It wasn't so very different from a rocket-handling simulator.

He straightened out the trajectory of the sounding rocket, sent it back towards the mysterious globe and then, as Beadle had done, put it in orbit. So far, so good. He cut the drive and the thing, of course, continued circling the metallic sphere. A brief blast from a braking jet—that should do the trick. With its velocity drastically reduced the missile should fall gently towards its target. But it did not—as von Tannenbaum, manning the radar, reported.

There was something wrong here, thought Grimes. The thing had considerable mass, otherwise it would never have shown so strongly in the screen of the MPI. The greater the mass, the greater the gravitational field. But, he told himself, there are more ways than one of skinning a cat. He actuated the steering jets, tried to nudge the rocket in towards its objective. "How am I doing, Pilot?" he asked.

"What are you trying to do, Captain?" countered von Tannenbaum. "The elements of the orbit are unchanged."

"Mphm." Perhaps more than a gentle nudge was required. Grimes gave more than a gentle nudge—and with no result whatsoever. He did not need to look at Beadle to know that the First Lieutenant was wearing his best I-told-you-so expression.

So . . .

So the situation called for brute strength and ignorance, a combination that usually gets results.

Grimes pulled the rocket away from the sphere, almost back to the ship. He turned it—and then, at full acceleration, sent it driving straight for the target. He hoped that he would be able to apply the braking jets before it came into damaging contact—but the main thing was to make contact, of any kind.

He need not have worried.

With its driving jet flaring ineffectually the rocket was streaking back towards *Adder*, tail first. The control box was useless. "Slovotny!" barked Grimes. "Fire!"

There was a blinding flare, and then only a cloud of incandescent but harmless gases, still drifting towards the ship.

"And what do we do now, Captain?" asked
Beadle. "Might I suggest that we make a full report to Base and resume our voyage?"

"You might, Number One. There's no law
against it. But we continue our investigations."

Grimes was in a stubborn mood. He was glad
that *Adder* was not engaged upon a mission of real
urgency. These bags of Fleet Mail were not important. Revised Regulations, Promotion Lists, Ap-
pointments . . . If they never reached their destination it would not matter. But a drifting menace to
navigation was important. Perhaps, he thought, it
would be named after him. Grimes's Folly . . . He
grinned at the thought. There were better ways of
achieving immortality.

But what to do?

Adder hung there, and the *thing* hung there,
rates and directions of drift nicely synchronised,
and in one thousand seven hundred and fifty-three
Standard years they would fall into or around Al-
gol, assuming that Grimes was willing to wait that
long—which, of course, he was not. He looked at
the faces of his officers, who were strapped into
their chairs around the wardroom table. They
looked back at him. Von Tannenbaum—the Blond
Beast—grinned cheerfully. He remarked, "It's a
tough nut to crack, Captain—but I'd just hate to
shove off without cracking it." Slovotny, darkly
serious, said, "I concur. And I'd like to find out
how that repulsor field works." Vitelli, not yet
quite a member of the family, said nothing. Deane
complained, "If the thing had a mind that I could
read it'd all be so much easier . . . " "Perhaps it's
allergic to metal . . . " suggested von Tannenbaum.

"We could try to bring the ship in towards it, to see what happens . . . "

"Not bloody likely, Pilot," growled Grimes. "Not yet, anyhow. Mphm . . . you might have something. It shouldn't be too hard to cook up, with our resources, a sounding rocket of all-plastic construction . . . "

"There has to be metal in the guidance system . . ." objected Slovotny.

"There won't be any guidance systems, Sparks. It will be a solid fuel affair, and we just aim it and fire it, and see what happens . . . "

"*Solid* fuel?" demurred Beadle. "Even if we had the formula we'd never be able to cook up a batch of cordite or anything similar . . . "

"There'd be no need to, Number One. We should be able to get enough from the cartridges for our projectile small arms. But I don't intend to do that."

"Then what do you intend, Captain?"

"We have graphite—and that's carbon. We've all sorts of fancy chemicals in our stores, especially those required for the maintenance of our hydroponics system. Charcoal, sulphur, saltpeter . . . Or we could use potassium chlorate instead of that . . . "

"It *could* work," admitted the First Lieutenant dubiously.

"Of course it will work," Grimes assured him.

It did work—although mixing gunpowder, especially in Free Fall conditions, wasn't as easy as Grimes had assumed that it would be. To begin with, graphite proved to be quite unsuitable, and the first small sample batch of powder burned slowly, with a vile sulphurous stench that lingered in spite of all the efforts of the air conditioner. But there were carbon water filters, and one of these was broken up and then pulverised in the galley food mixer—and when Grimes realised that the bulkheads of this compartment were rapidly acquiring a fine coating of soot he ordered that the inertial drive be restarted. With acceleration playing the part of gravity things were a little better.

Charcoal 13 percent, saltpeter 75 percent, sulphur 12 percent . . . That, thought Grimes, trying hard to remember the History of Gunnery lectures, was about right. They mixed a small amount dry, stirring it carefully with a wooden ladle. It was better than the first attempt, using graphite, had been—but not much. And it smelled as bad. Grimes concluded that there was insufficient space between the grains to allow the rapid passage of the flame.

"Spooky," he said in desperation. "Can you read my mind?"

"It's against Regulations," the telepath told him primly.

"Damn the Regulations. I sat through all those Gunnery Course lectures, and I'm sure that old Commander Dalquist went into the history of gunnery *very* thoroughly, but I never thought that the knowledge of how to make black powder would be of any use at all to a modern spaceman. But it's all there in my memory—if I could only drag it out!"

"Relax, Captain." Spooky Deane told him in a soothing voice. "Relax. Let your mind become a blank. You're tired, Captain. You're very tired. Don't fight it. Yes, sit down. Let every muscle go loose . . . "

Grimes lay back in the chair. Yes, he *was* tired

. . . But he did not like the sensation of cold, clammy fingers probing about inside his brain. But he trusted Deane. He told himself very firmly that he *trusted* Deane . . .

"Let yourself go back in Time, Captain, to when you were a midshipman at the Academy . . . You're sitting there, on a hard bench, with the other midshipmen around you . . . And there, on his platform before the class, is old Commander Dalquist . . . I can see him, with his white hair and his white beard, and his faded blue eyes looking enormous behind the spectacles . . . And I can see all those lovely little models on the table before him . . . The culverin, the falcon, the carronade . . . He is droning on, and you are thinking, *How can he make anything so interesting so boring?* You are wondering, *What's on for dinner tonight?* You are hoping that it won't be boiled mutton *again* . . . Some of the other cadets are laughing. You half heard what the Commander was saying. It was that the early cannoneers, who mixed their own powder, maintained that the only possible fluid was a wine drinker's urine, their employer to supply the wine . . . And if the battle went badly, because of misfires the gunners could always say that it was due to the poor quality of the booze . . . But you are wondering now if you stand any chance with that pretty little Nurse . . . You've heard that she'll play. You don't know what it's like with a woman, but you want to find out . . . "

Grimes felt his prominent ears turning hot and scarlet. He snapped into full wakefulness. He said firmly, "That will do, Spooky. You've jogged my memory sufficiently. And if any of you gentlemen think I'm going to order a free wine issue, you're mistaken. We'll use plain water, just enough to make a sort of mud, thoroughly mixed, and then we'll dry it out. No, we'll not use heat, not inside the ship. Too risky. But the vacuum chamber should do the job quite well . . ."

"And then?" asked Beadle, becoming interested in spite of himself.

"Then we crush it into grains."

"Won't that be risky?"

"Yes. But we'll have a plastic bowl fitted to the food mixer, and the Chief can make some strong, plastic paddles. As long as we avoid the use of metal we should be safe enough."

They made a small batch of powder by the method that Grimes had outlined. Slovotny fitted a remote control switch to the food mixer in the galley, and they all retired from that compartment while the cake was being crushed and stirred. The bowlful of black, granular matter looked harmless enough—but a small portion of it transferred to a saucer—and taken well away from the larger amount remaining in the bowl—burned with a satisfying *whoof!* when ignited.

"We're in business!" gloated Grimes. "*Adder* Pyrotechnics, Unlimited!"

They were in business, and while Grimes, Beadle and von Tannenbaum manufactured a large supply of gunpowder Slovotny and Vitelli set about converting a half-dozen large, plastic bottles into rocket casings. They were made of thermoplastic, so it was easy enough to shape them as required, with throat and nozzle. To ensure that they would retain the shape after firing they were bound about with heavy insulating tape. After this was finished there was a rocket launcher to make—a tube of the correct diameter, with a blast shield and with the essential parts of a projectile pistol as the firing mechanism.

Then all hands joined forces in filling the rockets. Tubes of stiff paper, soaked in a saturated solution of saltpeter and allowed to dry, were inserted into the casing and centered as accurately as possible. The powder was poured around them, and well tamped home.

While this was being done Spooky Deane—who, until now, had played no part in the proceedings—made a suggestion. "Forgive me for butting in, Captain, but I remember—with *your* memory—the models and pictures that the Instructor showed the class. Those old chemical rockets had sticks or vanes to make them fly straight . . ."

For a moment this had Grimes worried. Then he laughed. "Those rockets, Spooky, were used in the atmosphere. Sticks or vanes would be utterly useless in a vacuum." But he couldn't help wondering if vanes set actually in the exhaust would help to keep the missiles on a straight trajectory. But unless he used metal there was no suitable material aboard the ship—and metal was out.

Grimes went outside, with von Tannenbaum, to do the actual firing. They stood there on the curved shell plating, held in place by the magnetic soles of their boots. Each of them, too, was secured by lifelines. Neither needed to be told that to every action there is an equal and opposite reaction. The backblast of the home-made rockets would be liable to sweep them from their footing.

Grimes held the clumsy bazooka while the Navigator loaded it, then he raised it slowly. A cartwheel sight had been etched into the transparent shield. Even though the weapon had no weight in Free Fall it still had inertia, and it was clumsy. By the time that he had the target, gleaming brightly in the beam of *Adder's* searchlight, in the center of the cartwheel he was sweating copiously. He said into his helmet microphone, "Captain to *Adder*. I am about to open fire."

"*Adder* to Captain. Acknowledged," came Beadle's voice in reply.

Grimes's right thumb found the firing stud of the pistol. He recoiled involuntarily from the wash of the orange flame that swept over the blast shield—and then he was torn from his hold on the hull plating, slammed back to the full extent of the lifeline. He lost his grip on the rocket launcher, but it was secured to his body by stout, fireproof cords. Somehow he managed to keep his attention on the fiery flight of the rocket. It missed the target, but by a very little. To judge by the straight wake of it, it had not been deflected by any sort of repulsor field.

"It throws high . . ." commented Grimes.

He pulled himself back along the line to exactly where he had been standing before. Von Tannenbaum inserted another missile into the tube. This time, when he aimed, Grimes intended to bring the target to just above the center of the cartwheel. But there was more delay; the blast shield was befogged by smoke. Luckily this eventuality had been foreseen, and von Tannenbaum cleaned it off with a soft rag.

Grimes aimed, and fired.

Again the blast caught him—but this time he hung in an untidy tangle facing the wrong way, looking at nothingness. He heard somebody inside the ship say, "It's blown up!"

What had blown up?

Hastily Grimes got himself turned around. The mysterious globe was still there, but between it and *Adder* was an expanding cloud of smoke, a scatter of fragments, luminous in the searchlight's glare. So perhaps the nonmetallic missiles weren't going to work after all—or perhaps this missile would have blown up by itself, anyhow.

The third rocket was loaded into the bazooka. For the third time Grimes fired—and actually managed to stay on his feet. Straight and true streaked the missile. It hit, and exploded in an orange flare, a cloud of white smoke which slowly dissipated.

"Is there any damage?" asked Grimes at last. He could see none with his unaided vision, but those on the control room had powerful binoculars at hand.

"No," replied Beadle at last. "It doesn't seem to be scratched."

"Then stand by to let the Pilot and myself back into the ship. We have to decide what we do next."

What they did next was a matter of tailoring rather than engineering. *Adder* carried a couple of what were called "skin-divers' suits." These were, essentially, elasticised leotards, skin-tight but porous, maintaining the necessary pressure on the body without the need for cumbersome armor. They were ideal for working in or outside the ship, allowing absolute freedom of movement—but very few spacemen liked them. A man feels that he should be armored, well armored, against an absolutely hostile environment. Too, the conventional spacesuit has built-in facilities for the excretion of body wastes, has its little tank of water and its drinking tube, has its container of food and stimulant pellets. (Grimes, of course, always maintained that the ideal suit should make provision for the pipe smoker . . .) A conventional spacesuit is, in fact, a spaceship in miniature.

Now these two suits had to be modified. The radio transceivers, with their metallic parts, were removed from the helmets. Plastic air bottles were substituted for the original metal ones. Jointures and seals between helmet and shoulderpieces were removed, and replaced by plastic.

While this was going on Beadle asked, "Who are you sending, Captain?"

"I'm *sending* nobody, Number One. I shall be going myself, and if any one of you gentlemen cares to volunteer . . . No, not you. You're second in command. You must stay with the ship."

Surprisingly it was Deane who stepped forward. "I'll come with you, Captain."

"*You*, Spooky?" asked Grimes, not unkindly.

The telepath flushed. "I . . . I feel that I should. That . . . That *thing* out there is awakening. It was as though that rocket was a knock on the door . . ."

"Why didn't you tell us?"

"I . . . I wasn't sure. But the feeling's getting stronger. There's something there. Some sort of intelligence."

"Can't you get in touch with it?"

"I've been trying. But it's too vague, too weak. And I've the feeling that there has to be actual contact. Physical contact, I mean."

"Mphm."

"In any case, Captain, you *need* me with you."

"Why, Spooky?"

Deane jerked his head towards the watch on

Grimes's wrist. "We'll not be allowed to take any metal with us. How shall we know when we've been away long enough, that we have to get back before our air runs out?"

"How shall we know if you're along?"

"Easy. Somebody will have to sit with Fido, and clockwatch all the time, really concentrating on it. At that short range Fido will pick up the thoughts even of a non-telepath quite clearly. I shall remain *en rapport* with Fido, of course."

"Mphm," grunted Grimes. Yes, he admitted to himself, the idea had its merits. He wondered whom he should tell off for the clock-watching detail. All spacemen except psionic radio officers hate the organic amplifiers, the so-called "dogs' brains in aspic," the obscenely naked masses of canine thinking apparatus floating in their spherical containers of circulating nutrient fluid.

Slovotny liked dogs. He'd be best for the job.

Slovotny was far from enthusiastic, but was told firmly that communications are communications, no matter how performed.

The Inertial Drive was restarted to make it easier for Grimes and Deane to get into their suits. Each, stripped to brief, supporting underwear, lay supine on his spread-out garment. Carefully they wriggled their hands into the tight-fitting gloves— the gloves that became tighter still once the fabric was in contact with the skin. They worked their feet into the bootees, aided by Beadle and von Tannenbaum, acting as dressers. Then, slowly and carefully, the First Lieutenant and the Navigator drew the fabric up and over arms and legs and bodies, smoothing it, pressing out the least wrinkle, trying to maintain an even, all-over pressure. To complete the job the seams were welded.

Grimes wondered, as he had wondered before, what would happen if that fantastic adhesive came unstuck when the wearer of the suit was cavorting around in hard vacuum. It hadn't happened yet—as far as he knew—but there is always a first time.

"She'll do," said Beadle at last.

"She'd better do," said Grimes. He added, "If you're after promotion, Number One, there are less suspect ways of going about it."

Beadle looked hurt.

Grimes got to his feet, scowling. If one is engaged upon what might be a perilous enterprise armor is so much more appropriate than long underwear. He said, "All right. Shut down inertial drive as soon as we've got our helmets on. Then we'll be on our way."

They were on their way.

Each man carried, slung to his belt, a supply of little rockets—Roman candles, rather—insulated cardboard cylinders with friction fuses. They had flares, too, the chemical composition of such making them combustible even in a vacuum.

The Roman candles functioned quite efficiently, driving them across the gap between ship and sphere. Grimes handled himself well, Deane not so well. It was awkward having no suit radio; it was impossible to give the telepath any instructions. At the finish Grimes came in to a perfect landing, using a retro blast at the exact split second. Deane came in hard and clumsily. There was no air to transmit the *clang*, but Grimes felt the vibration all along and through his body.

He touched helmets. "Are you all right, Spooky?"

"Just . . . winded, Captain."

Grimes leading, the two men crawled over the surface of the sphere, the adhesive pads on gloves, knees, elbows and feet functioning quite well— rather too well, in fact. But it was essential that they maintain contact with the smooth metal. Close inspection confirmed distant observation. The 100-foot-diameter globe was utterly devoid of protuberances. The markings—they were no letters or numerals known to the Earthmen—could have been painted on, but Grimes decided that they were probably something along the lines of an integrated circuit. He stopped crawling, carefully made contact with his helmet and the seamless, rivetless plating. He listened. Yes, there was the faintest humming noise. Machinery?

He beckoned Deane to him, touched helmets. He said, "There's something working inside this thing, Spooky."

"I know, Captain. And there's something alive in there. A machine intelligence, I think. It's aware of us."

"How much time have we?"

Deane was silent for a few seconds, reaching out with his mind to his psionic amplifier aboard *Adder*. "Two hours and forty-five minutes."

"Good. If we could only find a way to get into this oversized beach ball . . . "

Deane jerked his head away from Grimes's. He was pointing with a rigid right arm. Grimes turned and looked. Coming into view in the glare of the searchlight, as the ball rotated, was a round hole, an aperture that expanded as they watched it. Then they were in shadow, but they crawled towards the opening. When they were in the light again they were almost on top of it. They touched

helmets again. "Will you come into my parlor
. . . ?" whispered Grimes.

"I . . . I feel that it's safe . . . " Deane told him.

"Good. Then we'll carry on. Is that an airlock, I
wonder? There's only one way to find out . . . "

It was not an airlock. It was a doorway into
cavernous blackness, in which loomed great,
vague shapes, dimly visible in the reflected beam of
Adder's searchlight—then invisible as this hemisphere of the little, artificial world was swept into
night. Grimes was falling; his gloves could get no
grip on the smooth, slippery rim of the hole. He
was falling, and cried out in alarm as something
brushed against him. But it was only Deane. The
telepath clutched him in an embrace that, had
Deane been of the opposite sex, might have been
enjoyable.

"Keep your paws off me, Spooky!" ordered
Grimes irritably. Yet he, too, was afraid of the
dark, was suffering the primordial fear. The door
through which they had entered must be closed
now, otherwise they would be getting some illumination from *Adder's* searchlight. The dense blackness was stifling. Grimes fumbled at his belt, trying
to find a flare by touch. The use of one of the little
rockets in this confined space could be disastrous.
But there had to be light. Grimes was not a religious man, otherwise he would have prayed for it.

Then, suddenly, there was light.

It was a soft, diffused illumination, emanating
from no discernible source. It did not, at first,
show much. The inner surface of the sphere was
smooth, glassy, translucent rather than transparent. Behind it hulked the vague shapes that they
had glimpsed before their entry. Some were moving slowly, some were stationary. None of them

was like any machine or living being that either of
the two men had ever seen.

Helmets touched.

"It's aware of us. It knows that we need light
. . ." whispered Deane.

"What is It?"

"I . . . I dare not ask. It is too . . . big?"

And Grimes, although no telepath, was feeling it
too, awe rather than fear, although he admitted to
himself that he was dreadfully afraid. It was like
his first space walk, the first time that he had been
out from the frail bubble of light and warmth, one
little man in the vastness of the emptiness between
the worlds. He tried to take his mind off it by
staring at the strange machinery—if it was
machinery—beyond that glassy inner shell, tried
to make out what these devices were, what they
were doing. He focused his attention on what
seemed to be a spinning wheel of rainbow
luminescence. It was a mistake.

He felt himself being drawn into that radiant
eddy—not physically, but psychically. He tried to
resist. It was useless.

Then the pictures came—vivid, simple.

There was a naked, manlike being hunkered
down in a sandy hollow among rocks. Manlike? It
was Grimes himself. A flattish slab of wood was
held firmly between his horny heels, projecting out
and forward, away from him. In his two hands he
gripped a stick, was sawing away with it, to and fro
on the surface of the slab, in which the pointed end
of it had already worn a groove. (Grimes could *feel*
that stick in his hands, could feel the vibration as
he worked it backwards and forwards.) There was
a wisp of blue smoke from the groove, almost
invisible at first, but becoming denser. There was a

tiny red spark that brightened, expanded. Hastily Grimes let go of the fire stick, grabbed a handful of dried leaves and twigs, dropped them on top of the smoulder. Carefully he brought his head down, began to blow gently, fanning the beginnings of the fire with his breath. There was flame now—feeble, hesitant. There was flame, and a faintly heard crackle as the kindling caught. There was flame—and Grimes had to pull his head back hastily to avoid being scorched.

The picture changed.

It was night now—and Grimes and his family were squatting around the cheerful blaze. One part of his mind that had not succumbed to the hypnosis wondered who that woman was. He decided wryly that she—big-bellied, flabby-breasted—was not his cup of tea at all. But he *knew* that she was his mate, just as he *knew* that those almost simian brats were his children.

It was night, and from the darkness around the camp came the roars and snarls of the nocturnal predators. But they were afraid of fire. He, Grimes, had made fire. Therefore those beasts of prey should be afraid of him. He toyed with the glimmerings of an idea. He picked up a well-gnawed femur—that day he had been lucky enough to find a not-too-rotten carcass that had been abandoned by the original killer and not yet discovered by the other scavengers—and hefted it experimentally in his hand. It seemed to belong there. From curiosity rather than viciousness he brought it swinging around, so that the end of it struck the skull of the woman with a sharp *crack*. She squealed piteously. Grimes had no language with which to think, but he knew that a harder blow could have killed her. Dimly he realised that a hard blow could kill a tiger . . .

He . . .

He was outside the sphere, and Deane was with him. Coming towards him was a construction of blazing lights. He was afraid—and then he snapped back into the here-and-now. He was John Grimes, Lieutenant, Federation Survey Service, Captain of the courier *Adder*. That was his ship. His home. He must return to his home, followed by this Agent of the Old Ones, so that observation and assessment could be made, and plans for the further advancement of the race.

The ship was no longer approaching.

Grimes pulled a Roman candle from his belt, motioned to Deane to do likewise. He lit it, jetted swiftly towards *Adder*. He knew, without looking around, that the sphere was following.

Although blinded by the searchlight he managed to bring himself to the main airlock without mishap, followed by Deane. The two men pulled themselves into the little compartment. The outer door shut. Atmospheric pressure built up. Grimes removed the telepath's helmet, waited for Deane to perform a like service for him.

Deane's face was, if possible, even paler than usual. "Captain," he said, "we got back just in time. We've no more than a few minutes' air in our bottles . . ."

"Why didn't you tell me?"

Deane laughed shakily. "How could I? I was being . . . educated. If it's any use to me or to anybody else, I know how to make wheels out of sections of tree trunk . . ."

Beadle's voice crackled from an intercom bulkhead speaker. "Captain! Captain! Come up to Control! It's . . . vanished!"

"What's vanished?" demanded Grimes into the nearest pick-up.

"That . . . That sphere . . . "

"We're on our way," said Grimes.

Yes, the sphere had vanished. It had not flickered out like a snuffed candle; it had seemed to recede at a speed approaching that of light. It was gone, and no further investigation of its potentialities and capabilities would be possible.

It was Deane who was able to give an explanation of sorts. He said, "It was an emissary of the Old Ones. All intelligent races in this Galaxy share the legends—the gods who came down from the sky, bearing gifts of fire and weaponry, setting Man, or his local equivalent, on the upward path . . ."

"I played God myself once," said Grime. "I wasn't very popular. But go on, Spooky."

"These Old Ones . . . Who were they? We shall never know. What were their motivations? Missionary zeal? Altruism? The long-term development of planets, by the indigenes, so that the Old Ones could, at some future date, take over?

"Anyhow, I wasn't entirely under Its control. I was seeing the things that It meant me to see, feeling the things that It meant me to feel—but, at the same time, I was picking up all sorts of outside impressions. It was one of many of Its kind, sent out—how long ago?—on a missionary voyage. It was a machine, and—as machines do—it malfunctioned. Its job was to make a landing on some likely world and to make contact with the primitive natives, and to initiate their education. It was programmed, too, to get the hell out if It landed on a planet whose natives already used fire, who were already metal workers. That was why It, although not yet awakened from Its long sleep, repelled our metallic sounding rocket. That was why you, Captain, got this odd hunch about a nonmetallic approach.

"Your plastic rocket woke It up properly. It assumed that we, with no metal about us, were not yet fire-making, tool-using animals. It did what It was built to do—taught us how to make fire, and tools and weapons. And then It followed us home. It was going to keep watch over us, from generation to generation, was going to give us an occasional nudge in the right direction. Possibly It had another function—to act as a sort of marker buoy for Its builders, so that They, in Their own good time, could find us, to take over.

"But even It, with Its limited intelligence, must have realised, at the finish, that we and It were in airless space and not on a planetary surface. It must have seen that we, using little rocket-propulsion units, were already sophisticated fire-users. And then, when we entered an obviously metallic spaceship, the penny must finally have dropped, with a loud clang.

"Do you want to know what my last impression was, before It showed off?"

"Of course," said Grimes.

"It was one of hurt, of disillusion, of bewilderment. It was the realisation that It was at the receiving end of a joke. The thing was utterly humorless, of course—but It could still hate being laughed at."

There was a silence, broken by Beadle. "And Somewhere," he said piously, "at Some Time, Somebody must have asked, 'Where is my wandering buoy tonight?' "

"I sincerely hope," Grimes told him, "that this Somebody is not still around, and that He or It never tries to find out."

THE MOUNTAIN MOVERS

Olgana—Earth-type, revolving around a Sol-type primary—is a backwater planet. It is well off the main Galactic trade routes, although it gets by quite comfortably by exporting meat, butter, wool and the like to the neighbouring, highly indus-trialised Mekanika System. Olgana was a Lost Colony, one of those worlds stumbled upon quite by chance during the First Expansion, settled in a spirit of great thankfulness by the personnel of a hopelessly off-course, completely lost emigrant lodejammer. It was rediscovered—this time with no element of chance involved—by the Survey Service's *Trail Blazer,* before the colonists had drifted too far from the mainstream of human cul-ture. Shortly thereafter there were legal proceed-ings against these same colonists, occupying a few argumentative weeks at the Federation's Court of Galactic Justice in Geneva, on Earth; had these been successful they would have been followed by an Eviction Order. Even in those days it was illegal for humans to establish themselves on any planet already supporting an intelligent life form. *But*—and the colonists' Learned Counsel made the most of it—that law had not been in existence when *Lode Jumbuk* lifted off from Port Woomera on what turned out to be her last voyage. It was only a legal quibble, but the aborigines, had no represen-tation at Court—and, furthermore, Counsel for the Defense had hinted, in the right quarters, that if he lost this case he would bring suit on behalf of his clients against the Interstellar Transport Commission, holding that body fully responsible for the plights of *Lode Jumbuk's* castaways and their descendants. ITC, fearing that a dangerous and expensive precedent might be established, brought behind-the-scenes pressure to bear and the case was dropped. Nobody asked the aborigines what they thought about it all.

There was no denying that the Olganan natives—if they were natives—were a backward race. They were humanoid—to outward appearances human. They did not, however, quite fit into the general biological pattern of their world, the fauna of which mainly comprised very primitive, egg-laying mammals. The aborigines were mammals as highly developed as Man himself; although along slightly different lines. There had been surprisingly little research into Olganan biology, however; the Colony's highly competent biologists seemed to be entirely lacking in the spirit of scientific curiosity. They were biological engineers rather than scientists, their main concern being to improve the strains of their meat-producing and wool-bearing animals, descended in the main from the spermatozoa and ova which *Lode Jumbuk*—as did all colonisation vessels of her period—had carried under refrigeration.

To Olgana came the Survey Service's Serpent Class Courier *Adder,* Lieutenant John Grimes commanding. She carried not-very-important dispatches for Commander Lewin, Officer-in-Charge of the small Federation Survey Service Base maintained on the planet. The dispatches were delivered and then, after the almost mandatory small talk, Grimes asked, "And would there be any Orders for me, Commander?"

Lewin—a small, dark, usually intense man— grinned. "Of a sort, Lieutenant. Of a sort. You must be in Commodore Damien's good books. When *I* was a skipper of a Courier it was always a case of getting from Point A to Point B as soon as possible, if not before, with stopovers cut down to the irreducible minimum . . . Well, since you ask, I received a Carlottigram from Officer Commanding Couriers just before you blew in. I am to inform you that there will be no employment for your vessel for a period of at least six weeks local. You and your officers are to put yourselves at my disposal . . . " The Commander grinned again. "I find it hard enough to find jobs enough to keep my own personnel as much as half busy. So . . . enjoy yourselves. Go your merry ways rejoicing, as long as you carry your personal transceivers at all times. See the sights, such as they are. Wallow in the fleshpots—such as *they* are." He paused. "I only wish that the Commodore had loved me as much as he seems to love you."

"Mphm," grunted Grimes, his prominent ears reddening. "I don't think that it's quite that way, sir." He was remembering his last interview with Damien. *Get out of my sight!* the Commodore had snarled. *Get out of my sight, and don't come back until I'm in a better temper, if ever . . .*

"Indeed?" with a sardonic lift of the eyebrows.

"It's this way, Commander. I don't think that I'm overly popular around Lindisfarne Base at the moment . . . "

Lewin laughed outright. "I'd guessed as much. Your fame, Lieutenant, has spread even to Olgana. Frankly, I don't want you in *my* hair, around *my* Base, humble though it be. The administration of this planet is none of my concern, luckily, so you and your officers can carouse to your hearts' content as long as it's not in *my* bailiwick."

"Have you any suggestions, sir?" asked Grimes stiffly.

"Why yes. There's the so-called Gold Coast. It got started after the Trans-Galactic Clippers started calling here on their cruises."

"Inflated prices," grumbled Grimes. "A tourist trap . . . "

"How right you are. But not every TG cruise passenger is a millionaire. I could recommend, perhaps, the coach tour of Nevernever. You probably saw it from Space on your way in—that whacking great island continent in the Southern Hemisphere."

"How did it get its name?"

"The natives call it that—or something that sounds almost like that. It's the only continent upon which the aborigines live, by the way. When *Lode Jumbuk* made her landing there was no intelligent life at all in the Northern Hemisphere."

"What's so attractive about this tour?"

"Nevernever is the only unspoiled hunk of real estate on the planet. It has been settled along the coastal fringe by humans, but the Outback—which means the Inland and most of the country north of Capricorn—is practically still the way it was when Men first came here. Oh there're sheep and cattle stations, and a bit of mining, but there won't be any real development, with irrigation and all the rest, until population pressure forces it. And the aborigines—well, most of them—still live in the semi-desert the way they did before *Lode Jumbuk* came." Lewin was warming up. "Think of it, Lieutenant, an opportunity to explore a primitive world whilst enjoying all mod. cons.!

You might never get such a chance again."

"I'll think about it," Grimes told him.

He thought about it. He discussed it with his officers. Mr. Beadle, the First Lieutenant, was not enthusiastic. In spite of his habitual lugubrious mien he had a passion for the bright lights, and made it quite clear that he had enjoyed of late so few opportunities to spend his pay that he could well afford a Gold Coast holiday. Von Tannenbaum, Navigator, Slovotny, Electronic Communications, and Vitelli, Engineer, sided with Beadle. Grimes did not try to persuade them—after all, he was getting no commission from the Olganan Tourist Bureau. Spooky Deane, the psionic communications officer, asked rather shyly if he could come along with the Captain. He was not the companion that Grimes would have chosen—but he was a telepath, and it was just possible that his gift would be useful.

Deane and Grimes took the rocket mail from Newer York to New Melbourne, and during the trip Grimes indulged in one of his favorite gripes, about the inability of the average colonist to come up with really original names for his cities. At New Melbourne—a drab, oversized village on the southern coast of Nevernever—they stayed at a hotel which, although recommended by Trans-Galactic Clippers, failed dismally to come up to Galactic standards, making no attempt whatsoever to cater for guests born and brought up on worlds with widely differing atmospheres, gravitational fields and dietary customs. Then there was a day's shopping, during which the two spacemen purchased such items of personal equipment as they had been told would be necessary by the office of Nevernever Tours. The following morning, early, they took a cab from their hotel to the Never-Never Coach Terminus. It was still dark, and it was cold, and it was raining.

They sat with the other passengers, all of whom were, like themselves, roughly dressed, in the chilly waiting room, waiting for something to happen. To pass the time Grimes sized up the others. Some were obviously outworlders—there was a TG Clipper in at the spaceport. Some—their accent made it obvious—were Olganans, taking the opportunity of seeing something of their own planet. None of them, on this dismal morning, looked very attractive. Grimes admitted that the same could be said about Deane and himself; the telepath conveyed the impression of a blob of ectoplasm roughly wrapped in a too gaudy poncho.

A heavy engine growled outside, and bright lights stabbed through the big windows. Deane got unsteadily to his feet. "Look at that, Captain!" he exclaimed. "Wheels, yet! I expected an inertial drive vehicle, or at least a hoverbus!"

"You should have read the brochure, Spooky. The idea of this tour is to see the country the same way as the first explorers did, to get the *feel* of it"

"I can get the feel of it as well from an aircraft as from that archaic contraption!"

"We aren't all telepaths . . . "

Two porters had come in and were picking up suitcases, carrying them outside. The tourists, holding their overnight grips, followed, watched their baggage being stowed in a locker at the rear of the coach. From the p.a. system a voice was ordering, "All passengers will now embus! All passengers will now embus!"

The passengers embussed, and Grimes and

Deane found themselves seated behind a young couple of obviously Terran origin, while across the aisle from them was a pair of youngish ladies who could be nothing other than schoolteachers. A fat, middle-aged man, dressed in a not very neat uniform of grey coveralls, eased himself into the driver's seat. "All aboard?" he asked. "Anybody who's not, sing out!" The coach lurched from the terminus on to the rain-wet street, was soon bowling north through the dreary suburbs of New Melbourne.

Northeast they ran at first, and then almost due north, following the coast. Here the land was rich, green, well-wooded, with apple orchards, vineyards, orange groves. Then there was sheep country, rolling downland speckled with the white shapes of the grazing animals. "It's wrong," Deane whispered to Grimes. "It's all wrong . . ."

"What's wrong, Spooky?"

"I can feel it—even if you can't. The . . . the resentment . . ."

"The aborigines, you mean?"

"Yes. But even stronger, the native animals, driven from their own pastures, hunted and destroyed to make room for the outsiders from beyond the stars. And the plants—what's left of the native flora in these parts. Weeds to be rooted out and burned, so that the grapes and grain and the oranges may flourish . . ."

"You must have felt the same on other colonised worlds, Spooky."

"Not as strongly as here. I can almost put it into words . . . *The First Ones* let us alone."

"Mphm," grunted Grimes. "Makes sense, I suppose. The original colonists, with only the resources of *Lode Jumbuk* to draw upon, couldn't have made much of an impression. But when they had all the resources of the Federation to draw upon . . . ''

"I don't think it's quite that way . . . '' murmured Deane doubtfully.

"Then what *do* you think?"

"I . . . I don't know Captain . . . ''

But they had little further opportunity for private talk. Slowly at first, and then more rapidly, the coachload of assorted passengers was thawing out. The driver initiated this process—he was, Grimes realised, almost like the captain of a ship, responsible for the well-being, psychological as well as physical, of his personnel. Using a fixed microphone by his seat he delivered commentaries on the places of interest that they passed, and, when he judged that the time was ripe, had another microphone on a wandering lead passed among the passengers, the drill being that each would introduce himself by name, profession and place of residence.

Yes, they were a mixed bag, these tourists. About half of them were from Earth—they must be, thought Grimes, from the TG Clipper *Cutty Sark* presently berthed at the spaceport. Public Servants, lawyers, the inevitable Instructors from universities, both major and minor, improving their knowledge of the worlds of the Federation in a relatively inexpensive way. The Olganans were similarly diversified.

When it came to Grimes's turn he said, "John Grimes, spaceman. Last place of permanent residence St. Helier, Channel Islands, Earth."

Tanya Lancaster, the young and prettier of the two teachers across the aisle, turned to him. "I thought you were a Terry, John. You don't mind my using your given name, do you? It's supposed to be one of the rules on this tour . . . "

"I like it, Tanya."

"That's good. But you can't be from the *Cutty Sark*. I should know all the officers, at least by sight, by this time."

"And if I were one of *Cutty Sark's* officers," said Grimes gallantly (after all, this Tanya wench was not at all bad looking, with her chestnut hair, green eyes and thin, intelligent face), "I should have known you by this time."

"Oh," she said, "you must be from the Base."

"Almost right."

"You are making things awkward. Ah, I have it. You're from that funny little destroyer or whatever it is that's berthed at the Survey Service's end of the spaceport."

"She's not a funny little destroyer," Grimes told her stiffly. "She's a Serpent Class Courier."

The girl laughed. "And she's *yours*. Yes, I overheard your friend calling you 'Captain' . . ."

"Yes. She's mine . . . "

"And now, folks," boomed the driver's amplified voice, "how about a little singsong to liven things up? Any volunteers?"

The microphone was passed along to a group of young Olganan students. After a brief consultation they burst into song.

"When the jolly *Jumbuk* lifted from Port Woomera
Out and away for Altair Three
Glad were we all to kiss the tired old Earth good-bye—
Who'll come a-sailing in *Jumbuk* with me?

Sailing in *Jumbuk*, sailing in *Jumbuk*,
Who'll come a-sailing in *Jumbuk* with me?
Glad were we all to kiss the tired old Earth
good-bye—
You'll come a-sailing in *Jumbuk* with me!

Then there was Storm, the Pile and all the engines dead—
Blown out to Hell and gone were we!
Lost in the Galaxy, falling free in sweet damn
all—Who'll come a-sailing *Jumbuk* with me?

Sailing in *Jumbuk*, sailing in *Jumbuk*,
Who'll come a-sailing in *Jumbuk* with me?
Lost in the Galaxy, falling free in sweet damn
all—
You'll come a-sailing in *Jumbuk* with me!

Up jumped the Captain, shouted for his Engineer, 'Start me the diesels, one, two, three!
Give me the power to feed into the
Ehrenhafts—You'll come a-sailing in *Jumbuk*
with me!' "

"But that's *ours*!" declared Tanya indignantly,
her Australian accent suddenly very obvious. "It's
our *Waltzing Matilda*!"

"*Waltzing Matilda* never was yours," Grimes
told her. The words—yes, but the tune, no. Like
many another song it's always having new verses
tacked on to it."

"I suppose you're right. But these comic lyrics
of theirs—what are they all about?"

"You've heard of the Ehrenhaft Drive, haven't
you?"

"The first FTL Drive, wasn't it?"

"I suppose you could call it that. The Ehrenhaft generators converted the ship, the lodejammer, into what was, in effect, a huge magnetic particle. As long as she was on the right tramlines, the right line of magnetic force, she got to where she was supposed to get to in a relatively short time. But a magnetic storm, tangling the lines of force like a bowl of spaghetti, would throw her anywhere—or nowhere. And these storms also drained the micropile of all energy. In such circumstances, all that could be done was to start up the emergency diesel generators, to supply electric power to the Ehrenhaft generators. After this the ship would stooge along hopefully, trying to find a habitable planet before the fuel ran out . . ."

"H'm." She grinned suddenly. "I suppose it's more worthy of being immortalised in a song than our sheep-stealing Jolly Swagman. But I still prefer the original." And then aided by her friend, Moira Stevens—a fat and cheerful young woman—she sang what she still claimed was the original version. Grimes allowed himself to wonder what the ghost of the Jolly Swagman—still, presumably, haunting that faraway billabong— would have made of it all. . . .

That night they reached the first of their camping sites, a clearing in the bush, on the banks of a river that was little more than a trickle, but with quite adequate toilet facilities in plastic huts. The coach crew—there was a cook as well as the driver—laid out the pneumatic pup tents in three neat rows, swiftly inflated them with a hose from the coach's air compressor. Wood was collected for a fire, and folding grills laid across it. "The inevitable steak and billy tea," muttered somebody who had been on the tour before. "It's *always* steak and billy tea . . ."

But the food, although plain, was good, and the yarning around the fire was enjoyable and, finally, Grimes found that the air mattress in his tent was at least as comfortable as his bunk aboard *Adder*. He slept well, and awoke refreshed to the sound of the taped *Reveille*. He was among the first in the queue for the toilet facilities and, dressed and ready for what the day might bring, lined up for his eggs and bacon and mug of tea with a good appetite. Then there was the washing up, the deflation of mattresses and tents, the stowing away of these and the baggage—and, very shortly after the bright sun had appeared over the low hills to the eastward, the tour was on its way again.

On they drove, and on, through drought-stricken land that showed few signs of human occupancy, that was old, old long before the coming of Man. Through sun-parched plains they drove, where scrawny cattle foraged listlessly for scraps of sun-dried grass, where tumbleweed scurried across the roadway, where dust-devils raised their whirling columns of sand and light debris. But there was life, apart from the thirsty cattle, apart from the grey scrub that, with the first rains of the wet season, would put forth its brief, vivid greenery, its short-lived gaudy flowers. Once the coach stopped to let a herd of sausagekine across the track—low-slung, furry quadrupeds, wriggling like huge lizards on their almost rudimentary legs. There was a great clicking of cameras. "We're lucky, folks," said the driver. "These beast are almost extinct. They were classed as pests until only a couple of years ago—now they've been re-classed as protected fauna . . . '' They rolled past an aboriginal encampment where gaunt, black figures, looking arachnoid rather than humanoid, stood immobile about their cooking fires. "Bad bastards those," announced the driver. "Most of the others will put on shows for us, will sell us curios—but not that tribe . . . ''

Now and again there were other vehicles—diesel-engined tourist coaches like their own, large and small hovercraft and, in the cloudless sky, the occasional high-flying inertial drive aircraft. But, in the main, the land was empty, the long, straight road seeming to stretch to infinity ahead of them and behind them. The little settlements—pub, general store and a huddle of other buildings—were welcome every time that one was reached. There was a great consumption of cold beer at each stop, conversations with the locals, who gathered as though by magic, at each halt. There were the coach parks—concentration camps in the desert rather than oases, but with much appreciated hot showers and facilities for washing clothing.

On they drove, and on, and Grimes and Deane teamed up with Tanya and Moira. But there was no sharing of tents. The rather disgruntled Grimes gained the impression that the girl's mother had told her, at an early age, to beware of spacemen. Come to that, after the first two nights there were no tents. Now that they were in regions where it was certain that no rain would fall all hands slept in their sleeping bags only, under the stars.

And then they came to the Cragge Rock reserve. "Cragge Rock," said the driver into his microphone, "is named after Captain Cragge, Master of the *Lode Jumbuk*, just as the planet itself is named after his wife, Olga.'' He paused. ''Perhaps somewhere in the Galaxy there's a mountain that will be called Grimes Rock—but with all due respect to the distinguished spaceman in our midst he'll have to try hard to find the equal to Cragge Rock! The Rock, folks is the largest monolith in the known Universe—just a solid hunk of granite. Five miles long, a mile across, half a mile high.'' He turned his attention to Tanya and Moira. ''Bigger than *your* Ayers Rock, ladies!'' He paused again for the slight outburst of chuckles. ''And to the north, sixty miles distant, there's Mount Conway, a typical mesa. Twenty miles to the south there's Mount Sarah, named after Chief Officer Conway's wife. It's usually called 'the Sallies,' as it consists of five separate domes of red conglomerate. So you see that geologically Cragge Rock doesn't fit in. There're quite a few theories, folks. One is that there was a submarine volcanic eruption when this was all part of the ocean bed. The Rock was an extrusion of molten matter from the core of the planet. It has been further shaped by millions of years of erosion since the sea floor was lifted to become this island continent.''

As he spoke, the Rock was lifting over the otherwise featureless horizon. It squatted there on the skyline, glowering red in the almost level rays of the westering sun, an enormous crimson slug. It possessed beauty of a sort—but the overall impression was one of strength.

''We spend five full days here, folks,'' went on the driver. ''There's a hotel, and there's an aboo settlement, and most of the boos speak English. They'll be happy to tell you *their* legends about the Rock—Wuluru they call it. It's one of their sacred places, but they don't mind us coming here as long as we pay for the privilege. That, of course, is all taken care of by the Tourist Bureau, but if you want any curios you'll have to fork out for them . . . See the way that the Rock's changing color as the sun gets lower? And once the sun's down it'll slowly fade like a dying ember. . . ."

The Rock was close now, towering above them, a red wall against the darkening blue of the cloudless sky. Then they were in its shadow, and the sheer granite wall was purple, shading to cold blue . . . Sunlight again, like a sudden blow, and a last circuit of the time-pocked monolith, and a final stop on the eastern side of the stone mountain.

They got out of the coach, stood there, shivering a little, in the still, chilly air. "It has something . . ." whispered Tanya Lancaster. "It has something . . ." agreed Moira Stevens.

"Ancestral memory?" asked Deane, with unusual sharpness.

"You're prying!" snapped the fat girl.

"I'm not, Moira. But I couldn't help picking up the strong emanation from your minds."

Tanya laughed. "Like most modern Australians we're a mixed lot—and, in our fully integrated society, most of us have some aboriginal blood. But . . . Why should Moira and I feel so at home here, both at home and hopelessly lost?"

"If you let me probe . . . " suggested Deane gently.

"No," flared the girl. "No!"

Grimes sympathised with her. He knew, all too well, what it is like to have a trained telepath, no matter how high his ethical standards, around. But he said, "Spooky's to be trusted. I know."

"You might trust him, John. I don't know him well enough."

"He knows *us* too bloody well!" growled Moira.

"I smell steak," said Grimes, changing the subject.

The four of them walked to the open fire, where the evening meal was already cooking.

Dawn on the Rock was worth waking up early for. Grimes stood with the others, blanket-wrapped against the cold, and watched the great hulk flush gradually from blue to purple, from purple to pink. Over it and beyond it the sky was black, the stars very bright, almost as bright as in airless Space. Then the sun was up, and the Rock stood there, a red island in the sea of tawny sand, a surf of green brush breaking about its base. The show was over. The party went to the showers and toilets and then, dressed, assembled for breakfast.

After the meal they walked from the encampment to the Rock. Tanya and Moira stayed in the company of Grimes and Deane, but their manner towards the two spacemen was distinctly chilly; they were more interested in their guidebooks than in conversation. On their way they passed the aboriginal village. A huddle of crude shelters it was, constructed of natural materials and battered sheets of plastic. Fires were burning, and gobbets of unidentifiable meat were cooking over them. Women—naked, with straggling hair and pendulous breasts, yet human enough—looked up and around at the well-clothed, well-fed tourists with an odd, sly mixture of timidity and boldness. One of them pointed to a levelled camera and screamed, "First gibbit half dollar!"

"You'd better," advised the driver. "Very commercial minded, these people . . ."

Men were emerging from the primitive huts. One of them approached Grimes and his companions, his teeth startlingly white in his coal-black face. He was holding what looked like a crucifix. "Very good," he said, waving it in front of him. "Two dollar."

"I'm not religious . . . " Grimes began, to be cut short by Tanya's laugh.

"Don't be a fool, John," she told him. "It's a throwing weapon."

"A throwing weapon?"

"Yes. Like our boomerangs. Let me show you." She turned to the native, held out her hand. "Here. Please."

"You throw, missie?"

"Yes. I throw."

Watched by the tourists and the natives she held the thing by the end of its long arm, turned until she was facing about forty-five degrees away from the light, morning breeze, the flat surfaces of the cross at right angles to the wind. She raised her arm, then threw, with a peculiar flick of her wrist. The weapon left her hand, spinning, turned so that it was flying horizontally, like a miniature helicopter. It travelled about fifty yards, came round in a lazy arc, faltered, then fell in a flurry of fine sand.

"Not very good," complained the girl. "You got better? You got proper one?"

The savage grinned. "You know?"

"Yes. I know."

The man went back into his hut, returned with another weapon. This one was old, beautifully made, and lacking the crude designs that had been burned into the other with redhot wire. He handed it to Tanya, who hefted it approvingly. She threw it as she had thrown the first one—and the difference was immediately obvious. There was no clumsiness in its flight, no hesitation. Spinning, it flew, more like a living thing than a machine. Its arms turned more and more lazily as it came back—and Tanya, with a clapping motion, deftly caught it between her two hands. She stood admiring it—the smooth finish imparted by the most primitive of tools, the polish of age and of long use.

"How much?" she asked.

"No for sale, missie." Again the very white grin. "But I give."

"But you can't. You mustn't."

"You take."

"I shouldn't, but . . ."

"Take it, lady," said the driver. "This man is Najatira, the Chief of these people. Refusing his gift would offend him." Then, businesslike, "You guide, Najatira?"

"Yes. I guide." He barked a few words in his own language to his women, one of whom scuttled over the sand to retrieve the first fallen throwing weapon. Then, walking fast on his big, splayed feet he strode towards the rock. Somehow the two girls had ranged themselves on either side of him. Grimes looked on disapprovingly. Who was it who had said that these natives were humanoid only? This naked savage, to judge by his external equipment, was all too human. Exchanging disapproving glances, the two spacemen took their places in the little procession.

"Cave," said Najatira, pointing. The orifice, curiously regular, was exactly at the tail of the slug-shaped monolith. "Called, by my people, the Hold of Winds. Story say, in Dream Time, wind come from there, wind move world . . . Before, world no move. No daytime, no nighttime . . ."

"Looks almost like a venturi, Captain," Deane marked to Grimes.

"Mphm. Certainly looks almost too regular to be natural. But erosion does odd things. Or it could have been made by a blast of gases from the thing's inside . . ."

"Precisely," said Deane.

"But you don't think . . . ? No. It would be impossible."

"I don't know what to think," admitted Deane.

Their native guide was leading them around the base of the Rock. "This Cave of Birth. Tonight ceremony. We show you . . . And there— look up. What we call the fishing net. In Dream Time caught big fish . . ."

"A circuit . . ." muttered Grimes. "Exposed by millenia of weathering . . ." He laughed. "I'm getting as bad as you, Spooky. Nature comes up with the most remarkable imitations of Man-made things . . ."

So it went on, the trudge around the base of the monolith, under the hot sun, while their tireless guide pointed out this and that feature. As soon as the older members of the party began to show signs of distress the driver spoke into his wrist transceiver, and within a few minutes the coach came rumbling over the rough track and then, with its partial load, kept pace with those who were still walking. Grimes and Deane were among these hardy ones, but only because Tanya and Moira showed no signs of flagging, and because Grimes felt responsible for the women. After all, the Survey Service had been referred to as the Policemen of the Galaxy. It was unthinkable that two civilised human females should fall for this unwashed savage—but already he knew that civilised human females are apt to do the weirdest things.

At last the tour came to an end. Najatira, after bowing with surprising courtesy, strode off towards his own camp. The tourists clustered hungrily around the folding tables that had been set up, wolfed the thick sandwiches and gulped great draughts of hot, sweet tea.

During the afternoon there were flights over the Rock and the countryside for those who wished them, a large blimp having come in from the nearest airport for that purpose. This archaic transport was the occasion for surprise and incredulity, but it was explained that such aircraft were used by *Lode Jumbuk's* people for their initial explorations.

"The bloody thing's not safe," complained Deane as soon as they were airborne.

Grimes ignored him. He was looking out and down through the big cabin windows. Yes, the Rock did look odd, out of place. It was part of the landscape—but it did not belong. It had been there for million of years—but still it did not belong. Mount Conway and Mount Sarah were natural enough geological formations—*but*, he thought, *Cragge Rock was just as natural*. He tried to envision what it must have looked like when that upwelling of molten rock thrust through the ocean bed.

"It wasn't like that, Captain," said Deane quietly.

"Damn you, Spooky! Get out of my mind."

"I'm sorry," the telepath told him, although he didn't sound it. "It's just that this locality is like a jigsaw puzzle. I'm trying to find the pieces, and to make them fit." He looked around to make sure that none of the others in the swaying, creaking cabin was listening. "Tanya and Moira . . . The kinship they feel with Najatira . . ."

"Why don't you ask them about it?" Grimes suggested, jerking his head towards the forward end of the car, where the two girls were sitting. "Is it kinship, or is it just the attraction that a woman on holiday feels for an exotic male?"

"It's more than that."

"So you're prying."

"I'm trying not to. He looked down without interest at Mount Conway, over which the airship was slowly flying. "But it's hard not to."

"You could get into trouble, Spooky. And you could get the ship into trouble . . ."

"And you, Captain."

"Yes. And me." Then Grimes allowed a slight smile to flicker over his face. "But I know you. You're on to something. And as we're on holiday from the ship I don't suppose that I can give you any direct orders . . ."

"I'm not a space-lawyer, so I'll take your word for that."

"Just be careful. And keep me informed."

While they talked the pilot of the blimp, his voice amplified, had been giving out statistics. The conversation had been private enough.

That night there was the dance.

Flaring fires had been built on the sand, in a semi-circle, the inner arc of which faced the mouth of the Cave of Birth. The tourists sat there, some on the ground and some on folding stools, the fires at their backs, waiting. Overhead the sky was black and clear, the stars bitterly bright.

From inside the cave there was music—of a

sort. There was a rhythmic wheezing of primitive trumpets, the staccato rapping of knocking sticks. There was a yelping male voice—Najatira's—that seemed to be giving orders rather than singing.

Grimes turned to say something to Tanya, but she was no longer in her place. Neither was Moira. The two girls must have gone together to the toilet block; they would be back shortly. He returned his attention to the black entrance to the Cave.

The first figure emerged from it, crouching, a stick held in his hands. Then the second, then the third . . . There was something oddly familiar about it, something that didn't make sense, or that made the wrong kind of sense. Grimes tried to remember what it was. Dimly he realised that Deane was helping him, that the telepath was trying to bring his memories to the conscious level.

Yes, that was it. That was the way that the Marines disembarked on the surface of an unexplored, possibly hostile planet, automatic weapons at the ready . . .

Twelve men were outside the Cave now, advancing in a dance-like step. The crude, tree-stem trumpets were still sounding, like the plaint of tired machinery, and the noise of the knocking sticks was that of the cooling metal. The leader paused, stood upright. With his fingers in his mouth he gave a piercing whistle.

The women emerged, carrying bundles, hesitantly, two steps forward, one step back. Grimes gasped his disbelief. Surely that was Tanya, as naked as the others—and there was no mistaking Moira. He jumped to his feet, ignoring the protests of those behind him, trying to shake off Deane's restraining hand.

"Let go!" he snarled.

"Don't interfere, Captain!" The telepath's voice was urgent. "Don't you see? They've gone native—no, that's not right. But they've reverted. And there's no law against it."

"I can still drag them out of this. They'll thank me after." He turned around and shouted, "Come on, all of you! We must put a stop to this vile performance!"

"Captain Grimes!" This was the coach driver, his voice angry. "Sit down, sir! This sort of thing has happened before, and it's nothing to worry about. The young ladies are in no danger!"

"It's happened before," agreed Deane, unexpectedly. "With neurotic exhibitionists, wanting to have their photographs taken among the savages. But not *this* way!"

Then, even more unexpectedly, it was Deane who was running out across the sand, and it was Najatira who advanced to meet him, not in hostility but in welcome. It was Grimes who, unheeded, yelled, "Come back, Spooky! Come back here!"

He didn't know what was happening, but he didn't like it. First of all those two silly bitches, and now one of his own officers. What the hell was getting into everybody? Followed by a half-dozen of the other men he ran towards the cave mouth. Their way was barred by a line of the tribesmen, holding their sticks now like spears (which they were)—not like make-believe guns. Najatira stood proudly behind the armed men, and on either side of him stood the two girls, a strange, arrogant pride in every line of their naked bodies. And there was Deane, a strange smile on his face. His face, too, was strange, seemed suddenly to have acquired lines of authority.

"Go back, John," he ordered. "There is

nothing that you can do." He added softly, "But there is much that I can do."

"What the hell are you talking about, Spooky?"

"I'm an Australian, like Moira and Tanya here. Like them, I have the Old Blood in my veins. Unlike them, I'm a spaceman. Do you think that after all these years in the Service I, with my talent, haven't learned how to handle and navigate a ship, any ship? I shall take my people back to where they belong."

And then Grimes *knew*. The knowledge came flooding into his mind, from the mind of Deane, from the minds of the others, whose ancestral memories had been awakened by the telepath. But he was still responsible. He must still try to stop this craziness.

"Mr. Deane!" he snapped as he strode forward firmly. He brushed aside the point of the spear that was aimed at his chest. He saw Tanya throw something, and sneered as it missed his head by inches. He did not see the cruciform boomerang returning, was aware of it only as a crashing blow from behind, as a flash of crimson light, then darkness.

He recovered slowly. He was stretched out on the sand beside the coach. Two of the nurses among the passengers were with him.

He asked, as he tried to sit up, "What happened?"

"They all went back into the cave," the girl said. "The rock . . . The rock closed behind them. And there were lights. And a voice, it was Mr. Deane's voice, but loud, loud, saying, 'Clear the field! Clear the field! Get back, everybody. Get well back. Get well away!' So we got well back."

"And what's happening now?" asked Grimes. The nurses helped him as he got groggily to his feet. He stared towards the distant Rock. He could hear the beat of mighty engines and the ground was trembling under the monolith. Even with the knowledge that Deane had fed into his mind he could not believe what he was seeing.

The Rock was lifting, its highest part suddenly eclipsing a bright constellation. It was lifting, and the skin of the planet protested as the vast ship, that for so long had been embedded in it, tore itself free. Tremors knocked the tourists from their feet, but somehow Grimes remained standing, oblivious to the shouts and screams. He heard the crash behind him as the coach was overturned, but did not look. At this moment it was only a minor distraction.

The Rock was lifting, had lifted. It was a deeper blackness against the blackness of the sky, a scattering of strange, impossible stars against the distant stars, a bright cluster (at first) that dimmed and diminished, that dwindled, faster and faster, and then was gone, leaving in its wake utter darkness and silence.

The silence was broken by the coach driver. He said slowly, "I've had to cope with vandalism in my time, but nothing like this. What the Board will say when they hear that their biggest tourist attraction has gone I hate to think about . . . " He seemed to cheer up slightly. "But it was one of *your* officers, Captain Grimes, from *your* ship, that did it. I hope you enjoy explaining it!"

Grimes explained, as well as he was able, to Commander Lewin.

He said, "As we all know, sir, there are these odd races, human rather than humanoid, all through the Galaxy. It all ties in with the Common

Origin of Mankind theories. I never used to have much time for them myself, but now . . . "

"Never mind that, Grimes. Get on with the washing."

"Well, Deane was decent enough to let loose a flood of knowledge into my mind just before that blasted Tanya clonked me with her boomerang. It seems that millions of years ago these stone space-ships, these hollowed out asteroids, were sent to explore this Galaxy. I got only a hazy idea of their propulsive machinery, but it was something on the lines of our Inertial Drive, and something on the lines of our Mannschenn Drive, with auxiliary rockets for maneuvering in orbit and so forth. They were never meant to land, but they could, if they had to. Their power? Derived from the conversion of matter, any matter, with the generators or converters ready to start up when the right button was pushed—but the button had to be pushed psionically. Get me?"

"Not very well. But go on."

"Something happened to the ship, to the crew and passengers of this ship. A disease, I think it was, wiping out almost all the adults, leaving only children and a handful of not very intelligent ratings. Somebody—it must have been one of the officers just before he died—got the ship down somehow. He set things so that it could not be re-entered until somebody with the right qualifications came along."

"The right qualifications?"

"Yes. Psionic talents, more than a smattering of astronautics, and descended from the Old People . . ."

"Like your Mr. Deane. But what about the two girls?"

"They had the old Blood. And they were highly educated. And they could have been latent telepaths . . . "

"Could be." Lewin smiled without much mirth. "Meanwhile, Lieutenant, I have to try to explain to the Olganan Government, with copies to Trans-Galactic Clippers *and* to our own masters, including *your* Commodore Damien. All in all, Grimes, it was a fine night's work. Apart from the Rock, there were two TG passengers *and* a Survey Service officer . . . "

"*And* the tribe . . . "

"The least of the Olganan Government's worries, and nothing at all to do with TG or ourselves. Even so . . . " This time his smile was tinged with genuine, but sardonic, humor.

"Even so?" echoed Grimes.

"What if those tribesmen and—women decided to liberate—I suppose that's the right word—those other tribespeople, the full-blooded ones who're still living in the vicinity of the other stone spaceship? What if the Australians realise, one sunny morning, that their precious Ayers Rock has up and left them?"

"I know who'll be blamed," said Grimes glumly.

"How right you are," concurred Lewin.

WHAT YOU KNOW

Lieutenant John Grimes, captain of the Serpent Class Courier *Adder*, was in a bitter and twisted mood. He had his reasons. To begin with, he had just been hauled over the coals by Commodore Damien, Officer Commanding Couriers, and still resented being blamed for the disappearance of Cragge Rock from Olgana. Then he had been told that his ship's stay at Lindisfarne Base was to be a very short one—and Dr. Maggie Lazenby, with whom he hoped to achieve something warmer than mere friendship, was off planet and would not be returning until after his own departure. Finally, he had seen the latest Promotion List and had noted that officers junior to himself had been given their half rings, were now Lieutenant Commanders. And some of those same officers, in Grimes's words, wouldn't be capable of navigating a plastic duck across a bathtub.

Ensign Beadle, his first lieutenant, was sympathetic. He said, "But it isn't what you do, Captain. It isn't what you know, even. It's whom you know . . ."

"You could be right, Number One," admitted Grimes. "But in my case I'm afraid that it boils down to who knows me . . . Did you ever see that book, *How to Win Friends and Influence People?* I often think that I must have read the wrong half, the second half . . ."

Beadle made a noncommittal noise. Then, "We're ready to lift ship, Captain. Mechanically, that is, Mr. Hollister, the new psionic radio officer, has yet to join—and, of course, there are the passengers . . . " Grimes allowed himself a sardonic smile. "I wonder what the Commodore has against *them*?"

Beadle took the question literally. "We're the only Courier in port, Captain, and it's essential that the Commissioner reaches Dhartana as soon as possible . . . "

' . . . if not before," finished Grimes. "Mphm. All right, Number One. Is the V.I.P. suite swept and garnished?"'

"I . . . I've been busy with the *important* preparations for space, Captain . . ."

Grimes scowled. "I sincerely hope, Number One, that Mrs. Commissioner Dalwood never hears you implying that she's unimportant. We'll make a tour of the accommodation *now*."

Followed by Beadle he strode up the ramp into the airlock of his little ship, his "flying darning needle." The V.I.P. suite took up almost the entire compartment below the officers' flat. As he passed through the sliding door into the sitting room Grimes's prominent ears reddened; with him it was a sign of anger as well as of embarrassment. "Damn it all, Number One," he exploded, "don't you realise that this woman is one of the civilian big wheels on the Board of Admiralty? You may not want promotion—but I do. Look at that table top! Drinking glass rings—and it must have been something sweet and sticky!—and bloody nearly an inch of cigarette ash! And the ashtrays! They haven't been emptied since Christ was a pup!"

"The suite hasn't been used since we carried Mr. Alberto . . ."

"I know that. Am I to suppose that you've kept

it the way he left it in loving memory of him?"

"You did say, sir, that bearing in mind the circumstances of his death we should leave everything untouched in case his department wanted to make a thorough investigation . . ."

"And his department did check just to make sure that he'd left nothing of interest on board when he disembarked on Doncaster. But that was months ago. And this bedroom . . . The way it is now I wouldn't put a dog into it. Get on the blower at once to Maintenance, ask them? no, *tell* them—to send a cleaning detail here immediately."

Grimes became uncomfortably aware that there was somebody behind him. He turned slowly, reluctantly, looked into the hard, steel-grey eyes of the woman who was standing just inside the doorway. She returned his stare coldly. She was tall, and she was handsome, with short-cut platinum blonde hair, wearing a beautifully tailored grey costume that looked like a uniform but wasn't, that looked more like a uniform than a deliberately casual rig of the day affected by Grimes and Beadle in common with all Courier Service officers. Her figure seemed to be that of a girl—but her face, although unlined, was old. There were no physical marks of age, but it was somehow obvious that she had seen too much, experienced too much. Grimes thought, *If she smiles, something will crack.*

She didn't smile.

She said—and her voice, although well modulated, was hard as the rest of her—"Mr. Grimes . . ."

"Ma'am?"

"I am Commissioner Dalwood."

She did not extend her hand. Grimes bowed stiffly. "Honored to have you aboard, Ma'am."

"The honor is all yours, Mr. Grimes. Tell me, is the rest of your ship like this pigsty?"

"We're having the suite put to rights, Mrs. Dalwood."

"Pray do not put yourself out on my behalf, Mr. Grimes. My lady's maid and my two robot servants are at this moment bringing my baggage aboard. The robots are versatile. If you will let them have the necessary cleaning gear they will soon have these quarters fit for human occupancy."

"Mr. Beadle," ordered Grimes, "belay that call to Maintenance. See that Mrs. Dalwood's servants are issued with what they need."

"Very good, sir," replied Beadle smartly, glad of the chance to make his escape.

"And now, Mr. Grimes, if I may sit down somewhere in less squalid surroundings . . ."

"Certainly, Ma'am. If you will follow me . . ."

Grimes led the way out of the suite. The two humanoid robots, with expensive-looking baggage piled at their feet, stared at him impassively. The maid—small, plump, pert, and darkly brunette—allowed a flicker of sympathy to pass over her rosy face. Grimes thought that she winked, but couldn't be sure. On the way up to his own quarters Grimes was relieved to see that Beadle had kept the rest of the ship in a reasonably good state of cleanliness, although he did hear one or two disapproving sniffs from his passenger. His own day cabin was, he knew, untidy. He liked it that way. He was not surprised when Mrs. Dalwood said, "Your *desk*, Mr. Grimes. Surely some of those papers are of such a confidential nature that they should be in your safe."

Grimes said, "Nobody comes in here except by invitation. I trust my officers, Ma'am."

The Commissioner smiled thinly. Nothing cracked. She said, "What a child you are, Lieutenant. One of the first lessons I learned in politics was never to trust anybody."

"In space, aboard ship, you have to trust people, Ma'am."

She sat down in Grimes's easy chair, extending her long, elegant legs. Grimes suspected that she looked at her own limbs with brief admiration before returning her regard to him. Her laugh was brittle. "How touching, Lieutenant. And that is why ships are lost now and again."

"Can I offer you refreshment, Ma'am?" Grimes said, changing the subject.

"And do *you* drink, Lieutenant?"

I know damn well that I'm only a two ringer, Grimes thought, *but I do like being called* Captain *aboard my own ship . . .* He said, "Never on departure day, Mrs. Dalwood."

"Perhaps I shall be wise if I conform to the same rule. I must confess that I am not used to travelling in vessels of this class, and it is possible that I shall need all my wits about me during lift off. Might I ask for a cup of coffee?"

Grimes took from its rack the thermos container, which he had refilled from the galley coffee maker that morning. After he had removed the cap he realised that he had still to produce a cup, sugar bowl, spoon and milk. His tell-tale ears proclaiming his embarrassment, he replaced the container, conscious of the woman's coldly amused scrutiny. At last he had things ready, finally filling the jug from a carton of milk in his refrigerator.

She said. "The milk should be warmed."

"Yes, Mrs. Dalwood. Of course. If you wouldn't mind waiting . . . "

"If I took my coffee white I should mind. But I prefer it black, and unsweetened."

Grimes poured out, remembering that the coffee maker was long overdue for a thorough cleaning. *Adder's* coffee had a tang of its own. Her people were accustomed to it. The Commissioner was not. After one cautious sip she put her cup down, hard. She asked, "And what is the food like aboard this ship?"

"Usually quite good. Ma'am. We carry no ratings or petty officers, so we take it by turns cooking. Mr. Beadle—he's my First Lieutenant—makes an excellent stew." Grimes babbled on. "It's a sort of a curry, actually, but not quite, if you know what I mean . . . "

"I don't, Lieutenant. Nor do I wish to. As I have already told you, my robots are versatile. Might I suggest that they take over galley duties, first of all thoroughly cleaning all vessels and implements, starting with your coffee maker? Apart from anything else it will mean that your officers will have more time to devote to their real duties."

"If you want it that way, Mrs. Dalwood . . . "

"I do want it that way."

To Grimes's intense relief the intercom phone buzzed. He said to the Commissioner, "Excuse me, Ma'am," and then into the speaker/microphone, "Captain here."

"First Lieutenant, Captain. Mr. Hollister, the new P.C.O., has just boarded. Shall I send him up to report to you?"

"Yes, Mr. Beadle. Tell him that I'll see him in the Control Room. Now." He turned to Mrs. Dalwood. "I'm afraid I must leave you for a few minutes, Ma'am. There are cigarettes in that box, and if you wish more coffee . . . ''

"I most certainly do not. And, Mr. Grimes, don't you think that you had better put those papers away in your safe before you go about your pressing business?" She allowed herself another thin smile. "After all, you haven't asked yet to see *my* identification. For all you know I could be a spy."

And if you are, thought Grimes, *I hope I'm the officer commanding the firing squad.* He said, "You are very well known, Ma'am." He swept his desk clean, depositing the pile of official and private correspondence on the deck, then fumbled through the routine of opening his safe. As usual the door stuck. Finally he had the papers locked away. He bowed again to Mrs. Dalwood, who replied with a curt nod. He climbed the ladders to Control, glad to get to a part of the ship where, Commissioner or no Commissioner, he was king.

Beadle was awaiting him there with a tall, thin, pale young man who looked like a scarecrow rigged out in a cast-off Survey Service uniform. He announced, before Beadle could perform the introductions, "I don't like this ship. I am very sensitive to atmosphere. This is an unhappy ship."

"She didn't use to be," Grimes told him glumly.

Usually Grimes enjoyed shiphandling. Invariably he would invite his passengers to the control room during lift off, and most times this invitation would be accepted. He had extended the courtesy to Mrs. Dalwood, hoping that she would refuse the offer. But she did not. She sat there in the spare acceleration seat, saying nothing but noticing everything. It would almost have been better had she kept up a continual flow of Why-do-you-do-this? and Why-don't-you-do-that?

Her very presence made Grimes nervous. The irregular best of the inertial drive sounded wrong to him as *Adder* climbed slowly up and away from her pad. And, as soon as she was off the ground, the ship yawed badly, falling to an angle of seven degrees from the vertical. It must look bad, Grimes knew. It looked bad and it felt worse. The only thing to do about it was to get upstairs in a hurry before some sarcastic comment from Port Control came through the transceiver. Grimes picked his moment for turning on the auxiliary rockets, waiting until the tall, slender tower that was *Adder* was canted away from the wind. That way, he hoped, he could make it all look intentional, convey the impression that he was using the quite stiff north-wester to give him additional speed. He managed to turn in his seat in spite of the uncomfortable acceleration and said, forcing out the words, "Letting . . . the . . . wind . . . help . . . us . . ."

She—calm, unruffled—lifted her slender eyebrows and asked, with apparently genuine unconcern, "Really?"

"Time . . ." Grimes persisted, "Is . . . money . . ."

"So," she told him, "is reaction mass."

Flushing, Grimes returned to his controls. Apart from that annoying yaw the ship was handling well enough. Beadle, and von Tannenbaum, the navigator, and Slovotny, electronic communications, were quietly efficient at their stations. They were certainly quiet. There was none of the usual good-humoured banter.

Sulkily Grimes pushed *Adder* up through the

last, high wisps of cirrus, into the purple twilight, towards the bright, unwinking stars. She screamed through the last tenuous shreds of atmosphere, and shortly thereafter von Tannenbaum reported that she was clear of the Van Allens. Grimes, still far too conscious of the Commissioner's cold regard, cut inertial and reaction drives, then slowly and carefully—far more slowly than was usual—used his directional gyroscopes to swing the sharp prow of the ship on to the target star. He applied correction for Galactic Drift—and then realized that he had put it on the wrong way. He mumbled something that sounded unconvincing even to himself about overcompensation and, after a few seconds that felt more like minutes, had the vessel headed in the right direction.

He wondered what would happen when he started the Mannschenn Drive—but nothing did; nothing, that is, worse than the familiar but always disquietening sense of *dejà vu*. He had a vision of himself as an old, old lieutenant with a long white beard—but this was nothing to do with the temporal precession field of the Drive, was induced rather by the psionic field generated by the Commissioner. He didn't like her and had a shrewd suspicion that she didn't like him.

She said, "Very educational, Mr. Grimes. Very educational."

She unstrapped herself from her chair. Slovotny and von Tannenbaum got up from their own seats, each determined courteously to assist her from hers. They collided, and von Tannenbaum tripped and fell, and Beadle fell over him.

"Very educational," repeated the Commissioner, gracefully extricating herself from her chair unaided. "Oh, Mr. Grimes, could you come to see me in ten minutes' time? We have to discuss the new galley routine.''

"Certainly, Mrs. Dalwood." Grimes turned to his embarrassed officers. "Deep Space Routine, Mr. Beadle." Usually he said, "Normal Deep Space Routine," but had more than a suspicion that things would not be at all normal.

Things were not normal.

Usually *Adder's* people were gourmands rather than gourmets, and a certain tightness of waistbands was an accepted fact of life. Even when whoever was doing the cooking produced an inedible mess bellies could be filled, and were filled, with sandwiches of the doorstep variety. But these relatively happy days were over.

As she had told Grimes, the Commissioner's robots were skilled cooks. To have called them chefs would not have been exaggerating. Insofar as subtlety of flavorings and attractiveness of presentation were concerned nobody could fault them. To the average spaceman, however, quantity is as important as quality. But there were no second helpings. The coldly efficient automatons must have calculated just how much nutriment each and every person aboard required to operate efficiently himself—and that was all that he ever got. Too, there was always at least one of the mechanical servitors doing something or other around the galley and storerooms, and Grimes and his officers knew that the partaking of snacks between meals would be reported at once to Mrs. Dalwood.

A real Captain, one with four gold bands on his shoulderboards and scrambled egg on the peak of his cap, would never have tolerated the situation.

But Grimes, for all his authority and responsibility, was too junior an officer. He was only a Lieutenant, and a passed-over one at that, while the Commissioner, although a civilian, could tell Admirals to jump through the hoop.

But he was hungry.

One morning ship's time, he went down to the solarium for his daily exercises. This compartment could, more aptly, have been called the gymnasium, but since it was part of the "farm" it got its share of the ultra violet required for the hydroponics tanks. Mrs. Dalwood and her maid, Rosaleen, were still there, having their daily workout, when Grimes came in. Always he had timed his arrival until the two women had finished, but for some reason he was running late. It was not that he was prudish, and neither were they, but he had decided that the less he had to do with them the better.

As he came into the room he noticed their gowns hanging outside the sauna. He shrugged. *So what?* This was *his* ship. He took off his own robe and then, clad only in trunks, mounted the stationary bicycle. He began to pedal away almost happily, watching the clock as he did so.

From the corner of his eye he saw the door to the sauna open. The Commissioner, followed by her maid, came out. It was the first time that he had seen her naked. He almost whistled, then thought better of it. She was a bit of all right, he admitted, if you liked 'em lean and hungry. He inclined his head towards her courteously, carried on pedalling.

Rather to his surprise she stood there, looking him over. She said, "Mr. Grimes, there is a little improvement in your condition, but that probably is due to a properly balanced diet.'' She walked towards him, her feet slim and elegant on the carpeted deck, her breasts jouncing over so slightly. ''Get off that thing will you?''

Grimes did so, on the side away from her. She stooped, with fluid grace, and tested the pedals with her right hand.

''Mr. Grimes! How in Space do you hope to get any benefit from these exercises unless you do them properly?'' Her hand went to the adjusting screw of the roller on top of the wheel, turned it clockwise. The muscles of her right arm stood out clearly under the smooth brown skin as she tested the pedals again. Then she actually smiled, saying, ''On your bicycle, spaceman!''

Grimes remounted. He had to push, hard, to start the wheel rotating. He had to push, to keep it rotating. Now and again he had ridden on real bicycles, but almost always had dismounted rather than pedal up a steep hill. She stood there watching him. Until now he would have thought it impossible actively to dislike an attractive naked woman. But there has to be a first time for anything.

The Commissioner turned to her maid. ''Rosaleen, you were last on the bicycle. Did you readjust it?''

The girl blushed guiltily over her entire body. ''Yes, Ma'am.''

''I see that I shall have to watch you too.'' The woman glanced at the watch that was her only article of clothing. ''Unluckily I have some work to do. However, you may stay here for another thirty minutes. The bicycle again, the rowing machine, the horizontal bars. And you, Mr. Grimes, will see to it that she does something about shedding that disgusting fat.''

Grimes did not say what he was thinking. He had little breath to say anything. He managed to gasp, ''Yes, Ma'am.''

Mrs. Dalwood went to her gown, shrugged it on, thrust her feet into her sandals. She walked gracefully to the door. She did not look back at the man on the bicycle, the girl on the rowing machine.

As soon as the door had shut behind her Rosaleen stopped rowing.

She said, ''Phew!''

Grimes went on pedalling.

''Hey, Captain. Take five. Avast, or whatever you say.''

Grimes stopped. He said, ''You'd better carry on with your rowing.''

The girl grinned. ''We're quite safe, Captain. *She* is so used to having every order implicitly obeyed that she'd never dream of coming back to check up on us.''

''You know her better than I do,'' admitted Grimes.

''I should.'' She got up from the sliding seat of the rowing machine, then flopped down on to the deck. She was, Grimes decided, at least as attractive as her mistress, and she had the advantage of youth. And there was so much more of her. The spaceman looked her over, studying her almost clinically. Yes, she had been losing weight. Her skin was not as taut as it should have been.

She noticed his look. She complained, ''Yes, I'm starved . . .''

''You get the same as we do, Rosaleen.''

"That's the trouble, Captain."

"But you have this sort of feeding all the time."

"Like hell I do. I have my nights off, you know, and then I can catch up on the pastries and candy, and the hot rolls with lots of butter, and the roast pork, with crackling . . ."

"Please stop," begged Grimes. "You're making me ravenous."

She went on, "But aboard your ship I have to toe the line. There's no escape."

"I suppose not."

"But surely *you* can do something. You've storerooms, with bread . . ."

"Yes, but . . ."

"You aren't scared of *her*, Captain?" She looked at him through her big, dark eyes. He had thought that they were black—now he saw that they were a very deep violet.

"Mphm." He allowed his glance to stray downwards, then hastily looked back at her face. There had been invitation in every line of her ample body. He was no snob, and the fact that her status was that of a servant weighed little with him. *But she was the Commissioner's servant.* A lady has no secrets from her lady's maid—is the converse true? Anyhow, they were both women, and no doubt happily prattled to each other, disparity of social status notwithstanding. She said plaintively, "I'm hungry, Captain."

"So am I, Rosaleen."

"But you're the Captain."

Grimes got off the bicycle. He said, "It's time for my sauna." He threw his shorts in the general direction of the hook on which his robe was hanging, strode to the door of the hot room, opened it.

She followed him. He stretched out on one of the benches, she flopped on one opposite him. She said, "I'm hungry."

"It's those damned robots," complained Grimes. "Always hanging around the galley and storerooms."

"They won't be there tonight."

"How do you know?"

"They're much more than cooks. Even I don't know all the things they've been programmed for. This I do know. *She* has been working on a report, and tomorrow it will be encoded for transmission. The way that *she* does it is to give it to John—he's the one with the little gold knob on top of his head—to encode. And James decodes each sheet as John finishes it, to ensure that there are no errors."

"Are there ever any?"

"No. But *she* likes to be sure."

"*She* would." He wondered when he was going to start sweating. The girl was already perspiring profusely. "Tell me, when does this encoding decoding session take place?"

"After dinner."

"And there's no chance of her breaking it off?"

"None at all. When *she* starts something she likes to finish it."

"Mphm." The sweat was starting to stream out of Grimes's pores now. The girl got up, began to flick the skin of his back lightly with the birch twigs. He appreciated the attention. "Mphm. And are you free while all this Top Secret stuff is going on?"

"Yes."

"And she should have her nose stuck into it by 2000?"

"Yes, Captain."

"Then meet me outside the galley at, say, 2015 . . ."

"*Yes!*"

"Thick buttered toast . . ." murmured Grimes, deciding that talking about food took his mind off other things.

"*Lots* of butter . . ." she added.

"And sardines . . ."

"Fat, oily sardines . . ."

"With lemon wedges . . ."

"With mayonnaise . . ." she corrected.

"All right. Mayonnaise."

"And coffee. With sugar, and great dollops of cream . . ."

"I'll have beer, myself, even though it is fattening."

"We can have beer with, and coffee after . . ."

The door slid open and Hollister came in. Naked, the telepath looked more like a living skeleton than ever. Grimes regarded him with some distaste and wondered if the psionic radio officer had been eavesdropping. To do so would be contrary to the very strict code of the Rhine Institute—but espers, in spite of their occasional claims to superiority, are only humans.

He said, "I'm just about cooked, Rosaleen."

"So am I, Captain." She got up from her bench, the perspiration streaming down her still plump body, went through into the shower room. Through the closed door Grimes heard the hiss of the water, her little scream as its coldness hit her. There was the whine of the blowers as she dried off, and then she ran through the hot room on her way back into the solarium.

"Quite a dish, Captain," commented Hollister.

"We," Grimes told him coldly, "are neither kings nor peasants."

He took his own cold shower, and when he stepped out into the gymnasium Rosaleen was gone.

Dinner that night was as unsatisfying as usual. A clear soup, a small portion of delicious baked fish with a green salad, a raw apple for desert. Grimes, at the head of the table, tried to make conversation, but the Commissioner was in a thoughtful mood and hardly spoke at all. Beadle, Slovotny, Vitelli, and Hollister wolfed their portions as though eating were about to be made illegal, saying little. The four officers excused themselves as soon as they decently could—Slovotny going up to Control to relieve von Tannenbaum for *his* dinner, Beadle to have a look at the air circulatory system, Vitelli to check up on the Mannschenn Drive. Hollister didn't bother to invent an excuse. He just left. Von Tannenbaum came down, took his place at the table. He was starting to acquire a lean and hungry look that went well with his Nordic fairness. The Commissioner nodded to him, then patted her lips gently with her napkin. Grimes, interpreting the signs correctly, got up to help her from her chair. She managed to ignore the gesture.

She said, "You must excuse me, Mr. Grimes and Mr. von Tannenbaum. I am rather busy this evening."

"Can I, or my officers, be of any assistance?" asked Grimes politely.

She took her time replying, and he was afraid that she would take his offer. Then she said, "Thank you, Mr. Grimes. But it is very confidential work, and I don't think that you have Security clearance.''

It may have been intended as a snub, but Grimes welcomed it.

''Good night, Ma'am.''

''Good night, Mr. Grimes.''

Von Tannenbaum turned to the serving robot which was waiting until he had finished his meal. ''Any chance of another portion of fish, James?''

''No, sir,'' the thing replied in a metallic voice. ''Her Excellency has instructed me that there are to be no second helpings, for anybody.''

''Oh.''

In sulky silence the navigator finished his meal. Grimes was tempted to include him in the supper party, but decided against it. The fewer people who knew about it the better.

The two men got up from the table, each going to his own quarters. In his day cabin Grimes mixed himself a drink, feeling absurdly guilty as he did so. ''Damn it all,'' he muttered, ''this is *my* ship. I'm captain of her, not that cast iron bitch!'' Defiantly—but why *should* he feel defiant?—he finished what was in his glass, then poured another generous portion. But he made it last, looking frequently at his clock as he sipped.

2014 . . .

Near enough.

He got up, went out to the axial shaft, tried not to make too much noise going down the ladder. He paused briefly in the officers' flat, on the deck below and abaft his own. Faint music emanated from behind the door of von Tannenbaum's cabin—Wagner? It sounded like it—and loud snores from inside Beadle's room. His own air circulatory system could do with overhauling, thought Grimes. Slovotny was on watch, and Hollister, no doubt, was wordlessly communicating with his psionic amplifier, the poodle's brain in aspic. Vitelli could be anywhere, but was probably in the engineroom.

The V.I.P. suite was on the next deck down. As he passed the door Grimes could hear the Commissioner dictating something, one of the robots repeating her words. That took care of her. Another deck, with cabins for not very important people . . . He thought of tapping on Rosaleen's door, then decided against it. In any case, she was waiting for him outside the galley.

She whispered, "I was afraid you'd change your mind, Captain."

"Not bloody likely."

He led the way into the spotless—thanks to the industry of the robot servitors—galley. He was feeling oddly excited. It reminded him of his training cruise, when he had been a very new (and always hungry) cadet. But then there had been locks to pick . . .

He opened the door of the tinned food storeroom, ran his eye over the shelves. He heard Rosaleen gasp. "New Erin ham . . . Carinthian sausage . . ."

"You'll have Atlantan sardines, my girl, and like 'em . . . Ah, here we are . . . A can each?"

"*Two* cans."

"All right. Here you are. You can switch on the toaster while I rummage in the bread locker . . ."

He thrust the cans into her eager hands, then collected bread, butter and seasonings. He tore open the wrapper of the loaf, then put the thick slices on the rack under the griller. The smell of the cooking toast was mouth-watering—too mouth-watering. He hoped that it would not be distributed throughout the ship by the ventilation system. But the Commissioner's overly efficient robots must, by this time, have put the air out-take filters to rights.

One side done . . . He turned the slices over. Rosaleen asked plaintively, "How *do* you work this opener?"

A metallic voice replied, "Like this, Miss Rosaleen—but I forbid you to use it."

"Take your claws off me, you tin bastard!"

Grimes turned fast. Behind him the toast smouldered unheeded. His hands went out to clamp on the wrists of the robot, whose own hands gripped the girl's arms. The automaton ignored him. If it could have sneered it would have done so.

"Mr. Grimes! Rosaleen!" The Commissioner's voice was hard as metal. In her all-grey costume she looked like a robot herself. "Mr. Grimes, please do not attempt to interfere with my servitor." She stood there, looking coldly at the little group. "All right, John, you may release Miss Rosaleen. But not until Mr. Grimes has taken his hands off you. And now, Mr. Grimes, what is the meaning of this? I seem to have interrupted a disgusting orgy. Oh, John, you might extinguish that minor conflagration and dispose of the charred remains."

"Supper," said Grimes at last.

"Supper?"

"Yes, Ma'am. Rosaleen and I were about to enjoy a light snack."

"A light snack? Don't you realise the trouble that went into working out suitable menus for this ship?" She paused, looking at Grimes with an expression of extreme distaste. "Legally, since your superiors, in a moment of aberration, saw fit to appoint you to command, you may do as you like aboard this vessel—within limits. The seduction of my maid is beyond those limits.''

''Seduction?'' This was too much. ''I assure you that . . . ''

''I was not using the word in its sexual sense. Come, Rosaleen, we will leave Mr. Grimes to his feast. He has to keep his strength up—although just for what I cannot say.''

''Ma'am!'' The girl's face was no longer soft, her voice held a compelling ring. ''Since you use that word—it was I who seduced the captain.''

''That hardly improves matters, Rosaleen. The commanding officer of a warship, even a very minor one, should not allow himself to be influenced by a woman passenger.''

''You said it!'' snapped Grimes. This could mean the ruin of his career, but he had been pushed too far. ''You said it, Mrs. Dalwood. I should never have let myself be influenced by you. I should never have allowed your tin dieticians to run loose in *my* galley. I should have insisted, from the very start, on running *my* ship *my* way! Furthermore . . . '' He was warming up nicely. ''Furthermore, I doubt if even your fellow Commissioners will approve of your ordering an officer to spy on his captain.''

''I don't know what you're talking about, Mr. Grimes.''

''Don't you, Mrs. Dalwood? Who put you wise to this little party in the galley? Who would have known about it, who could have known about it but Hollister? I shouldn't like to be in your shoes when the Rhine Institute gets my report on my psionic radio officer. They're no respecters of admirals and their female equivalents.''

"Have you quite finished, Mr. Grimes?'' With the mounting flush on her cheeks the Commissioner was beginning to look human.

"For the time being.''

"Then let me tell you, Lieutenant, that whatever secrets Lieutenant Hollister may have learned about you are still safely locked within his mind. If you had been reading up on the latest advances in robotics—which, obviously, you have not—you would have learned that already psionic robots, electronic telepaths, are in production. This has not been advertised—but neither is it a secret. Such automata can be recognised by the little gold knob on top of their skulls . . . ''

The robot John inclined its head towards Grimes, and the golden embellishment seemed to wink at him sardonically.

"You tin fink!'' snarled the spaceman.

"I am not a fink, sir. A fink is one who betrays his friend—and you were never a friend to me and my kind. Was it not in this very vessel, under your command, that Mr. Adam met his end?''

"That will do, John!'' snapped the Commissioner.

"I still resent being spied upon!'' almost shouted Grimes.

"That will do, Lieutenant!''

"Like hell it will. I give you notice that I have resigned from the Survey Service. I've had a bellyful of being treated like a child . . . ''

"But that is all that you are.''

"Captain,'' Rosaleen was pleading. "Please stop it. You're only making things worse. Mrs. Dalwood, it was my fault. I swear that it was . . . ''

"Anything that happens aboard *my* ship is *my* fault,'' insisted Grimes.

"From your own mouth you condemn yourself, Lieutenant. I am tempted, as a Commissioner, to accept your resignation here and now, but I feel . . ." Her features sagged, the outlines of her body became hazy, the grey of her costume shimmered iridescently. "Leef I tub . . ." She was her normal self again. "But I feel . . ." Again the uncanny change. "Leef I tub . . ."

This is all I need . . . thought Grimes, listening to the sudden, irregular warbling of the Manneschenn Drive, recognising the symptoms of breakdown, time running backward and *dejà vu*. He had another vision—but this time he was not an elderly Survey Service Lieutenant; he was an even more elderly Rim Runners Third Mate. They'd be the only outfit in all the Galaxy that would dream of employing him—but even they would never promote him.

The thin, high keening of the Drive faded to a barely audible hum, then died as the tumbling, ever-precessing gyroscopes slowed to a halt. From the bulkhead speakers came Slovotny's voice—calm enough, but with more than a hint or urgency. "Captain to Control, please. Captain to Control . . ."

"On my way!" barked Grimes into the nearest speaker/microphone. "Carry on with emergency procedure."

"All hands secure for Free Fall. All hands secure for Free Fall. The inertial drive will be shut down in precisely thirty seconds."

"What is happening, Mr. Grimes?" demanded the Commissioner.

"It should be obvious, even to you."

"It is. Just what one could expect from this ship."

"It's not the ship's fault. She's had no proper maintenance for months!"

He pushed past the women and the robot, dived into the axial shaft. The greater part of his journey to Control was made in Free Fall conditions. He hoped maliciously that the Commissioner was being spacesick.

At least neither the Commissioner nor her robots had the gall to infest the control room. Grimes sat there, strapped into the command seat, surrounded by his officers. "Report, Mr. Vitelli," he said to the engineer, who had just come up from the engineroom.

"The Drive's had it, Captain," Vitelli told him. A greenish pallor showed through the engineer's dark skin, accentuated by a smear of black grease. "Not only the governor bearings, but the rotor bearings."

"We have spares, of course."

"We should have spares, but we don't. The ones we had were used by the shore gang during the last major overhaul, as far as I can gather from Mr. McCloud's records. They should have been replaced—but all that's in the boxes is waste and shavings."

"Could we cannibalise?" asked Grimes. "From the inertial drive generators?"

"We could—if we had a machine shop to turn the bearings down to size. But that wouldn't do us much good."

"Why not?"

"The main rotor's warped. Until it's replaced the Drive's unusable."

Beadle muttered something about not knowing if it was Christmas Day or last Thursday. Grimes ignored this—although, like all spacemen, he dreaded the temporal consequences of Mannschenn Drive malfunction.

"Sparks—is anybody within easy reach? I could ask for a tow."

"There's *Princess Helga*, Captain. Shall I give her a call?"

"Not until I tell you. Mr. Hollister, have you anything to add to what Mr. Slovotny has told me?"

"No, sir." The telepath's deep-set eyes were smouldering with resentment, and for a moment Grimes wondered why. Then he realised that the man must have eavesdropped on his quarrel with the Commissioner, had "heard" Grimes' assertion that he, Hollister, had carried tales to Mrs. Dalwood. *I'm sorry*, Grimes thought. *But how was I to know that that blasted robot was a mindreader?*

"I should have warned you, sir," admitted Hollister. The others looked at Grimes and Hollister curiously. Grimes could almost hear them thinking, *Should have warned him of what?*

"*Princess Helga* . . ." murmured Grimes.

"Light cruiser, Captain," Slovotny told him. "Royal Skandian Navy."

"And is the Federation on speaking terms with Skandia?" wondered Grimes audibly. He answered his own question. "Only just. Mphm. Well, there's no future—or too bloody much future!—in sitting here until somebody really friendly chances along. Get the *Princess* on the Carlotti, Sparks. Give her our coordinates. Ask her for assistance. Perhaps her engineers will be able to repair our Drive, otherwise they can tow us to the nearest port."

"Shouldn't we report first to Base, Captain?" asked Slovotny.

Yes, we should, thought Grimes. *But I'm not going to. I'll put out a call for assistance before Her Highness shoves her oar in. After that—she can have a natter to Base.* He said, "Get the signal away to *Princess Helga*. Tell her complete Mannschenn Drive breakdown. Request assistance. *You* know."

"Ay, Captain." Slovotny busied himself at his Carlotti transceiver. The pilot antenna, the elliptical Mobius strip rotating about its long axis, quivered, started to turn, hunting over the bearing along which the Skandian cruiser, invisible to optical instruments, unreachable by ordinary radio—which, in any case, would have had far too great a time lag—must lie.

"Locked on," announced the radio officer at last. He pushed the button that actuated the calling signal. Then he spoke into the microphone. "*Adder* to *Princess Helga*. *Adder* to *Princess Helga*. Can you read me? Come in, please."

There was the slightest of delays, and then the swirl of colors in the little glowing screen coalesced to form a picture. The young woman looking out at them could have been Princess Helga (whoever *she* was) herself. She was blue-eyed, and hefty, and her uniform cap did nothing to confine the tumbling masses of her yellow hair.

"*Princess Helga* to *Adder*. I read you loud and clear. Pass your message."

"Complete interstellar drive breakdown," said Slovotny. "Request assistance—repairs if possible, otherwise tow. Coordinates . . ." He rattled off a string of figures from the paper that von Tannenbaum handed him.

The girl was replaced by a man. He should have been wearing a horned helmet instead of a cap. His eyes were blue, his hair and beard were yellow. He grinned wolfishly. He demanded, "Your Captain, please."

Grimes released himself from his own chair, pulled himself into the one vacated by Slovotny. "Lieutenant Grimes here, Officer Commanding Courier Ship *Adder*."

"Captain Olaf Andersen here, Lieutenant. What can I do for you?"

"Can your engineers repair my Drive?"

"I doubt it. They couldn't change a fuse."

"What about a tow to Dhartana?"

"Out of the question, Captain. But I can take you in to my own Base, on Skandia. The repair facilities there are excellent."

Grimes weighed matters carefully before answering. Skandia, one of the small, independent kingdoms, was only just on speaking terms with the Interstellar Federation. At the very best the Skandians would charge heavily for the two, would present a fantastically heavy bill for the repair work carried out by their yard. (But he, Grimes, would not be paying it.) At the worst, *Adder* and her people might be interned, could become the focus of a nasty little interstellar incident, a source of acute embarrassment to the Survey Service. *And so,* Grimes asked himself mutinously, *what?* That Promotion List had made him dangerously dissatisfied with his lot, the Commissioner had strained what loyalties remained to the breaking point.

The Commissioner . . .

"What exactly *is* going on here?" she asked coldly.

So she was getting in his hair again.

"I'm arranging a tow," Grimes told her. "The alternative is to hang here . . . " he gestured towards the viewports, to the outside blackness, to the sharp, bright, unwinking, distant stars . . . "in the middle of sweet damn all, thinking more and more seriously of cannibalism with every passing day."

"Very funny, Lieutenant." She stared at the screen. "Is that officer wearing *Skandian* uniform?"

"Of course, Madam," replied the Skandian Captain, who seemed to be very quick on the uptake. "Captain Olaf Andersen, at your service." He smiled happily. "And you, if I am not mistaken, are Mrs. Commissioner Dalwood, of the Federation's Board of Admiralty. According to our latest Intelligence reports you are *en route* to Dhartana." He smiled again. "Delete 'are.' Substitute 'were.' "

"Mr. Grimes, I forbid you to accept a tow from that vessel."

"Mrs. Dalwood, as commanding officer of this ship I must do all I can to ensure her safety, and that of her people."

"Mr. Slovotny, you will put through a call to Lindisfarne Base at once, demanding immediate assistance."

Slovotny looked appealingly at Grimes. Grimes nodded glumly. The grinning face of the Skandian faded from the screen, was replaced by a swirl of color as the pilot antenna swung away from its target. Sound came from the speaker—but it was a loud warbling note only. The radio officer worked desperately at the controls of the Carlotti transceiver. Then he looked up and announced,

"They're jamming our signals; they have some very sophisticated equipment, and they're only light minutes, distant."

"Are you sure you can't get through?" demanded the Commissioner.

"Quite sure," Slovotny told her definitely.

She snorted, turned to Hollister. "Mr. Hollister, I'll have to rely on you."

"What about your own chrome-plated telepath?" Grimes asked her nastily.

She glared at him. "John's transmission and reception is only relatively short range. And he can't work with an organic amplifier, as your Mr. Hollister can."

"And *my* organic amplifier's on the blink," said Hollister.

"What do you mean?" demanded Grimes.

The telepath explained patiently. "There has to be a . . . relationship between a psionic communications officer and his amplifier. The amplifier, of course, is a living dog's brain . . . "

"I know, I know," the Commissioner snapped. "Get on with it."

Hollister would not be hurried. "The relationship is that which exists between a kind master and a faithful dog—but deeper, much deeper. Normally we carry our own, personal amplifiers with us, from ship to ship, but mine died recently, and so I inherited Mr. Deane's. I have been working hard, ever since I joined this ship, to win its trust, its affection. I was making headway, but I was unable to give it the feeling of security it needed when the temporal precession field of the Drive started to fluctuate. The experience can be terrifying enough to a human being who knows what is happening; it is even more terrifying to a dog. And so . . ."

"And so?" demanded the woman.

"And so the amplifier is useless, possibly permanently." He added brightly, "But I can get in touch with *Princess Helga* any time you want."

"You needn't bother," she snarled. Then, to Grimes, "Of all the ships in the Survey Service, why did I have to travel in this one?"

Why? echoed Grimes silently. *Why?*

Even the Commissioner was obliged to give Captain Andersen and his crew full marks for spacemanship. *Princess Helga* emerged into normal space/time only feet from the drifting *Adder*. At one moment there was nothing beyond the courier's viewports but the blackness of interstellar space, the bright, distant stars—at the next moment she was there, a vague outline at first, but solidifying rapidly. She hung there, a great spindle of gleaming plastic and metal, the sleekness of her lines marred by turrets and antennae. Another second—and the shape of her was obscured by the tough pneumatic fenders that inflated with almost explosive rapidity. Another second—and *Adder's* people heard and felt the thump of the magnetic grapnels as they made contact.

Andersen's pleasant, slightly accented voice came from the transceiver. "I have you, Captain. Stand by for acceleration. Stand by for resumption of Mannschenn Drive."

"I suppose that your temporal precession field will cover us?" asked Grimes.

"Of course. In any case there is physical contact between your ship and mine."

"Where are you taking us?" demanded Mrs. Dalwood.

"To Kobenhaven, of course, Madam. Our Base on Skandia."

"I insist that you tow us to the nearest spaceport under Federation jurisdiction."

"You insist, Madam?" Grimes, looking at the screen, could see that Andersen was really enjoying himself. As long as somebody was . . . "I'm sorry, but I have my orders."

"This is piracy!" she flared.

"Piracy, Madam? The captain of your ship requested a tow, and a tow is what he's getting. Beggars can't be choosers. In any case, Space Law makes it quite plain that the choice of destination is up to the officer commanding the vessel towing, not the captain of the vessel towed."

She said, almost pleading but not quite, "In these circumstances the Federation could be generous."

Andersen lost his smile. He said, "I am a Skandian, Madam. My loyalty is to my own planet, my own Service. Stand by for acceleration."

The screen went blank. Acceleration pushed the group in *Adder's* control room down into their chairs; Mrs. Dalwood was able to reach a spare seat just in time. Faintly, the vibration transmitted along the tow wires, they heard and felt the irregular throbbing of *Princess Helga's* inertial drive—and almost coincidentally there was the brief period of temporal/spatial disorientation as the field of the cruiser's Mannschenn Drive encompassed both ships.

"You realise what this means to your career," said the Commissioner harshly.

"What was that?" asked Grimes. He had been

trying to work out how it was that *Princess Helga* had been able to start up her inertial drive before the interstellar drive, how it was that there had been no prior lining up on a target star.

"You realise what this means to your career," repeated the woman.

"I haven't got one," said Grimes. "Not any longer."

And somehow it didn't matter.

The voyage to Kobenhaven was not a pleasant one.

The Commissioner made no attempt to conceal her feelings insofar as Grimes was concerned. Rosaleen, he knew, was on his side—but what could a mere lady's maid do to help him? She could have done quite a lot to make him less miserable, but her mistress made sure that there were no opportunities. The officers remained loyal—but not too loyal. They had their own careers to think about. As long as Grimes was captain they were obliged to take his orders, and the Commissioner knew it as well as they did. Oddly enough it was only Hollister, the newcomer, the misfit, who showed any sympathy. But he knew, more than any of the others, what had been going on, what was going on in Grimes's mind.

At last the two ships broke out into normal space/time just clear of Skandia's Van Allens. This Andersen, Grimes admitted glumly to himself, was a navigator and shiphandler of no mean order. He said as much into the transceiver. The little image of the Skandian captain in the screen grinned out at him cheerfully. "Just the normal standards of the Royal Skandian Navy, Captain. I'm casting you off, now. I'll follow you in. Home on the Kobenhaven Base beacon." He grinned again. "And don't try anything."

"What can I try?" countered Grimes, with a grin of his own.

"I don't know. But I've heard about you, Lieutenant Grimes. You have the reputation of being able to wriggle out of anything."

"I'm afraid I'm losing my reputation, Captain." Grimes, through the viewports, watched the magnetic grapnels withdrawn into their recesses in *Princess Helga's* hull. Then, simultaneously, both he and Andersen applied lateral thrust. As the vessel surged apart the fenders were deflated, sucked back into their sockets.

Adder, obedient to her captain's will, commenced her descent towards the white and gold, green and blue sphere that was Skandia. She handled well, as well as Grimes had ever known her to do. But this was probably the last time that he would be handling this ship, any ship. The Commissioner would see to that. He shrugged. Well, he would make the most of it, would try to enjoy it. He saw that Beadle and von Tannenbaum and Slovotny were looking at him apprehensively. He laughed. He could guess what they were thinking.

"Don't worry," he told them. "I've no intention of going out in a blaze of glory. And now, Sparks, do you think you could lock on to that beacon for me?"

"Ay, Captain," Slovotny replied. And then, blushing absurdly, "It's a damn' shame, sir."

"It will all come right in the end," said Grimes with a conviction that he did not feel. He shrugged again. At least that cast-iron bitch and her tin boyfriends weren't in Control to ruin the bitter-

sweetness of what, all too probably, would be his last pilotage.

Adder fell straight and true, plunging into the atmosphere, countering every crosswind with just the right application of lateral thrust. Below her continents and seas expanded, features—rivers, forests, mountains, and cities—showed with increasing clarity.

And there was the spaceport, and there was the triangle of brilliant red winking lights in the center of which Grimes was to land his ship. He brought her down fast—and saw apprehension dawning again on the faces of his officers. He brought her down fast—and then, at almost the last possible second, fed the power into his inertial drive unit. She shuddered and hung there, scant inches above the concrete of the apron. And then the irregular throbbing slowed, and stopped, and *Adder* was down, with barely a complaint from the shock absorbers.

"Finished with engines," said Grimes quietly.

He looked out of the ports at the soldiers who had surrounded the ship.

"Are we under arrest, Captain?" asked von Tannenbaum.

"Just a guard of honor for the Commissioner," said Grimes tiredly.

Grimes's remark was not intended to be taken seriously—but it wasn't too far from the mark. The soldiers were, actually, members of the Royal Bodyguard and they did, eventually, escort Mrs. Commissioner Dalwood to the Palace. But that was not until after the King himself had been received aboard *Adder* with all due courtesy, or such courtesy as could be mustered by Grimes and his officers after a hasty reading of *Dealings With Foreign Dignitaries. General Instructions*. Grimes, of course, could have appealed to the Commissioner for advice; she moved in diplomatic circles and he did not. He *could* have appealed to her. He thought, *As long as I'm Captain of this ship I'll stand on my own two feet*. Luckily the Port Authorities had given him warning that His Skandian Majesty would be making a personal call on board.

He was a big young man, this King Eric, heavily muscled, with ice-blue eyes, a flowing yellow moustache, long, wavy yellow hair. Over baggy white trousers that were thrust into boots of unpolished leather he wore a short-sleeved shirt of gleaming chain mail. On his head was a horned helmet. He carried a short battle-axe. The officers with him—with the exception of Captain Andersen, whose own ship was now down—were similarly uniformed, although the horns of their helmets were shorter, their ceremonial axes smaller. Andersen was in conventional enough space captain's dress rig.

Grimes's little day cabin was uncomfortably crowded. There was the King, with three of his high officers. There was Andersen. There was (of course) the Commissioner, and she had brought her faithful robot, John, with her. Only King Eric and Mrs. Dalwood were seated.

John, Grimes admitted, had his uses. He mixed and served drinks like a stage butler. He passed around cigarettes, cigarillos, and cigars. And Mrs. Dalwood had *her* uses. Grimes was not used to dealing with royalty, with human royalty, but she was. Her manner, as she spoke to the King, was kind but firm. Without being disrespectful she managed to convey the impression that she ranked with, but slightly above, the great-grandson of a piratical tramp skipper. At first Grimes feared (hoped) that one of those ceremonial but sharp axes would be brought into play—but, oddly enough, King Eric seemed to be enjoying the situation.

"So you see, Your Majesty," said the Commissioner, "that it is imperative that I resume my journey to Dhartana as soon as possible. I realise that this vessel will be delayed for some time until the necessary repairs have been effected, so I wonder if I could charter one of your ships." She added, "I have the necessary authority."

Eric blew silky fronds of moustache away from his thick lips. "We do not question that, Madam Commissioner. But you must realise that We take no action without due consultation with Our advisors. Furthermore . . . " he looked like a small boy screwing up his courage before being saucy to the schoolteacher . . . "We do not feel obliged to go out of Our way to render assistance to your Federation."

"The *Princess Ingaret* incident *was* rather unfortunate, Your Majesty . . . " admitted Mrs. Dalwood sweetly. "But I never thought that the Skandians were the sort of people to bear grudges . . . "

"I . . . " he corrected himself hastily . . . "We are not, Madam Commissioner. But a Monarch, these days, is servant to as well as leader of his people . . . "

Grimes saw the generals, or whatever they were, exchanging ironical glances with Captain Andersen.

"But, Your Majesty, it is to our common benefit that friendly relations between Skandia and the Federation be re-established."

Friendly relations? thought Grimes. *She looks as though she wants to take him to bed. And he knows it.*

"Let me suggest, Madam Commissioner, that you do me—Us—the honour of becoming Our guest? At the Palace you will be able to meet the Council of Earls as soon as it can be convened. I have no doubt—*We* have no doubt that such a conference will be to the lasting benefit of both Our realms."

"Thank you, Your Majesty. We are . . . " She saw Grimes looking at her sardonically and actually blushed. "I am honored."

"It should not be necessary for you to bring your aides, or your own servants," said King Eric.

"I shall bring John and James," she told him. "They are my robot servitors."

Eric, whose face had fallen, looked cheerful again. "Then We shall see that all is ready for you." He turned to one of his own officers. "General, please inform the Marshal of the Household that Madam Commissioner Dalwood is to be Our guest."

The general raised his wrist transceiver to his bearded lips, passed on the instructions.

"John," ordered the Commissioner, "tell Miss Rosaleen and James to pack for me. Miss Rosaleen will know what I shall require."

"Yes, Madam," replied the robot, standing there. He was not in telepathic communication with his metal brother—but UHF radio was as good.

"Oh, Your Majesty . . . "

"Yes, Madam Commissioner?"

"What arrangements are being made for Lieutenant Grimes and his officers, and for my lady's maid? Presumably this ship will be under repair shortly, and they will be unable to live aboard."

"Mrs. Dalwood!" Grimes did not try very hard to keep his rising resentment from showing. "May I remind you that I am captain of *Adder*? And may I remind you that Regulations insist that there must be a duty officer aboard at all times in foreign ports?"

"And may I remind you, Mr. Grimes, that an Admiral of the Fleet or a civilian officer of the Board of Admirality with equivalent rank can order the suspension of any or all of the Regulations? Furthermore, as such a civilian officer, *know* that nothing aboard your ship, armament, propulsive units or communications equipment, is on the Secret List. You need not fear that our hosts' technicians will learn anything at all to their advantage." She added, too sweetly, "Of course, you might learn from them . . ."

King Eric laughed gustily. "And that is why We must insist, Lieutenant, that neither you nor your officers are aboard while repairs are in progress. Captain Andersen, please make arrangements for the accommodation of the Terran officers."

"Ay, Your Majesty," replied Andersen smartly. He looked at Grimes and said without words, *I'm sorry, spaceman, but that's the way it has to be.*

Grimes and his officers were housed in the Base's Bachelor Officers' Quarters, and Rosaleen was accommodated in the barracks where the female petty officers lived. They weren't prisoners—quite. They were guests—but strictly supervised guests. They were not allowed near their own ship—and that hurt. They were not allowed near any of the ships—in addition to *Princess Helga* and *Adder* there were three destroyers, a transport and two tugs in port. Captain Andersen, who seemed to have been given the job of looking after them, was apologetic.

"But I have to remember that you're spacemen, Lieutenant. And I have to remember that *you* have the reputation of being a somewhat unconventional spaceman, with considerable initiative." He laughed shortly. "I shudder to think what would happen if you and your boys flew the coop in any of the wagons—yours or ours—that are berthed around the place."

Grimes sipped moodily from his beer—he and the Captain were having a drink and chat in the well-appointed wardroom of the B.O.Q. He said, "There's not much chance of our doing that, sir. You must remember that the Commissioner is my passenger, and that I am responsible for her. I could not possibly leave without her."

"Much as you dislike her," grinned the other. "I think that she is quite capable of looking after herself."

"I know that she is, Captain. Even so . . . "

"If you're thinking of rescuing her . . . " said Andersen.

"I'm not," Grimes told him. He had seen the Palace from the outside, a grim, grey pile that looked as though it had been transported, through space and time, from Shakespeare's Elsinore. But there was nothing archaic about its defences, and it was patrolled by well-armed guards who looked at least as tough as the Federation's Marines. He went on, almost incuriously, "I suppose that she's being well treated.''

"I have heard that His Majesty is most hospitable.''

"Mphm. Well, we certainly can't complain, apart from a certain lack of freedom. Mind you, Mr. Beadle is whining a bit. He finds your local wenches a bit too robust for his taste. He prefers small brunettes to great, strapping blondes . . . But your people have certainly put on some good parties for us. And Rosaleen was telling me that she's really enjoying herself—the P.O.s' mess serves all the fattening things she loves with every meal.''

"Another satisfied customer,'' said Andersen.

"But *I'm* not satisfied, Captain. I know damn well that the repairs to my Mannschenn Drive took no more than a day. How long are we being held here?''

"That, Lieutenant, is a matter for my masters—and yours. We—and our ships—are no more than pawns on the board.'' The Captain looked at his watch. "Talking of ships, I have some business aboard *Princess Helga*. You must excuse me.'' He finished his beer and got to his feet. "Don't forget that after lunch you're all being taken for a sail on the Skaggerak . . . ''

"I'll not forget, sir,'' Grimes informed him.

He was, in fact, looking forward to it. He enjoyed the sailing excursions in stout little wooden ships as much as any Skandian, already had proved himself capable of handling a schooner under a full press of canvas quite competently, was realising that seamanship and spacemanship, the skilled balancing of physical forces, have much in common.

He sat down again when Andersen had left the almost deserted wardroom, then saw Hollister coming towards him. The telepath said in a low voice, "I'm afraid you'll not be taking that sail, Captain."

Grimes was going to make some cutting remark about psionic snooping, then thought better of it. He asked, "Why not, Mr. Hollister?"

The psionic communications officer grinned wryly. "Yes, I've been snooping, Captain. I admit it. But not only on you. Not that it was really snooping. I've maintained contact of a sort with John . . . "

"The tin telepath . . . "

"You can call him that. He's very lonely in the Palace, and he's going to be lonelier . . . "

"What the hell are you talking about?"

"*She* has been getting on *very* well with the King. *She* has persuaded him to release us, even though the Council of Earls is not altogether in approval. We should get the word this afternoon, and we shall be on our way shortly afterwards. *Adder* is completely spaceworthy."

"I know. Captain Andersen's as good as told me. But why is John so lonely that he's spilling all these beans to you?"

"*She* wanted to make a farewell gift to His Majesty—and he, it seems has always wanted a robot valet. Humanoid robots are not manufactured on Skandia, as you know."

"And so John's been sold down the river. My heart fair bleeds for him."

"No, Captain. Not John—James. John's 'brother.' They think of each other as brothers. They feel affection, a real affection, for each other . . . "

"Incredible."

"Is it, Captain? I've heard about the Mr. Adam

affair, and how a mere machine was loyal to *you*."

"Then not so incredible . . . "

One of the wall speakers crackled into life. "Will Lieutenant Grimes, captain of the Federation Survey Service Courier *Adder*, please come at once to telephone booth 14? Will Lieutenant Grimes, captain of the Federation Survey Service Courier *Adder*, please come at once to telephone booth 14?"

"Coming," grumbled Grimes. "Coming."

He was not surprised to see Andersen's face in the little screen, to hear him say, "Orders from the Palace, Lieutenant. You're to get your show on the road at 1500 hours Local. Mrs. Dalwood will board at 1430. You, your officers, and Miss Rosaleen Boyle will board at 1330. You will find all in order, all in readiness."

"Thank you, Captain."

Andersen grinned. "Don't thank me. Thank His Majesty—or Commissioner Dalwood."

Grimes returned to the table where he had left Hollister. He said, "You were right."

"Of course I was right. And now, if I may, I'll give you a warning."

"Go ahead."

"Watch John. Watch him very carefully. He's bitter, revengeful."

"Are you in touch with him now?"

"Yes." The telepath's face had the faraway expression that made it obvious that he was engaged in conversation with a distant entity. Suddenly he smiled. "It's all right. He has assured me that even though he feels that Mrs. Dalwood has betrayed him and his brother he is quite incapable of physically harming any human being. The built-in safeguards are too strong for him to overcome."

"Then that's all right." Grimes knew that he should be worrying nonetheless, but the Commissioner was a big girl and could look after herself. And how could the robot harm her in any way but physically? "You've been snooping in its—his—mind, so you know how he ticks."

"Yes, Captain."

Grimes strode to the reception desk and asked the attractive, blonde petty officer to have *Adder's* crew paged.

Mrs. Dalwood looked well. She was softer, somehow, and she seemed to have put on a little weight!—although not as much as Rosaleen. She sat at ease in her day room, admiring the beautiful, jewel-encrusted watch that now adorned her left wrist. Grimes sat on the edge of his chair, watching her, waiting for her to speak. To one side stood the robot John, silent, immobile.

"Well, Lieutenant," she said, not too unpleasantly, "you managed to get us upstairs without any major catastrophes. I hope that we shall reach our destination in a reasonably intact condition. We should. As you must notice already, the work carried out by the Skandian technicians is of excellent quality . . . Like this watch . . ." She turned her wrist so that Grimes could see it properly. "It seems strange that a robust people such as the Skandians, space Vikings, should be such outstanding watchsmiths, but they are, as you probably know. His Majesty insisted that I accept this keepsake from him.

"Yes. Things *could* have been worse. Much worse, as it turned out. His Majesty and I reached an understanding. Together we accomplished more, much more, than the so-called diplomats..."

I can imagine it, thought Grimes—and to his surprise experienced a twinge of sexual jealousy.

Her manner stiffened. "But don't think, Mr. Grimes, that I shall not be putting in a full report on your conduct. It is my duty as a Commissioner to do so. I cannot forget that you gave me your resignation . . . "

Suddenly John spoke. He said tonelessly, "He is thinking of you."

The Commissioner seemed to forget that Grimes was present. Her face softened again. "He is? Tell me . . . "

"He misses you, Madam. He is thinking, *I really loved her. She reminded me so much of my dear old mother.*"

Grimes laughed. He couldn't help it. Mrs. Dalwood screamed furiously, "Be silent, John. I forbid you to speak, ever, unless spoken to by me."

"Yes, Madam."

"And as for you, Mr. Grimes, you heard nothing."

Grimes looked at her, into the eyes that were full of appeal. He remembered what he had heard of Mrs. Commissioner Dalwood before ever he had the misfortune to meet her. The beautiful Mrs. Dalwood, the proud Mrs. Dalwood, the so-called *femme fatale* of the Admiralty who could, and did, compete with much younger women on equal terms. In a less permissive society she could never have attained her high rank; in Earth's past she could have become a King's courtesan.

And in Skandia's present . . . ?

Grimes said softly, "Of course, King Eric's very young . . . "

"Mr. Grimes, you heard nothing . . . "

He could not resist the appeal in her voice, the

very real charm. He thought, *I may not be an officer much longer, but I'll still try to be a gentleman.*

He said, "I heard nothing."

Commodore Damien looked at Grimes over his desk, over the skeletal fingers with which he had made the too-familiar steeple. He said, without regret, "So I shall be losing you, Grimes."

"Yes, sir."

"Frankly, I was surprised."

"Yes, sir."

"But not altogether pained."

Grimes wasn't sure how to take this, so said nothing.

"Tomorrow morning, Grimes, you hand over your command to Lieutenant Beadle. I think that he deserves his promotion."

"Yes, sir."

"But how did you do it, Grimes? Don't tell me that . . . ? No. She's not your type, nor you hers."

"You can say that again, sir."

"It can't be what you *do*. It can't be what you know. It must be *whom* you know . . . "

Or what you know about whom, thought Lieutenant Commander Grimes a little smugly.

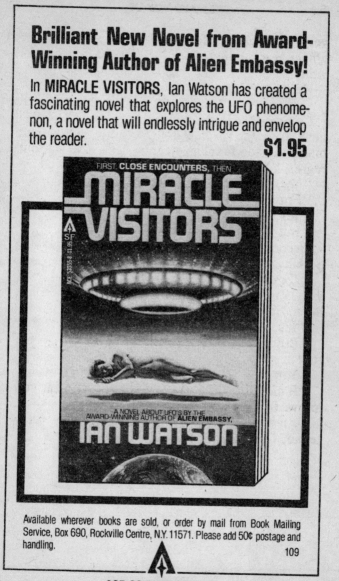

There are a lot more
where this one came from!

ORDER your FREE catalog of ACE paperbacks here. We have hundreds of inexpensive
books where this one came from priced from
75¢ to $2.50. Now you can read all the books
you have always wanted to at tremendous
savings. Order your *free* catalog of ACE
paperbacks now.